THE LOST MASK

BOOK 2

THE BONE MASK CYCLE

ASHLEY CAPES

For Brooke

CHAPTER 1

Vinezi hauled himself up the stony sides of the regeneration pool, gasping and spitting grey and pink gunk sharp with the tang of blood. He blinked stinging liquid from his eyes. His slick fingers gripped the rim and he growled, straining to lift his bulk free of the slush. Where was his strength? Something was amiss.

"Help me," he snarled at the shadows beyond the pool of light.

One of his brothers leapt across the cavern, boots echoing on stone. "Here." It was Tarvilus. The younger man caught Vinezi's arm and heaved. Together they worked to free him. Fluid soon sloshed to the tiled floor and he shivered in the chill air.

"Find me...a robe," he managed, heaving in air as his knees wobbled. Even his chest strained at the activity. Ridiculous, he'd followed the instructions in the Genus exactly. To the damnable letter. Not a whit of variation. His idiot brothers had made a mistake – that was the only answer.

He sighed.

No. It was hardly their fault. Both his brothers would have done their best with what was available. He was standing at least. And he was alive. His oldest memories were intact. He was Vinezi still – bones could not lie, they remembered everything. Everything returned to bone eventually.

The Crucible had delivered its promise. He was reborn.

He twisted with a grunt, enough to see the artefact where it lay in the centre of the pool. Old bone woven in criss-crossing patterns, ringed by a silver band, it peeked above the surface of the murky pool.

Tarvilus returned, a heavy red robe in his hands. His dark beard and the collar of his own robe glistened with fluid from the pool. "It's the last we have," he said.

"Fine." Vinezi spread his arms, allowing his brother to help him into the robe. "Clean yourself up too. And what happened this time?"

Tarvilus produced a rag, wiping the fluid away. "An accident, Vinezi."

He frowned. "With the mercenary at the inn?"

"No. You don't recall?

"No."

"This is the second time you have been regenerated," Tarvilus said. His expression grew into one of worry. "Don't you remember the acor and Tantos? The throne room?"

"I..." He frowned. There was nothing there...except. Almost. Laughter? Darkness and crashing through glass. Tantos and his blasted mask; yet nothing added up.

Memories of his youth were clear as daylight. The taste of mud as Marinus Compelled him, forcing him with magic to lie across the earth, bones aching, while the others laughed. Even Father. Vinezi sneered – what a coward he'd been as a boy.

"How are your legs?"

Vinezi waved a hand. "Well enough. What do you mean by 'accident'?"

"I think it's best for your recovery if you try and remember for yourself."

"I do not."

His brother sighed. "After the...miscalculation at the Iron Pig we regenerated you. I stole bone from your body but left the rest behind. You recovered quickly and we resumed the search."

"And?"

"You don't remember anything after?"

"No. A curse upon you, Tarvilus, tell me," Vinezi shouted. He gaped as the room spun, reaching out. His flailing hand caught something firm. A shoulder. An arm slipped around his back.

"This isn't good, brother. You remembered more easily last time."

Sweat had formed on Vinezi's brow. "Just tell me."

"You need to remember the details for yourself – your mind needs the practice – but everything transpired as we'd hoped until the old man and the Renovar girl interrupted. Tantos lost control and we had to flee the palace."

"We broke through the windows." Feet pounded on cobblestones and red fire glowed in the sky. He blinked. The cavern was dim, quiet.

"Good. But in the Second Tier one of the explosions had damaged a nearby building. It collapsed and crushed you."

Nothing. "Truly?"

"Julas cut a finger free – only your hand was visible

in the rubble. We had no time; the search parties were closing in."

Only a finger? Was that why it was harder for him to remember? The Genus always specified a larger bone for regeneration via the Crucible, but nowhere did it mention a minimum. "Next time take my skull," he said. "And where is your brother?"

"Below. In the city."

"Why?"

"To watch. Much has happened."

"I need to rest. Tell me after." He took a step and his leg collapsed. Tarvilus caught his weight and together they walked to a bench at the edge of the cavern. Not a large room, it was nonetheless lined with benches for witnesses. Regeneration had once been a holy rite not the befouled by secrecy and common blood.

His neck ached from supporting his head. He lifted a hand. Fluid from the pool still coated his skin – but there was a patch of fur spreading from wrist to knuckle. "What is this?"

Tarvilus swallowed. "I could only take one. A young man. The village is already suspicious after the last time."

"That's not enough flesh or blood for the ritual."

"Forgive me. I had to improvise."

"Tarvilus."

"I used animal flesh. I skinned them as best I could."

Vinezi shuddered. There. He was part animal now. How fitting – perhaps one of them had been a slinking fox or some other sneaking thief? Father would have roared with laughter. "No more."

Tarvilus waited.

"Send for Julas. I need to know what's happening. We will form new plans while I recover." He paused. "Do I remember true – the Sea God has died?"

"Yes. Its bones are even now being harvested by the Anaskari."

"Fortunate." He smiled – cheeks reacting slowly. "That ought to make our task easier. Go now, find our little brother."

Tarvilus stood and strode for the exit. He hesitated, a mere dark figure beyond the pool of light. "Do you think Marinus will find us?"

"Stop asking me that."

"I know he will come for us."

"It won't matter. We will have our own Greatsuits by then."

"Don't underestimate him."

"Never will I, brother." Vinezi closed his eyes and leant back. "Tarvilus?"

"Yes?"

"You did exceptionally well. Thank you."

His younger brother left but there was a snap to his footfalls. Vinezi smiled again. This time the muscles in his cheeks were quicker to respond.

There would be no more accidents.

CHAPTER 2

Kanis paced the deck, only half-aware of the creak of ropes and shouts of men in the rigging, sparing not even a glance for inky clouds massing on the horizon. A chill wind pressed pants and vest against him but barely bothered his bare arms.

He almost sighed. The closer they drew to Anaskar the harder it was to avoid thinking about her. Would he see her there? Maybe not. Years had passed; there was no guarantee Flir would even be in the city anymore. An easier question – would she still be angry? He chuckled. Of course she would. And she'd hardly be happy with him looting her new home either.

But being at least a little angry was natural for Flir.

And her temper kept things interesting, no point denying that.

"Kanis, the storm." Yaev gave him a look. The first mate's beard was crusted with brine and the scar on his cheek pink in the cold. "Did you hear me?"

"Huh?"

"Thinking about her again?"

He affected a look of nonchalance. "No."

Yaev snorted. "You're no actor, Kan."

"Fine, give me something else to worry about then." He turned to the rail and leant against it, staring across the grey of flashing waves to the storm clouds. They were breaking apart already and the storm would be no more than a squall when it hit his small fleet. Only a dozen ships in total, one wing of his 'V' formation trailing to port, but twelve would be enough to surprise Anaskar.

"Maybe you should worry about her. You dilar have a knack for causing trouble – and it's worse when you're together."

He smiled. Like the brawl in temple, right before the end. "We did have some good times."

"She'll try and stop you."

"I know."

"And you don't have a problem with that?"

"Of course I have a problem with it – namely, how do I convince her to join us?"

Yaev groaned. "You burned that bridge years ago."

"True."

He'd lied to her. No hiding that fact now but he'd had no choice back then. There was no way she'd have gone along with the coup otherwise. And King Chaak had been a tyrant – after a fashion. To further cloud the skies, she'd loved him despite all her denials. Flir wasn't one to be honest with herself when it came to love.

If he could talk to her...maybe there would be a chance? But then, maybe not. Her last words, shouted from the royal docks, hadn't been encouraging.

He sighed. "What else is afoot, Yaev?"

"I've got three things. Take your pick."

"You choose – anything to break the eternal dullness

of this trip."

Yaev ignored him. "First, that storm."

"Nothing to its bite," he said. "Take another look."

He did so and grunted. "Fine. Second, the new cabin boy was caught trying to steal some of the acor."

Kanis turned, a frown on his face. "That's more like it. Little fool, what's he want with it? Impress me, Yaev, what's the third problem?"

"It's that weasel Vinezi left behind."

"Oh?"

"His fever isn't breaking. He demands to see you."

Kanis snorted. "I'm almost disappointed. Atilus will recover, we're not lucky enough for him to die."

"And if he doesn't?"

"We don't need him to sack Anaskar, Yaev." He raised a hand and began counting off items on his fingers. "We have the acor. We've been taught to use it. We have our catapults. We have a dozen ships with us. We'll have a city on its knees. Don't worry so much."

Yaev raised an eyebrow. "Well I still don't trust Vinezi. And you tried to tell me not to worry when I warned you about the new Conclave."

Kanis paused to shout up to a man working on the rigging. "Watch that line." He glanced back to his mate. "They'll have no idea we're betraying them until it's too late. And as for Vinezi, I'll be keeping an eye on him."

"But I was right, Kan. And the Conclave will send ships after us eventually. They want what we want."

"Then they shouldn't have given me command, don't you agree? And we're too far ahead now." He slapped the rail, ignoring the creak. "Let's start with young Skink."

Yaev led him below decks to the darkened hold. They picked their way through barrels of acor and stores marked with the ice-peaks of Renovar; the familiar symbol a dire reminder of home. A single lamp swung overhead. To be safe, it was a good distance from the sealed cases of acor, which in turn kept the hold quite dark.

Skink lay shackled in place, knees pulled up against his chest. His bare feet twitched when Kanis knelt before him.

"I'm s-sorry, dilar. Please, f-forgive me."

"That depends."

"On what?" He swallowed.

"Why did you steal the acor? What were you going to do with it?"

Skink looked down, shoulders hunched. "Sell it."

Kanis glanced at Yaev, who shrugged. It made no difference to his first mate. "Why?"

He opened his eyes, his bottom lip quivering. "I-I...for money, dilar."

"I know, Skink. But we're about to steal a lot of gold, jewels and silks from the richest city in the world. Even as cabin boy, your share of whatever we take could see you clear of never working another day for years. Why steal acor?"

"It's not enough," he said.

"Greedy whelp," Yaev said.

"I didn't take much. I need to make a lot of money back home. My father owes gold." His eyes were wet. "I don't even know how much. Mother told me I had to get some acor."

Kanis raised an eyebrow. "Well, little Skink, I don't know if I believe you."

"Dilar, I would –"

"No need," he interrupted. "I'll think about your fate

and when I return, we'll talk again."

He left the boy huddled in his chains and climbed the ladder back to the cabins, moving aft until he reached Atilus' cabin door.

"You believe the boy?" Yaev asked.

"Yes."

"And?"

"Let him sweat tonight. Tomorrow I'll Bind him to me."

"Him?"

"Don't give me that – he'll prove useful. Trust me, I always know."

Yaev muttered beneath his breath.

Kanis grinned. "Have I been wrong before?"

"Yes."

"Well, not recently, anyway." He pushed the door open. A man lay on a narrow cot beneath a porthole, beyond which the dark sea toiled. His face was pale, even with the Anaskari tan, and sweat soaked rags on his temple. The room smelt of illness – closed up air, herbs and sweat.

Yaev opened the window, letting a blast of cold sea air in.

Atilus groaned.

"Atilus?"

The man turned his head, breathing hard. "Kanis you half-wit, I need a proper healer." His accent was slight.

"No port for two weeks, perhaps more."

"Then try something else," he snapped.

"Why?"

His eyes blazed, partly in rage, partly from the fever, no doubt. He pointed at his own chest. "Because if I die, the proper use of the acor dies with me."

Kanis narrowed his eyes. "What have you been

holding back?"

"Enough."

"Tell me."

"When I am recovered."

"Your own goals are at risk if our attack fails."

"At risk, yes. But you will have nothing."

Kanis swore. He was right, the bastard. But that didn't mean a healer could be produced from the heavens. "I'll check the other ships."

"Good." Atilus lay back and Kanis left the room, motioning for Yaev to lock the cabin behind them.

"Damn him."

"Do you believe him?"

Kanis shrugged. "We don't have a choice, do we?"

CHAPTER 3

Seto rubbed at a spot of grime on the golden, gilded arm of his throne. Father had often let him sit on it as a child. A tiny step toward a typical preparation for a prince – preparation that not so long ago, he would have looked back on as pointless. No longer. Now he would be sitting on the throne often. And at the very least, he'd ensure it remained clean.

His father's unsmiling face loomed in memory.

"So, Father, is this not a triumph? Your son – your only worthy son – is King." King of two realms. One of deceit, and one of...deceit.

He snorted. How often Father came to mind, now when the clamouring of a thousand problems pummelled him. The shattered harbour, the poor tatters of the navy and the great, rotting intrusion of the Sea Beast. Near to two weeks since its breach and so little progress in harvesting its precious bones.

"No greater commodity," he whispered.

Footsteps approached. "Sire?"

He didn't turn from the Swordfish banner; an orange

splash against grey stone. "Yes?"

"Ah, Luik requests that you join him in the city jail at your earliest convenience."

A Braonn page, dressed in yellow and grey, and beginning to sweat despite the cold hall, stood with arms at his side. Seto smiled. "Surely Luik didn't use those actual words?"

"That is his request, Your Majesty." A slight frown creased his smooth brow.

"Indeed." He rose and descended from the dais. He still had to meet with the council an hour after daybreak, but there was time if he hurried. *What now, Luik?*

He waved to the boy. "Off you go, then."

The lad swallowed as he bowed.

Seto swept through the corridors, the glittering trim on his robes catching dust as he slipped into the secret ways. *How long before such freedom was denied?* Already, the wet-nurses of the palace, or the council, if he was feeling generous, did their best to either curtail or at the very least, monitor his every move. *How was he to run both his Kingdoms with worriers like Nemola underfoot all the time?*

Seto slapped a hidden switch and crossed a corridor, its warmth rushing over his cheeks, then it was back into the darkness of the ways. Only twice since having the throne dumped in his lap, had he encountered Mascare in the passages, and each time, their challenge was answered with a royal response.

By the time he crossed beneath the walls and snuck into the cobblestone of the Second Tier, sweat had formed at his temples, even in the cool of morning. He exhaled and rolled up his sleeves. *Most unbecoming.* Dawn light softened the hard edges of the buildings, their upper storeys casting deep shadows. His footfalls echoed on the cobbles of the empty street and from afar came the crash of waves, a gentlemanly rhythm.

He passed two women drawing water from a well, their discussion hushed, arms straining. He nodded to them as he passed.

Anaskar City Prison was a squat building. Well-fortified, its heavy doors possessed twin steel bands and thick bars on the windows. He rapped on the door. A hatch soon opened and a face bearing a faded bruise blinked at him.

"Your Majesty?"

"I certainly am. Now do open up."

The door swung wide and Seto swept in. "Where is Luik?"

"The big guy, My Lord?"

He sighed. "Yes, the big guy."

"Bottom floor. It's –"

"I know the way, thank you." He held out his hand.

"My Liege?"

"The key, my dear fellow. The key."

The Jailor fumbled at his belt, eventually handing the ring over. Seto took it and opened the first door. Immediately beyond, he turned down a set of steps and then a second, and after unlocking another door, a third. He wrinkled his nose at the bottom. Prisons. All the same. Dead sweat, bad hay and human waste.

Seto strode toward a pair of figures at an open cell near the end of a row. He ignored the rather unimaginative calls from the inhabitants, and stopped before two guards. One gaped and the other combined a bow with frantic brushing at his silver and blue uniform. Comical.

"That will be all, gentlemen."

"Yes, Your Majesty," they chimed as they left.

Luik stood within the open cell, his nasty-looking mace belted over a dark tunic. "Glad you're here, Seto. Fancy robe you've got there."

"Never mind that. And why am I here exactly, Luik? This lump?" He gestured to the occupant, who lay in a heap on the floor. "You know I've had to leave off preparing for a meeting to come here."

"You seem heartbroken."

Seto grinned. "Well?"

"You won't believe me, so I'll let you look. Just remember, doesn't make sense. I figured that much out already."

Seto bent by the body. A familiar face, covered in grime and twisted into a mask of death, stared up at him.

Vinezi.

He sucked in a breath. "Impossible."

"I thought so too."

Seto prodded the body with his toe. Soft. And the smell another clue – enough to know the prisoner had been dead for some time. Weeks. There was no way the corpse before him could have set off the explosion at the Iron Pig, let alone attacked the palace.

"See his neck?"

Seto's brows drew together. Vinezi still wore the blindfold from the interrogation, it had fallen down around his throat. "By all the Ocean Gods."

"There's more."

"I couldn't be more surprised, Luik."

He pulled up Vinezi's pant cuff. "Someone cut his foot off." Only a festering stub remained.

Seto raised an eyebrow. "I retract my earlier claim. Who cut him?"

Luik sighed. "I'll be back."

Seto bent down to address the corpse. "Dead all along it seems. Then who was your friend? A brother?" He rose, meeting Luik and one of the jailors outside.

Luik gestured. "This is Adilo, Your Majesty."

"Who visited the prisoner, Adilo?"

He swallowed. "It was weeks ago now, Sire, but one of the masks, ah, Mascare-is, well, he came in and said he wanted 'the big prisoner' that was just put in." He spread his hands. "We took the mask, but when we got to the cell, the prisoner wasn't in good shape."

"Continue."

"He was dead, Sire. I'd say whoever dropped him off had worked him over, broken something inside. Anyway, the mask screamed at us, as if it were our fault, then demanded an axe. Took a bit, but we found one." Adilo scratched at his cheek. "Well, I don't really understand the point of what happened next. But I won't never forget it-is. He took the axe and chopped the fellow's foot right off. Snatched it up and told us to move the body down here-is, and not to disturb it until he returned. We've been waiting since. Only sent word because of the smell."

What madness was afoot? Seto almost smiled at his own joke. Instead, he saved it for the guard. "You did the right thing, Adilo. Know that I am pleased. Return to your post now."

He bowed and scurried off.

"What's happening, Seto?" Luik's voice was a little unsteady.

"This man died some weeks ago."

"Right after Flir and I dumped him here by the looks of things."

"And then, he did not escape as we assumed – as we witnessed – but instead, has lain in this corner of the prison ever since?"

"Doesn't seem real." Luik shook his head. "And then some mask comes and hacks off a foot? Imposter?"

"Baffling but it would appear so. Arrange to have the body taken to the palace."

"Seto?"

"I will investigate this further. I've no idea what it could mean. But we have to accept that there may be two of Vinezi out there."

"Twins? Or brothers?"

Seto shrugged. "Possibly." It wasn't something that could be solved right away. The pit of dark stone and human refuse was not the venue either. "It's more likely that this body, whoever he was, was no more than a ploy."

"Doesn't explain why he's missing a foot."

"Nothing does." He pointed toward the entrance. "Have anyone who has been on guard duty since his arrival report to the palace. Then go find Flir."

"Yes, Seto."

CHAPTER 4

Sofia pulled her mount to a halt, calling for Notch. She rubbed her mare's neck, leaning over to murmur in the horse's ear. Notch turned his own horse. Beneath shadows of the treeline his face was creased with worry and his beard had grown heavier.

"What's wrong?" he asked.

She glanced over her shoulder. "I just..." A week had already passed and they were only now reaching the Bloodwood, how could they catch up? And how could she turn her back on Anaskar, on her city? From her position on the edge of the Bloodwood, in the middle of the once-paved road, the city was lost beyond the horizon but it would still be perched on the black coast, its walls rebuffing the distant sea. She sighed. Damned either way. Seto would be furious; not that the old man needed her, just her bone masks. But then, he couldn't use Osani anyway.

And only she could use Argeon.

"Is this the right choice?"

Notch rested his hands on the pommel. "We can turn

back."

She said nothing, running a hand over the saddlebag where both Argeon and Osani sat. Were they talking to each other even now, as Tantos claimed they could? Or was it another diversion, a half-truth? Gods, it wasn't as though she could trust her brother. Had he lied about Father? Or worse, had he told the truth?

"Sofia?"

"No. I'm just being...I don't know. Maybe it's selfish." Did he think she was selfish too? His face gave nothing away. She adjusted her cloak in the cold. The crimson robes of the Mascare were packed away, for now Notch believed it best to appear as simple travellers. "But I need to know the truth about Father."

He hesitated. "Seto will understand your choice, Sofia."

"Hmmm." Would he? Would anyone back in the city? Pietta? Or Emilio? How could she explain it to them, especially with the city under threat? The Masks were meant to protect Anaskar. "I doubt that."

"You might be surprised."

"You're not much of a liar, are you, Notch?"

He chuckled. "I guess not. Well, either way, he'll manage. We should keep moving."

Sofia exhaled and pulled her horse into line behind Notch. The Bloodwood closed around them as long branches spread over the road; big, broad leaves rustling in the breeze where it danced across the treetops. Sofia reached for one but paused. Notch assured her stories about the Bloodwood were lies, that the trees didn't suck the blood of unwary travellers, but perhaps there was another reason for the name. She tugged at a leaf as they passed a low branch. It came free with a tiny pop.

Red veins ran through the green leaf, ending in a

blush at the tip. She shuddered. Blood followed her still. Splashing over her hands as she drove the blade into Oson's stomach. Spreading across the Mascare's back in the Carver's room. Staining the carpet in her father's study.

"Sofia." Notch had stopped beside her. "The deeper we go, the more careful you should be."

"With the trees?"

"The Braonn are very attached to the forest. Some consider it a grave insult to raise a hand against a tree."

Sofia nodded slowly. History lessons with Father. "As their Gods, Tira and Areth ask."

"Right. Protectors of the forests."

They rode on. So much of the wood appeared similar to what had come before. "Have you seen any sign yet?"

He shook his head. "That'd be pushing the limits of our luck. Weeks have passed since he'd have come this way. If he did."

She frowned. "This is hardly a good time to start having doubts."

"I'm only saying he might not have taken the Southern Road into the Bloodwood. There are other trails."

"He was being pursued; wouldn't he take the path of least resistance?"

"You know Danillo best. What do you think?"

"He'd make it difficult. He'd go deep. He wouldn't stay on the main road long."

"We'll find something." Notch said, nudging his horse back into motion. The clomp of hooves was dulled by a thick loam coating the road. "There's a settlement where we can ask. Demarc. We'll reach it by noon."

The morning wore on. Notch set a steady pace, not overtaxing their mounts. They stopped twice, once to eat travel rations and once to let a Braonn cart pass. Two men crowded the driver's seat. The Anaskari man inclined his head, but the driver glared, his pale skin covered in bruises. In the back rode four Braonn children, already dressed in palace livery. Wide eyes stared from sombre faces, though one, a girl, waved at Sofia. Indentured, each of them.

She waved back.

Beside the children were a pair of heavily armed Braonn. Bigger than the driver, they reminded her of Luik. Bows were slung across their shoulders and each carried long knives belted over green tunics.

"Heading for the Palace," was all Notch said.

Sofia didn't speak again until the trees thinned ahead. A dozen low-rooved buildings of log and thatch appeared. The homes surrounded a dirt square with a single well. One building, much larger than others, boasted a stable. Not much else seemed of note. Both Braonn and Anaskari folk mingled before the buildings, some offering a greeting to Notch as he dismounted before the building that must have been Demarc's inn.

"It's smaller than I expected," she whispered, removing her cloak and fastening it to her saddle. Beneath the leaves it wasn't exactly hot, the winter sun being smothered by green, but nor was the day cool. Or she was simply nervous. She hesitated over the masks. No-one could use them, and she wasn't going far. They would be safe.

"It's a stopping point really," Notch said. "We'll reach a larger, older village tomorrow."

She trailed him to the door, which he pushed open, entered and closed gently. "Doors are rarely slammed in the wood," he told her. "It's how they honour the trees from which they were made."

"Truly?"

Notch didn't answer, instead moving across the crowded room. The inn, such as it was, had curved seats with a long bar, though most people stood around tall tables with circular tops. Anaskari traders in their blues, yellows and oranges and even a few Shields from the city, mingled with paler Braonn, their blue eyes striking in large groups. Everywhere she turned, another face with clear blue eyes. Some were even green.

Instead of tension, the murmur of purposeful conversation filled the room. Expressions were calm, or if animated, it was with interest, even excitement. Trade – how swiftly it connected people.

She glanced back through a window at the horses. Both appeared safe.

Notch stopped before an old man drinking alone. He leant against one of the odd, tall tables. His hair was yellow but his face lined, as if every part of him had aged except his hair.

He blinked at first, then put his drink down with a smile. "Notch, what brings you to the thins of Demarc?" His accent was light.

Their hands met in a warrior's grip. "We're searching." He introduced Sofia. "Gelehn here is one of the best hunters in the Bloodwood, though he's far from his part of the forest."

"As folks here on the fringes are quick to remind me," he grumbled. He raised an eyebrow. "And what do you mean, 'one of'?"

"Fine. The best."

"Better." He winked at Sofia. "How'd you get mixed up with Notch then?"

She laughed. "He seems a man of his word."

"That he is, girl." To Notch he said, "And what are you searching for here in the Wiraced?"

"A Mascare who fled the city. He's an imposter and we've been given the job of recapturing him. He would have passed this way some weeks ago."

Gelehn shook his head. "That I can't help you with. Haven't been here long, but I know someone who might have heard something – nothing gets by Pan."

"I'd hoped you would."

Sofia brightened. Notch was quicker than she gave him credit for, already they had something to go on. Good. Every clue, every advantage was vital. They followed Gelehn from the tavern and crossed the dirt to one of the smaller buildings, built up against the tree line. Beyond the screen of trunks a man toiled in a large, enclosed garden of dappled light. When he saw them the thin man straightened and wiped sweat from his brow. A dark streak of dirt was left behind.

Gelehn stepped over the low stone fence, switching to Braonn. "Pan, can you help us today?"

The farmer drove a hoe into the turned earth. "Might be, Gelehn. Who are your city friends?"

"This is Notch and Sofia. They're chasing a fugitive from Anaskar."

The man's eyes widened. "In a red robe? One of them Mask-fellows?"

"Yes. Did you see him?" Sofia asked.

"I did. He damn near smashed through my fence, he did." The man waved to a corner of the garden, its fencing newly tied. "Hope you have better luck than them others."

Sofia straightened. "Others?"

"I'll show you." Pan took them to the fence, which he

stepped over carefully with some show, as if to school them, and to a small clearing beyond a fallen trunk covered in moss. He pointed to a great heap of white ashes and burnt log endings. "There." Within, hints of blackened steel poked through the ash, and something that might have been a skull. She looked away. It could have been Father in there.

"You burnt them?" Notch asked. His Braonn was passable but the farmer followed.

"After the fellow that was running burst my fence, he stopped here and killed them that was following him. He took off again, and more Shields and another Mask came through Demarc later, but by then, we'd already burnt the bodies. Bad luck to just leave them."

Sofia turned to Pan as Notch knelt by the ashes. "But he was well, the man being chased?"

Pan pursed his lips. "Well, he looked tired but made short work of that lot." He pointed.

Notch stood. "When was this, Pan?"

"Weeks back now. I'd just put the potatoes into the ground."

Gelehn thanked the farmer and led them back to their mounts. "This Mascare you're chasing, he sounds dangerous. At least, more than usual. Sure just the two of you are up to it, Notch?"

"Don't worry about us, Gelehn. Sofia has hidden talents and I've still got a few tricks up my sleeve."

He chuckled. "Well, good luck to you both. I've work of my own to be about. Be safe, Notch."

"And you, Gelehn."

The old man strode off and Sofia caught her saddle. A wave of dizziness stopped her words. Sweat had built up beneath her clothing.

Notch reached out. "The withdrawals?"

Her vision had grown foggy. She closed her eyes a moment and it passed. "I think so."

"Can you stand?"

"Yes. I'll put Osani on again later, when we're out of sight." She clenched her teeth. Damn you, brother. "It'll pass."

"Why don't you wait here while I top up our supplies?"

Sofia murmured assent as she checked on the masks. How frequent the attacks had become. She'd used what little medicine Mayla had been able to provide mere days out of Anaskar. Only wearing Osani put a stop to the fever and side effects. Argeon would too...but how much of Tantos was in the mask now? No. Better to leave it in her bag, hidden away. Not that Osani was much better. If Argeon had been difficult to communicate with, Osani simply refused to acknowledge her.

But he protected her from the *lenasi* cravings at least. Better, from the pain too.

And at least they'd finally had word of Father.

"Ready?" Notch was stuffing flasks and packages into his saddlebags. How long had she stood by the horses?

"Ready." She mounted up. "Where to now?"

"To Irihs." He kicked his horse into a trot, leading them deeper along the leaf-strewn trail. "I'll bet my sword that your father passed by, maybe even through. He'd need supplies, possibly medicine if he was wounded. Even a small cut can sometimes turn into a problem if not tended."

"Think we'll be lucky there too?"

"The Braonn know their forest, Sofia. Someone will help us." A slight frown crossed his brow.

"Notch?"

"Folks in Ihris might not be as welcoming as they were here. Resentment lingers."

"So we're going to be in danger."

"No more than on any other day of your life."

"I'm looking for something more specific than philosophy right now."

He grinned. "Sorry. Just keep a closer eye on those masks perhaps, and leave the talking to me."

"Fine, but I speak better Braonn than you."

"That's a relief."

"What is?"

"To spend time with someone so refined in manner."

"But it's true, Notch. And I have a larger vocabulary."

He laughed. "Well, leave the sword play to me at least. Agreed?"

"Agreed."

CHAPTER 5

The council wore near identical looks of shock at his robes, the hems covered in webs and dust of the ways and filth from the prison. Seto bit his tongue to keep from sighing as he paced before the fire, its warmth soothing his bones. They weren't listening; that old busybody Nemola was the worst. The man's eyes tracked every swish of Seto's robe from where the advisor sat at the grand table, its polished surface catching the firelight.

Seto stopped before a painting – one of many that towered over him from the walls. Menfolk of the Sword-Fish line. This man, dressed in full armour and his dark eyes brooding, was all-too familiar, especially for someone Seto so rarely thought of before taking the throne.

Father.

Seto spoke without turning. "Nemola, my robe isn't going anywhere."

The councillor cleared his throat. "Your Majesty, I –"

He waved a hand as he returned to his seat. "No matter, Nem, old boy. What matters is that we return our focus to the future. Or rather, the present. I need reports, after which Flir ought to have arrived to update us on remaining acor deposits in the city and the palace."

The council exchanged glances. So similar, robes trimmed in royal orange, faces lined, brows furrowed. More than one member swallowed. Only Brunetti appeared unperturbed – an ex-soldier, he was used to such tension. And living in the palace had its share of tense moments, now that any portion of it could explode. Not only were the poor fools adjusting to the new order – a much more efficient order if the truth were known – but they had to live in constant fear. Tempers frayed as easily as the cheapest, dockside linen.

Even Captain Holindo was not immune to the tension. He barely acknowledged Solicci whenever the two shared a room. But then, perhaps that was no surprise, after what Solicci had been part of. The Captain's shock at Solicci and Cera's scheming had been genuine as far as Seto was concerned. Surprising too.

The scarred Captain spoke first. "King Oseto, I regret to report little progress in tracking down Vinezi. Early this morning we captured one of his lackeys, but the man died from his wounds. The good news is that we believe Vinezi has not left the Second Tier yet."

Seto tapped the arm of his chair. No need to immediately share what Luik had discovered. "You found nothing on his body?"

He shook his head.

"And word from Wayrn?"

"Returned to his search for trails beneath the city."

Seto turned to Solicci. The man had lost weight since his brief interrogation and release, his cheeks sinking and his nose becoming an even sharper hook. Seto had him watched constantly of course. So too the man's nephew, who'd replaced Sol as head of House Cavallo, but so far, Solicci had proven a useful administrator and interim head of the Mascare. The man's outrage at Tantos' false Mascare had seemed genuine too. Was he trustworthy? He was certainly useful. Seto had mined the traitor for insights into the subtler relationships in the palace as much as he had any other man in the room.

"No word on the whereabouts of either Danillo or Sofia Falco, nor Captain Medoro. Not from my earlier party, nor from Captain Emilio. It has nearly been two weeks, I doubt we will catch up to them. Maybe if Emilio had left the same day..."

"We had to search the city too," Holindo added, not quite addressing the man, but rather the space between Solicci and Seto.

"Of course, Captain."

Seto exhaled slowly. To avoid thinking on Notch and Sofia, and the masks...it took some effort. He'd been doing well up to that point. Inevitable, really. Those two... they'd have to talk fast indeed when they returned. Or better, were dragged back.

Possibly in chains. "Send more men."

"Yes, Your Majesty."

Next was General Tadeo. Hailing from the edge of the Bloodwood, the man's partial Braonn heritage found him exiled by Otonos until Seto ordered him back from the Far Islands. His brother had many failings, chief among them an inability to recognise – and make good use of – talent. "Tadeo? News from the eastern seas?"

"No big storms as yet, but it was a comfort to have your Storm Singer along, Your Majesty."

Abrensi inclined his head, a half-smile on his face.

That one bore watching. Ever since Abrensi 'saved the city' he'd been enjoying his new-found fame a little too much. But then, Abrensi had been the same, even before Father 'put him out of sight.' For an undisclosed reason at that. How reliable was Abrensi truly?

Seto accepted a drink from a servant. "Then you both feel that the sea is not impassable yet? You saw no ships from Renovar?"

"Hard to say. But we saw no such ships."

Abrensi clicked his tongue. "If the weather worsens quickly, the invasion may not eventuate."

Holindo crossed his arms. "There's no guarantee of that – we may have as little as a week to finalise the city's defences."

Seto frowned into his fire-lemon. "And I find myself unconvinced yet."

"Sire?" Solicci asked.

"Again, I feel Renovar has nothing to gain by invading, and everything to lose. None of our investigations have borne fruit yet. Our envoy will not send word back for weeks, and that is only if they survive the seas. I fear we do not have all the pieces."

"Doubtless not. But we cannot fail in our preparations."

"Certainly." He tented his fingers. "I will see Ambassador Lallor again."

A page appeared. He cleared his throat, glancing at the assembled dignitaries. "Your Majesty, Luik and Flir have returned."

"See them in," Seto said.

Flir strode into the room, dressed in her street clothes, face smudged and hands filthy. Luik appeared somewhat cleaner, having taken the trouble to wipe his face it seemed.

"Well, we found another one." Flir slumped into a chair. "Every time I think we've found the last, there's another. It's beyond dozens now." Seto schooled his features. Some of the council, especially Nemola, had yet to grow accustomed to Flir's casual attitude. It was a blessing, really, no-where else in the palace could he get such directness.

"And it is neutralised?"

"Drowned it. The powder's useless now."

Luik nodded. "We tested it after, like the others and it wouldn't catch. Pevin was right again."

Flir sighed at mention of Pevin, but continued. "This one was by the First Tier wall. We should have been more thorough there."

"I will put people on it immediately," Seto said.

Solicci leant forward. "I still wonder why there have been no more explosions. If Pevin is correct, and more deposits exist, why not explode them?"

"They're waiting for numbers and co-ordination?" Holindo said.

Seto took another drink. "That's what I believe. Vinezi is scrambling to gather more recruits and cannot act as he wishes."

"Or they're waiting for the invasion, to have a simultaneous strike," Flir said. "That's how I'd do it."

Silence fell over the council room. Seto stood, pacing by the fire again. She was correct. He should have seen it himself, but with so much on his plate, a buffet of troubles, really, he was half-blind. "Certainly we will address that too." Seto paused. "I think that will be all for today's meeting."

Nemola rose halfway in his seat. "But Your Majesty, the matter of the deposits in the palace remains."

Captain Holindo added his own voice. "And the corpse of the Sea Beast."

Seto nodded. "Captain, remain with me. Councillors, I appreciate your time but that will be all. Nemola, we search the palace periodically, as you know."

The men filed out, Solicci bowing deepest. Neither Flir nor Luik moved, seated near the Captain. "To my rooms." Seto strode into the corridor without waiting to see if they followed. The Queen's Harper was in need of attention too. The palace would swallow him if he let it. Too many people depending on him – as the Water Rat – to let that happen. "And I won't have it," he muttered beneath his breath.

Seto passed tall statues of the Ocean Gods, their oft-times aggressive poses a stark reminder of Anaskari history. A bloody one, but then, what nation wasn't steeped in blood? Seto murmured a greeting to the group of Shields at his chamber door and wove through a gaudy room of orange and silver to a large sitting chamber. Three chairs surrounded a small table, its bone inlay depicting ships cresting waves.

He lowered himself into the deepest chair, stretching his legs out on a footrest. Behind him, a low fire crackled from a hearth.

"Where are you, Seto?" It was Flir, from another room.

Captain Holindo cleared his throat. "King Oseto, My Lady."

"Thanks, but I'm hardly a Lady, Holindo."

Luik's head poked around the door. "In here," he called over his shoulder. The mercenary-turned-chef took a chair. Flir was next, slipping into the final chair, leaving Holindo to stand. He glanced at the seating arrangement, but said nothing. Seto noted Flir and Luik grinning at one another.

"I am considering taking one other into our confidence," Seto announced.

Flir rested her feet on the table's crossbeam. "In regards to harvesting the Beast?"

"Sire, I hope it is not Solicci you are considering."

"No, Captain. I am watching that one."

"It still galls me. Had I known what Cera and he were up to –" he began.

Seto held up a hand. "You have established your trustworthiness, my good man."

He bowed.

"Who then?" Luik asked.

"Lavinia."

"A logical choice."

Seto tented his fingers. "Indeed. I believe she can offer insights on the Beast. I remember some considerable lore had been gathered by her father. The Storm Singers have a long history with the Beast that we ought to draw upon."

"Sounds good," Luik said.

Flir shook her head. "Only if she keeps her secrets."

"What do you mean?" Luik asked.

"Abrensi. I don't know about him."

Seto murmured his agreement. "I may visit him first. Assess him."

"My Liege?"

"Yes, Holindo?"

"Can I offer a suggestion? I know it's not my place to do so."

"Do so, please."

"Demand to see the Storm Singer's knowledge. You are, after all, King," he rasped. "It is your right."

Seto gave a rueful smile. "So it is. But I wish to make allies, rather than resentful subjects."

"Of course, sire."

"And how goes the management of the corpse?"

"There have been no more attacks but the stench is horrific. The people protest and there have been two riots in the last week. I've tripled the Vigil, and boosted the presence of Mascare and Shield." He paused to drink from a glass on the table when his voice became strained. "Tensions are high. I fear there is risk of disease. It has to be controlled and I'm speaking with the healers and priests about how to do it."

"Good. And the actual harvesting?"

"The work is difficult and slow. We lost another man to the poison."

"That's ten so far," Luik said quietly.

Seto frowned. One was too many, but the beast was both too dangerous and too valuable. It had to be harvested. And kept out of unsavoury hands. "And the bones we have freed?"

"The first quarter of the beast has yielded well over a dozen wagon loads, all stored beneath the palace as requested."

"Very well. What else do you require?"

"I have a report in my quarters, should I find it, Sire?"

"Yes."

Holindo slipped from the room and Seto straightened on the chair. "Luik, have you filled Flir in on our discovery?"

"I have. She wanted to see for herself."

"It's him."

"I know, Flir. What I wish to know, is what it means. The man you deposited at the jail is the same man I captured, the same one I saw in the palace, the same man Notch saw outside the inn and also the man Luik followed from the explosion in the market. At most of those appearances, he would have been dead."

She threw up her hands. "He's a ghost."

"A twin, Seto," Luik said. "A brother with a close resemblance."

He sighed. "And I favour a fake, a decoy. Either way, we need to find Vinezi, or whoever he is, soon. I don't want another explosion."

"Any ideas?"

"Yes. One I should have implemented weeks ago. I blame myself of course, I shouldn't have let the palace take up so much of my attention. I honestly felt Luik would find him," he held up a hand at Luik's expression, "by which I mean, that Vinezi wouldn't have been so crafty. We had him beaten and his network smashed. I should have immediately engaged the people of the street through my own contacts."

"How much could you cover?"

Seto considered it. "The whole of the Lower Tier and good portions of the Second."

"Really?" Flir said.

"I don't mean I have so many men, you know that. Rather, I could place someone or contact informants and exploit relationships, and have eyes where we need them. It would be a complete mobilisation, to the detriment of other...projects, but I suspect we have no choice."

"Off to the inn then?" Luik said.

"Indeed."

CHAPTER 6

Sofia shivered beneath Osani as the forest closed around her. Woody scents mixed with the faint rot of loam stirred by hooves. Notch led his own horse through the trees, finding a thin path in the dying light. She patted her mare's neck, keeping close behind.

The trickle of water over stone grew. "How did you know where it was?" she asked.

Notch didn't turn. "I've travelled the Bloodwood several times, remember."

"And when will we reach Irihs?"

He stopped at the edge of the small stream. It cut deep into the earth, running clear over stone. His mount bent her head to drink. "Before noon tomorrow. Earlier if we push on, but I think we should camp here."

Her own horse drank. "Here? We should keep going a little further, shouldn't we?" In the failing light, with only a blush of colour in the distance through the western tree line and Notch's face a pale blur, there seemed little to recommend it as a site, aside from the stream.

"We have water and space here. And we're not visible

from the road." He picketed his mount to a tree. The harness jingled in the evening hush. "I know you want to hurry, but by now, anything that has happened to your father has already happened."

Sofia swallowed. He was right, but it didn't change anything. Father still needed her. "That's not reassuring, Notch."

"I know, I'm sorry. But it's safer to travel by day. And we need to stay safe if we're to help the Lord Protector."

"Safe from what? Bandits?"

"They are rare here but other things too. Simpler ones. Like injuring a horse in the dark. And Seto would have sent people to round us up, you can bet on that." He rubbed the horse's neck. "And then there's always the chance that some aggressive Braonn might take exception to our passage. I'd rather post a watch than stumble into something."

"I know there's going to be hostility, but are the Braonn truly likely to attack us?"

"I don't know. The deeper we end up, the higher the risk. Not everyone in the south is happy with the remnants of our rule."

"I know that."

"But you haven't seen it here. Without Luik or the caravan, there were places I might have been attacked or worse. It wasn't so many years ago."

"And my father?"

"He probably faced the same threats. I don't know."

"How far have you been into the wood?"

"To a section of the forest which conceals the First Tree. Luik took me to its borders, but not inside. No Anaskari are permitted inside its groves."

"I hope we won't have to travel so far." She tied her

own horse.

"Me too." He said. "I'll dig a fire pit – why don't you find fuel. Fallen wood only," he added.

Sofia hesitated.

"Make sure you get twigs and logs. Search the undergrowth for dry wood."

She nodded and moved between the trees in the dying light, reaching through the damp undergrowth to first collect twigs, then small branches and larger ones, holding them in the crook of her arm. Something rustled leaves in the distance and she flinched, losing a log. She snatched it up with a growl. Stupid. Afraid of the dark, Sofia?

Back in the camp she placed the pile beside Notch's own. He looked up from where he knelt, tinderbox in hand.

"I don't know, is this enough?" she said.

Notch chuckled. "It's fine."

"Stop that. How would I know?"

"Sorry." He began arranging the kindling in a tent formation, twigs beneath sticks and the bigger branches atop. He struck the flint, sending sparks into the dark until a tongue of flame grew. He kept feeding twigs, some barely thicker than a hair, to the small blaze and eventually the fire took hold.

"There." He stood, fetching a pan from the packs, which he rinsed in the stream before placing it beside her. Next he took a short bow and several arrows from where they were slung across the saddle. "How about rabbit? Or something with meat on its bones at least."

She held her hands out to the fire. "Yes, please."

Notch's footsteps, light as they were, faded into the trees. She removed Osani to wipe at her face. It wasn't long before she was blinking away a blurring of her vision. Her pulse had crept up again and a tremble snuck into her hands. She muttered a curse. Back already? The *lenasi* cravings barely gave her any respite. Damn Miandra and damn Tantos again. She replaced Osani.

Her head cleared.

The tremor in her limbs disappeared and air flowed through her lungs unimpeded.

But from the mask there was a great void of silence. Osani's face, just as white and aged as Argeon's once was, did not appear. And the only time she'd worn Argeon since, his blackened face remained white; whatever Tantos' death did to the mask itself, did not impact the way it appeared in her mind. Even so, she hadn't been able to keep it on. An image of Tantos had appeared with Argeon, so strong, so real. She'd snatched the Greatmask off and switched to Osani.

The Cavallo mask was a mystery. His presence, vast, lurked beyond a wall of some manner. As if she'd been blocked from truly seeing him. As her father had attuned Argeon to the Falco House, so obviously, had Solicci ensured none but a Cavallo might use Osani.

But wearing Osani continued to banish the effects of *lenasi* withdrawal, and it wasn't as if she knew how to use a Greatmask properly anyway. With a sigh she lay back, letting warmth from the fire set her boots to steaming while she waited for Notch.

"Sofia."

She opened her eyes. Notch stood over her, holding out a bowl. She took it, blinking at the steaming food, accepting a spoon next.

"You fell asleep."

Her head throbbed and her feet burned, but she

raised the mask and spooned the hot meat and stew into her mouth nonetheless, pulling her feet in to cool. Rabbit. "Notch, this is pretty good." She took another bite. The symptoms lurked, but while she ate, weren't overpowering.

He laughed. "You're just hungry."

Sofia smiled around another mouthful. "So do you know anyone in Irihs?"

"Luik has a cousin there. If we cannot learn anything from the traders, we'll find her."

"Good." She stood, collecting Osani and stretching her legs. "I can watch first, I'm wide awake now."

"Good, I'm getting tired." Notch scooped up a few more mouthfuls and unpacked his bedroll, laying it out after brushing sticks and stones from the ground. "Wake me when you get sleepy."

She sat on a log, put her back to the fire and strained her ears. The darkness between pale tree trunks was still. Only the crackle of the flames and Notch's breathing reached her. Osani was warm on her skin but distant. Again, she called to him without response. No doubt it would stay that way.

*Father, if only Argeon could reach you...*She straightened on the log. Why couldn't he? She'd never tried, but maybe there was a way? *Idiot.* She had one of the most powerful objects in the world and she hadn't thought to use it?

Tantos or no, she had to try.

Sofia crept to her bags. Notch stirred but didn't wake. She took Argeon back to her seat and paused. Would her brother be there again? Or was it only the echo of him she'd seen before? No more hesitation. Sofia raised the mask. In the void Argeon was quiet, not restless as she often expected. Nor did the mad drive of Tantos lurk within, only Argeon's vast calm. How to explain what she wanted? Nothing she'd heard or read about the masks suggested they could be used for scrying, but she had to try.

Images.

Her father in his robe, pacing the study. His stern face smiling, eyes creased. His laugh – so rare, but so loud. His arms lifting her into a carriage, his voice calling to Mother. Next, the question, but what image represented searching?

A rich gold splashed across the void – and beyond it, some hint of her father.

"Father? Is that you?"

Who speaks?

Was his voice deeper somehow? Sofia gripped her thighs. Had it worked? "Father, where are you – it's Sofia."

Young woman, I am not your father. Where are you – and what is wrong with your Novatura? The voice sounded agitated.

"Novatura?"

A sigh. *Yes. Are you even wearing it, or just touching it? Is that why your voice is so faint? I'm sending someone to –*

Sofia tore the mask from her face with trembling hands. Who was out there? She stood, drew her knife and crept between the trees, placing each foot in a deliberate step. She completed a circuit of the camp, heart thumping. Nothing. Sofia turned back to the fire. Should she wake Notch? No, there was no-one out there. Let him sleep. She turned back to the dark. No light, no sounds, no irritated voices.

Just who had Argeon connected her with? She raised the mask. Whoever it was seemed far away. Surely she was in danger? She placed the cool bone against her face.

Be sure, Sofia.

Into the void she spoke. "Are you there?"

No response.

She tried again, and received the same silence. Even Argeon barely flickered his attention to her.

By the time Notch was due for his shift, she'd almost dismissed the voice. But she told him as he drank from his flask. "It felt distant. I don't think anyone is close, but it seems worth mentioning."

"Could you tell anything about the voice? It wasn't Argeon or the Old One?"

"No. There was an accent that I couldn't place." She shook her head. "Not even an accent. An inflection. I don't know how to describe it."

"Well, I'll be watching." He already had his sword drawn, resting it across his knees. "Get some sleep, Sofia."

She prepared her own bedding and lay back.

*

Ihris spread around its trees. Most buildings had space enough for a small family only – many appeared suited to a single person. They were squat, with thatched rooves and not one of them over a single storey. Vines and moss grew across the surface of the buildings but all were built of wood, which surely was hypocritical? To revere the woods yet cut them to make their homes? Maybe Luik could explain it.

There was no strict boundary to the town, it simply began with a home nestled between two broad oaks. Moss climbed the walls and a flowering plant grew over the doorway. A white petal fluttered to the ground as she rode by.

Most people, their clothing green, grey and brown to blend with the forest, moved between homes without giving Sofia even a glance. Many wore longbows and quivers, both women and men. One large man, chest bare, sweated as he heaved slate across the path ahead.

Some of the Braonn however, cast unfriendly looks their way. One woman stood, arms folded, and watched them pass. Notch nodded to her but she did not respond.

"Chilly," Sofia said.

"It'll probably get worse."

"Wonderful." The Braonn continued to move from their homes to watch them pass. Muttering darkened some doorways. Several doors slammed and Sofia flinched. The significance of the action was not lost on Notch either, who tapped his horse's flanks, moving into a fast walk.

Further along, they passed a young couple standing around a small garden plot beside a home. Inside a sapling had been planted, it's broad leaf shot through with red veins. The young man's expression was expectant. The woman smiled and took the man's hand and he gave a cry of happiness.

"What was that?" Sofia asked once they'd passed.

"Part of an old Braonn courting ritual. She accepted him so they'll care for the tree now, to symbolise their commitment to one another."

More and more houses popped up, stretching back into the trees on all sides. There was no centralisation, just more houses, the mossy slope of their rooves making odd patterns.

"How do you find anything? A tailor, or somewhere for fletching?"

Notch pointed to a home with a man passing quivers

to children. "Each family's responsible for their own tools, clothes and weapons. For gathering food. The Braonn don't buy much, they mostly barter with a neighbour."

"Then who are the traders you mentioned?"

"At the edge of town there's a Trade House where people get materials they cannot easily provide for themselves. Some steel items, some medicines, food for the few travellers who aren't taken in to Braonn homes."

"They do that?"

"That's one of the reasons I know Luik has a cousin here – he'd stay here when he travelled."

The Trade House was much larger than the other buildings. A wide bench rested across its front, where a smiling man stood, sleeves rolled up. He stopped smiling when they dismounted and approached. Behind him lay shelves of assorted items, many jars – some of which looked to be jam, along with weapons and even a few bolts of Anaskari silk.

"What do you want?" His Anaskari was fair.

Notch answered in Braonn, stating their purpose then gesturing to Sofia.

She continued. "He would have come through some weeks prior, dressed as a Mascare, in red robes. He may not have worn a mask, but he would have sounded educated. He was a little older than my friend here and finally, he was being pursued. Others may have passed this way, close behind."

The man worked his jaw a moment. "You know this is a Trade House, missy?"

"Of course."

"Then I think it only fair that you offer something in exchange for information."

Notch leaned in. "Then you saw him? He came here?"

"You know, Ihris could use another horse. We have few at the moment."

Sofia blinked. Notch's face was turning red and his lips made a white line. "A horse?"

The Trader folded his arms. "Yeah. A horse."

Notch withdrew some Anaskari silver. "Three silver pennies."

He shook his head. "Don't want Anaskar coin. You know my terms."

Sofia put a hand on Notch's arm, which had begun to tremble. "Agreed. Take mine," she said. "Now what do you know?"

He grinned at her. "I saw a man like you describe. He traded for food and headed toward Avaon."

Sofia drew breath. "When?"

"Must be over a full turn of the moon."

"And those who followed?"

"Three Masks, but none of your fancy Guards. They paid too."

Sofia thanked him and joined Notch, who was already transferring supplies from her horse to his own, the stronger of the two. He handed the reins to the Trader. "Here." Notch said. "The saddle is a gift for your generosity of spirit."

The man gave a mock bow and led the horse away. Notch shook his head, switching to Anaskari. "That was robbery. We could have asked any other person in Ihris and found the same information."

"Not the people I saw, Notch. And Father didn't speak to them, he spoke to the Trader."

He grunted. "Well, you can ride. I don't want to overburden Swift now that she's carrying everything." Notch helped her mount up, then slung a pack over his shoulder. "At least we're on the right path."

She flicked the reins gently. "I hope so. We're so far behind."

Notch led them into the trees. "We'll find him."

CHAPTER 7

Ain fell back against cold stone of the palace dungeon, Schan close by.

In the dim light a slender arm stretched through the bars, long fingers still more than a foot from being able to touch him or Schan.

"What does it want?" Schan breathed.

"The egg?"

Ain gaped as the creature's skin changed colour to match the bar, and then the light inside the cell, blending the dark grey and grime. Its body was too broad to fit between the bars, but not by much. Ain inched away. The arm strained, clawing toward him.

Light burst into the cells.

The creature fell back, seeming to melt into a wall as a pair of guards approached, boots scraping on stone. One held a torch, the other chains. Both wore shiny breastplates and hard expressions. The one with chains motioned for Ain to turn around. A long scar crossed his throat.

Ain glared at the man.

The guard only repeated the motion.

Ain folded his arms.

The Anaskari exchanged a few words. The one with the torch shrugged. Chain-man leant against the bars. "Do as I say," he rasped. "The King wishes to speak with you. He didn't specify what condition you were to be in. Cooperate."

The man spoke Medah. And more than competently. Ain frowned. "Why would I trust an Anaskari dog?"

The guard growled. "Last chance."

Ain snorted, then did as he was told. He exchanged a glance with Schan, who shrugged.

"Hands behind your back." The key turned in the cell door as Ain complied. The guard continued. "Not your friend. Move across the cell, warrior. And no moving. Giovan likes to use his knife."

Cold steel clapped over Ain's hands with a clanking. Then he was jerked toward the door, pushed outside and marched down the hall. He twisted his neck. Schan watched from the cell. The older man mouthed the word "strength" and then Ain stumbled over the threshold and a door slammed shut.

Had the creature followed? Or was it watching Schan? Wherever it lurked, Schan could take care of himself. Even locked in a cell.

His guards did not speak as they marched him along dim corridors of stone. Ain couldn't stop a fresh bout of shivers. Damn the cold. Anaskar was a nightmare of chill and unforgiving stone. Outside was worse, the cutting wind.

And paths.

A constant, hideous mess of them. Everywhere. From youngest whispers to the oldest thump of boots on stone from centuries past, the whole palace was littered with them. Their rumbling filled his head until it throbbed, assaulted by their persistent creeping from even the city below. Grinding his teeth, he was able to push it back for the most part but the pressure remained.

After twisting through a maze of dark corridors he found himself blinking in new light, as the guards stopped before a plain door and knocked. Ain flexed his hands while the guard waited, anything to distract from the paths.

"Come, Holindo."

Holindo opened the door and dragged Ain into warmth. An old man with silver hair sat in a rich room. Wooden chairs and the table, both set with some manner of bone, rested in the centre. On the table, strangest of all – most wasteful of all – were red flowers in a clear vase. Their stems drank deeply of water.

Ain licked parched lips. He studied the silver-haired man. Black clothing, no distinction to it. He wore no jewels or obvious marks of status, but his authority was clear, even without the deferential pose of the guards.

"Thank you both." The old man looked to Giovan. "Ensure we are not interrupted."

The guard left without a word. Holindo stood beside the old man but did not take his eyes from Ain. No-one spoke. Sands. He wouldn't indulge them. Let his captors speak first. Curiosity be damned. Just sit still and block out the paths.

"Welcome to Anaskar." The old man's Medah was perfect. "I wonder if it meets your expectations?"

"Not at all."

He laughed. "Sometimes I must agree. But I am being ill-mannered. I haven't introduced myself. I am King

Oseto and I have brought you here to make you an offer."

Ain narrowed his eyes. "You jest?"

"His Majesty does no such thing," Holindo snapped.

The old man raised a hand. To Ain, he smiled, though it was predatory. "Indeed I do not. Now, Ain, Pathfinder of Cloud Oasis, would you like to hear my proposal? I trust the chatter of the paths is not too great here in the palace?"

"You know a lot about me, King Oseto."

"Your name from conversations with your warrior, your skill set via your cloak and as I understand, it has been the responsibility of the Cloud to send Pathfinders on the Search for the last few decades."

Ain smothered a spark of surprise. "You don't expect me to be impressed, surely?"

"I expect you to be interested." The King toyed with a petal. "Your skills as a Pathfinder are useful to me. It's my hope that they're worth your life. And Schan's life. That is what I'm offering you. Help me locate what I seek, and you shall both be set free to return to your Oasis."

Ain shook his head. "Your word is worth nothing. I hardly trust it, the word of a usurper."

"Very well." The King stood. "Back to your cell then."

Holindo called for Giovan and the King walked to a second door, one built to resemble the wall. He passed beyond without a backward glance, and before Ain could react, he was hauled to his feet.

"Guess you like it down there," Giovan snickered.

Ain gave no reply. For days now, ever since he'd been captured, he'd known his fate. They would execute him; a fitting reward for failure, perhaps. And all the time in the cell, staring at the steel door where the egg had been locked away, choking down bread and water, waiting for them to come, hope draining from his body like invisible blood, and suddenly the King of the devils offered him a chance to see Silaj again.

It had to be a lie.

CHAPTER 8

Flir rubbed her temples with fingertips, turning from the calm man waiting in the sunlit street with a beatific smile. Why couldn't he let it rest? "Pevin, can you at least stand a bit further away while you stare like that?"

He took a single step back. "Of course, dilar."

Luik grinned at her.

"Don't you laugh, Luik, or I'll smack your fat head into the harbour."

He glanced down the quiet street to the Lower Tier wall, as if to draw attention to the considerable distance, but said only, "Give him something to do."

She turned to her follower. "Pevin, go find us some food, will you?"

"Certainly." He turned with a nod, starting back up the cobbles toward the clamour of conversation from a market.

"Meet us at the Beast," she called after him.

He turned to bow again, before quickening his step. Flir let her shoulders slump. If only he didn't know. Or better yet, no-one knew. At least Luik, and Notch when he was around, never treated her differently. No dilar, just Flir. No ridiculous lies about the Goddess Mishalar, just Flir.

She started toward the harbour. "How do you think Notch and Sofia are doing?"

"I wouldn't worry about them, Flir. Notch knows what he's doing and Sofia has the Greatmasks."

"You're right I suppose. But I'll admit, I wish I was with them."

Luik gave a grunt.

Was he agreeing or not? She waved an arm at the tall buildings, mostly warehouses or large workshops and shipyards. "All this running around, looking for acor, maybe it's a goose chase and there's none left."

"Sure of that?"

"No, I'm not."

"Well, Vinezi's still out there. Or his brother."

"That's just what we need, two Vinezis."

"We've got a possible riot to break up at least."

She cracked her knuckles. "Good."

"Seto wants us to defuse trouble, Flir. Not start it."

Flir shrugged.

The street fed into a busy thoroughfare. Women with baskets of silver-scaled fish and vegetables, men in overalls and the city Vigil all went about their business, but children, idle merchants and even a few nobles by their dress, paraded toward the corpse of the Sea Beast. They laughed and shouted as they bounced along.

One man was waving his hands and a dried fish-head charm swung from his neck. "You've never seen anything like it, Puco. They're actually cutting it up-is, but it's so big it's taking forever."

Puco's bushy eyebrows rose. "I should have come

home sooner. Reckon we could take a piece for luck?"

"We'll ask when we get there," the first man said, as the two passed by.

Idiots. It wasn't a novelty at a market.

Flir let Luik make a path with his broad shoulders, rather than accidently flinging someone into a wall herself. Even so, it was slow going. "Seto needs to do something about this. Ban gawkers already."

"Think they'd listen?" Luik said over his shoulder.

"Good point."

The watery sun fell behind a cloudbank and the street darkened a shade as the Sea Beast came into view, its black bulk towering over the street. It remained in the wreckage of the wall, but significant portions had been cut away over the weeks since its death. A rotten piece of fruit it was. Black and slime-covered on the outside; pinker flesh within. In places it still hung from the massive white rib bones. Scaffolding had been erected around the beast's body and the Guard were tiny where they cut into the flesh.

Their spoils would be heading to two places. The flesh itself dumped in the harbour to disintegrate, as early on Seto discovered that the flesh would not burn under any flame. The precious bones, however, were placed in massive wagon beds and transported to the palace. As far as the populace knew, it was so the beast's skeleton could be reassembled in the palace grounds. Flir smiled. It had to be one of Seto's more brilliant deceptions – it so naturally fit his love of the grandiose.

The wind changed and the fetid stink of old fish ran through the crowd. Groans and curses went with it, and Flir spat. "No wonder there's been rioting. I couldn't live with this."

Luik grunted his agreement, a hand over his face.

At the barricade, which blocked off a good deal of the streets surrounding the corpse, they were given cloths soaked in lemon to tie around their faces. Flir knotted hers with a sigh. It didn't remove the smell, but it made being near the corpse bearable. Captain Holindo himself handed them out.

"How goes it?" Flir asked.

"We lost two more men today. A vein exploded. We tried to clean them, but there was too much blood." Holindo's jaw worked beneath the cloth. "This creature had better be worth the cost."

"At the least, we're protecting the people from it," Luik said.

Holindo nodded.

"Has there been any further trouble?" Flir asked. Both Shield and Vigil lined the barricades day and night, to protect the people from the corpse but also to safeguard the precious bones. The Mascare were present too, their red robes stirred by the chill sea breeze. While there was shouting and pleading from the crowds, much of it directed at the Guard, no-one shouted at the Mascare whenever one of the masks completed a circuit.

The Captain pointed to a section of crowd pushing up against the barricade, waving their fists and shouting. Many were fishermen and all had the look of Lower Tier folk, their clothing drab. "There, see that lot?"

"They look unhappy."

"They are and they should be," he rasped. "They want the beast gone and so do I. It's as I feared, there are reports of people falling ill."

"From the smell?"

He spread his hands. "Perhaps, but likely from the sea.

Dumping the flesh in the harbour will now stop."

"That's what's making people sick? They aren't eating it are they?"

"I hope not. First, the flesh we cut away disintegrated as it sunk. It didn't seem to be doing any harm. Why would it? The beast has swum the sea for centuries."

Luik slapped his thigh. "The fish!"

"Right. That's what we think. The dead flesh is poisonous and fish are eating that flesh, then our fishermen catch those fish, feed them to their families or sell it in the markets." He paused to swallow. "People have been sick for days it appears, and not every symptom worsens at once. With others it may have been fear; they did not want to tell us."

Flir turned from the angry people. "Does Seto know?"

"I've sent a runner. He should –"

A cry cut across the staging area. A man clung to the scaffold, his saw clattering to the cobbles far below. Holindo charged forward, shouting orders over the now hushed crowd.

"Come on." Flir ran after. Another workman climbed across scaffolds, calling for his friend to hold on. The stricken man's legs dangled.

"His gloves will be wet from the monster," a Shield cried.

Flir kept running, dodging a half-loaded wagon, shouldering men aside and skidding to a halt beneath the scaffold. Some of the men she'd knocked to the ground shouted but she ignored them. The dangling man's friend closed in and stretched a hand down. The workman caught it. A cheer rose from the Guard and other workers, echoed in some spots from the crowd.

Flir released a breath as the man was pulled up.

A sharp splitting sound and a scream followed as part of the scaffold snapped, sending one of the men tumbling through the air. Flir dashed across the stone, spread her arms and braced herself.

Luik shouted but his voice was lost in the rush and thump as the falling man crashed into her grip. A shock of pain thundered through her bones but she stood firm. The dazed man babbled as she set him aside, neck craned. The second workman clung to a sturdy part of the scaffold, edging toward a second structure.

The stunned crowd began to urge him on.

His hand slapped around the other scaffold and then he was safe. Cheers rose again, and this time everyone was staring at her. Standing beside Luik and Captain Holindo, arms burdened with food, was Pevin. His eyes brimmed with tears, an exultant expression on his face.

Flir groaned.

CHAPTER 9

After fending off waves of adoration and speaking with the man she'd saved, tears streaming down his face into his already soaking cloth mask, Flir hid in the command post with Luik and Holindo. Pevin she made wait outside the tan-coloured tent, but let him dig into the food.

What she really wanted was a bath, now that she reeked of Sea Beast. Although, saving a life was probably worth a bit of stink.

Luik thumped her arm. "Good job, Flir."

She thumped him back. "Thanks. You can get the next one."

Holindo poured them each a small glass of fire-lemon, regarding Flir with a touch of awe. He'd removed his cloth-mask, as had Luik, and Flir did the same. In the tent the smell of the beast wasn't too bad, masked by crushed rosemary.

Flir smiled at him. "Now don't you start acting like Pevin."

He blinked. "I won't. Only, that was impressive."

She accepted her drink and drained it with a nod. "Well, I won't be around all the time, so don't get used to it. Now, what about this illness?"

Holindo reached into a stack of papers and shuffled them. "Too early to tell if it's contagious. Over a hundred reported cases, and I've only today started taking reports. Symptoms include a blue skin pallor, odd growths and breathing problems. One boy's stomach grew so swollen that he died. There must be more but the people aren't talking much. They're afraid."

Luik's face was set.

Flir leant forward. "For how many days now?"

"Earliest case is two days old – but it must have started sooner."

She stood. "Take me to one of them, Captain."

Luik joined her. "You sure?"

"We need more information."

Captain Holindo gestured through the tent wall, in the direction of the barricade. "We can ask them, though I don't like our chances."

Flir pulled open the tent flap and headed for the row of angry faces at the barricade. Pevin fell into step beside her and Holindo motioned for a pair of Shields to join him. She brought the small party to a halt by the largest contingent of citizens. The shouting and jeers eased to muttering when the people recognised her.

A voice from the back of the press of bodies shouted. "No-one to catch here, lovely."

Flir glanced at Holindo, who nodded. Being gentle would win her more ears. The folk in the Lower Tier were afraid of the illness. They wanted help, not violence. Most of all, they wanted answers. Just like the people in Caldtha, where the plague slaughtered without pause.

Bodies in ice drifts flashed before her mind's eye.

"Who is here to waste time in misplaced anger?" She raised her hands when the voices swelled and waited for them to stop. "And who is here to find help for their loved ones?"

An old woman sneered. "Think you can help us, girl?"

"Who else has offered?"

Quiet. Then the muttering renewed. "Not them damn Shields, that's for sure. All they do is shout or rough us up-is."

Behind her, one of the guards snapped. "It's for your own damn good, you half-wits."

Holindo whirled on the man. A stone bounced off the Captain's armour before he could speak. Flir leapt onto the barricade, leaning down to point her finger at the people. "Stop this. Don't you want to help your families?"

A young woman spun on the crowd. "She's right-is, just listen, will you?"

Flir raised her voice. "The new king will listen to me. If someone will allow it, I will come with them to their home, to see a sick loved one. I want to understand what is happening. Then, tomorrow, I will bring back the full might of the palace and put an end to this illness."

The muttering faltered. Hopeful faces raised and Flir spoke to the young woman. "What's your name?"

"Ana, My Lady."

"Ana, will you take me to your home?"

She pressed her hands together. "Oh, My Lady, yes. Please, it's my father, Delamo. He has so much trouble breathing, he does."

"Lead the way." Flir jumped down into the crowd. They surged along the streets, half-carrying her between shadows of tall buildings, her feet brushing the cobblestones every other step. Somewhere beyond, Luik's voice mingled with Pevin and Holindo's shouts. They would follow.

Having left her cloth in the tent, she wrinkled her nose when the crowd took her past one of the drainage grates; a bad sign if she could smell it too, over the miasma created by the rotting corpse. Beside her, Ana chewed her lip as she fluttered along the cobblestones, leading Flir deeper into the poorer parts of the Lower Tier.

"Here." Ana stopped beside a green door in a small building wedged between others of a similar, dark stone. Refuse clogged the street. Ana's door was newly, if crudely, repaired. Someone had obviously kicked it in.

Stove, table and chairs, candles and a pile of blankets were crammed into the first room, and in the second an older man lay wheezing on one of two cots. Ana knelt by his side, near to displacing a boy. "Delamo, my father," she told Flir. "Father, can you hear me?" To the boy, "How is he?"

The boy sniffed. "The same, Mother." He frowned up at Flir.

Ana stroked her son's face. "This lady is going to try and help your grandfather-is, don't worry now."

Flir moved closer. Delamo's skin was tinted blue, even in the poor light of the bedroom it had a vibrancy. He didn't quite glow, yet no healthy man ever looked so damn strange. His chest rose and fell in a sharp rhythm, strained. The air seemed to claw its way along his throat. His hands twitched constantly.

The only good sign, not that she was a healer, was that he ran no fever.

"How long has he been like this, Ana?"

"Four days now, My Lady."

"Good."

She blinked. "How so?"

"I'm only guessing, but if it was an especially vicious illness, he might not have survived the first night." She held up her hands when mother and child brightened. "I'm not a healer, remember. But I've seen a deadly sickness devour a village in my homeland, and none of them lasted beyond two days."

"He's strong," Ana said.

"He works for us on the wharves," the child added.

Flir gave him a big smile. "Then let's try and get him back there."

"But how?" Ana stood, lowering her voice. "A dock-healer has tried herbs and potions and nothing has worked."

"I am going to the King after I see some more people. He's a very clever man."

"King Oson?" Ana's expression was not confident.

"No, King Oseto."

"And he will save my father?" Her eyes were wide.

"I don't know, but he'll try." Seto would know something about the sickness, surely. "Has your father been eating a lot of fish lately?"

"We all do."

Flir paused. "And you're not sick, not your son?"

"No. Should we stop eating the fish? Only, it's all we have most of the time-is."

What could she say? "Just be careful, check whatever you eat very carefully."

"What do I look for?"

"Discolouration." Flir said. Was that even the right thing to suggest? "And anything out of the ordinary."

Ana took her arm. "Thank you, My Lady."

"I'm not really a lady."

Pevin entered the house. He made a swift bow. "Dilar."

"Pevin, where's Luik and Holindo?" She ignored the confused look from Ana.

"Both outside, speaking with the people. Luik doesn't look too comfortable."

The big sissy. He'd never been good with sickness. "Ana, look after your father. I'll be back as soon as I can."

Ana nodded, eyes filling.

Outside, Flir joined Luik and Holindo, who stood listening to a breathless young man. The crowd had grown, more men in overalls and worn clothing waiting in the street. "She's awake but she won't answer me and she never turns from the wall."

"For how long, son?" Captain Holindo's voice was quieter, as if tired. He swallowed after he spoke. His throat was obviously giving him pain; he took a small pouch from his belt and removed a pinch of herb, which he chewed on.

"Since yesterday."

"Let's go," Flir said to Holindo. Luik drew in a breath but said nothing. The young man took them to a nearby home. This time, Holindo joined her. Pevin she left outside with Luik and the crowd, Luik especially appeared pleased enough to stay outside. "Find out who's in the most trouble," she told them.

The young man knocked on the door. The wood parted a crack, enough for an eye to fix on the young lad, then beyond to Flir, Holindo and the crowd. "Mother, some people from the palace want to help Bel."

The door swung open. A squinting woman waved them in. "About time-is."

She led them to the corner of a kitchen, to a cot

stretched out beside a closed door. A girl's slim form faced the wall. She groaned when her brother knelt and touched her shoulder.

"Bel, it's just me." He paused. "There's some people here from the palace who want to help you."

Still nothing. The young man rubbed his arms. "Please, Bel. You're in pain."

Flir squeezed closer. "Bel, my name is Flir and I want to help you. I'm going to speak to the King today."

The mother snorted but Flir ignored her.

"It's true, Bel – look," her brother said.

She turned, squinting over her shoulder. "Really?"

Flir knelt. "Yes. Now can you tell me what's wrong? I need to know so I can tell the King."

Bel looked at her brother and mother, to everyone in the room and then back to Flir. Flir stood, motioning for them to leave the room. The family complained but Holindo placated them as he ushered them out.

"All right, where does it hurt?" The girl didn't have the blue pallor, no hint of fever or any overt signs of illness.

She turned. "Here." Bel lifted her shirt and Flir steeled the muscles in her face. A pointed fin grew from her side, the skin around its exit red and inflamed. "It hurts all the time-is, but sometimes really bad."

"Bel, we're going to get you all fixed up right now. I'm taking you to the palace, all right?"

Bel's face brightened. "Can Alfeo and Mother come?"

Flir scooped her up, blanket and all. "We'll send for them."

On the step to the door, Flir explained what was happening and charged along the street, heading for the palace.

"They won't let us in," Bel's brother called.

"I'll send someone."

Flir ran, cobblestones flashing beneath her feet. By Mishalar, trouble was coming.

Chapter 10

Notch led Swift to a thick clump of grass just off the trail. Luik had taken him on narrower paths, but this trail was not well used. Animal droppings were frequent, as were weeds. Nettles tall as the horse's shoulders lined the path and twice he'd had to move fallen branches.

Sweat itched beneath his leathers as he waited. He took a long drink from his flask.

Who would Seto send into the trees to catch them? Surely not Luik and Flir? The old fox needed them to prepare for the invasion. Notch chewed the inside of his cheek. Gods, if any of them were to...no, no point going there.

"Notch, what are you looking at?" Sofia stared down at him.

"Nothing. We should eat." He rummaged through the packs and threw her an apple, crunching into his own. The juice was always better than the flesh. He smiled, cheeks full. "This might be the best apple I've ever had."

Sofia shook her head, her own smile wide, but her expression faded. She inched her hand toward the bag that hid the Greatmasks.

Four Braonn had slipped from the trees, striding down the path to spread into a half circle before them. Notch put his hand on his hilt but didn't draw. The Braonn wore their greens, but kept their bows slung over their shoulders. The leader bore similar tattoos to Wayrn – linking his family to the First Tree.

All four were young men, or boys if he had to draw a line.

"You shouldn't be here," the leader said in Braonn.

Notch raised a hand to prevent Sofia answering. The kids weren't here to talk. They were trying to prove something to themselves, to each other. How much worse had the resentment grown? In truth, he'd expected an easier time. Naïve of him probably. But was it a bluff? Best to put a stop to it either way.

"Are you sure you want to be here?" he replied, speaking clear as he could.

The leader sniggered. He'd understood. "I'm sure, Anaskari. This is our forest. You are the one who needs to understand. You're not in your monstrous city now."

Notch stepped away from the horse, motioning for Sofia to stay. She kept her hand inside the pack. He rolled his shoulders, stretching his arms before removing his leather armour and tunic, dropping the dark cloth to the earth. The chill beneath the trees must have had his scars standing out, from the look on the leader's face. The longest one, which ran from shoulder to chest, was especially pale.

Keeping eye contact with the leader, Notch drew his blade and he went to his knees, movements deliberate, before pulling one of his knives and slapping the blades together.

"*Ma dirra o curiga.*"

A slave's duel.

Two boys stepped back. The leader's eyes were wide.

Notch repeated his challenge.

Finally the group turned to run, the leader being pulled along the trail by one of his fellows. Notch grinned at their backs.

"What the hell just happened?" Sofia said. "And why did you take your clothes off?"

He ducked into the tunic. "They had to see my scars. That way they'd be too afraid to accept my challenge."

"I didn't follow all of that. What did you say to them?"

"In an old slave's duel, the loser must become the other's slave. Or die." Notch chuckled. "Those boys weren't going to try it."

"That sort of thing doesn't happen in Anaskar. How'd you find out about that?"

"Luik taught it to me, in case I was ever accosted alone."

Sofia wiped her brow. "Glad he did."

"The fever?"

"It's fine, I'll just wear Osani again."

Notch frowned. She needed a proper solution soon. Using the mask was one thing, but what if she couldn't wear it for some reason? How long before the cravings posed a real problem? He didn't want her burning up.

They wove deeper into the forest. Birds chattered and leaves whispered underfoot, but none of the sounds were unnatural. Hopefully the youths were the last of the trouble they'd face from the Braonn. No need to let Sofia know that their behaviour was more aggressive than he'd expected.

The nearer they came to the First Tree, the worse the

tension would become. The oldest families in the forest were hardly friendly toward the Anaskari. If only there was a way to know if Danillo had flown that far into the forest? Or whether something more sinister had befallen him? Hard to imagine. The man was invulnerable. Even without a Greatmask, Sofia's father was a force of nature. As a young Shield, and a star pupil at that, Notch had sparred with Danillo. He'd been hopelessly out-matched.

Even so, the Bloodwood had seemingly swallowed up the Lord Protector.

But Danillo wasn't a coward; he would have fought tooth and nail to return, to protect his daughter and take back his position.

"Where could he be, Notch?" Sofia's voice echoed behind the mask.

He shook his head. How closely their thoughts had taken them. "Deep is my guess."

"I keep asking myself why he didn't come back, if he's able."

Notch hesitated. "He might be hurt."

"Or dead." Her voice cracked on the word.

Notch looked up at her. Her shoulders were set and she stared to the thickets of tree trunks ahead, Osani cloaking her face. "Have you searched for him again?"

"No. That voice, I don't trust it. And I don't know if it's even possible to use the mask that way. It might not even be safe to wear Osani." She shrugged. "But nothing's happened yet."

"Then we'll find him without the masks," he said, giving her a smile.

Night came and went. He woke at the smallest sounds after his watch, and when morning came his head was thick with the remnants of sleep. He splashed chill water from the stream they'd camped near, flinching as it ran down his neck. Damn winter, too cold beneath the trees, too cold everywhere.

A heavy mist half-concealed Sofia as she loaded Swift, who stomped a hoof. Another cold breakfast, but it was too damp to bother with a fire now. Nor would Sofia want to, the way she tied off each saddlebag with a snap was a clear indicator of her sense of urgency.

"Ready?" he asked, stepping into the camp.

"Ready."

He led Swift along the still-narrow trail, mist peppering his face. It dampened everything, the ground, the gleaming trunks and the leaves, the horse's flanks and their bags. He shook drops from his hair as he walked, boots muffled by the loam.

At noon, vibrant autumn colours appeared ahead.

Which made no sense. Elsewhere stood evergreens and their bloody leaves beside empty elms. Autumn was gone. He slowed. "Wait. Something's wrong."

"What?"

"Look at the leaves. They're too bright; the reds and yellows."

She glanced around. "It's winter. And aren't a lot of trees in the Bloodwood always green anyway?"

"A part of the forest that never turns green," he said. "It sounds like...legends of the Autumn Groves."

"Is it dangerous?"

"I don't know. Luik told me that most Braonn believe the Autumn Groves are a place of ill fortune, due to the unchanging trees. Others say all Braonn ancestors came from the Groves." Notch said, shrugging his pack higher. "I've never seen them. And I don't remember it lying between Irihs and Avaon."

"We're taking a different path though."

"Hmmm."

"We can't waste time on a detour to double back."

He hesitated. The trees lifted their arms to collect water in their orange and brown leaves. Some patches of yellow peeked through, and spots of crimson, but the misted rain muted them all. The trail widened, broad enough for two wagons to pass. Twin sets of old grooves told as much. Only now there was no traffic, only thin, pale weeds. Beneath the trees were few shrubs, and even fewer leaves.

In fact, barely a dozen leaves sat on the ground in any direction.

The drip of water to the earth grew loud.

"Notch?"

"Your father might have passed this way."

"So we should keep going. What else do the legends say?"

He shook his head as he moved into the trees. "I don't know any more. We'll just keep our eyes open."

"How far does it stretch?" Sofia asked, voice soft. Once again, she wore Osani.

Notch wiped moisture from his face. "Hard to say."

"Do you feel anything?"

"Like what?"

"I don't know. Something unusual."

"I feel cold."

Sofia snorted. "Fine. Just be on the lookout for Father."

Swift nickered when he rubbed her neck, moving deeper into the hush. No birds sang, no small creatures rustled about in the leaves on the ground – there were none to slip through. Twice he went for his sword at a shape on the trail ahead, but it was no man. Large wooden statues stood beside the trail. The first was taller than a rider on a horse, carved as a man with wings folded around his shoulders, but had no head. He gripped a blade and long pitchfork. The grooves in the wood were wind-worn, save for the section shorn off by the head. There the jagged teeth of a saw left behind rough edges.

The second statue was the same, a tall, winged figure looming from pale mist, barely a few dozen yards along the trail. Only it was of a woman and her head was intact. Her expression was serene, though unlike the first statue, she held a carven spade and a net.

"What are they?" Sofia asked.

Notch had to laugh. "I wish I knew. I'm not much of a guide, am I?"

"You're doing fine." Sofia leant over to touch the woman's net. "What is this for? If they're carved of Braonn Gods I've never heard of them as having wings."

"Nor I." The same hush was magnified here, his voice echoed in the mist. "But they don't help us, whatever they are."

"True." Sofia pulled away and tapped the horse's flanks.

By late afternoon the rain eased. They passed no more statues and the road remained true, never forking, but Notch found himself squinting at the light. Even with the overcast sky, barely visible through the autumn canopy, the afternoon was too bright – as best he could tell, light still fell from directly above. Sofia had been right; something was strange here. Time passed slower in the Grove.

Notch swore. "I don't like this."

Sofia stopped the horse. "What?"

"The sun is in the wrong place. We've been travelling

for hours and it's barely moved."

Sofia craned her neck. "Then the Grove is cursed?"

He shook his head.

"All we can do is keep going."

"I guess so."

By nightfall, or what ought to have been nightfall, since the light had not changed enough for darkness, Sofia gave a shout. "There. Notch, quickly." She kicked Swift into a trot and he gave chase. Up ahead, Sofia dismounted and knelt by a dark shape. She waved back at him.

He thundered to a halt at her side. "Another clue?"

"Yes."

A pair of corpses lay heaped across one another in the centre of the trail. One Shield and a Mascare, both armed – yet none had drawn. Scuff marks cut into the forest floor, as if quite a battle had taken place. And yet, no other bodies waited on the damp earth.

Notch pointed. "Look." Both men had giant purple bruises spreading beneath their skin. The Shield's entire throat and chin were covered. Peeling back the mask revealed a similar wound on the Mascare, though it trailed down the man's throat toward the chest. Notch gave the wet robe a jerk, tearing the fabric. He did the same with the undershirt. The purple bruising spread further, from throat down to nipple.

"What could do that?" Sofia whispered.

"I've never seen such wounds. It's no illness, and yet – it does have the look of a bruise."

"A fresh bruise. Shouldn't they have faded?"

"Not after death. Could your father have done this?"

"Perhaps with a poison. I don't know them all."

Notch nodded. It didn't explain the scuff marks, as

many as half a dozen men, maybe more, could have made them. But it was a start. Anyone could have killed the men, but if they had been travelling the Grove, then so had the Protector. "We're on the right path."

"How long have they been dead?"

He shrugged. "In this place? I don't know. From their bodies, several days. But it must be more than that."

Sofia stood, turning a slow circle. "So you feel it too."

Notch grunted, digging through the clothing on the bodies, relieving them of their silver. From the mask he added a belt of poisons to his takings and took a fine dagger from the Shield. Probably a gift for a promotion, given the Swordfish on his tunic.

He held up the belt. "Can you use this?"

"Notch, they're dead."

"We've established that."

She snatched it from him, running a finger across the coloured vials. "I only recognise some, but I'll take it."

Notch rose, knees creaking inside. "Good. I hate to rob a corpse for nothing."

Sofia frowned. "That's a bad habit, Notch."

"I'm a mercenary, My Lady."

"I know, I know." She mounted up and kicked the horse into a trot.

He whispered a Soldier's Prayer for the Shield, hoping it would do for the mask too, and followed.

CHAPTER 11

In the smaller room set off from the regeneration chamber Vinezi held his hands before a brazier, arms outstretched. No tiled floor here, just stone. But it was warmer at least. With one hand he pulled back the fingers of the other, locking his elbow. He continued to do this while he waited, changing arms regularly. The restoration of his strength was more tedious that the last time – dim memories of his first recovery were surfacing.

It had taken a day to recover. No more. He'd spent most of it eating, stretching and building endurance with heavy stones – but that seemed enough. Yet how many hours since his latest regeneration and the notion of re-entering the city remained ludicrous. He fatigued too easily, like an invalid. How many times had he dozed off on the bench before coming to the warmth of the fire?

The murmur of voices drifted in from an adjoining chamber as his brothers finally returned.

"...and you shouldn't have taken the risk," Tarvilus was saying as they entered.

Julas strode beside him, fake mask in hand, red robe

swirling. He limped. Was that new? Vinezi frowned. Or could he simply not recall? The youngest, Julas bore more resemblance to his mother than their father. For that alone, he might have been Vinezi's favourite. "No progress without taking a few chances – isn't that what you always tell me?"

"What is this?" Vinezi asked.

"How do you feel?" Julas joined him at the brazier, eyes roving.

"Adequate." He switched hands. "What is afoot? Risk?"

Tarvilus folded his arms. "He's let one of the experiments loose."

"Which experiment would that be?"

"You don't remember?" Julas frowned. "Didn't the regeneration work properly? You look well enough, aside from the discolouration."

Discolouration? Ah. From the animal parts no doubt. "It is simply slower this time. And tell me about..." He trailed off. Maybe the experiments were familiar after all. Using bone charms...for something. With Renovar...no, Anaskari recruits? "It's gone."

Julas shrugged. "It's nothing really. We have been trying to imbue power into some of the recruits via the bone fragments you stole."

"Stole from where?"

"Home. Ecsoli."

"Ecsoli is no longer our home," Vinezi said with a frown.

"It's more our home than this place. Anaskar is so small." Julas said. "Why didn't Those Who Fled build something bigger?"

"Not to mention their pitiful Mascare," Tarvilus said.

Vinezi let them blather a moment. A memory danced

beyond his grip...if only...yes! Many of the pieces his brothers spoke of had to be the off-cuts and fragments salvaged from the Carver's Quarters...some few pieces tied to a ship's anchor before...before...deceiving Harbour Warden, yes. And not long after, when the shoreline was gone – raising the mutiny. "That is a very limited crop of bone." His tone cut into the discussion.

Tarvilus shook his head. "It was your idea."

"I see." No memory of that. "Then do keep going."

"Some respond better than others. We haven't had any deaths since the first. Just wearing the charm seemed to energise one man, Alvetti. Perhaps he has a strong link to his ancestors?" Julas said. "He's an Anaskari Shield and I own his gambling debt but he jumped at the chance to try."

Vinezi raised an eyebrow. "And Tarvilus is angry because?"

"He thinks Alvetti isn't ready for the plan. Too rash."

"Alvetti *is* rash," Tarvilus said. "Worse than Julas."

Vinezi growled. How much longer would he have to be in the dark when it came to his recent memories? "What plan?"

"Don't worry, I've set it in motion. We'll soon have access to every bone in the city," Julas said.

Vinezi rolled his shoulders. "A promising claim – I assume this plan you mention is mine?"

"Of course," Julas said. He glanced around. "What's left to eat?"

"Little," Tarvilus said.

"Well, what have you been doing while I was in the city?"

"Restoring our brother. Some of the others have been hunting – it's not easy to feed even our small party on this blasted mountain," he said. "Why don't you check on them yourself?"

"Enough," Vinezi snapped. Julas hung his head and Tarvilus looked away. "Julas, you will find food soon enough but first, tell me exactly what you have done."

He sighed. "Only what was planned."

"But too soon," Tarvilus interjected.

Vinezi snapped his fingers. "Enough."

"Sorry, brother."

Julas moved a little closer to the brazier. "I opened the Harvest Chamber beneath the harbour and we swam down. Don't worry, no-one saw us. We surfaced beneath the palace with the acor – and I judged it dry so we began to stack it beneath the palace." He paused to scratch his neck. "It's taken forever but there's finally enough acor to blow the palace apart from the inside."

The general thrust of what Julas said was...like a twinge, playing on his mind. It sounded an approximation of what they'd discussed when it first appeared that Tantos had his own agenda...but surely it was more of an end game should Marinus and the others be able to follow from across the sea? Yes, that was it. Better that no-one should have access to the city and its secrets.

Yet with the Sea God dead, such a gambit might not be required.

"How much did you use?" he asked.

"Not all of it. Enough to take out a good deal of them – we need the advantage. It's not exactly easy for what – less than a dozen of us now? – to take an entire city."

"Tell him what else you did," Tarvilus said with a shake of his head.

"I decided to test Alvetti. The charm I gave him is one of the Keystones – so he can find the store of acor. I told him to lead the King beneath the palace storerooms in time for the explosion. I'm curious to see if Alvetti survives. Either the struggle or the explosion. No matter if he fails to bring the King near, the explosion will kill them all."

Tarvilus threw his hands into the air. "And what happens if we blow the store of bones into the sky?"

He shrugged. "We pick them up – it's not as if they will be harmed."

"You don't know that for sure," Vinezi said. He kept his voice even. Julas may have made a mistake – he may not have.

"Surely, brother. It's the bones of a Sea God, not mere stone."

"Perhaps. And you have set this in motion?"

"Alvetti has a letter which the King will believe comes from you. The old man will capture Alvetti and once inside, the Shield will strike. He has his Keystone and the others are waiting to lay the trail for the explosion. They simply await Alvetti's capture and then his signal." He shook his head. "You should both be pleased – I've salvaged a serious set-back."

Vinezi closed his eyes. "That is yet to be seen. For one, I am not ready to venture into the city."

"What now, then?" Tarvilus said. "I don't think you've thought this through, Julas. If Alvetti is captured they will take his Keystone. It could lead them to us – think you can handle that freak of a Renovar girl, Flir? With a few dozen Shield on top?"

"It's more than you've done to bring us closer to the bones."

"Stop this," Vinezi said. "They won't know what the Keystone is for. Don't forget how much the New Land has forgotten of its own history."

Tarvilus muttered to himself, sounds of vague agreement.

"Let's just wait and see what happens," Julas said. "And while we do, let's find some food. I need something; my stomach is eating itself."

"Find the others and see what they have," Vinezi said. "I too, find myself ravenous and I fear this recovery will be a long one."

CHAPTER 12

Seto knocked on Ambassador Lallor's door, standing alone in the lamplight of the guest wing. After a moment, a Renovar servant opened the door. Her eyes widened. "Your Majesty."

"If you could run and tell the Ambassador that I'm here to speak with him?"

"At once." She rushed into an adjoining room, speaking urgently in Renovas, soft enough that he couldn't make out many words.

Lallor appeared, expression one of surprise. He looked exhausted beneath it, shadows lurking under his eyes. "King Oseto, this is a rare honour. Can I offer you something to drink?"

"Please." He joined Lallor in the Ambassador's sitting room, which was dominated by the tapestry of a snowscape. The scene covered a window, showing a hunting party chasing a white bear into a stand of black trees.

A platter sat on a small table, a single steaming cup next to a pot. The servant returned and poured the pale lavender liquid – picha – into a second cup.

"You brought the herbs from home?" Seto asked as he sat across from Lallor, accepting the cup and sipping. Sweet against his tongue.

"This represents my last haul, over a month old now. It is much better fresh, Your Majesty." He took his own sip and replaced the cup. Did his hand waver slightly? "I admit, I am surprised by your visit."

"You may have gathered that I do not enjoy formal meetings."

"I believe it so." He smiled, but it faded. "I imagine you wish to discuss the invasion again?"

"I do. Have you received word? From the Conclave or your own contacts perhaps?"

"No, alas. Though it is still my firm belief that there is no invasion, Your Majesty. I am waiting on official response to my letters, but the sea is unkind."

"Indeed." Seto waited.

"I just do not believe it." Lallor shook his head. "There is simply no valid reason, not with our trade ties."

Seto nodded. "And it leaves you in a dangerous position."

"Yes." He took a long drink. "There is something, though I hate to spread rumour."

"I have little else now."

"Ships are coming. Some say for war, some say chasing a traitor – though I put little stock in that. Traitor to who and why?" He spread his hands. "In any event, how many ships is unclear, I cannot offer more, nor guess at the purpose behind their coming."

The man did appear sincere. Once again, doubt returned. An invasion would have had some manner of precursor. Like the evacuation of Lallor for one. Unless the man was out of favour. "And your unofficial sources?"

"Merchants mostly. Some I have sailed with in the past, but their news was old when they arrived."

Seto took another sip and nodded. Much as he suspected. "Thank you, Ambassador. We will speak again."

"Of course, Your Majesty." He stood to see him out. "King Seto, I firmly believe there is no invasion but that doesn't mean something isn't afoot. I am seeking answers, let me assure you."

"As am I, Ambassador."

He bowed and Seto left, striding the halls with a slight frown. The same conclusions came to mind. Pevin had not lied – he'd not lie to Flir. His devotion appeared genuine. And Lallor too was suspicious of the 'invasion.' The man's own life hung in the balance of course. He would have to be watched.

But the very idea of invasion was implausible. Trading partners did not launch surprise invasions.

And what exactly was the nature of Vinezi's involvement?

He sighed. All this had been chewed over before – and so much to attend to yet, with at least one more urgent meeting looming. Seto paused at a junction and glanced down the empty hall before slipping into the ways.

It took long enough to exit the palace and reach the Harper, but once he'd collected Luik from the common room and descended to the basement, he'd forgotten about time. Plans had to be set in motion.

Three men waited in the shadows, voices hushed. They stopped speaking and moved toward a table and a worn map where it sat beneath the single lamp hanging from the roof.

"Gentlemen." Someone snickered and he flashed a grin. "Thank you for coming so swiftly."

Seto splayed his fingers on the table. In the dim room, faces were almost suggestions. Luik receded behind him and his three 'seconds', the other Rats, waited.

Two old companions, and one, younger, a replacement for Tulio. But in one respect only. Ugly as sin and an unimaginative, if skilled thief, Enzo – the Slick Rat, was working out well enough. The man spoke now, pointing to the wharves. "I can cover the harbour, I'm recruiting fast now. Trust me."

The other Rats chuckled, and even Seto smiled. An old joke, that one. "Very well. I will continue to monitor the Palace, and I require the rest of you to split the Second Tier and the aqueducts. I have a man of my own down there, Wayrn, he may have useful information by now. Send word if you cross paths."

The older Rats nodded, they knew Wayrn.

The Blood Rat pointed. "I'll start with the underground then. There's a few groups I can introduce myself to. They've kept out of our way so far." The man was half-Braonn, in addition to his own responsibilities, he would handle the runaways that lurked beneath the city quite well.

To the thin man, the aptly named Perfume Rat, Seto drew several circles with his finger on the map. "Start with the pillow talk in our softer establishments, but don't neglect these inns. Gently with the Storm's End; it's mine now."

The Perfume Rat rubbed his chin. "Times are changing, aren't they?"

"Indeed." The man referred to Seto's new role of course. "But don't let that stop you here. If Vinezi is not found, who knows what else he may explode? It hurts us all."

The three Rats nodded and slipped from the room.

Seto bowed his head a moment. How long before his new concerns clashed with the old? Bah. No time for that.

Luik came forward. "Think they'll find him?"

"No-one else is better poised." Seto tapped his fingers on the table. "And yet, why does Vinezi elude me still?" Failure was...unpleasant. A taste he'd long since done with. Not since the little bastard of a brother left him for dead, clinging to the splinters of the *East Wind*, had he tasted failure. No, that wasn't right. Not since Tulio.

"You'll get him," Luik said.

He folded the map. "In time, yes. But will it be soon enough?"

"My gold's on you."

"Bless you, Luik. Now, back to the palace. You said Flir wanted to see me also?"

"About the Sea Beast and the illness. She has something to show you."

"More pleasant news I assume?"

"It's another one of those things you have to see for yourself."

*

Seto strode into the Healer's room, Luik in tow.

Mayla, clear eyes flashing at the intrusion, closed her mouth when she saw who had entered. She gave a short bow. "King Oseto."

"Good evening, Mayla."

Flir turned from where she paced before the patient.

"Finally."

Seto raised an eyebrow. So impudent – she thought he'd been taking a leisurely meal perhaps? "Finally, Flir?"

"Yes. I've been waiting over an hour. I had to send Holindo away and Pevin's in the hall, probably in a panic that he cannot keep me under his gaze."

"I saw him, he's fine." Seto gestured to the young girl, who slept beneath a thin blanket, a sheen of sweat on her brow. "How is your patient?"

Flir looked to Mayla, who stepped forward and paused, smooth hands on the blanket. "I have given her something to help her sleep, and ease any pain. I had to have a chirurgeon help me."

"Please."

She lifted the blanket and he drew in a breath. A fin, sharp and blue, protruded from the girl's side. Stitches ran in a neat line beneath the fin. Luik made a sound and Seto turned. The big man had stepped back across the room a little. "You're safe, here, you know," Seto told him.

"If you say so." He didn't look convinced.

Seto turned back to the girl, bending to stretch a hand. Mayla intercepted him. "My apologies for touching the royal person, but it might not be safe. We do not know enough."

"Certainly."

Flir pointed. "That's one of the worst cases, Seto. And I promised this girl you'd be able to save her, do you understand?" Her eyes were hard.

"I believe I do." She'd told him little of the plagues in Renovar, but it was enough.

"Many more people are sick and more will follow. They eat the fish, which have already eaten pieces of the

Sea Beast we've dumped in the harbour. Some people are even falling ill from the toxic air. We need to get rid of that bloody corpse."

"Are all inflicted citizens reacting this way?"

"I don't know. Many more have breathing problems and fevers. Some turn bluish and die. The more I asked, the more I heard. Whole streets around the corpse are ill. We have to contain it. Bel is the only one like this, so far."

"That you know of," Mayla added.

Seto nodded. "I will take steps." To Mayla, "You didn't remove the fin?"

"It's hard to believe but it has grown from her flesh, not her skin. If we cut it away we do not know exactly what will happen. I want to be certain."

Seto closed his eyes a moment. What curse had befallen his city? How the Gods mocked him. His old desire come true, and it was a bitter poison. "And you will continue to help her?"

"Of course, my King."

"Flir, will you and Luik join me in my sitting room?"

"Right." She thanked Mayla as the two left and once they were gone Seto sat on a divan. Mayla moved across the room, clinked with bottles and returned with a cup of fire-lemon. "Here."

"Thank you, Mayla."

"I wondered when you'd come to visit me."

"Well, I had intended to, but I have been so busy."

She snorted. "Too busy to make time for an old friend?"

"Forgive me."

"It's been too many years."

"Dark years?"

"Very."

He hesitated. "My brother won your support?"

"I kept my head."

He raised his glass to her. "Of course."

She pointed at him. "Enough of that, Seto. I have to ask, because you're usually too smart for your own good. Do you know what trouble you're about to get into?"

"With the illness?"

"That too, but I meant with the Water Rat."

"Ah."

"Well?"

"That's an unresolved issue at this point."

She considered him. "Resolve it, sooner rather than later. Because you've got some hard decisions coming up with this sickness, Seto. I suspect a lot of your people are going to die. Are you ready for that?"

"I don't see how I could be."

"Good answer." She sipped her drink. "So long as you make sure your city's ready."

He finished his drink and stood. "I'll call upon you, of course."

"You're in trouble if you don't. Anaskar's been lucky, but I've seen cities that weren't."

"In Renovar?"

"And to the South, beyond Wiraced. Just keep one thing in mind, the lives of few for the lives of many. Sometimes all."

Seto nodded. "Sadly, to that I must attend, even now." He bade her goodnight, promising to call again, and slipped through dark passages to his sitting room, where Flir, Luik and a weary Captain Holindo awaited.

He waved the Captain down as he sat. New chairs had been added, so that all could now sit. Seto eased himself into a chair, an ache in his bones, deeper than usual. A crafty enemy, old age. No way to stave it off either.

"We will meet with Mayla and others tomorrow to discuss the illness that spreads from the great corpse. I hope we are closing in on Vinezi, and that preparation for the city's defence continues as expected. To both ends, Captain, you'll be receiving a lot more men shortly. Someone else will iron out details."

"I'll put them to good use."

"I know you will." Seto opened his mouth to continue but stopped at a knock on the door. "Come."

A page appeared. He swept a deep bow. "A note for you, Your Majesty. Lord Cavallo deemed it urgent."

Seto accepted the letter. "Very well." He waited for the boy to depart before breaking the seal. Cheap wax, but the insignia was odd. Wavy lines. Within, two lines in a dancing script.

"What is it?" Flir asked.

He narrowed his eyes then read aloud. "It says, 'Deliver the bones to me and there will be no more explosions, I will spare both palace and city. Another letter will come.' It is signed 'Vinezi'."

Luik shook his head. "He knows."

Flir swore. "How did the weasel find out?"

Seto folded the letter. "So the game changes yet again."

"What do we do?"

"We gather everyone." Seto straightened. "Then I move my pieces and he moves his."

"Let's make it a good move," Luik said.

CHAPTER 13

Flir tapped her foot, ignoring Seto's glance. The council room was stuffed with robes and the clash of voices, none of it really cutting to the matter at hand. Beyond the invasion, nothing was more important than stopping the spread of illness. And yet, they blathered on about who would provide which resources to which task. A job for an administrator, not decision-makers. Be a king, Seto.

And yet, for some reason, the old Rat held back. Was he waiting for something? Flir nudged Luik. "Look."

"What?"

"By the door."

Solicci approached, his thin face and hook-nose obvious tells even at a distance. Did he feel exposed, now that he wore no mask?

Seto stood, no robes this time, just his familiar black tunic and pants, raising his hands. The bickering eased to a hush. "Please, now that I have considered your input, I will set to work. We must go swiftly to action. First, we will close movement between Tiers, save royal business. A ten street radius will be cordoned off around the beast. Assign forces from your Houses to Solicci for this. In addition, seafood is not to be collected, sold or consumed until further notice. We must monitor the harbour most closely. Further, the corpse's flesh will now be transported to the Wards where it cannot harm the populace. The bones will be retained."

Nemola cleared his throat. "The restriction on fish I understand. It will strain our food supplies, which of course it is necessary, but with respect, surely the King's commemorative project can wait while the growing crisis is dealt with?"

"Even the bones may be toxic, and they will not decompose so quickly. They must be hidden away until such time as they can be properly destroyed. Preferably after the coming invasion," Seto said smoothly.

Solicci leant forward. "The quicker such a feat is achieved, the sooner we will be able to repair the wall."

Nemola frowned but the rest of the council murmured their agreement; the threat of invasion too strong. Brunetti folded his arms over his big chest. "Accept it, Nemola. It's safest."

"Very well." But Nemola had other concerns. "There's still the acor in the palace. What of that? Why haven't we found it yet?"

Seto motioned to Flir.

"Luik and I have covered every inch of the palace twice. I'm starting to think it was the bluff of a defeated man, though we haven't given up yet."

Nemola pursed his lips but sat back.

Seto stood. "Please follow Solicci for further instructions on the city's management of the sickness."

The council and Shield filed out, leaving Flir and

Luik alone with Seto. He stared out the wall of windows, looking over a city brighter in the morning light. The sea beyond remained calm, though the horizon was grey.

"You shouldn't let them waste time with pointless discussion, Seto."

He winked. "I let them feel they have contributed, as though I am listening and considering. Then, when I make decisions it is often the ones they believe they had a hand in."

"That's just as dangerous as trampling them. They'll begin to believe their own opinions more valuable than they really are."

"Not unlike someone I could name."

Flir grinned. "True. Luik is awfully opinionated."

Seto glared a moment, before breaking into laughter. "Come now, we have more work to do." He stood, but blinked, swaying on his feet. Luik caught his elbow.

"You haven't been sleeping."

Seto removed Luik's hand with some ceremony. "Neither of my kingdoms sleep, how can I? Now pay attention here, Solicci has sent us the man who was given the note. I want every detail."

Flir exchanged a glance with Luik. Seto's colour *was* a little off and dark shadows, dark even for Seto, ringed his eyes.

"Stop that." He spoke over his shoulder as he led them from the council rooms and quickly into the ways. Flir brushed at a cobweb in the shadowy halls, soon following by sound alone.

When they emerged into the light, it was to a plain storeroom. A Mascare and Shield stood waiting. The mask opened the door with a bow. Seto collected the Shield and stepped through, letting the mask close the door. Another simple room. Flir rolled her eyes. Its plainness was in itself dramatic. A single table and chair beneath a single lamp. Not unlike the basement of the Harper.

A man of middle years, a shopkeeper perhaps, stood before the table. He continually made adjustments to his tunic, belt and rings, giving a little jump when they entered. Seto sat and Flir flanked him, Luik taking the other side. So, what would Seto open with? The threat? The seemingly understanding grandfather?

"Thank you for waiting. Lino, is it?"

"Yes, sir."

"Do you know who I work for, Lino?"

"No, sir. Someone important? It must be, or I wouldn't have been brought to the palace, now, would I?" He finished with a weak laugh.

"That's very apt of you, Lino. I work for the new King, Oseto."

Flir fought off a smile. That explained the plain clothes.

"The King, sir?"

"Yes, and he's worried about the city. You remember the explosions?"

He nodded, near-to jumping on the spot. "Of course, sir. I do, it was terrible. Just one street over one of them was. Destroyed my cousin's seamstress shop."

"Most regrettable, I do sympathise. But we think the man who gave you the letter is involved somehow. He is a dangerous man, Lino, and we need your help putting a stop to his evil."

"How might I help?"

"Simply tell us about the man who delivered the note."

Lino linked his fingers and rubbed his thumbs together.

"Well, he was a local man with a slight limp. Not one of them sneaky forest folk," he said, apparently unaware of Luik, whose mouth twitched at the comment, "and he smiled when he gave me the note. He seemed to have a trace of an accent."

"How so?"

"Can't really describe it, I'm sorry sir."

"Not to worry. What did he say, exactly?"

Lino glanced to the dark ceiling. "Well...he said 'take this to the King, it's urgent' and he smiled at me."

"And did you read it?"

Lino shook his head. "No, sir, never!"

"That is well," Seto said. "Was he alone?"

"He was alone, sir."

"And where were you when he gave you the letter?"

"In my shop. I make candles on Trader's Row."

"And why do you think he chose you, Lino?"

"I've been wondering that ever since I got here." Lino sighed. "You see, I took the letter to the gates myself."

"And they believed you?"

"Well, my little brother is a Shield you see."

"Ah. And your brother's name?"

"Alvetti."

"Well, I think your brother can help me catch this man."

"I bet he'd love to stop the fellow behind the explosions."

"Of course, he would. Thank you, Lino. You will be compensated for giving so freely of your time." To the guard he gestured. "See him home, will you?"

"Yes, sir."

Lino attempted a bow as he was pulled, gently, from the room.

Seto drummed his long fingers on the table. "So. A betrayal."

Flir moved around to the light. "Alvetti, the Shield?"

"Yes. Solicci told me that the Shield on the gate claimed he did not know who brought the letter."

"You want us to round him up?"

"Bring him to the council room. I'm going to visit Abrensi while you're out, but I will wait for you after."

"And the messenger – one of Vinezi's men?" Luik asked.

"Doubtless."

"If we see him, do we take or follow? Might lead us to Vinezi if we let him."

"Take either. I don't want to rush."

"We'll be quick as we can." Flir led Luik from the room, striding through the halls. Lamps were spaced widely here in the servant's halls and she passed few people, though each bowed as she did. Silly. She wasn't a lady, wasn't a hero. She was just one of the few people willing to get things done.

"Slow down, will you?"

"You can keep up," she said. "Besides, I don't want to run into Pevin – he's probably finished his errands by now."

He grunted, matching her stride. "What errands?"

"He didn't really say. Seto's still having him watched. He doesn't completely buy Pevin's devotion, I suspect."

"Probably for the best. Gate first, then the barracks?"

"Yes. And Alvetti better be there because I'm not trudging through a dozen taverns and inns," Flir growled. "Or whorehouses for that matter."

"Think Vinezi has him in his nest?"

"Looks that way." She crossed an intersection, closing

in on a long staircase leading down to the ground floor. Their boots clapped on the stone steps. "What would have made you turn on everyone, Luik? Poor pay?"

"When I was a Shield? Pay was poor but...nothing would have made me do that."

"Nothing? The old King didn't strike me as a person to inspire loyalty."

"Which old King?"

"Pick one."

"Genatos was like Seto – only not as noble, down inside, I think. Otonos...well, you're right. He was no good. But that's not who I'd have betrayed. The Shield. They deserved my best."

"Well, Alvetti found something worthwhile." Flir leapt down the last few steps and crossed the marbled floor to the great double doors. She gave the King's Swordfish a shove, splitting the body from fin, light and chill air rushing through.

Winter lurked on the landing. She exhaled, breath steaming. Below, across tidy lawns dotted with feature gardens, quiet fountains and statues of Kings, Heroes and Gods, stood the gatehouse and massive gates. They made even the wall seem modest. How heavy was the Gate? With both hands, she probably couldn't open it. Probably.

The Captain at the gatehouse checked his ledger, nodding as he rubbed at his stubble. "Alvetti's got some time to himself. Most likely down at the Strong Arm."

"Second Tier, near the silk market," Luik said.

"Right." The Captain paused. "He in any trouble? He likes to gamble, but he's a good lad."

Flir shook her head. "Nothing like that. Thank you, Captain."

Outside, she tapped her foot while men rushed to open the gates. "What do you know about the Strong Arm?"

"Been a soldier's tavern for a long time. Generations. Quieter, not much in the way of trouble. Older soldiers mostly."

"That the kind of place young Shield frequent?"

"Not often. Reckon I was one of the youngest when I used to visit."

The streets were full. The flow of people led to and from market squares. In no other city were there so many specific markets. Another curious Anaskari custom. A pair of Mascare walked in a pool of their own space. Flir inclined her head and a mask dipped. They knew her and Luik now. In the palace, people called them The Pale Girl and the Tree Trunk. One of those strange mixes of affection and distrust. Was it painful for Anaskari pride, to have two foreign heroes?

Clamour from the silk market jumped up over the crowd, the riot of waving colours on flagpoles like a beacon, for the people who could afford it anyway. Before the old square, the 'Seta Piazza', stood a sturdy inn. The Strong Arm. Two storeys of stone, its beaten iron sign recently polished, it appeared orderly.

Flir pushed on the heavy door and stepped inside. Shield, both in uniform and out, lined tables in a room with a high ceiling. A fire roared in the corner, lighting the way for serving girls, who carried more platters than mugs. Most of the men were older. They sat and spoke quietly, few glancing up when Flir entered, but one short man slapped his table.

"Luik, you giant." He crossed the room to thump Luik on the back. "Didn't think I'd see you here again. What happened? By the Gods, you didn't re-enlist, did you?"

He laughed. "It's good to see you, Gin, but no. Flir and I are looking for an off-duty Shield. Alvetti?"

Gin jerked a thumb over his shoulder. "Blond lad in the corner. Dicing." He rolled his eyes. "Come visit again, we'll tell tales."

"I will."

Flir followed Luik to the table. Four men diced. The youngest was out of uniform and his blond hair, rare for Anaskari, had been cut close. He looked up, eyes widening. Before Flir could speak, Alvetti overturned the table with a crash.

She leapt back, but Luik sidestepped and caught the fleeing man. "In a hurry, aren't you?"

The young Shield slumped against him. Flir smiled. The Tree Trunk was quicker than he looked. When he wanted to be anyway.

"What's going on?" A big man in an apron, whose arms alone were half the size of Luik's chest, came around the bar. Most of the inn was on its feet.

Flir stepped forward. "Just a gambling debt, nothing too serious. Do you have a room we can use to discuss it with him?"

"I might remember you," he said to Luik before giving them both a look then a short nod. He produced a set of keys and unhooked one. "Round back. Second on right. You break something I break you, got it?"

"We'll be gentle, Balsa," Luik said.

He gave another nod.

Behind the bar was a door and a staircase. Luik hauled Alvetti up the stairs and into the room. A clean bed lay beneath a window, shelves set high. Luik dumped Alvetti on the bed and stood before him.

"He doesn't smell too good, does he?" Luik said.

"Not really."

Alvetti frowned. "I'm too busy to bathe in winter."

"Aren't we lucky?" Flir said. "Now. Tell us about the man who hired you. He has a limp."

"Who?"

She kicked the bed. The damn thing still creaked; she'd barely put any effort into the kick either. The young soldier flinched.

"Next time it's your face."

Alvetti shuddered. "Julas is the man that owns me."

"Where is he?"

"I don't know." He slumped against the wall, head in his hands. "He bought my debts and now I have to do whatever he tells me."

Flir glanced at Luik. "Like delivering letters?"

"All over the city. Mostly to...people from other nations. There's a Mascare too, but a lot of the time I'm told to listen to people in inns or markets. I blend in as a Shield in a lot of places."

"Who gives you these assignments?"

"The Mascare, Julas."

"Where?"

"He finds me."

Flir leant closer. The little idiot might be useful yet, but who was the mask? Another fake? "You're going to help us, Alvetti."

"He'll kill me."

"Not if I kill him first."

"You can't do that. He's too smart."

"Let me worry about that. Help us trap him and I'll have the palace clear your debts."

The young man's eyes lit up, but he looked away.

"You're lying."

"I understand. You should be wary." She pulled a folded piece of paper from her leathers, and flipped it open. "See that seal on the bottom? It gives me permission to do things others cannot. It might be squashing pieces of you into a box and dumping you in the harbour, it might be paying off your debts. Which sounds better?"

Alvetti gaped at the seal. "You can help me?"

"Come with us to the palace and you can speak with King Oseto about your role in catching Julas."

He swallowed. "And what will that be?"

"The hardest role, kid." Luik said. "Bait."

His eyes widened. "And you'll protect me?"

She nodded.

"All right. I'll go with you."

Flir snorted. "You didn't really have a choice."

CHAPTER 14

Skink was waiting for Kanis in his cabin, having been deposited there earlier. He was tied to a chair, eyes wide. As was customary, Yaev remained out of sight. Above decks probably. His friend didn't approve, but wasn't willing to object too loudly. After all, who would want to contradict the will of the Goddess?

"Nice to see you, Skink," Kanis said, pausing by a series of costumes hanging from pegs.

The old Captain's quarters had been refurnished with a wide desk and a proper bed beneath the row of portholes on the stern. The new pegs were installed by a carpenter before leaving Whiteport – a short stopover to resupply. A longer stay would have been pleasant. He could have hidden away in the Far Islands for the rest of his life. And maybe he should, after they finished with Anaskar.

Kanis ran silk between forefinger and thumb. The deep purple was cut to conceal. Formal robes after the Goddess herself. "Do you know what these are for?" He waved a hand at the row of costumes.

"No, dilar."

He moved to the next costume, red robes of Anaskari cut; the famous Mascare. "To keep life interesting."

"D-dilar?"

"Look at this one." He raised a deep green tunic. "How simple, but in the forests of Braonn, I would blend in quite naturally. There are threads of brown woven within the green here."

"What are you going to d-do to me? I truly am sorry, dilar."

"I know, I know." Finally to a coat of black with gold buttons, three lines crossing on the collar. Heavy boots, polished back and plain black pants with a heavy belt, its buckle carved from onyx to resemble a snowflake. Not something he'd wear anytime soon. "Kink, I'm going to spare you."

"Oh, thank you, dilar, thank you!" His eyes shone.

Kanis shook his head. "Not yet, son. There's a condition. I'm going to Bind you. Do you know what that means?"

His expression crumbled. He fell back against his ropes. "I think I do, dilar. I will be your slave."

"Good. That's a start. But it is more than that. You will live only for me. To be bound to a Dilar is a holy rite. It is everything. You will have no desire that is not one I have given you. No dream, no hope – and yet, you will not know a second of sadness either. Or fear." Or happiness, for that matter. "Do you understand?"

Skink met his eye. "Do you mean, if I see my family again, I won't even care that they need me?"

"Not unless I tell you to."

He looked away.

"Don't worry, Skink. Who knows, maybe I'll release

you someday?"

Skink turned back. "That's possible?"

"Yes."

"Then I will serve you faithfully."

"Yes, you will." Kanis stood before the boy. "Hands out now." Skink complied and he took them. The boy was sweating.

"It won't hurt," Kanis said. "Just repeat these words 'My eyes, my heart, my mind for Mishalar' until I say stop."

Skink swallowed then started the chant, his voice squeaking at first.

Kanis waited.

The longer Skink spoke, the more he calmed, until finally his heart beat steady and slow enough. Kanis matched his breathing to the boy's and the familiar warmth soon bloomed from his chest, running down his arms and into his hands, where it spread into Skink.

The boy's voice faltered but he kept chanting up until the warmth reached his own chest, enveloping his heart.

And then he stopped.

Kanis released the boy and checked his eyes. Calm, expectant. Barely a spark, and yet his spirit lurked somewhere back there. They always did. But for now, the boy was malleable. No will of his own. Kanis drew a knife and sliced through the ropes.

"Skink, go and lie down. Rest until I need you."

Skink stood and walked to Kanis' bed, lying down and laying still, breathing evenly.

Perfect. The young were usually easier, not like some men or women. They always had to fight. Kanis returned above decks. Yaev stood beside the helmsman, his face set. Kanis gave him some space, moving to one of the rails and glancing across the water.

Sometime overnight, they'd drifted out of formation enough that it was now being corrected. Men swarmed over the other ships, readying planks as they pulled closer. One of his own men roared to keep steady. Sailors clung to ropes and beams above, just in case a rough patch of sea tangled ships.

But the transfer looked to be smooth enough. Two ships across, a figure in grey and black furs crossed makeshift gangways, hunched but moving swiftly. A 'proper' healer as Atilus wanted. It had taken most of the night to locate him, coordinating by shouts with the closest ships and flags to bring the outliers closer, and now Svek the healer was scurrying toward him, weighed down by heavy leather bags.

Yaev appeared beside him. "He'd better know what he's doing."

"I agree."

"Skink?"

"Resting."

Yaev grunted, but said no more.

Svek arrived, placing his bags down to bow. "Dilar."

"Up you get, Svek. I have a patient with a fever, can you tend to him?"

He shrugged. "I will cure him."

"That easy? You haven't seen him yet," Yaev said.

Svek waved his hands. "Not to worry, you eastern folk are always suspicious at first, but my results will speak for themselves."

Yaev flushed. "You should have left that Chosen People rubbish at home, highlander. We're born of the same ice."

"Of course we are," Kanis said, glaring at Yaev. "Why don't we move it below decks? I'm sure Atilus is fuming by now."

"Of course, dilar," Svek said. He collected his bags and followed Kanis down the nearest ladder, with some mumbling, and to Atilus' cabin. This time he'd had someone open up the room earlier and it didn't smell so bad.

Atilus groaned, stirring on his cot, blankets twisted. The man placed a bone charm aside, muttering something at it under his breath. A curse?

Svek clicked his tongue. "He's bad."

"Can you restore him?"

"Assuredly, but I can't have anyone hovering over me."

Kanis stepped into the hall, Yaev following. He scratched at his beard. "I wonder."

"About?"

Yaev's expression was dark. "Just how much Atilus is holding back."

"I don't want to risk a mistake with the acor. That demonstration was impressive, in a terrifying way."

"No. I mean about he and Vinezi. And you know what I think. They have goals they aren't going to share."

"Such as?"

"Such as we're fodder for some larger scheme. Who knows what he's up to in Anaskar? He's not interested in looting the city."

"Of course not, but we are." He shrugged. "And whatever he wants he's welcome to it so long as we get our share. I told you, Yaev, I'll be watching them."

"Don't get so confident that you end up snowblind."

"Stop that. You sound like my grandmother."

"A wise woman."

"Just let me worry about him. I've already dreamt of the city in flames. If I do so again, you know Mishalar foretells it."

Yaev grunted. "You didn't mention that."

"That's because I didn't want to mention it until I dream it a third time. To be sure."

"Fair enough."

"Come on, let's go get something to drink. Watching Svek do all that work is making me thirsty."

CHAPTER 15

Notch paused. "Look."

Ahead, the trees remained brown and orange for the most part, their trunks gleaming in a faint rain, but the forest was changing, as hints of green appeared in the dim light. He exhaled. Good. Any longer in the Grove and he'd snap.

"This is the end of the grove then?" Sofia straightened in Swift's saddle where she rode beside him.

"Looks like it."

"Finally. I'm starving," she said.

"I think we should eat here."

"Why?"

He pointed. "The rain's harder beyond." Puddles were forming across the trail, green leaves battered by the water. And yet, here in the Autumn Grove the rain fell gently, the thunder of water distant. It should have been louder, seeing as it fell mere yards away.

Sofia slipped down and picketed Swift to a tree. "Is there any chance of shelter? I'm getting sick of the rain, even when it's light."

"Not much. And I think we should camp here too."

She stretched. "Good idea. It must be close to evening and it seems safe."

He snaked a hand into a saddlebag and withdrew two apples, throwing one to her. "I'm not sure about being safe."

"Well, we'll be drier at least." Her voice echoed behind the mask.

"You're right about that." He turned a half circle. There had to be some fallen branches somewhere, or at least – wait. A flash of colour, ducking behind a stand of thick trunks. Purple and pink? "Someone's watching us."

"Where?"

"Those trees, four close together." He drew his sword. "Can you use Argeon?"

Sofia hesitated, reaching into the saddlebags. "Are we in danger?"

"Let's be ready."

"I'll try." She switched masks, the blackened bone of Argeon a stark contrast to Osani. With the white stripe, she had a fearsome look. In her robes the effect would have been more powerful still.

"Good." He advanced on the trees, footfalls muted on the damp earth. Stopping but a few paces away, he raised his voice. "Who hides there?"

Silence.

Sofia nudged him. He'd spoken Anaskari. "Show yourself," he said, this time in Braonn.

A rustling, then two small figures emerged from behind the trunk.

Two Braonn children. They moved with hands at their backs. Both wore muted greens and browns. No purple or pink. Notch lowered but didn't sheathe his blade.

Each boy cast frequent glances at Sofia's mask.

Notch motioned for her to speak. His accent might trouble them.

"Were you watching us before?"

The boys looked at each other a moment. Neither seemed inclined to answer.

Sofia removed her mask. "Were you playing perhaps?"

Upon seeing her face they relaxed. The taller boy nodded and the other smiled. "Yes. We play here often."

"In the Autumn Grove, all alone?"

One of the boys frowned. "Autumn Grove?"

"Yes. This place." She gestured to the trees.

The boys conferred, then gave an answer that had the sound of Braonn, but were not words he knew. Sofia hesitated a moment before continuing. Had she understood? "And when you play here, do you ever see other people like us?"

They nodded.

"Recently?"

Two more nods.

"What happened?"

The boys giggled, edging away. Notch pounced, but they scattered. Their bare feet kicked up wet leaves as they ran, and he'd barely taken a step after them before they disappeared into the trees.

"Did they seem to move too fast?" Sofia asked.

He scratched at his beard. "I thought I was close enough to touch them, but here, who knows?"

Sofia replaced Argeon. "Well they know something."

"I don't like our chances of catching them."

"They might have seen Father."

He sheathed his sword. "Or they might be toying with us. I'm not sure, Sofia. You feel it too; there's something odd about the Grove."

She hesitated.

"We don't have any proof those children saw Danillo." He didn't mention the flash of colour from before. It didn't mean anything. Probably imagined it anyway.

"They might have witnessed the fight back there."

He waved to the trees. "We'll never find them. Even if we did, they probably wouldn't understand our questions. Were they speaking a Braonn dialect? It didn't sound exactly familiar."

"Part of it I couldn't follow."

"Who knows how much they really understood from you? And your father wouldn't have followed them either. I doubt he ever saw them, being chased as he was."

"True."

"Let's eat for now. In Avaon there might be word. If not there, somewhere else."

"You're probably right." Sofia turned back to the horse. Notch followed, casting another glance over his shoulder. The trees were empty.

*

After a long night at watch, and another cold meal beneath scant shelter of the only fallen branches in half a mile of the Grove's edge, Notch was once again trudging along beside Swift.

The rain had stopped, and a winter sun peered from the clouds. It did nothing to warm the forest but the light was natural again. Upon crossing the Grove's threshold into the evergreens, tension flowed from his muscles.

By noon, they reached the outskirts of Avaon, the largest settlement yet. He paused. "I've travelled some of the way beyond here, Sofia. As a caravan guard, we'd take the western paths to the Jin-Dakiv lands."

"The Jin-Dakiv? Are they really all blind?"

He shook his head. "No, just their priests. But they are secretive folk, we barely crossed the border before we had to stop and trade, basically on the side of the road."

"But you know Avaon?"

"Well enough. Beyond is the centre of the Bloodwood and the First Tree."

"Father might be there."

"I hope not." He gave Swift a pat and she started forward again.

Similar houses to those in Irihs appeared first; small, thatched and covered in moss, but beyond them lay larger structures. Some with stone bases. Most were in ruin, the flow of Braonn never glancing at the run-down buildings. Each one was being reclaimed by the forest.

Sofia spoke softly. "Avaon has stone buildings?"

He gave her a look. "You seem surprised?"

"Something to do with Seto's grandfather, perhaps?"

"Older. King Menate. He decided that living in each other's lands was the best way for our two peoples to learn about each other, to prevent more fighting."

"Only it didn't work," Sofia said.

"Right. The buildings ended up being used to prepare Braonn children to work in Anaskar, as an odd penance for the Braonn Rebellion. And resentment continued to grow." He glanced around, then back to her. "I would have thought you'd know the history well."

"As a Carver I was lucky to get the learning I did. The only reason I know languages and a bit more, is because Father was careful. It was only me and Tantos and..." She trailed off, wiping at the sweat at her temples.

It was still best to hide the masks but she was already suffering from the *lenasi* withdrawal. How long could she hold off?

"Let's just say there are gaps in my education, all right?"

"I understand."

"But I've always meant to ask, why do the Braonn still send their children to us? Surely the debts are paid?"

"I asked Luik the same thing once. He said some people here see it as a way to escape the isolated life of the Bloodwood, a way to join the 'rich lives' of the northerners. Sometimes, when Braonn return home, they're given positions of power."

"That's a foolish risk."

"And when has a young person ever been open to reason?"

"I'm hardly old, Notch and I'm reasonable."

"You're unique."

"Thank you, I think."

"There's more. You mentioned the debts? Luik knows families who owe debts that supposedly travel back beyond the Rebellion, as far as two hundred years. Some were placed into service as payment for Anaskari aid in driving off the Ulag Clan."

Sofia nodded slowly. "The Black Raiders ravaged the Bloodwood for generations. But didn't they die out?"

"Only beneath the swords of our ancestors."

Sofia fell silent.

Deep in the settlement now, and as with Irihs, unfriendly eyes watched them. Notch kept a hand on his hilt as he walked. Men folded their arms from doorways and women turned away. Children pointed but their parents hushed them.

"Where are we going?"

"To find a Trader. Or even a hunter."

Again, the tension hadn't been so high the last time he'd travelled the Bloodwood, but he'd been with Luik then. It all came back to that. He was Anaskari, with another Anaskari, deep in a place where his people were rarely seen, let alone welcomed.

Another ruin loomed. Twice as tall as any other, its windows were crammed with flowerbeds and the crumbling tops of walls snaked with dark vines. By its empty doorway, a group of men barred the way.

All had bows slung over their shoulders. Many stood with crossed arms, but no drawn weapons. The eldest, a man with grey at his temples, raised a hand when they approached. His tunic had a giant tree stitched in gold. Notch motioned for Sofia to dismount.

Grey-hair spoke in Anaskari. "You must turn back, strangers."

Notch stopped. "We seek a Mascare who may have passed through. We would appreciate it if we could continue."

"No Mask has come through Avaon, and so you will have to leave."

Sofia stepped forward and bowed, speaking in clear Braonn. "We have tracked him and his pursuers as far as the forest just behind us, is it not possible to continue?"

He shook his head. "Be that as it may, there is nothing for you beyond Avaon. Even were you not Northerners. And further, it is on my mercy only, the mercy of peace, that I will not have you killed for what you are."

"Please."

The leader gestured to the men surrounding him. "Escort them from Avaon. If they resist, kill one and send the other away to explain the price of trespass."

Sofia opened her mouth to speak again, but Notch touched her arm. It was a time to obey. He fell into step beside one of the men, keeping close to Sofia. The Braonn flanked the horse and the group walked in silence. Notch kept his hand near his blade, but the Braonn, each man with a tight mouth, made no hostile move.

People stopped their tasks to stare at the escort. At the edge of the settlement, the men stopped. One pointed to the path leading away. "If you go now, we won't hurt you."

Notch moved to lead Swift away. She glanced over her shoulder. "They're only watching us."

"I'll settle for that."

"Will you just? And what are we going to do now?"

"Well I don't want them taking up their bows. And as for your question, I don't know."

"Do we have a map?" She twisted her torso to rummage through the saddlebags.

"Wait until we stop a moment."

He followed the path until it reached a small clearing, Avaon no longer visible through the trees behind them. Giving Swift her feedbag, Notch joined Sofia on a smooth rock where she frowned over a map, bright in the patch of light.

"I don't know where we are."

He pointed to a faint circle drawn in the trees. "Here."

"Then where would my father go if not Avaon?"

"East toward the coast, maybe further into the Bloodwood. It's hard to know. How close was pursuit at this point? The answer is either in Avaon itself or on the outskirts."

"Can we circle Avaon?"

"Traces of his passage would be hard to find unless there'd been another fight. It's been too long. And we'd be lucky to stumble upon anything useful at this rate."

"Then we're back to finding a hunter or tracker."

"If the Braonn find us snooping around, blood will be shed. And we're outnumbered, Sofia, even with the Greatmasks."

Sofia scowled. "I don't know how to use them anyway."

"You did some impressive things in the Sea Shrine."

She shrugged.

"Well, it's up to us then," he said. "No-one is going to talk in Avaon."

"Where do we start?"

"East."

"Why east?"

"It's as good as any side of the settlement and it's closer to the river." He bent to take a flask from his pack, raising it. Cool water slid down his throat and he turned back toward Avaon. The man with the First Tree on his chest would kill them. The Bloodwood was a different place now. Old resentments had come to the fore. Did Seto know? Did anyone in Anaskar know?

Maybe charging into the Bloodwood was a mistake.

"Notch, what is it? Are we leaving?"

"When Luik and I travelled through the forest as mercenaries it was in a company of mostly Anaskari with a few Braonn men too. Even an older soldier from the Far Islands. Now and then we were chasing thieves, but mostly guarding caravans bound for Avaon itself or sometimes Jin-Dakiv. When we came through settlements or passed people on the paths, anyone with tanned skin got their share of dark looks, but we were always allowed to enter Avaon."

"And today we were stopped."

"Why now? What exactly is happening in the Bloodwood?"

Sofia straightened. "Trade has slowed over the last few months. I overheard Father, he wanted to investigate but then Tantos...disappeared."

Notch sighed. "Maybe we don't have much choice. We're blind out here. I'll check to see if we've been followed, then it's back toward Avaon before we lose the light. There must be information we can use somewhere."

Sofia nodded.

Notch snuck into the trees, choosing his footfalls. The old growth was not easy to traverse but at least he didn't snap any branches. His circuit of the clearing was slow. He narrowed his eyes at more than a few trees. Had there been a flash of green clothing? Pale skin – the glint of an eye? He crouched by a stump. No surprise if the Braonn did have them followed, to ensure they headed away, to carry out the promise.

He inched his sword from its scabbard.

Something cold rested against his neck. "Be still," a voice said in Braonn.

Notch cursed.

CHAPTER 16

Sofia paced the small clearing, sweat building at her temples. She'd have to wear Osani soon but not until Notch returned. How long should it take him to check for trouble? Was something wrong? Swift snickered. Sofia moved over to rub her neck. "Don't worry, girl."

Leaves rustled and Notch stumbled into the clearing, a group of Braonn on his heels. Six men, all armed with bows, hand axes and daggers. Notch's own weapons were missing and a thin cut bled on the side of his neck. His lips were set. One of the Braonn, a tall man, gestured at her and a pair started forward.

Notch shook his head when she met his eyes. She let a man take her by the arm, the other leading Swift, who clopped along behind her. Her pulse quickened. Were the Braonn taking them to be killed? Interrogated? Escorted from the forest?

They couldn't be allowed to find the Greatmasks. So far, her captors weren't looking in the saddlebags at least. The men smelt of leather and sweat and no-one spoke as the group crossed, single file, into the forest, pushing through the undergrowth to a winding game trail beyond. The footing was slick with old, damp leaves and she slipped to a knee. One of her captors muttered something, but helped her up. No other sounds, and Notch not close enough to hear if she whispered.

The narrow trail broadened as it turned toward Avaon, but a tall-man, his blond hair visible above the others at the head of the group, didn't return to the settlement. His path veered away, though glimpses of smoke from home fires were never far.

A dark building loomed ahead, crumbling stone visible beneath the weight of vines and moss. A temporary roof of branches stretched across the building and a guard stood at the door, arms folded. He let them in, a sneer on his face, but again, no-one spoke.

Inside, light filtered through the makeshift roof, mottling the leaf-strewn floor. In a dim corner, a man sat on a crate, eating stew from a bowl. The tall Braonn and the eating man conferred, voices a bare murmur.

After a time the tall man nodded, leaving his fellow in the shadow. He stopped before her. "Hands up." He looked to Notch. "You too."

"What do you want?" she said, raising them.

"No speaking," he growled. The Braonn tied her wrists together, the rope digging into her skin. A second captor tied Notch, then they were pushed toward the opposite corner, where a trapdoor was thrown open. Wide steps led down to darkness. One of their captors waved his hand. Notch hesitated until the man raised a knife.

She followed him into the darkness, moving slowly. The shape of the steps gradually resolved, as did the dank stone floor of an empty room below. The hatch thumped closed, plunging their prison into darkness.

Scraping followed as something heavy – the crate – was dragged over to rest atop the trapdoor.

That was that.

"Shouldn't we have fought them?"

Notch shifted in the dark. "Too many."

"Well, what do we do now?" Sweat formed on her temples, despite the chill beneath the ground. "Wouldn't they have killed us already?"

"It might be a good sign. When they took me, they were talking about waiting for someone. The tall one must have seen that I understood enough, so they stopped."

"We shouldn't have given up, Notch. I could have used Argeon."

"You said you can't use it, so you'd likely be dead. Me too."

"And how much better off are we now?"

"We're alive."

Her stomach started to churn. Gods, the Masks. Had they been found yet? How bad would the withdrawals be without them? "I need to wear one of the Greatmasks again, if they haven't been stolen already."

"How are your bindings?"

"Tight. Do you have a knife, hidden somewhere?"

"Taken."

"Then what do we do?"

"Wait for our chance. Can you hold on?"

"We're going to find out." Sofia sat against the wall opposite Notch. Only a patch of his shoulder caught what little light slipped through the trapdoor. Cold seeped through her clothing, an odd contrast to the sweat at her temples and running down her neck.

With nothing else to do, she dozed.

The room shifted in and out of focus, light blurring.

Sometimes it seemed Notch called to her but her lips wouldn't move. She answered in her mind, but the conversation stopped. From somewhere came laughter, as if someone stood above her head, walking on the ceiling. Sweat dampened her hair and undergarments.

Other sounds filtered through the fever, but they were soon lost in the dark.

When a wave of light burst upon her face, she groaned, squeezing her eyes shut. Voices followed, but the words weren't making...Braonn. She stretched stiff muscles, raised bound hands to shield her eyes.

Two Braonn men stood by the wall, placing torches in iron rings. One was the tall man who'd captured them. The other leant close; a Braonn man with circle tattoos running down his neck and crossing the backs of his hands. Were the tattoos dancing? Green eyes glittered, before he clicked his tongue. "Useless. This one is barely conscious."

"The other is well enough, Efran."

The two crossed the room where Efran nudged Notch with his boot. "Wake up, soldier." His Anaskari was good. "Two things. Your name and your purpose in Wiraced."

Notch squinted. "Notch. We're searching for a fugitive."

Efran exchanged a glance with his taller counterpart.

Sofia squinted, holding a breath and releasing it slowly. The room grew steady, though her arms were still damp with sweat.

"And this fugitive?"

"A rogue Mask. Others were sent after him, they would have been here before us. We think he's passed through or beyond Avaon."

"That I do not believe."

"It's the truth. Surely someone saw other searchers?"

Efran drove his foot into Notch's ribs. Sofia cried out and the tall man glanced at her, but Efran bent by the gasping Notch. "You are in Avaon to cause discord. No Mask has been seen in or near Avaon. Try again."

Notch pulled himself back upright, but said nothing, only glaring up at Efran.

"Answer me."

"I have no answer to satisfy you. You've already made up your mind."

Efran nodded to the tall man, who gripped Notch by the shoulders, holding him down. Then the tattooed man approached Sofia. A knife appeared in his hand and she blinked – was there a yellow glow in his veins? Sofia shrank back. The glow faded. Perhaps she'd imagined it? "So, young lady. Let's see if you will be more forthcoming?"

"No," Notch shouted, struggling.

"Mor, hold him." Efran turned back to lift her chin with the point of his blade. "Now, tell me your purpose. On whose orders do you and your *cana* come?"

Cana. Braonn for 'Mask.' She swallowed, throat dry. Speaking was an effort. "The man we chase is powerful."

"So powerful that you require two special *cana*? Unlikely." He dug the point in deep enough to free a trickle of blood. "'Tis you two here as Mascare, are you not?"

She tried again but only croaked. Efran shouted for water, and a guard brought a cup. She drank and breathed easier. "No. We seek a fugitive. We tracked him to the Autumn Grove, where we lost the trail."

He stared into her eyes. "As I suspected." He withdrew the knife and straightened. "Very well, until tomorrow, when we will talk again. With company."

"Company?"

Mor joined Efran, who paused on the stair. "Your reticence means I must resort to other measures to learn the truth. And I don't want to dirty my hands." He opened the trapdoor and the two left, slamming the lid as they went.

Notch hobbled over. "You're sweating too much."

"There isn't much pain right now at least. How are you?"

"It's nothing. But you'll need more water."

"I won't hold my breath waiting for them to bring us any."

"They want us alive long enough to talk at least."

"But we can't tell them anything."

"Then we'd better think of something good," he said. "Efran will have someone torture us, where he'll pit us against one another. Using my pain to make you talk and the other way around."

Sofia closed her eyes. "Even though we know nothing."

"Yes." Notch sat back and swore. "This is my fault. I thought it would be safer here – it always was before."

"It's not your fault."

"It feels like the beginning of an attack. They're closing down the wood, pushing foreigners out and barring access. Weaning off trade. I'd be surprised if the amount of indentured servants hasn't dropped too."

Could it be true? Father would know. And here she was, stuck in a hole in the forest, with no way to be certain, no way to warn anyone of anything. Facing torture and death at the hands of furious Braonn. "They risk everything. It would mean war, outright war."

"Not something Anaskar can afford, with Renovar on the seas. But I don't think the Braonn would launch

a large-scale attack. It would be something quieter."
Notch smiled, and Sofia smiled back at his attempt at
reassurance. The expression was more one of sadness,
but he was dear to try. Like Father would have.

"An assassination?"

"Maybe." He shrugged. "Not that they wouldn't feel
they have cause."

"I still don't want them killing Seto."

"Me either."

"So what now?"

"Now I get to work, scraping these ropes against the
stone."

"Good idea." Sofia dragged her bindings across the
floor, the quiet rasp seeming so ineffectual. Sweat dripped
to the stone as she worked and the night wore on.

CHAPTER 17

As much as escape loomed in his dreams, there was the Egg too. Large, gold, beautiful, clamouring for attention. Beating like a heart, or a persistent wind. Over Schan's worries and an echo from the strange offer from the King of the Devils, Ain stared at the dungeon's stronghold.

Within waited the Egg. Its song was muted, but it slipped between the bars nonetheless. The strange creature, whose skin changed, had not appeared again. But it was out there too, somewhere. Waiting.

"Ain, are you listening, lad?"

Schan stood before him, face expectant. Ain shook his head. "I'm sorry."

The warrior held a bowl of water. "I asked if you were thirsty."

Ain accepted it and drank deeply. "Yes, I was. Thank you."

"You were thinking about it again, weren't you."

He nodded. "Who else will protect it? It needs help."

"So do we," Schan said, controlling his voice. "Ask to see the King again. We can use his offer to escape. Or better, to strike him while we do so."

A door clanged open and two guards marched a

prisoner down the cells. The man was snarling and muttering meaningless words. Upon catching sight of Ain and Schan, the fellow screeched, pointing a dirty finger at them. One of the guards thumped him and he fell silent.

Before tossing the prisoner into a nearby cell, the guard snatched a pack from the man and marched it to the storeroom. He'd barely opened the door when he stumbled back, throwing his hands up.

A fiery yellow shape streaked from the room and angled for Ain's cell. He fell back as it slipped through the bars, feathers fluttering, coming to rest on his shoulder. A bird? He froze, but it only adjusted its heavy claws and clicked its beak. Ain turned his head, a tiny movement, coming eye-to-eye with the bright bird.

The pupil expanded, ringed white. Its beak was a milky brown, hooked at an orange tip. Close up, it looked to have a big wingspan but he could hardly measure it.

The guards shouted and pointed, but Ain paid them no heed. A slender hand, a bare mottling of light, slipped into the cell near the floor, dragging a fallen feather through the bars. The creature tucked it away somewhere, because the feather disappeared as a rippling of light receded into the shadows. Biding its time. The creature wanted the bird.

Was it some manner of egg-snatcher? The fell-lizard in the desert was the same.

But the bird was safe now. Ain smiled at the magnificent creature. Warmth spread through his chest. Nothing could come between them. "I'll protect you."

The bird clapped its beak.

Schan crept closer. "Beautiful."

Ain held up his hand, but the bird didn't hop on. It

flexed its claws and remained in place. One of the guards had already left, the other staying back to watch. Ain straightened. His limbs tingled, muscles bunching as his pulse jumped. The cell grew lighter. Or could he see clearer in the dark all of a sudden?

"Something's changing," he said.

"What?"

"I feel different. Like in the passage, when I held the egg. It refreshed me." Ain flexed his fingers. If only a rock was in reach; he'd try crushing it. "I see more clearly, for one. Both with my eyes and to the shape of the paths." They remained a mess, but they extended so much further now – out into a strange, slithering darkness that swallowed each path. Was that the limits of his new vision or something else?

"So the bird's doing it?"

"Have you heard of anything like that before?"

"None of our legends speak of such a thing."

"Hmmm." Ain shifted. There was no fear, it lay muffled beneath a wondrous golden blanket, and yet..."The beak is quite close to my face."

"Yes, it is." Was Schan grinning?

"It's not funny. It could be dangerous."

"She looks calm to me."

"She? How can you tell?"

"I just can. And she likes you anyway."

"Thank the Sands," he said. "But I think I agree." He gazed at her. How beautiful her beak, the fierce eyes and magical feathers. All he had to do was keep her safe, even if it cost him his life...his life? Ain frowned. Too far. Sands, how difficult it was to keep control of his thoughts.

New footfalls echoed down the block. A familiar

guard, Giovan, marched up to the cell. His eyes widened at the bird, then he cast a look of suspicion over Ain and Schan. The Warrior glared back and Ain took a step forward. Giovan raised an eyebrow but only conferred with his fellow soldier, one of which pointed to the guard room, then back to Ain.

"What are they up to then?" Schan said.

"They want her too, no doubt. I won't let them take her."

"Careful. You might not have a choice."

He turned to face Schan and the bird adjusted its grip. "I can't."

Schan said nothing.

The door to the cell block opened again and a man in red robes and white mask of bone appeared. His step slowed when he saw the bird, and he moved forward to grip the bars, ignoring the guards.

"You. Where did you find the bird?" The man's Medah was fair, though it sounded as though he'd not spoken the language for a long time. His voice was flat, almost toneless.

"An egg. And she is staying with me."

The Mask tilted. "And where did you find the egg?"

Ain moved a step closer. The Mask wasn't simply demanding the bird, as he might well have. Was he afraid? "What does it matter?"

"I see."

"Do you?"

"It has you." The mask turned and left without another word.

Ain turned to Schan. "What does he mean?"

"The egg had a hold on you, Ain. Why not the bird?"

"I don't think so."

"I think we'll find out soon enough. That Mask will return."

And return the mask did.

Only now King Oseto walked beside the Mascare. Enough time had passed between visits, the bright bird only occasionally shifting its weight, that Schan had been able to try convince him to take the King's offer once again. His friend knew where to press. Silaj. His unborn child. He might see them again. Still Ain hesitated. Going home as a failure. How differently they'd see him. Those Pathfinders that returned were ruined, treated as useless.

But if he stayed in Anaskari, and waited for a chance to strike...

Maybe.

The King stopped before the cell. His eyes were all-knowing. "So, Pathfinder. Solave. Bird of the Sun. I am impressed with your resolve, misplaced though it seems to be."

"How so?"

"You don't seem ready for her power." The King raised an arm, pursing his lips. A musical whistle followed, something that gave Ain pause. The bird leapt from his arm and flew directly to the King's wrist, whistling in response. The same tune. The bird kept whistling and the King smiled at it. "Hello, little one."

Ain gaped. His heart had flown across the cell and he staggered as the warmth left his body. The cell was darker, dirtier. Beauty was gone. He caught the bars. "She's mine."

The Guard and Mask flanked the King, who stepped back smoothly. "She belongs to no-one. But you belong to her."

Cold steel bit into his shoulder as he pressed himself

into the bars. "Return her to me."

Giovan snickered.

Ain growled but Schan took his arm. "Steady, lad."

King Oseto stroked the bird, which nuzzled his hand. "And now, once again I will make a generous offer. Help me find what I seek and you and your Warrior will be set free."

Ain snarled. "Give her to me."

The King held his gaze a moment, then shook his head. "Very well." He turned to drift from the cell, whispering to the bird as he left, accompanied by the Mask.

"Sands bury you!" Ain slammed his body into the bars, grasping after the bird, shouting, screaming, curses mixed in with his gasps. Blood thundered in his ears and he shrugged off hands that tugged at him from every corner, throat hoarse when something knocked him to the cold stone.

A haze of rage cleared.

He blinked up at Schan's worried face.

"Here." Schan helped him into a sitting position. Ain spat blood, but the strength flowed from his body with each new tear. How could she leave him? And to go with the King of the devils, Sands why? Did she truly possess him? A terrible emptiness filled his chest.

Giovan had turned back to the other guards, who spoke a moment, then as one, reached for the torches. One at a time, each torch was snuffed, until only a single point of light remained, bobbing toward the door.

Groans and curses came from other cells but Ain only stared into the dark, Schan's words as tiny, useless things.

She was gone.

CHAPTER 18

Seto paced before the open window while he waited for Wayrn. A welcome chill kept him alert where wind swept up from the black rooftops below, blending into evening shadow. Sooner or later, he needed an unbroken night's sleep. But some conversations could not wait.

He turned at a faint sound from the corner of the room.

The Solave. Magnificent Bird of the Sun. Not seen in perhaps two decades by his best guess. He knew of a Solave's love of music and the fact that they'd been revered since the time of the Landing, but little else. She had a power, that much was clear. The Solave stirred in her cage, hidden beneath a large, dark drop cloth. Best that she remain hidden. And he could feed her later. He took a step forward. Although, if he did so now he could concentrate on –

Stone slid across stone and a tapestry picturing the Great Landing billowed.

Wayrn stepped from the hidden passage. "Seto." His eyes were weary and while his black clothing appeared to have been brushed, traces of webbing remained on his shoulders and his boots were damp.

"How was your trip?" Seto took up a glass of fire-lemon and handed it over.

Wayrn accepted the drink and sipped, giving a small sigh when he moved to stand in front of the fire. "Fruitless, for the most part. I did find Kael and his band of children but they've seen nothing of Vinezi."

Seto frowned. "As expected. You said, 'for the most part'?"

"Well, they mentioned another beast."

"As the one you and Notch dispatched some time ago?"

"Yes. Only, this one wasn't as large to hear them tell it. They thought it walked upright."

"Hmmm. This bears investigating, though it is not your first concern of course."

"I'll tell the Shield we're going back down there," he said, a sigh implicit if not present in his voice.

"I know you feel your talents are not being...utilised to their fullest, Wayrn, but you have contacts beneath the city now."

"I understand."

"Well, do not rush away. Take the remainder of tonight to rest and renew your search tomorrow." He paused. "The children truly had no information of use?" He'd been relying on them more than he'd like to admit.

"There's a new 'watcher' they thought I should speak to but I couldn't locate him. He's supposed to forage near one of the harbour mouths."

"He's a Scrapper?"

"Yes, though he calls himself a Watcher. He appears to be proud of it too," Wayrn said, and this time the sigh escaped. "Kael seems to think this Bodol fellow would know if anyone tried to enter the city via the underground."

"I've not heard of him." That in itself was unusual. Seto took another sip. "Take care when you return."

"I'll take some steel with me too, Seto."

"As you should. Enjoy your respite, Wayrn. I expect another report the moment Bodol is found."

Wayrn bowed and returned to the ways.

Seto tapped a finger on his own glass of Fire-Lemon a moment, then left his chambers. Time for his next meeting. Easier if he made everyone come to him but there was something to be said for the charm of surprise. He waved off his guards and strode down the corridors, slowing as he approached Abrensi's quarters.

Had he forgotten something? The memory of claws gripping his wrist hit, strong enough that he turned half a step. Was the Bird of the Sun truly safe, hidden in his rooms? The cage, was it shut? Had he opened it before Wayrn arrived? Perhaps if he checked on it just before he spoke to the Storm Singer...Seto shook his head. "No, little one, your charms are strong but not strong enough," he whispered.

His two kingdoms needed him, one powerful bird atop was too much. It had already ensnared Ain, it would have no more thralls.

"How exciting it is to have more problems than answers," he muttered.

"Sire?" One of the Shields on the door looked to him.

"Nothing, my good man. Is Abrensi in?"

"He is, Your Majesty." Both guards reached to open the Storm Singer's doors.

Seto swept inside. Of all his problems, the Solave was one which would wait. The corpse of the Sea Beast was a bigger fish, in every sense of the word, and Abrensi was about to earn his keep once more. Besides which, the visit was overdue – for his own reasons – even if Abrensi had been requesting to speak with him for days now. Of course, a King's tardiness might be expected.

The Storm Singer's room overflowed with musical instruments. Flutes and pipes, hand drums and sets of polished stones with tiny mallets in silver settings. Seto paused at a magnificent harp that dominated an entire corner of the room. Its strings gleamed in the lamplight, the gold foil worked into the huge bones. Much finer than his own instrument, locked away in the Harper. His fingers itched, but he did not touch it. Even had playing been a choice, one never touched another musician's instruments uninvited.

The rest of the furniture stood crammed into corners and had been set aside, or more often, become resting places for more instruments, including several he did not recognise.

"Ah, Your Majesty."

Abrensi smiled at him from the entryway to another room. As ever, his eyes were bright and he appeared amused with something no-one else was privy to. A familiar expression. When the man was younger, it had been the same, only now there were traces of bitterness.

"Abrensi. I am impressed with your collection."

The Storm Singer sketched a bow. "Before my time in the...finer accommodations of our city, I collected much. I travelled a little to do so." He shrugged. "But I am hardly telling you anything new, am I? You yourself know the obsessions of a musician and a traveller. Though I understand you no longer play?"

"Regrettably, yes. But today, I'm here on more official business. I know you wish to speak with me and I have questions of my own."

Abrensi gestured to a pair of chairs, skipping over to remove a small horn from one. He brushed at dust. "I apologise, time is dusty, dusty, dusty."

"No trouble." Seto gestured to Abrensi's robe. It was rumpled, but the silver star had changed. It was now crossed by a golden bolt of lightning. An auspicious alteration – when had Abrensi commissioned it? Seto's memory of the Storm Singers and their rituals was admittedly hazy. Too much time abroad as a young lad. "That is a fine addition."

"Ah, thank you. As the elder Singer, I thought a mark to be fitting. It further signifies that I will take a senior role in training Lavinia's children – and subsequent Singers."

"Isn't her brother attending to that now?"

"He is, but Tenefio will bow to my superior knowledge when he returns. It is for the greater good. Which is a good thing, isn't it?"

Seto offered a sound of agreement. Had the man always been this...scattered? "And have you heard from him?"

"He is due to return in a matter of weeks. I asked him to stay in the mountains, that way he can protect the children if something...dire occurs here during the invasion."

Seto nodded. A wise choice. "That is in fact related to my purpose here."

"That and to discuss my requirements?" He paused. "Notch assured me you would be willing to listen."

"I am, Abrensi."

"More than can be said of your brother, no?"

"True."

"And how is he?"

Otonos was in pain, as he ought to be. Checking on the fool was probably a good idea, it had been a good while now. "He clings to life."

"Hmmm. Again, I felt you would be more receptive to my concerns. I remember you as a fine man – rational. Awfully rational. And if you will forgive me, better than your brother, better than your father."

"And you must know, Abrensi – that is a bare compliment. I could overturn the nearest rug and find something better than my brother."

"And your father?"

Seto raised an eyebrow. "You are more forward than I remember."

"Thank you."

"Come, let us speak plainly."

"Very well, my King, though I thought I was." Abrensi toyed with the horn. "Your father committed a grievous sin against the city. You know of which I speak?"

"Magic."

"Yes. For my part in it, I am unable to...make amends. But isn't loyalty a strange beast? How it pulls us into darkness. Promises light. Don't you think it is so?"

"Sometimes." Seto suppressed a frown. Father kept his secrets next to his skin – something useful the man passed down – and exactly what happened during his scourge against people who could perform anything even slightly resembling magic, was a dim chapter in Seto's memory. Where had he been at the time? The Far Islands? Travelling back from Renovar? Even in the aftermath, he'd learned little of the motivations.

But then, he'd had other things on his mind at that point.

"I have learnt that my art, King Oseto, my art is my

only true loyalty. And so, I wish to expand upon what we have here. To create a place for developing magic in our city. Storm Singers, Witches – whoever. From any class. To that end, I wish for your support." He paused, a big grin. "And your money."

Seto clasped his hands together, placing them in his lap. "Abrensi, I don't know what to think of you."

"That pleases me, Your Majesty."

"Should it?"

He shrugged. "Being predictable is awfully... predictable, Majesty."

"Indeed," Seto said. "Tell me then, why did my father put you in that cell? And more importantly, why did you stay there? You are powerful, people love the Storm Singers. Why? Tell me that and we can continue speaking of what I believe may be a noble goal. Tell me that and you take another step toward my full trust."

Abrensi held his gaze. All trace of mockery was gone from his eyes. "Life is precious, it is not in my nature to cause harm through purpose."

"A fine philosophy." Seto waited.

Abrensi gave a long sigh. "I stayed there because it was safer. For everyone."

"How?"

"Because I would not raise my hand against a fool, because I might have raised many hands in doing so." Abrensi stood, pacing the room. "Such is a Storm Singer's draw, My Liege. You are right. The people love us. But that matters not. Both your father and brother are of the past. You and I speak now of tomorrow. Its glories."

Seto leant forward. How to handle Abrensi? A push, or an open hand? Above all, he needed the man cooperative. Perhaps his secrets could wait a little longer.

Lavinia might know more. "Do you know what I wish for, Abrensi?"

He paused. "No. I would like to know."

"The Anaskar of old. The city I remember my grandfather loving so dearly. Vibrant, open and bustling with people from all over the lands. Renovar Ice-Hands, smiling children from the Far Islands, folk from Holvard back in our shipyards and even a truer peace in the south and west. And I believe your goal will be an important step, but there are threats most immediate."

"The Sea Beast."

"That is only one, but yes."

"An important one. You need its bones."

Seto nodded. Time to tread lightly again. For if nothing else, life was about the control of information. Who it flowed toward, and who it flowed from. For who it ought to stop. "I need its toxins contained. Bones and all."

"And because Greatmasks can be made from them."

Seto arranged a frown. "That seems most unlikely."

Abrensi laughed. "Come now, Your Majesty. I am no fool. I, we Storm Singers, have long known that about the Sea Beasts."

"Beasts?"

"Your father never told you?"

Seto shook his head. "He was meagre with details. Especially after I was no longer considered suitable for the throne."

"He loved to limit those around him, didn't he?"

"Indeed."

"Well, only Kings and First Singers share such information typically, though I assumed all Kings would at least have the foresight to share with their family."

Abrensi said, voice hardening. Seto could have laughed –
but it would have been a laugh of shame. How close his
own thoughts about hiding information had just echoed
his father's actions. "Well, let me tell you now. No-one
knows how to Awaken a Greatmask, let alone take bones
from the beast, that's something we've never known.
Maybe the Carvers did, once. Maybe the Lord Protector
knows? But most of what I learnt of the Sea Beasts is
about controlling them."

"Abrensi, there is much for us to discuss it seems."

"Most certainly, Your Majesty." He grinned again.
"Chief among them, my plans for the future."

"Let's call them 'our plans' shall we?" He smiled back.
"But first the Beast."

"Very well."

"I wish for your advice and your skills, if applicable, to
help remove the Beast from the wall. The city is at risk
from illness."

"As your men have no doubt discovered, harvesting is
dangerous without the proper equipment and magics. It
is beyond me, I am sorry to admit."

Seto let his shoulders slump a little. Of course. Why
would there be a simple solution? "And the illness the
Beast creates?"

He raised an eyebrow. "You wish for me to 'sing' it
away?"

"An interesting proposal. Is it possible?"

Abrensi opened his mouth, expression hardly
encouraging, but paused. "You know, I have never tried
to cure illness with song. Who is to say it is not possible?
Lavinia and I will investigate and send word of our
progress."

"Quickly too, Abrensi."
"As possible, my King."

CHAPTER 19

Flir pointed to the plush chair. "Stay seated."

Alvetti opened his mouth a moment, then sank back down. Luik snorted from across Seto's sitting room. Heavy curtains kept the night's chill out, swallowed the lamp light and smothered the very windows. "Why can't I look around?" the Shield said.

"You're in debt, right?"

"It's not my fault, I'm just having a bad run. My luck will change, it always does."

"Well I don't trust your pockets."

His brows drew together. "My pockets?"

"They might take a liking to some of those lovely baubles on the mantle."

"You think I'd steal from the King?" he spluttered.

"I don't want to find out."

He crossed his arms, slumping deeper into the chair. "How much longer will we have to wait? It's been...I don't even know how long."

Luik groaned.

A valid question, but one she'd given up asking years

ago. Seto kept his own time. If she could be sure the old Rat wasn't but moments away, she'd go visit Bel. See how the poor girl was doing. But knowing Seto, he'd swan in the very instant she left. After, she could check on Bel after.

Someone knocked at a door. "Come in," Flir shouted.

Pevin appeared, trailing a page, who directed him to the chairs. "Palliv ae ishkor, dilar." *I couldn't find you, dilar.* There was no reproach in his voice, only the unending devotion and a hint of apology. As if Pevin were at fault for her efforts to avoid him.

"Who's this then? He doesn't look like the King. He's like you," Alvetti said.

Pevin glanced at the young soldier, but did not answer. Flir pointed at Alvetti. "Be quiet." To Pevin. "Can you do something for me, Pevin?"

"I crave such an opportunity."

"I'm sure you do. I would like a report on a patient named Bel, if Mayla the healer is awake. Can you do this?"

"Of course." He strode from the room and Flir grinned. At least he was useful for something.

"For someone who complains often, seems like you enjoy ordering him around," Luik said.

"He'd be upset if he didn't have something to do."

"Sad thing is, I think you're right."

Finally Seto himself appeared. His orange robes of state were creased from sitting and he went immediately to a decanter on a sideboard. He took a long gulp of Fire-Lemon before nodding to her and Luik. On Alvetti he trained weary eyes as he sat.

"So. You are the traitor who would plunge the entire city into darkness?" The old Rat's voice was soft.

Alvetti cringed. "My King, no, I am only, I mean, he

only has me deliver letters and I didn't know —"

"Enough!" Seto roared.

Flir blinked. Was Seto actually angry? Alvetti's face was white. He heaved himself from the chair and fell to his knees. "Please, My Liege. Let me make it right."

"Ha! What can you offer me?" He stood, towering over the soldier. "I ought to stain my carpet with your very lifeblood."

"No," Alvetti screeched. "I will serve you."

Seto moved back to take another drink. Flir took her cue. Maybe it was just one of the old routines. "Do you mean that?"

"Of course, yes, yes."

"It will be dangerous." She stared at him. Had Seto shocked him so much that he'd give in so quickly? Would Alvetti even be able to handle being bait?

"I want to help you." He twisted back to look over his shoulder at Seto. "Please, Your Majesty. I do."

Seto frowned down at the Shield. After a long moment he spoke. "Then you will have to grow accustomed to Luik here. He's going to be spending a lot of time with you. You may not always see him, but he will be nearby."

"Yes."

"You will show him the Mask, you will show him this Julas."

"I can do that."

"If that is true, your life will remain yours."

"Thank you, my King."

"We shall see, Alvetti." Seto called through the door. Two of the Honour Guard entered, Swordfish on their breastplates. Seto directed them to take Alvetti to be fed and bathed, and then, only once the door had closed behind them, did he smile. "How was my performance?"

"Masterful."

"Well, I have no more in me tonight." He collapsed into an armchair. "I could sleep a week."

Luik crossed his arms. "Maybe you should."

"If but one of my kingdoms would permit such a luxury." He gestured with his glass. "Will you take a drink?"

Luik shook his head but Flir pulled herself from the chair and poured a small glass. Nothing like the icy fire of Renovar spirits, but still, the sweetness of the lemon was nice. "Luik and I have been...thinking about how to use Alvetti." Arguing was more accurate.

"Good."

"I think we should hit hard. The moment we know where Vinezi is, the moment it's confirmed, clamp him down. Above ground and below, street level and the rooftops. A coordinated strike of Shield and your men. No mistakes this time."

"And if we catch only more imposters? Or secondary men like this Julas?"

"It will be more than we have now."

Seto nodded. "And Luik is afraid to risk all those men, am I right?"

"If that slimy bastard's triggered another place with acor, we're all dead," Luik said.

"That might be true of the palace already," Flir said. "But I think he's bluffing."

"Not much of a gambler myself."

Seto held up a hand. "Circles, my friends. We risk talking in circles. There are risks, true. Luik, your alternative?"

"Something simpler. I put on the old uniform and spend time with Alvetti. Flir shadows us. Between the two of us, we can handle anything Vinezi's got."

Seto pulled himself from the chair. "I wonder."

"What?"

He paced; stride cutting the carpet. "Are we making the same mistake? Alvetti and Lino were easily picked up, were they not?"

"We're good at what we do," Flir said.

Seto's face was troubled. "But let's not assume no-one could be smarter than us. Even the letter itself, I wonder. Perhaps it *is* a familiar ruse to have us swoop in on another Iron Pig?"

Flir pursed her lips. It was exactly Vinezi's style. "Wouldn't he love that?"

"So he would."

"You think Alvetti is not our bait, but in fact Vinezi's?"

Luik leant forward. "And if we put him back on the streets, he'll lead us into an even bigger trap?"

"At first I thought that, but no longer. For why would Vinezi attempt the same ploy twice? We would see through it. I fear something worse." Seto stopped, then swore. He charged for the door. "I fear that a fox has been let loose amongst the hens."

Flir leapt after him, catching the old man in the hall. No guards. "Which way?"

"Split up and find him," Seto shouted, dashing down a corridor. Flir sprinted in the opposite direction, Luik's heavy tread fading. Wait. If Alvetti the runt was up to something, wouldn't it be assassination? No wonder he'd given-in so easily. She glanced over her shoulder – Luik had followed Seto. Good.

The guards took Alvetti to be fed and bathed. Kitchens first.

She skidded down a side passage. Shapes lay on the

stone floor. The honour guard. One man dead, his neck at an angle. The other breathed but a knife protruded from his shoulder and there was a huge dent in his breastplate. Flir scooped him up, ran to the nearest door and thumped on it until a surprised man answered.

"Find a healer." Flir dumped the wounded soldier in his arms and ran on. A trail of blood led along the corridor. Some luck, Alvetti was wounded. She followed the splashes, which eventually became drops, down narrow passages and once through the ways, snatching a nearby torch before plunging into shadow.

Beyond, the spots stopped at a door to a stairwell. She leapt down, finally bursting onto a landing. Nothing. She crossed the stones to another door – leading to second stairwell. Longer than the first, it opened into a storeroom.

Beneath the palace.

Flir ran from crate to crate, ducking between stacks of fruit and vegetables, the blood trail thinning as Alvetti headed into the next storeroom, this one lined with weapons and armour packed in straw, until finally the trail stopped at a wall. Crates of fire-lemon had been tossed aside, shoved away from the wall to reveal a small pile of spots, as if he'd stopped there a moment.

But it was only a featureless wall. No doors, no keyholes – and she'd combed the storerooms herself while looking for acor. Except, still the blood. Smeared slightly. By feet passing through the wall?

Flir trailed a hand over the stone. Dust drifted down. She stopped. "What's this?" A pattern was visible beneath the dust. She used both hands, clouds rising, then stood back. Differing stones were arranged in the wall to represent a Mask. How had no-one seen the symbol? Or had they – and left it hidden? The dust, the stacks of Fire-Lemon. Some crates were old, likely from decades past. How had the little whelp known about it?

Because surely it was the door to another passage.

Why else the blood with a smear trailing beneath the wall itself?

But without a key or latch, she wasn't going anywhere. The pattern of the Mask had no openings. No other crates had been shifted, so there were no latches elsewhere, surely? Only one choice left. She drove her palm into the wall. The brickwork shook and she clicked her tongue before crossing the room where she stretched her legs. "Ready, wall?"

Flir charged. Mere feet from the wall, she leapt into a flying kick. Her foot smashed through the mask, dust and bricks crashing around her as she stumbled into a wide passage. Scrambling over the rubble, she retrieved her torch and ran on. Shockwaves travelled her body from the impact, but they were as water sliding away.

Light flickered ahead. The time for stealth was long past – since she'd just kicked a wall down, Alvetti would know someone was coming for him.

Inside a large chamber set with a single torch, the traitorous Shield bent over a trail of dark powder. Acor. It led to a stack of barrels nestled against support columns. He spun, one arm wrapped with a bloody, makeshift bandage.

"So. The little girl."

"So. The little idiot." Flir dropped her torch and stomped it out. Alvetti glanced at the torch on the wall.

"Ready to die?" Flir asked.

"If you're not, this might end badly for you."

He watched her. His trail led to an open passageway,

beyond which lay more flickering light. And faint voices.

Flir darted forward, but Alvetti was fast – too fast? – he intercepted her, swinging a blow from his good arm. She blocked it with her forearm, throwing a counterpunch, but he'd already skipped away, closer to the torch. Flir hesitated for half a breath. She felt his strike – he was stronger than he should have been. But then, something had to have dented the honour guard's armour, and the traitor wore no mace, no hammer.

She leapt after him, dragging his shoulder back. Instead of casting him across the room, as she should have been able, Flir found stiff resistance. Alvetti dipped, attempting to use her momentum against her. He flung his elbow back, but she was already pivoting, kicking high and hard.

Her foot cracked his jaw. Blood sprayed from his mouth as he crumpled to the ground.

"What are you?" She stood over him, blocking the torch. She couldn't douse it yet, not without being sure that he was done. Who knew where he'd get to in the dark?

He reached his knees. Blood ran down his chin and his jaw hung, words distorted. "I am the future, bitch."

"You don't have a future."

Blood bubbled. "And I'm not the only one."

He swung, but she batted his fist aside. Another kick, this one shattering ribs. He screamed, the echo ringing in the chamber.

Flir knelt and lifted his head by the hair. "What does that mean?"

A hand whipped up to her wrist, pulling at her, but she ground her teeth. He was too strong for a normal man, but not strong enough. She broke his grip and another bone cracked, the snap buried in a second scream.

"Someone opened the back door." Alvetti's voice was a shriek of laughter and pain.

Footsteps thundered up the passage. Many footsteps. Flir swore. The doorway was empty yet but at any moment – steel flashed. She flinched back, but something tore into her thigh.

She lashed out, backhanding her captive with a shout.

A knife protruded from her leg and Alvetti lay still.

She ripped the cloak from the body and tore it into strips, before pulling the blade from her leg with a grunt. She wound a bandage tight and ran for the passage, kicking and breaking the trail of acor as she did. The wound impeded her movements, but the pain wasn't too bad. And she was on top of the bleeding at least.

Two figures appeared from a bend in the passage, paused, then charged with torches held high. Dressed as Shield. Beyond, four more men crowded the passage. Wide as it was, they'd be able to flank her if she wasn't quick. Flir met them with a crash, flinging the closest into a wall. The second slashed at her but she parried the blade with Alvetti's knife, following up with a heel to the breastplate. The man flew into the infiltrators, his curse lost in a clatter. Flir knelt by the first man but he was dead.

She paused.

His hair was wet, why?

It didn't matter. More men piled up behind the first group of tangled limbs. Flir spun, grabbed the man she'd smashed into the wall and hurled him at the newcomers, scattering them. His torch spluttered where it had fallen onto the stone. She snatched it up before it reached the trail of acor running up the middle of the passage.

She froze, torch in hand. What if one of the other —
fire bloomed.

CHAPTER 20

Someone shouted in Renovas, the panic in their voice filtering down through the darkness. And stone. Flir blinked grit, shifting her arms and legs. The grinding and tumbling of rock followed as she raised her torso. Light hurt her eyes. What the hell happened?

"Dilar, you are safe?" Pevin stared down at her, his eyes wide. Dust caked his skin and his hands bled. He dropped a brick. It clinked amongst more bricks. Flir shrugged off a pile as she stood. Much of the passage had collapsed, the edge of the debris covering her. An ache lurked behind her eye and her neck was sore, but her limbs responded well enough. Even the wound in her thigh was a bare twinge.

"Dilar, what happened here?"

"An explosion." She dusted herself off. "I guess even a small amount of acor can be serious. You saw how much is back in that other room?"

"I did. Half the palace might have gone up."

"Someone tried to do just that and get away." She put weight on her thigh. Not bad. "Only it didn't work."

"There are black marks on the ground. They stop before the chamber."

"Show me."

He led her along the passage. Uneven gouges, running in a line and blackening the floor, stopped before the chamber. "Maybe it would have worked." She said. But Alvetti would had to have been some distance away – or the trail of acor was awfully long. So why the big explosion? Unless, one of the men in the passage had been carrying more? Laying the rest of the trail.

"I need to see the other side of the blockage."

"I have no idea how that could be accomplished. It was hard enough finding you here."

"You followed the trail of blood?"

He frowned. "Actually no. I always know roughly where you are."

"You're a Heart-Hound?"

"No, not that. I only know where you are, dilar."

Flir closed her eyes. Even in a land distant from home, she was not free of the lies, the cruel trick played upon her by the Gods. "Wonderful, Pevin. Let's go find Seto."

"Of course."

She strode along, Pevin struggling to keep up at first. "You're upset, aren't you?"

"Yes."

"I hope I haven't angered you."

She stopped. "Pevin, who are you following?"

He opened his mouth then closed it. "I'm not sure how to answer this question – I mean, I'm following you, dilar."

"Who?"

"You, the dilar."

"You're not, Pevin. You're following Flir, the

mercenary."

His face broke into a serene smile. "Of course, dilar."

She resumed walking, skipping up the stairs. "Don't call me that."

"Sorry –" A slight pause, as if he'd omitted the word, but still thought it.

Halfway up the spiral, Flir ran into Luik and Seto, along with half the Honour guard. Or Luik at least; she bounced off his frame and even though he winced, he caught her shoulders before she fell back into Pevin.

"Flir, you all right?"

"I'm fine. I found Alvetti. He was trying to blow the palace into the heavens."

"Show me," Seto said.

Flir took them to the chamber. Alvetti's corpse rested some distance from the passage opening, mute beside the trail of acor. She gestured to the rigged barrels. "We can probably find another use for that." Then to the rubble. "There were maybe ten of them, maybe less. I'm guessing Alvetti let them in somehow, and they brought the acor with them."

Seto nodded, eyes roving the pile. His expression was hard.

"So where are we, Seto?"

"No idea. The Mascare passages do not lead to this place."

"There was a symbol on the brickwork in the storeroom. A mask. Someone, Alvetti I guess, had moved a lot of crates to get to it. As if he knew exactly where to look."

Luik kicked a shard of stone. "Know where the passage led?"

"I think I can guess," Seto said. "Come with me."

"Wait." Flir pointed to Alvetti, speaking to the Honour

Guard. "Put his body somewhere, can you? I want to examine him later."

"Why?" Seto asked as two of the Honour Guard stepped forward.

"There's something strange about him. He was too strong for a regular man."

"Hmmm." Seto took them back up the stairs and into the ways, setting a line of single file torches. Cobwebs glistened in the torchlight, footfalls echoed. They twisted and turned through the passages and finally, after she'd lost her sense of direction, emerged into a room lined with armour. Suits from different periods of Anaskar history, each with a plaque explaining its use.

"Where now?"

"We should be directly above the cave in."

Luik whistled. "I'll be impressed if you're right."

"Impressed? Don't forget whose palace this is, Luik." The old rat nodded to Flir. "What do you think?"

"You want me to put a hole in the floor?"

"If you're not strong enough..."

She snorted. "You don't need to goad me. Now get out of my way. All of you."

Luik chuckled as he backed against a wall. Seto joined him, waving for the Honour Guard to do the same. "If I fall through, you're in trouble."

"You'll be fine."

Flir grunted and Pevin skipped aside when she snatched a steel armour stand and gave it a shake, armour sliding off with a clatter.

"They're antiques, Flir," Seto said.

"Really?" She grinned, then thumped the base onto the floor. A deep rumble followed. She smashed it down again, then switched her grip. With a low roof, she swung an abbreviated arc, pounding the same piece of stone. Again and again she swung, each crash rattling the armour stands. Shards of stone sprayed the room.

A significant hole had appeared, but beneath was more stone. "Thick floors."

"Built to endure," Seto said.

Flir kept working until the base caught. Wrenching it free, she paused. A small opening lay in the floor.

"One more I should say," Seto observed.

"Nice to have your help." Flir heaved the stand again. This time the base crashed through. She tossed it aside, knocking over another suit of armour, and bent by the larger opening.

She looked up at Seto and gestured. "It's dark down there, but I think I see rubble."

"As I said."

Flir waved him back again, then took the edge of the flooring. Straining a moment, she tore a piece free. Choosing the next piece with some care, she tore up another flagstone and kept on until an opening wide enough to climb down was revealed.

One of the honour guard stared at her. She winked and he flinched. "All right, who's going down first?"

"Is it safe?" Seto asked.

"I hope so," she said.

Seto gestured to a guard. "Find us some more torches. Flir, why don't you lower Luik and me down?" Seto said.

The senior officer of the Honour Guard moved forward. "My King, it may not be safe."

"True enough. Let's move into the next room and throw a torch down there."

Luik raised a hand. "Won't that risk another explosion?"

"Exactly. And if anyone is lurking below, it should

give them a nasty surprise."

Flir took a torch from a guard as Seto herded everyone from the room. Flir joined him in the entryway to the passage and leant out, tossing the flame into the hole. It flew with a whoosh.

Then nothing.

No explosion. No sound but Luik's breathing and the tap of Seto's foot.

"Down we go then."

Flir braced herself over the floor, then took Luik's hands. "Ready?"

"Lower away."

She let him down the hole, bending her knees. She scratched her ear, holding Luik with one hand.

"I'm close enough now." Luik's voice floated up.

Flir stretched her arm then let him go. His feet clapped to stone. In the torchlight he hulked, casting great shadows. "Anything?"

He shook his head and the shadow shook with him. "Not much. There might be some hints of armour, and further along the passage just extends into the dark."

Seto tapped her shoulder. "My dear?"

Flir lowered Seto, then one of the guard. By the time a man returned with torches he was the last, as she'd just dropped off Pevin. She lowered him, then caught the ledge and dropped down herself.

The new torches were lit and a line formed. The passage was long. At its head, Luik and Seto were crouched around another mask-symbol, this one on the floor. "How did you open the last one?"

Flir waved them aside and brought her knee up. "Like this." She stomped and brick crashed, her foot bursting through.

"You're enjoying this, aren't you?" Seto said.

"A little."

Flir cleared a section of the floor, revealing a stair. Luik joined her. Once they'd opened the way, Seto motioned them in, handing over a torch.

The stairway led down.

And down.

Down into darkness that dampened and dripped until she heard Luik's stomach grumble. "We should have brought food."

"It hasn't been that long," Seto said.

"It's been close."

"Captain, I'd wager that we've neared the harbour?"

The Shield nodded, scratching at his moustache. "I would agree, Sire. The landings have been growing longer. We must have passed the Antico Gate some time ago."

"And you've all marked the footprints?"

Flir pointed. "They're the only sets. Before the traitors, I'd say no-one else had been here for a long time."

"How are the torches?"

"We have enough," the Captain answered.

"Then onward."

The echo of their passage continued until the stairs ended, delivering them beneath an arch. Once again, the Mask symbol graced the brickwork, but this time there was no door.

Beyond, a massive chamber swallowed the sound of their footfalls. Torchlight strained at the edges of the dark.

"Spread out," Seto said. "Be alert."

The rasp of steel followed.

Flir raised her own torch; keeping close to Seto. Luik flanked the King as the Shield spread across the floor.

They crossed a wide space, slowing when large shapes loomed. Flir put a hand on her knife, but it was a pair of tower-like stone staircases. Several Luiks, standing end on end, would have reached the top. She raised her torch. Spanning the stairs was a steel bridge and underneath, almost hidden beneath the scuff of their boots, a lapping of water. Its surface reflected the torchlight.

"What is this?"

"I've no idea, Flir." Seto placed a hand on a stair. "There seems to be a regular opening here."

Luik stood on tiptoes, torch high above his head. "Can't tell how far the water stretches."

"It feels big."

"So we're under the harbour itself?" Flir bent by the water's edge. Only black at the edge of the stone. Underground lake or underground pool? No way to tell.

Seto joined her. "Possibly."

"King Oseto."

One of the Honour Guard waved them over. He stood by the water's edge, something shapeless in one hand. "I found these by the water." He held some sort of smock. Small puddles surrounded a heap of other bag-like shapes, and evidence of splashing covered the stone beneath the soldier's feet. "A staging area, My Lord."

Seto glanced at the wet ground. "I see." Next he took the bag from the soldier. Flir moved her torch closer. The cloth was multi-layered and had been sliced open. "It's like a big wineskin."

Seto rubbed the surface between thumb and finger. "Heavily oiled."

"Acor," Luik said.

Flir nodded. It explained the wet hair on the men she'd met in the tunnel. "So they swam down beneath the harbour, dragging their powder behind. Found this lake and waited –"

"– for Alvetti to let them in," Seto finished.

"How did Vinezi know about any of this? The entry in the storeroom, how to open the passages, the lake here?"

Seto threw the skin down. "I don't know. But I am fed up."

"So what now?" Flir asked.

"Now some unlucky Shields are going to have a new guard duty and a cold swim, and the rest of us are going to sweep the palace. Again."

"Right." Part of her sweep would have to include Mayla's rooms. How did Bel fare? She waved Pevin over as she fell into step with Luik, Seto ranging ahead and directing his men.

"What did Mayla have to say?" she asked Pevin.

"That your patient was making progress. She wouldn't tell me much." He gave a rueful smile. "I don't think she trusts me."

"Pevin, I don't even know if I trust you yet."

His smile faded. "Even after my devotion?"

"We've had this argument before, haven't we? You're not devoted to me, you're devoted to a lie."

"Then I hope to prove myself."

"Can I stop you trying?"

"No, dilar."

"Don't call me that."

"Of course."

CHAPTER 21

The trapdoor inched open and Notch hid his hands and the frayed rope.

New light fed into the cellar, a suggestion of moonlight in the room above, barely enough to cast whoever had opened it into silhouette. Sofia had succumbed to the fever again. At least the way she'd slumped covered her wrists.

But he was no-where near free. Efran and his torturer would have some fun.

"Notch?" A whisper.

He tensed. The figure climbed into the room, no lamp, no torch. Was it a ruse?

"Notch, I'm getting you out of here."

A familiar, older voice. Speaking Anaskar with a Braonn accent. "Gelehn?"

"Of course. Who else is going to haul you out of trouble? Hurry." The old hunter crossed the floor, a knife in hand. Notch raised his bonds and Gelehn sliced them.

"Thank you." Notch worked some feeling back into his hands. "Sofia too."

Feet crossed stone. A pause. "Is she well? Her skin burns."

Notch joined the hunter. "She's running a fever. I have something in our bags that will help, unless Efran took them."

Gelehn lifted Sofia and started up the steps. "Don't worry about Efran and his men."

At the top, Notch paused. Bodies lay across the floor and a stillness filled the room – but not the stillness of death. The nearest man wore an expression of peace and his chest rose and fell in a gentle rhythm. "They're all asleep?" he whispered.

Gelehn nodded and wove through the men. Near to twice as many Braonn as he'd noted during their capture, but none so much as stirred as Notch passed. Not even when Sofia groaned in her fever-sleep.

Outside, Swift and their belongings waited in the dark trees, trunks but pale smudges beneath the moon. Notch helped set Sofia on the horse and checked for the masks. Untouched. Fortune had blessed them. Generously.

"How did you put them to sleep?"

"A powder. But we should hurry, I wasted much time gathering your possessions. Efran had taken a liking to your saddlebags there. He was some distance away when we surprised him."

"Where is he now?"

"The others are diverting him." Gelehn led them along a trail barely visible. "Nonetheless, let's put some distance between them, before he returns."

"You saw him? And who is 'we'?"

"We did. And his kind travel well." Gelehn didn't elaborate.

"So can you tell me what was in his veins?"

"Ah, you saw that? It's sap from the Summer Groves. It grants him endurance, among other things."

"I've never heard of this."

Gelehn grunted. "They're new to us too. What he's done is unnatural."

"Something's happening in the Bloodwood, isn't it?"

"Of course it is." He paused. "Exactly 'what' is the problem."

Notch led the horse up a small slope. "How did you find us?"

"Passing through Avaon, all people could talk about was you and the girl. And then Efran. Didn't take much to put it together."

"Glad you did."

Sofia groaned again and Notch cursed himself. He stopped the horse, which gave a snort, and rummaged through the bags. He found Osani – or so he thought – and placed it over her face.

Her laboured breathing eased.

Gelehn joined him. "She seems better already."

"She does. They're strange creatures."

Gelehn chuckled. "Women?"

"Greatmasks."

The hunter gave a shiver. "Well, we'd better keep moving. Let's get you two out of range, then we can talk about your path."

"We have to pass Avaon and find the rogue's trail."

"Leave that to this old hunter."

The night passed slowly. At one point he found himself blinking, leaning on Swift as he walked. A few steps later, the forest came into focus again and he shook his head. Stay alert. Gelehn's insistence on speed suggested that Efran might be able to catch them.

Light bloomed between trunks, as if a silver ball spread across the horizon. The path widened and the dawn grew until the red and orange of the leaves became vivid. Notch slowed. Autumn colours. He frowned at Gelehn's back. "Gelehn, this is the Autumn Grove."

The hunter stopped, facing ahead. "I know."

"Gelehn?"

"You have to come with me, Notch. Both of you." The hunter turned. Regret was plain on his face, but his mouth was firm. "I don't have a choice."

Notch rested a hand on his blade, but did not draw. He stopped closer to Sofia and the horse. "You always have a choice."

"My people don't think so." Gelehn made no move to his own weapons, but a long knife was within reach.

"Which people?"

"The Oynbae. You'd call us Butterfly-Eaters."

Magic-users. Stories he'd laughed over with Luik while travelling the forest. "That's how you put them to sleep."

"Not I, Notch, but that doesn't matter. What matters is that you cooperate. It's what's best for everyone."

His sword rang free. "I'm not convinced."

"We only want to talk, and to protect you from the Sap-Born."

"Then let us go. Point us in the right direction."

"You have to see the Oyn-Dir first."

"No."

"I don't want to fight you, Notch."

He hefted his blade. "I agree. You don't."

Gelehn blew a piercing whistle and movement exploded. From several directions figures in autumn colours charged, springing up from the ground in fountains of loam, ducking around from behind broad trunks and swinging down from the leaves.

Notch raised his sword, but a ring of blades, bows and slingshots, bulging with bright yellow pods, surrounded him.

No-one spoke.

Gelehn called from beyond the circle. "Notch, put down your sword."

"I don't trust you, Gelehn, much less anyone pointing sharp things at me."

"Would you trust me?" A woman's voice spoke in Anaskari, her accent slight. The circle parted and one of the Oynbae approached, a small smile on her face. Her hair was tied up in a high tail and her skin was...beyond smooth. The look she gave him was predatory.

He did not lower his blade. Underestimating a beautiful woman – any woman – was idiocy. "Not at all."

"Well," she removed a pair of leather gloves and cupped her palms, raising them to her lips, "leave that up to me." Then she blew. A puff of powder flew into his face and Notch coughed. Idiot. He should have known what was coming.

He coughed again. His sword point waivered and he dropped to his knees. The whole forest blurred and then it was gone. He couldn't open his eyes.

There'd been nothing in her hands.

*

Notch opened his eyes to a wooden room, bare of furniture but remarkably, one which appeared to be without seam. No joins, no windows or doors, but all smooth walls. High above lay a circular opening. It let daylight in, but no hope of escape. The walls grew narrower the higher they went, like a funnel – and he lay in the bulb at the bottom.

Sofia.

He shot to his feet.

He'd been drugged by the Oynbae woman somehow – the Butterfly-Eater. He slammed his fist into the wall. Some guardian, Notch. No sword, no supplies. Nothing. And now they had Sofia and the Greatmasks too.

"Notch?"

The voice was faint. From beyond the wall. He pressed his ear against the cool wood.

"Sofia?"

"Thank Ana of the Sea. What's happening? Are you stuck in a wooden cell too?"

"Yes," he said. "It was Gelehn. He rescued us from Efran and led us into a trap."

"The Hunter? But why? And where are we?"

"Back in the Autumn Grove. They want us for something."

"A strange woman came, asking me questions. She seemed Braonn, only different. She wore gloves for one thing."

That one. "They're the Oynbae. Luik called them Butterfly-Eaters." He laughed. "I never really believed him. But they have some strange magic, whoever they are. They used it to put me to sleep."

A groan of pain.

"Sofia?"

"It's fine, I'm just stiff. My muscles, it's hard to move. I feel like I slept encased in stone."

"How about your fever?"

"Gone. For now. Notch, what do we do?"

"Wait."

"Great advice."

"We can only hear what they have to say. What did the woman want to know?"

"She asked questions about Argeon and Osani. I couldn't answer many, so she left."

"Nothing else?"

"She said her name was Nia and that she'd return. I thought she was reasonable."

"She didn't put you to sleep with a strange powder."

"Well she's got the Greatmasks and all our possessions."

A shadow fell across the floor. Notch moved from the wall, craning his neck. A silhouette waved down at him. "Here you go."

Something dropped.

He reached to catch a water flask. Next came an orange. Then the figure left.

Notch uncorked, sniffed and shrugged. They'd already put him to sleep once. He drank deeply and put the flask aside, tearing into the orange and taking a bite, sucking the juice.

"What's happening?"

"They're feeding us," he said between bites. It was the finest orange ever grown.

"No-one's giving me any food. What have you got?"

"An orange."

"You sound like you're inhaling it."

"I'm sure yours is coming." He swallowed the last bite and sat against the wall. "Well?"

"Notch – wait. It's a ladder."

"Ladder?" Notch whipped his head back, smacking into the wall. "Gods be damned."

A new voice, fainter than Sofia's drifted through the wood. "Will you join us?"

Sofia, louder. "Where?"

"At a feast in the Centre. To discuss something of vital importance to both our peoples."

"How can I trust you? You've imprisoned us."

"Only temporarily."

"Then you'll let us go?"

"First, you must meet my father, the Oyn-Dir. He will decide your fate."

"What about –"

"Your servant is being cared for."

Notch thumped the wall. "One orange?"

Muffled laughter from the newcomer, then Sofia spoke again. "He should be with me."

A pause. "Very well, I will ask."

Notch paced until Sofia called his name. He returned to the wall, pressing his ear against the wood. "So they want to talk at least," he said.

"But what about? Both our peoples?"

"They want something." He took another drink. "So we're stuck here a little longer."

Sofia paused. "Can I ask you something...about brothers?"

"Of course."

"Did yours ever let you down?"

"No." He corked the bottle. "But I let him down."

"Oh."

"Raf was..." He clenched a fist. Each remembrance was like a new blade between his ribs. Maybe only the angle had changed, now that he'd consigned the King to a miserable wasting into death. Now Notch held the blade. Father's voice echoed. *You failed him.* And maybe it was true. Easier to blame Otonos than to admit he'd let Raf down. "All Otonos cared about was winning. It didn't matter how many of us – or the Medah – died. There wasn't an honourable bone in his body."

"You mean, the way he dishonoured the fallen?"

"Raf tried to stop him but the King was blind with rage. Otonos lashed out and I was too slow."

She was quiet a moment. "Notch, I'm sorry."

"Thank you."

"Do you think he'd forgive you if he could?"

Notch closed his eyes. The one question he'd never have an answer for. "I like to think he would. But I'll never know."

"So am I supposed to forgive Tantos?"

"I can't tell you, Sofia."

"I know. But, I feel him. Whenever I touch or even look at Argeon. Sometimes just a hint, but he's there."

He waited.

"Whenever I finally talk to Father, I might know. Who was telling the truth. But if I never see him again..."

He sighed, then shook his head. Come up with something better than sighs, Notch. "Even if that happens, I think you'll know."

"How?"

"Just decide if you'll feel worse if you don't forgive your brother."

She was quiet a moment. "Have you forgiven yourself?"

"No."

She was silent a moment.

"I'm not much help, I know," he said.

"No, it's just that I don't know if I even want to forgive him."

He kept his voice gentle. "Then don't decide today."

Something dropped into the room. A rope ladder,

swaying slightly. "Sofia."

"You too?"

Nia's voice called down from above. "Climb, warrior."

The rope was coarse beneath his fingers. He gave it a tug and put a boot in the first rung. Time to meet the Oyn-Dir.

CHAPTER 22

Sofia climbed free of the hole to stand on the clear floor of the Autumn Grove. The odd light, even at high noon, once again spread through the forest. She'd been underground, the hollow room dug into the earth. Impressive – but what did Nia and her people want?

Notch stood beside her as the woman wrapped a ladder around a stump. Beyond, a village wove its way between the trunks. As with the rest of the Bloodwood, small homes were spread without order, only with more statues similar to those she and Notch encountered. Large and small, sometimes in groups but just as often alone and towering as high as several men, none were broken here. Instead, each statue was free of grime and debris. A woman in a soft pink tunic rose on her tiptoes to brush at the folded wings of a male figure.

"Tira and Areth," Nia said as she stood, joining her. "Our Gods and Guardians. Protectors."

Sofia nodded. "Like you?"

"Perhaps. I am a warrior like your servant, only I also fight with means other than steel." She said it, not as a dismissal, only a fact.

Notch joined them. "And what was that powder you used on me?"

She laughed. "Have you never touched a butterfly's wings?"

More of the Oynbae appeared and Sofia noted that while Notch still had more questions for Nia, as she did herself, he left off and straightened, body taking on a stance of readiness. The newcomers lined up before her and Nia. One held her packs. Swift, who nickered upon seeing her, waited in the clearing, but the rest of their belongings were no-where in sight. "Before we take you to see the Oyn-Dir, would you do us the honour of dressing formally?"

Sofia glanced at Notch, who shrugged. She accepted the pack. "What do you mean?"

"Your robe and mask. You're here as an envoy of the Anaskari."

"Not as a prisoner?"

She shrugged. "I don't know yet."

"I see." She cast another glance at Notch. This time he gave a slight nod. An opportunity. If the Braonn let her wear Argeon she might be able to use it to escape.

Maybe.

Unless giving her the mask was meant to be a sign of trust?

Nia waved for Notch to turn around. He rolled his eyes but did so. The line of Oynbae closed around her, adding their bodies to a screen provided by Swift. The privacy wasn't really necessary but it was a nice gesture. Sofia removed her plain cloak, replacing it with the heavy crimson robe of her order. Not that she'd ever truly joined. As before, it cut the chill in the air. She paused over the masks.

Osani was safer, perhaps, but Argeon she could use. Sometimes.

Yet, what if Tantos lurked within?

Nia glanced over her shoulder. "Is there a problem?"

"No." She took the black mask and put it on, holding her breath.

Nothing.

Was it disappointment that squirmed in her chest?

First she would see if the Oynbae were sincere. There was no need to cause bloodshed with a botched escape attempt. "I'm ready."

"Wonderful." Nia led them through the trees. Sofia straightened her shoulders. If they wanted a Mascare, they would have one. The small party moved into a lane of pale statues alternating with broad tree trunks. People paused, lowering tools or bowls, to watch them pass. But this time, no slamming of doors, no scowls. Curiosity, and even some smiles. She would have smiled back if they'd been able to see it.

Bright lamps lined the trees ahead, containing a liquid that glowed without wick. Or was it more strange powder? There was a lavender tint to the woods here. More guards met them before a broad open area – the largest clearing she'd seen.

Wing-shaped tables, each with their own glowing pot, were occupied by murmuring men and women. Sitting in autumn colours, warriors had lain their bows and knives down, and were joined by a row of men and women with the look of hunters more typical to Braonn. Was Gelehn among them? His actions made some sense at least, yet where had he delivered them? From the danger of Efran to a newer danger?

The tables were arranged in a semi circle before an empty dais with its own two tables. Flanked by yet more statues of the Guardians, tables on the dais were only empty for moments. Figures in white filed from the trees, moving to take seats around the tables. All wore gloves of black, and did not move like simple attendants. Several chairs remained empty.

The entire clearing rose to its feet in silence.

A single man clad in a bright yellow robe, arms folded in large sleeves, walked onto the dais and took a seat. His white hair grew wild, swept back from his forehead in peaks. When he sat, he waved for those assembled to be seated.

He lifted his voice to cross the clearing, his Braonn having what she assumed was an old inflection, nothing she'd been taught at home. "Daughter, please show our guests to my table."

Guests. That hopefully answered one question. At least a hundred eyes tracked her as she followed Nia to the dais. At the Oyn-Dir's gesture, Sofia sat across from him. Nia hissed when Notch took a seat beside her. A collective gasp swept the clearing. Had he breeched protocol?

"I stay with you," he said.

Nia flanked him.

The Oyn-Dir raised his hands. The crowd hushed and the old man turned back to them. "Welcome, friends." He spoke now in Anaskari.

"Thank you, Oyn-Dir." Sofia replied in Braonn.

"Is your warrior able to follow us?"

Notch answered. "My Braonn is adequate only, My Lord."

"Then I will address most of our comments here in

Anaskari, though I will, after our conversation has come to an end, speak to my people in our tongue, of course."

"Thank you," he said, though his expression remained wary.

The Oyn-Dir turned back to Sofia. "Let me begin by apologising for circumstances surrounding our introduction. We were not sure you would speak with us."

"Our rescue was certainly appreciated," she said. Diplomacy first. It was not yet the time to mention their own pressing task, if at all.

"It was beyond fortunate. In truth, without your masks we would never have found you."

"You tracked us by them?"

"We did. For those attuned to the mysteries of the earth, objects of power have their own deep songs."

"But why were you searching for us?"

"Tira and Areth have provided an opportunity amidst this time of chaos. It is only my regret that we could not intercept you prior to Efran's strike."

"Then you only desire to speak with us?"

"I would not have you leave before that at the very least, yes."

Maybe prisoners yet. "We have our own task. It is of some urgency."

"Of course. But if you would indulge us first?" He motioned to one of his white-clad protectors, who clapped his hands. Food appeared from the trees, carried on smooth wooden platters. "Let us eat while we talk."

Dishes of berries and plates surrounded steaming hunks of meat – venison mostly, but rabbit too. Some manner of sweet sauce was ladled across the meat. Sofia's mouth watered. "It smells wonderful. I will have to remove my mask."

"Of course."

She did so, the air cool on her face. Notch had already taken a mouthful of the deer. Sofia took her own first bite. Delicious.

The Oyn-Dir continued as she ate, speaking around servants who brought cold water and sweet wines. "We are in need of a new peace. The old one was imbalanced at best."

"I didn't know there was war," Notch said.

He nodded. "Truly spoken, Warrior. However, there will be."

"Between who?" Sofia said.

"Braonn and Anaskari. Even now, there are preparations for assassination."

Sofia half-rose. "What?"

"Efran and the Sap-Born. He has taken control of the First Tree, our seat of governance, driven us, his own people, from its shade and now he sows for dark fruit from violence and hatred. Surely you have noticed a slow in trade, a trickle only of indentured servants?"

"We had discussed it of late."

"It is a precursor. Doubtless if your Kingdom was not beset with so many troubles, you might have noticed it much earlier. But that is to Efran's credit. He knows when to strike."

"Not his credit, Father," Nia said. "His detriment. He is a dangerous fool, seeking to bring such attention on our forest."

"But why now?" Notch said. "What's changed here?"

The Oyn-Dir answered. "Old debts that ought to have been paid by now evoke, for Efran, a chance for both vengeance and freedom from Anaskari ties. He has recently grown in power, both political and personal."

Sofia glanced at the audience. Soft conversation had already resumed. "And you wish for me to help you stop him?"

"Of course," the older man said. "War serves no-one. We have never wanted it."

Nia raised an eyebrow. "Never?"

He shrugged. "Perhaps in my youth, but that brings life to no-one. Tira and Areth would tell me what, daughter?"

"Life is green."

"Exactly. And so we must turn to the Anaskari themselves. We are not strong enough, alone."

"You have to play a dangerous game, don't you?" Notch asked.

"Yes. Already Efran is not satisfied with exile for us, with driving us from the First Tree. All he would need is exactly this sort of 'infraction' we commit now to feel justified in putting us to death." He leant forward. "And so we ask, in part, that you convince your King and the other owners of such Greatmasks to help us put a stop to Efran."

Notch shook his head. "Forgive me, Oyn-Dir, but that would be near impossible. You're talking about Anaskar mounting an invasion. Sofia could not convince King Oseto to do so now, not with the Renovar attack poised. Perhaps not even if there were no invasion from across the sea."

Sofia nodded her agreement.

"It is a risk, we understand. The alternative is the death of your King. If that were to happen, there would be war anyway."

"Violence to prevent violence," Nia said. "It's a poor choice, but the only one left. Efran's people are hunting us, despite our efforts to hide the Autumn Grove. If you don't help us, we will be driven from our home or killed. Efran will not tolerate such opposition as we represent."

Sofia raised a hand to stall Notch, and in part to bury the question of how someone hid an entire grove. "We would not wish to see that. But how does Efran believe he can achieve this?"

"He and his lackeys have been...changed by something I had never thought to see. A violation of the old ways. Somehow they have taken the sap of the Amber Trees from the Summer Grove into their veins. Warriors are now 'born' of the trees, changed irrevocably."

Nia shook her head. "It's a perversion."

"And now they claim to have a secret that will render the Greatmasks obsolete. They will send their assassins and then use the secret as blackmail, to force the Anaskari out of the forests. They will cancel all debt, free those in servitude."

"Can he truly do as he claims?"

"I do not know. He operates as if it is true, and his preparations are coming to a close. He has been readying a force of some size."

Notch put his cup down. "How many men? And how long has Efran known this secret?"

"Not long enough to act yet, though I suspect he has sent an assassin in the past. Doubtless more than one. They were assumed failures. Efran hinted as much during his speeches before the First Tree. His men number in the hundreds only, but that alone is a significant threat. The Sap-Born are not like other men."

"How so?"

"Their touch is death. I know not how, I know only what I have seen."

The table fell quiet. Nia had crossed her arms, but her eyes were far away.

Sofia broke the hush. "And the other part of your request?"

"That once Efran is dealt with, you agree to a longer view for peace. A sharing of children. We will educate our young in each other's homes."

"It sounds difficult." Sofia controlled a frown. And something that had been attempted unsuccessfully in the past. But what a stupid thing to say. It was a noble idea, and yet how could she possibly achieve any of it? "And I would love to be part of such a peace, but I do not have that power. Even if I did, I am on a grave mission of my own."

Father and daughter exchanged a glance, but neither spoke a moment. Notch shifted in his seat and Sofia opened her mouth but the Oyn-Dir spoke first. "Sofia –"

Nia leant forward. "No, Father. They will abandon us."

"Nia, that is not true."

"Of course it is, once they know – what reason would they have to help us?"

He slapped the tabletop, rattling cups. "Enough." Conversation ceased and those gathered had turned to stare up at the dais. Again, he raised his hands and the murmur resumed. To Sofia, he said, "Of your task we know, Sofia."

Whatever had passed between them didn't seem resolved, but Nia was not speaking. Sofia paused. "Then you've seen the rogue we seek?"

He smiled. "Rogue? No, Successor, your secret is safe here. I have met your father, long ago. I had even sent messengers to him about our current predicament, but there was no response. For a long time I did not understand why. I thought perhaps the Sap-Born had stopped them. Good men and women, each. But I recently learnt why else that might be."

"You know where my father is?"

His expression grew sombre. "Efran has him."

CHAPTER 23

Sofia shot to her feet. "Then he's alive?"

Voices hushed in the audience once more, and some of the hunters rose. The Oyn-Dir stood and lifted his voice. "Be calm, friends." He continued to explain that all was well and the feasters returned to their meals, casting glances up at the dais. The Oyn-Dir's face softened. "I would not wish to promise such a thing, Sofia, and offer false hope. Our scouts saw his capture and I suspect he lives, but only as Efran's prisoner."

"Where?"

"In the deepest of the forest, beyond the First Tree no doubt, but we do not know. I can only surmise that Efran keeps your father alive to learn whatever secrets he needs to support his claim of being able to circumvent the Greatmasks."

"Help me rescue my father and I will do anything you ask, anything in my power," Sofia said.

"Sofia, no," Notch said. "Don't make promises you might not be able to keep."

"I'm not sparing anything, Notch."

The Oyn-Dir smiled, gentle still. "We will accept your words for their intent. If you cannot make them come true, no-one at this table will hold you accountable."

She slumped in her seat. Finally, word that Father lived. The knot of stone in her stomach loosened – not completely, but enough. One step closer. Their journey had not been in vain. "Thank you, Oyn-Dir. We have searched long for traces of him."

Tears glistened in Nia's eyes but her face was set. "And so now you will continue to search for him, and leave us to our fate?"

"No." Sofia looked from face to face, including the white clad protectors who stood behind the Oyn-Dir. "Notch and I will stop Efran when we rescue my father."

Nia's bearing eased. Her father made a sound of doubt. "That would not be an easy task."

"I believe nothing is easy, but I haven't stopped trying."

The Oyn-Dir sighed. "Of course, if you attempt this, there will be no-one to vouch for us with your King should it come to war. Perhaps your Warrior –"

Sofia shook her head, even as Notch bristled. "Notch stays with me. When we deal with Efran, war will be averted."

"Only if you succeed."

"We won't fail. I am Casa Falco, I am Successor, I carry two Greatmasks, I am a match for these Sap-Born."

"Confidence is not enough," Nia said.

"It won't have to be," Notch growled.

Her eyes flashed. "No-one speaks to the daughter of the Oyn-Dir that way, Warrior."

"And no-one tells me where I can and cannot go."

"Think you're a match for everyone here?"

"Give me a sword and let's see."

The white-clad guards stood. Sofia snatched up Argeon and put the mask on. "Stop." Her voice stunned the crowd. Nia and Notch fell back; the Oyn-Dir's eyebrows were raised. His guards froze. "This is not the way," she said into the heavy silence. "We are to be allies. Let's not ruin that before we start. There are other paths."

Notch exhaled and raised his hands. "I apologise to you both. I was being rash."

Nia's lips were pressed together, but she eventually gave a short nod.

Sofia kept the mask on. "I believe I can contact the King without leaving the Autumn Grove, using Argeon. If that fails I could try to teach one of you to use Osani perhaps. It would be very difficult. But I meant what I said earlier. I will do what it takes to find my father," she said. "In the meantime, surely you can call people to your side? From other villages. I even saw Shields in Demarc. I could order them here. If you had some wax and paper maybe?"

The Oyn-Dir thanked her. "We have indeed called many to defend us, though those on the Fringes are not as...eager to help."

Nia snorted. "They are barely Braonn, Father."

He waved the matter aside. "In any event, Lady Sofia, we can offer our own help in your task. We Oynbae have our skills. Alone they are not a match for the entire Sap-Born force but with a Greatmask at her side, my daughter might transform you both into an invincible force that will bring even Efran and his ilk down."

"Father," Nia gasped.

"Is this not what you wanted? The chance for justice, which you have begged me for so often?"

She bowed her head. "Revenge is unclean. My needs

should not come before the Oynbae. It is a selfish wish."

"Even so, I believe Sofia and Notch need your help. I do not doubt their courage or the power of the Masks, but you are the most skilled. You know the forest, you know its depths where they do not."

She lifted her chin. "I will help them."

"Good. An agreement has been reached." He stood, shouting to the crowd. "The Oynbae are saved."

A cheer washed over the dais. Sofia accepted the Oyn-Dir's hand, letting him present her to the crowd. Notch's face was uncertain, and beneath Argeon, her own was a mirror.

*

Two days had passed and still she could not locate anyone with Argeon. Sofia leant against a tree, high on a platform used by lookouts. The path south of the clearing was empty, her view only partially obscured by a riot of yellow leaves in the afternoon sun. Each day she'd climbed the tree to attempt her sending. And while the solitude was welcome, they were all wasted moments.

She toyed with the tiny carven oar Mother had given her.

It brought a measure of peace; an echo of Mother's calming voice, as if from above her, when she was being tucked into bed. A warm memory, but no answers.

Father was alive. He was waiting. Who knew what Efran had done to him in order to steal her order's secrets? But whatever Efran learnt, whatever secret could supposedly combat the Greatmasks, would die with him.

She thumped the wooden platform.

Was there even a need to seek a position of elevation?

There were so many reasons the sending might fail; people probably needed masks to receive her voice, Argeon wasn't cooperating, the Grove itself blocked her somehow – the possibilities were as abundant as her ignorance when it came to using a Greatmask.

And yet, above all was the strange voice, the man who answered her when she'd searched for Father.

The man who mentioned a *Novatura* and wanted to send someone to her.

Was he listening?

So far, he'd not heard any of her attempts. But still, how hard was she trying? Father needed her. And while the man who'd intercepted her call had not struck her as malevolent in any way, who knew what he was? If there was a chance he'd be able to help find Father, why not? The voice seemed knowledgeable at least.

She had to keep trying, regardless.

New images.

Seto's sunken eyes as he held court in the Harper. His silvery hair. The way he spoke with his hands, the long fingers.

Argeon help.

"Seto?" She waited, holding his image. "Can you hear me?"

Nothing.

Did Argeon even know what she wanted? Was the last time a fluke?

Seto holding a fork, gesturing with a cup.

"Seto," she shouted.

Only her voice echoed among the trees. She climbed down, nodding to her 'escort.' The Braonn warrior followed her to a small clearing where Notch sat watching the Oynbae practicing their strange art.

To one side a group of younger men and women practised with slings, hurling hard yellow pods at leaf-filled targets hanging between trees, while closer, three women dressed in brown and orange stood in a triangle. All wore gloves and all had incredibly smooth skin, something Sofia was slowly becoming used to. It was almost like watching a living mask. The smoothness came from some kind of powder but she couldn't be sure if they applied it or if it was part of their skin. Nia was the same, though the Oyn-Dir was not. Whatever its purpose, she had not seen displays of their power beyond sparring.

She sat beside Notch on a stump. A large tree, it looked to lie exactly where it had fallen. Rather than create benches from it, the Oynbae simply carved seats – grooves really – in the trunk.

Notch raised an eyebrow. "No luck?"

"None," she said. "Father can't afford this."

"At least we know he's alive."

"Do we?"

"He's valuable to Efran."

Sofia made a sound of agreement. True enough, but it wasn't proof. And Efran could be doing anything to him. She lowered her voice. "We should sneak away."

In the clearing, one of the women dived forward. The other two sprang away, then skipped into another stance. The woman who'd rolled came to her knee with both palms poised beneath her face, but, seeing no-one before her, moved seamlessly into another movement. Again, the other two leapt in different directions.

As they sparred, or chased one another, the warrior tasked with chasing the other two changed. Sofia lost track of any pattern in the role shifting and their ceaseless movement continued with barely any pause.

How long had she been watching them?

"Notch, you didn't answer me," she said after a time.

"I know." He pointed. "Look how they're always moving, always aware of where the opponent is." He was sitting straighter, eyes tracing every movement.

"Yes, it's wonderful. Notch, I believe the Oyn-Dir but I can't wait any longer. Efran could be torturing Father right now for all I know, and I can't go to him. We're prisoners in all but name. You know it, Notch. You have a minder too." She looked to a second warrior, who sat some distance from Notch.

"His name's Ren." Notch shook his head. "And you're right."

"Well?"

"How far do you think we'd get, Sofia? We don't know where to find him and they'd catch us, they know their forest. They'd probably send Gelehn after us again."

"Have you seen him?"

"No. He's avoiding me. I am a little surprised."

She shrugged. "Well, we have to try something."

"I agree. What about Osani?"

"Useless. I can't get through to him so I won't be able to teach the Oynbae anything there."

"The Oyn-Dir suggested that I might still carry word to Seto."

"It would take too long."

"That's what I told him."

"And I need your help."

He snorted. "I'm not helping much now. I don't know anything about the Greatmasks, Sofia. Only what I've seen you do."

A shout brought the training – or was it a display? –

to a halt and the women bowed to each other and made room for another trio. One of the women who'd been sparring approached.

Nia. She brushed leaves from her knees and sat beside them. Despite her efforts, there was not even a trace of sweat at her temples.

"How goes it?"

"Not well. I cannot reach Seto."

"And must you reach your King? Can someone else be reached, who can then speak to the King?"

Sofia put her head in her hands a moment. "I'm a fool."

Nia grinned. "You're welcome." She stood and rejoined her fellow warriors, casting a glance at Notch. Sofia noted the way he watched her, a mixture of admiration and wariness. Was he interested in the woman? He probably didn't even know how obvious his behaviour was becoming.

But then, there wasn't time to figure it all out and Nia's idea was a good one. "Notch, why didn't I think of that?"

"You're trying too hard is all." He rested a hand on her shoulder a moment. "And I didn't think of it either."

"Well, who should I try next?"

Notch straightened. "I know who. Metti, the Harbour Witch. She's usually holding a bone of some sort."

"Think Argeon will be able to find bone?"

"Yes. Remember – the things that I fought in the aqueducts? I think they're all related to the Sea Beast. Like off-cuts or something. And those things that spewed from the sewers, the ones that attacked you."

An echo of Veddir's pleas, gurgling in the carriage. "I remember." She shuddered. "But what does that have to do with Metti?"

"I gave her a bone from the beast Wayrn and I killed. I think Argeon would be able to find it, he's made of bone, right?"

"Why not? Nothing else has worked." She paused. "Wait. I've never met her, let alone seen her."

"Does that matter?"

"I usually have to give Argeon images and impressions. Maybe I should try someone else first? Someone I know. Luik maybe?"

"It won't hurt."

Sofia replaced Argeon, the must of ages in her nose. The thin shadow of Tantos had returned. It lurked. Yet nothing of him was there, only the suggestion of his voice, a half-seen view of his profile.

Enough of that.

Luik.

The big man's pride in his cooking when he served at the table. The scars on his forearms, his broad shoulders and the brief but careful way he spoke. His sudden grin when he and Notch were up to something. She drew in a breath at the sense of him, present as if he sat beside her.

"Luik? Can you hear me? Luik, it's Sofia."

Then he was gone.

"That nearly worked, didn't it?" Notch said.

"He was so close, Notch, but I lost him."

"Try again."

Sofia closed her eyes. Bringing Luik back was easy enough, at least – the images of him. "Luik?" The longer she sat, the quieter the clearing grew. When she opened her eyes the next bout of sparring was already finished. Only Ren and her own guard remained, both stood together some distance away.

"No luck?" Darkness was falling and Notch had taken

to performing stretches on the loam. He paused when she growled her answer.

"No. It's useless."

"Why don't you try Metti? I'll describe her."

She threw up her hands. "Go ahead."

"Well, her face is like a mask."

"How?"

"Just let me finish." He took a breath. "She's old, but her skin is smooth, only it's stretched. It's the same for her hands. She sits in a deep chair before a warm fire and the room's dim. She wears black and white robes, and she had a kitten in her lap when I was there."

Sofia nodded slowly. The woman was easy to visualise, but how accurate was her picture? How long her hair, was she slender, graceful? No way to replicate those small details. "Keep going, but more big things. Things that struck you."

"All right. She's pretty rigid. I thought she could be a corpse at first, but there's a heat to her skin. It's unsettling."

"Perfect. More." A sense of Metti wavered somewhere, growing in her awareness.

"She held a bone, the one I gave her was long, maybe a rib."

The sense of the witch surged around her. "Metti?"

Who is there? Who intrudes? The voice was shocked, but a power burned within.

"Sofia Falco."

Truly? How can we speak thusly?

"Greatmask Argeon. I believe he can focus on your bones."

Ah. The Sea Beast. How curious. And wonderful.

"Metti, I need your help." Sofia relayed the Oyn-Dir's request. "It's urgent. They will not let us leave to find my father until Seto agrees to send help. Can you convince him?"

How little you ask, my dear.

"Please."

Worry not. I do not wish to see harm come to your father any more than you do. I will relay the message. She paused. *And give Notch my greetings. I feel him there, beside you. It seems he has proven a good protector.*

"He has."

I will keep a bone close by. Call me again at dawn, I should have an answer by then. I suspect we will speak often.

Metti was gone before Sofia could thank her, although, perhaps it was more that Sofia herself and Argeon were pushed back.

She threw her arms around Notch. "It worked."

"I heard." He squeezed her a moment. "I guess we'll be packing and heading back into the forest soon."

"As soon as Metti sends word, Notch."

CHAPTER 24

Waves slammed against the walls below, and Flir smacked the parapet as she turned. A morning wind tugged at her clothing but she pushed through it on her way back to the stairwell. Pacing had long since grown dull. And taking in some air, while welcome at first, no longer offered much of a respite.

Alvetti's body had revealed no truths. He appeared a typical soldier, fit, young and strong, with only his weapons, an empty purse and a small bone charm set to string around his neck. Nothing to hint at his strange strength. The charm was smooth with age, shaped as a tiny open hand but nothing anyone recognised.

She kept it just in case, but ultimately, it was another dead end.

At least Lavinia would be done by now, surely?

Pevin shadowed her down the steps, as was customary, but said nothing. A wise choice. Mayla's rooms were under guard, though they did not impede her progress. Flir entered on soft feet, motioning for Pevin to wait outside. She closed the door quietly. Mayla stood beside

Lavinia, who hummed something of a lullaby over the small figure of Bel.

The girl still slept, face clear of stress, and astonishingly, the fin had thinned and receded.

"It's working?"

Lavinia turned with a smile. "Flir. Not quite."

"But it's smaller."

"Yes, but within an hour, it will return."

"It's progress."

"True. Abrensi is a clever man. His song has some effect on the illness but the fin is persistent. I feel we may have to learn more, in the Tier."

Mayla nodded as she placed a fine cup, decorated with painted leaves, on a bedside table.

"Have you asked Seto?"

"His majesty would approve, I'm sure."

Flir stroked Bel's hair. "I don't know if I agree with that, but I like your idea."

"Then would you accompany me now, if I were to go?"

"I know just the house."

"Good." Lavinia gathered up her cloak. "I will bring Bol and Manico for protection of course."

"Think I'm not enough?"

"Oh, I apologise. I didn't mean to insinuate –"

Flir laughed. "Don't worry so much, I'm just having a joke."

"Oh."

Mayla cleared her throat. "I'll look after the patient then, will I?"

"That would be welcome, thank you," Lavinia said.

"And what do I tell her family, while you're out saving the city?"

"The truth," Flir said. "The song is working but she's not cured yet."

Mayla crossed her arms.

"That sounds fair, Mayla," Lavinia said.

"Of course it does. Get going then, before I go and find the King myself."

Flir grinned. "He's too busy to stop us."

She waved her hands. "Out, the both of you."

Flir chuckled as she skipped from the room. Two of the guards, obviously Bol and Manico, detached from the door as Lavinia followed. Pevin trailed at a respectable distance. By the Goddess, he was persistent. "Where exactly should we start?"

"A house with a green door."

"You know the people?"

"Not really. A young woman, Ana, showed me her father. He's sick with the fever and I promised to help them."

On the streets, a light rain slanted between buildings. Flir shrugged it off, but Lavinia wrapped her cloak. The Shield marched on. At the breach, the Sea Beast carcass was significantly smaller in places. With the added men the beast was finally shrinking, the Shield and labourers swarming over the corpse and the staging area.

Its dark bulk still towered over the area and the scaffolds remained in place, but fewer ribs were visible now; many had been shorn away. The softer, pink and bloody under-flesh gleamed in the mist and the creaking of winches and rasp of saws cut through pauses in shouts. The men with saws wore heavy masks to protect from the bone dust, and the expressions she could see were tense.

She had forgone a mask herself, the smell less

offensive in the poor weather.

When Seto barred the area around the wall and closed the Tiers he'd put an end to casual onlookers. Few locals watched now and the Shield, Vigil and labourers were left to do the dangerous job. Lately none of the workers had fallen seriously ill, but enough were showing early signs of sickness. Holindo's reports were requesting more men and more rotation, so as not to expose them to long periods with the Beast. A good idea. If she had to estimate, there was at least another two week's worth of work at full capacity.

"That is taking a long time," Lavinia said.

"Too long."

"But it is progress at least," Pevin added.

Moving deeper into the Lower Tier, Flir asked for directions several times, until she and Lavinia stood before the green door. A pair of thugs had appraised them outside a taproom, but Flir had Lavinia flash the star crest on her robe and their eyes widened. They made clumsy bows and sought less revered prey.

She knocked, and Ana answered. Her face was drawn, a blue tint to her skin.

"You came back." Her voice was listless as she showed them into the candle-crowded kitchen and then the second room. Again, Flir asked Pevin to wait outside. He complied without complaint.

"I brought someone – is your father..." Flir stopped. "No."

Ana's son, his arms crossed on his chest, lay deathly still on one of the cots. Delamo leant against a wall.

"Who is it, daughter?"

"Lady Flir."

He spun, jaw clenched. His colour was fine but his

eyes burned, and not with fever. Accusation. She doubted
he saw the Shields or Lavinia. "Too little, too late, girl."

Mishalar. Not again. "I should have come sooner."

"Any fool can see that," he shouted.

Flir said nothing. The boy's skin was both blue and
pallid. Deep, dark rings fell as far as his cheeks.

Lavinia stepped forward. "Sir, would you permit me
to treat your daughter?"

Ana had slumped against the door frame. "I'm fine-is.
I just need to rest."

Lavinia took her hand. "We both know that's not true,
dear." She led Ana to the other cot. "Lie down."

Delamo scooped up the cold boy and stumbled into
the kitchen. Flir let him pass but could not meet his eyes.
Just as in Caldtha. Once again, she'd broken a promise.
Only this time, there'd been no Gods involved.

Lavinia began to hum, almost beneath her breath, as
she removed a pouch of the herbal mixture Mayla had
prepared. Flir took it and went to the stove. Without
asking, she found a kettle and set it over the heat.
Delamo watched her, his grandson lying on the table. He
was placing hunks of dark bread over the boy's eyes. For
the Death Deity that the Anaskari seemed to believe in –
what was his name? It didn't matter.

Bol and Manico positioned themselves within reach
of Lavinia.

Flir's mouth twisted. Watching water boil? She turned
and met his eyes. "What happened?"

"I recovered. By myself."

"And your grandson?"

"Gian did not."

"Ana?"

"Same. She is getting no better. We've sent dozens of

messages to the palace-is." His jaw worked. "Not a one got further than the Tier gate."

"Lavinia will help."

"That so? She some witch?"

"Storm Singer."

Incredulity passed over his face. Lavinia's voice rose in the bedroom and Delamo took half a step forward. "The Storm Singer is in my home? Helping my daughter?"

"Yes. Go, listen. You'll feel a little better. She won't mind."

Flir attended to the kettle, finding a mug and mixing herbs into the boiling water. A bitter smell rose in the steam. She stirred it and handed the mixture to Ana, who took drowsy sips. Lavinia's voice grew louder, the same sequence of notes. Even Delamo's face had eased, some of the lines of grief fading.

She slipped out into the faint rain and slumped against the wall. Too little, too late.

"Dilar?" Pevin's face was full of concern.

She waved him away, pushing off the clammy stone and heading deeper into the Tier. The people she passed were not well. Some slumped in mouths of alleys, some vomiting, others unmoving. An older woman pulled a young man along. His eyes were vacant, a blue tint to his skin. A small dog trailed them, sniffing at the rivulets running between cobblestones.

By an unfinished house crammed between leaning buildings, its roof a caving mess and one wall tumbling into the street, a stench drove her back. Flir raised an arm, covering her mouth as she crept forward.

Bodies.

Over a dozen, all soaking blue, their limbs twisted and gnawed by scavengers.

She found three more such houses before stepping into an inn, dripping on the wooden floor. Two men sat at tables, opposite ends of the room. Both heads were down.

The innkeeper raised a club. "Stop."

She paused.

"Not another step till I see your skin."

"I'm not sick."

The thin man grunted, moving round the bar. He relaxed once he was close enough to see her skin. "You a southerner, then? If so, I want to see some money first."

"Renovar."

A shorter grunt. He went back to the bar and she followed. "Fine. What do you want?"

"To know what's happening."

He raised an eyebrow. "Ain't seen that big dead fish in the wall?"

"I meant in the Tier, with the people."

"Death, that's what's happening. People are dying faster than we can get them into the ground or onto pyres." He spat. "I'd say we're about a day or two away from city-wide riots at this rate. Can't turn anywhere without running into someone blue. I've been keeping them out myself. Want to keep my regular customers safe."

All two of them? But she only nodded.

"And what the hell is the palace doing? Forget the King's fancy bone collection – he ought to just put that thing to torch."

"It doesn't burn."

"Eh?"

"I saw them try it."

"Well, something else then. Something better," he added, rapping the bench top.

"Think there's going to be a cure for this sickness?"

He shook his head. "Not until that heap of pus and bones is gone."

"That bad?"

"There's talk of people growing fish parts before they die. Some end it early by throwing themselves into the harbour. Surprised the place isn't clogged with 'em by now. You know, some streets are already barricaded?"

"Really?"

"It's a good idea it is."

"I'd say so." Flir placed a silver penny on the bar. "Thank you for the information."

The coin disappeared into a pocket before he gave his own thanks. Flir strode back into the cold. The rain eased to a mist, but a chill wind now rushed through the streets. She made her way through more helpless-looking people, through refuse and narrow streets, until she reached the wharves. Those that weren't either shattered or under repair were crowded with ships and people shouting for passage.

One woman, clutching a wide hat and heavy bag, waved a purse at sailors lining the rail of one of the bigger ships. The moment it appeared in her hand, the crowd stripped it from her, tossing her to the ground. Flir shouldered people aside and pulled the woman to her feet.

"Thank you," she gasped.

Her hat had been trampled and her golden hair was plastered to her head, but she set her lips and headed for the next ship.

How many had come here, hoping to flee the inexorably sickening city? Certainly enough had stormed the gate of the Lower Tier, demanding to be free. But like all other gates in Anaskari, they stayed sealed. And the few remaining ships were to remain at dock themselves.

Nothing good would come of letting the illness spread to other nations.

Flir moved away from the clamour, leaning over the water. Dark shapes bobbed. Well over a dozen. The rain hit the surface like hundreds of needles. Several bodies even floated beneath the boards, knocking together. Out beyond the boats, chunks of rotting flesh bobbed. They twitched as fish nibbled at them.

Further still, the black smudges of funeral pyres lined the horizon.

"We're in trouble, Seto."

CHAPTER 25

Ana's colour was much better when Flir returned, dripping on their doorstep. Delamo was not smiling but he let her in and she was able to speak to Ana briefly, before leading her little group back into the streets. The rain had eased, but she was already wet.

"Will she recover?"

Lavinia smiled. "I believe so."

"Good. Now all you have to do is sing your song again – a few thousand times. We'll have the city cured in no time." She set off, heading for the Beast.

Lavinia hurried after. "You don't sound confident."

"Look at all the houses, Lavinia. We're outnumbered. And now we know the illness can spread between family members."

"That's not certain yet and we know Ana has been eating fish." The Storm Singer put a hand on her shoulder. "And Delamo recovered on his own. That is hope."

"For some."

"You're afraid."

"I know what's coming. Seto will have to seal off

sections of the Tier to prevent spreading and burn other parts. People will riot. People will die. Anaskar's economy is probably under threat. There are worse things ahead. How do you think the city will cope with the invasion that's coming?"

"It will cope by standing together."

"It has no choice," Pevin said.

"If you say so."

Lavinia quickened her stride again. "Will we visit other families?"

"Not right away. I think we should tell Seto about your success, and try to impress upon him the severity of the situation."

"I'm sure the King is duly concerned."

"Yes, but he's duly concerned about everything and he's only one man."

"Back to the palace then," Lavinia said.

"And hope he's in."

It took longer than she'd hoped to return. The Tiers were clogged with desperate people, most with wide eyes. Hawkers and charlatans shouted above the din, waving phony cures. Sadly, people flocked to them.

"I should stop them," she growled.

Lavinia shook her red curls. "More would only spring up, like terrible mushrooms."

Flir grunted. "It's going to be dark soon, at this rate."

"I should have arranged for a carriage earlier."

"It would have taken too long and someone would have tried to stop us. Or worse, sent an escort." Flir pointed to a carriage jammed at an intersection. The driver's face was red with fury and he cracked his whip but the press did not ease. "Or we'd be stuck anyway."

Seto was 'in' when Flir and Lavinia finally returned to

his chambers; he was pacing the sitting room. Abrensi stood by a window, tapping a foot, and Luik sat in one of the chairs.

Seto came to a halt. "Where have you been?"

"Tending to your city, Your Majesty."

He raised an eyebrow.

"We tested your song on a patient in the Tier."

"What?"

Abrensi spun. "Alone?"

Flir snorted. "She had me."

"And Bol and Manico, of course," Lavinia added.

"And Pevin," Flir said, gesturing to the man, who'd made himself unobtrusive, standing in a corner.

"Yes, dilar."

"This is irresponsible, even for you, Flir," Seto said.

"It was my choice, My Liege," Lavinia replied.

"Of course, my dear. But your safety is paramount."

"Is it? The Sea Beast is no more." Was there a hint of sadness in her tone?

"True, but who's to say what the depths of the oceans hold?" Seto replied.

Abrensi put his own glass aside, tapping the rim with a fingernail. "Nor are our skills limited to the rebuttal of frustrated relics of the past."

Flir downed her drink in a single gulp. "All that's well and good but it's not important. It worked. We've cured a young woman, the song worked." She outlined their achievements, and the information she received from the innkeeper. "So we'd better follow up on this success now."

Abrensi grinned. "Wonderful, wonderful. I think I know what to do next."

"And what is that?" Seto asked.

"A performance. On a grand scale. A mass healing, if you will."

Luik nodded. "Gather the Tier and sing to them all at once. That way you prevent the possibility of individually healed people being reinfected."

"Precisely."

"Be prepared to sing again." Flir said. "Because until the Sea Beast and the mess in the harbour are dealt with, it'll be for nothing."

"True," Seto said. "But we cannot let people simply die while the clean up continues." He threw a log onto the fire, kicking stray embers from the hearth into the flames. He massaged his temples a moment, then spun to thump the back of an armchair.

Flir stepped forward and Luik straightened in his own chair. "Seto?"

"I am well." He shook his silvery head. "Only angry with myself. I should have never let matters get this far out of hand. If I wasn't so damn weary, I would have picked up on all of this. The sneak attack, Vinezi, the mistake of dumping the flesh in the harbour. All of it."

"How would you have known about the harbour?" Flir said. "The beast came from the sea. Who knew that even its flesh would turn toxic once it died?"

Abrensi opened his mouth but closed it. Seto hadn't noticed. His smile was one of regret. "And the rest of it?"

"Vinezi is no fool, Seto. And you have to delegate more," Flir said.

He laughed. "I thought I was."

"Then let me help you now. I think we need to burn parts of the Tier, to prevent the spread, but even before that, we need to finish the Sea Beast. Get it out of there."

"Holindo thinks it will be at least another two weeks,"

he said.

"We need something quicker. There will be more riots before then. Bad ones – not to mention the invasion."

"I'm open to suggestions." He looked around the room. "Anyone?"

Only the snap and crackle of the fire followed his words. Flir poured herself a drink, swirling the liquid gently.

A page appeared in the doorway. "Your Majesty, Healer Mayla wishes to see you and Storm Singer Lavinia. Most urgent, if you were willing."

"It's Bel." Flir charged from the room. She didn't wait to see who followed, skidding down the corridors. At Mayla's door she entered without knocking. "What is it?"

Mayla turned from an empty cot. "Quickly. Bel is missing."

"What? How?"

"I left for stores." Mayla frowned. "And I thought I locked the door, but when I returned she was gone."

"Could she have wandered off?"

"Possibly. Lord Abrensi's song seemed to banish the illness, but why would she leave?"

"Maybe she's hungry?"

"I am feeding her."

"I'm just thinking out loud, Mayla. What about Bel's family?"

"In one of the guest rooms on the lower floors but I've already checked. She is not with them. I was able to keep Bel's disappearance from them for now, in case it is nothing."

"Then let's not worry them further. Bel might be close by, I'll start a search."

Flir ran to the door, bumping into Luik, who sprawled

in the corridor. "Sorry." She helped him up as Seto and the Storm Singers arrived, Pevin and Shield in tow.

"I'm fine." Luik rubbed his back. "The stone broke my fall."

To Seto she said, "Bel's missing. Seems like she just walked away."

"Why would she do that?" Lavinia asked. Abrensi's brow was furrowed.

"Let's find out." Flir divided them into groups, ignoring Seto's good natured head-shake. He was used to her decisiveness. Pulling Pevin into a run, she criss-crossed the halls. Tapestries and narrow windows flashed by, but no sign of Bel.

She stopped a servant. "Excuse me, have you seen a girl walking the halls?"

The young woman trembled under her gaze. "No, My Lady."

Flir hurried on, screeching to a halt near a set of double doors leading to the gardens. A small green cup, painted with leaves, lay on the floor. "There."

She charged into the darkening evening. The paved path, winding between low shrubs, was slick with rain from earlier. No chance of footprints. Had Bel even gone this way?

"Why head out into the dark and the cold?" Pevin asked.

"Maybe the fever came back and she's delirious? I'm going to look." Her feet smacked across the stone, chill air on her hands and face. The garden grew, wider shrubs with dormant flowers. Lemon trees spread on lattices and beyond, stone seats for ladies and their servants. But still no sign of Bel's passage. She followed a wall to a point of disturbance.

Slipping through an opening in a hedge, she made only two steps before tripping. Flir cursed in the dark, feeling around. A hunk of stone, its bottom covered in earth. Pulled from the garden beds?

If only she'd thought to bring – light bloomed beyond the hedge.

"Dilar?"

"Don't call me that."

Pevin appeared, head protruding between leaves, lamp outstretched. "Does this help?"

"Shine it here." Flir stood, pointing to the ground. A large piece of stone had been removed, then used to dig at the earth under a shrub near the garden's outer wall.

Beneath the stones, the piles of dirt, torn grass and shrubs, all glinting yellow in the lamplight, was the lid of a hatch. She pulled it open to reveal steel rungs leading down into darkness.

"Get Seto."

CHAPTER 26

Seto eased himself onto the bed.

Enormous thing it was, too large and too soft. Not like his narrow but sturdy cot at the inn. Another thing of Otonos' he'd have to get rid of, as soon as he had time. Like the dreadful, ancient paintings of slaughtered deer from the Old Land.

He groaned, closing his eyes and settling into the bed. No point removing any clothes, he'd just be up again in a few hours. The city never truly slept. He knew that. His bones knew it when they creaked, but right now nothing was better than the prospect of true quiet.

A muffled ruffling of feathers came from the cage, hidden by a heavy blanket. Even the lure of the Solare couldn't rouse him. It was fine. He'd feed her when he woke. If he ever drifted off! What would the Gods expect in return for shutting out every light and smothering every voice – for just a single night?

He turned onto his side. "More than you have, Seto."

Better yet, what would they want to banish the hatch Flir found? The way it leapt into his mind and mocked him. If only she hadn't discovered it.

But she had.

And everything it implied, just like the passage Alvetti

had revealed.

He didn't know the palace as well as he thought. Worse, someone knew it better. Vinezi perhaps? How had Bel even stumbled upon the opening – or had she been shown? Taken? Though it made little sense, for who would take a recovering tier girl?

He'd sent Flir down the hatch to discover more and to buy himself a moment to stop. To think, to rest. The Storm Singers he left to work on refining their song. Luik was to speed up the process of dealing with the carcass somehow.

He'd been reluctant, Seto knew, but the man hid his discomfort and eventually agreed.

"You would have fallen ill by now, if it was bound to happen," Seto told him.

"Think so?"

"I do. So stop worrying and help me help the city."

Luik had nodded and headed off with a frown on his face, but he was the right man for the job and he'd be fine. Seto hoped.

On the bed, he rearranged his blankets. And now to sleep.

A knock on the door to his chambers. "Your Majesty?"

Seto groaned.

"Your Majesty, someone wishes to speak with you. Forgive me. She assures me it's a matter of some urgency," one of his guards said.

"Send them away at once," Seto shouted.

The door to his rooms opened and footsteps approached.

"By the Gods!" Seto rose, fumbling for a lamp. Someone was about to get a thrashing. And then his guard too, for good measure. A knife came to hand as he spread his feet, facing the chamber door.

It swung open and a woman dressed in a black and white chequered robe entered, followed by a tall man with a scowl.

Nothing else about him registered, for the woman was a living mask. Her skin had been stretched so tight as to be reflective, but beneath waited age. Years beyond his own, beyond even his father's years had the man been alive. But her eyes held a fire; it reached out and seemed to heat the very room.

She held a large bone in her hands. Wisps of smoke rose from between her fingers.

"King Oseto. May we speak?"

He did not put his knife away. "Madam, I regret to admit I have not had the pleasure of meeting you and your cheerful companion before tonight. But certainly speaking together would be marvellous. We can begin with whether you're going to keep your heads. Then, how you gained entry."

A crack in the mask that might have been a smile. "Sofia and Notch have a message for you."

Now he lowered the knife. "Is this a jest?"

"No, Your Majesty. My name is Metti and I have spoken with Sofia, I assure you. There is unrest in the Bloodwood. She needs your help."

Notch's Harbour Witch. How else would she have entered the palace? Reached his rooms. Spoken with Sofia. "Does she indeed?"

"Yes. She has word of an assassination plot. The Oyn-Dir has told her so."

Seto raised an eyebrow. If the leader of the Braonn was trying to warn him... "Perhaps we ought to sit." He took them to a pair of chairs at a small table, clearing maps from its surface.

The scowling man helped Metti into one of the seats. Pain flashed in her eyes, like wind across a lake, and then she was arranging her hands together on the tabletop.

"Will your man sit?"

"Guingera?"

"I'm fine."

Seto nodded. "Very well. Please, continue."

"I will attempt a summation. Sofia and Notch are gentle prisoners, if that is possible, of the Oynbae. There they have learnt that Danillo Falco is being held by a cult conducting experiments in the Summer Groves. These 'Sap-Born' have a power Sofia could not explain fully, but the Oynbae are afraid of them. They are actually requesting that you protect them."

"I see." That was a serious fear indeed. When had the Braonn asked directly for help in recent decades? Or even centuries? "And the assassination attempt?"

"Will come from these Sap-Born. Sofia wonders if you've marked the slowing of indentured servants, the stalling of trade?"

"Hmmm." Typical of late, not to notice. "That's all she knows?"

"Only that it is precursor to whatever form their attempt may take. She and Notch are set to foil it, should they convince the Oynbae you are sending aid."

"Are you able to contact her?"

"No. She must use the Greatmask to initiate contact. I sensed her concern."

"Very well." Seto tapped a finger on the tabletop. "You know how thin the city's resources are stretched. The threat of invasion?"

"All with ears know this, Your Majesty. Quite the

opportunity for those more resentful Braonn."

"Indeed. And did Sofia convey specifics? How many men does the Oyn-Dir require?"

"She mentioned only a request for speed."

"Then let it be done. Tomorrow a company will ride forth – though it will not be as many as I might have once sent." He paused. "And what of you, Metti?"

"Me?"

"I believed my father succeeded in driving most or all of the magic-users from Anaskar, yet the Harbour Witch is alive and well."

"Very nearly. I lost a great many friends over that tantrum."

"Well, I have long thought him a fool – not only for that reason, let me add, but it is wonderful to hear that you are alive."

Guingera growled. "Metti isn't going to work for you."

Seto pursed his lips. "What about 'with' me then, my good man?"

"Of course, my King," she said. "But understand, I am feeling my age. The years weigh upon me and I do not travel well. Further to this, I would require remuneration and I would assist the crown under my own conditions."

"In a place of your choosing I expect?"

"Yes."

"That sounds reasonable. But I would require a reliable manner with which to contact you."

"That can be arranged."

"Good. We seem to have something of an agreement blossoming."

"I agree. What would you have me do?"

"Simply continue to communicate with Sofia, for now."

"And in the future?"

He spread his hands. "I can hardly know exactly until a problem arises."

"And you have so many to choose from."

Was she smiling? Difficult to say, with her mask-like face. He smiled. "More than I deserve, I will say. And what of remuneration?"

She leant forward, a slow movement. "Bones."

Seto permitted a frown. "Does the entire city know their secret then?"

"Doubtful. My knowledge only comes from Sofia confirming my own suspicions."

"Then I have no objection, should you prove, as I'm sure you are, able to keep the secret. They are used in your magic?"

"With them I achieve many of my aims, yes."

"Like gaining entry to the palace and my rooms?"

"Certainly. Do not be hard on your people, Your Majesty. I can be very persuasive."

"As proven." Seto rose. "This has been delightful and beneficial, however I find myself weary. Can I trust you are able to see yourself out?"

"Of course. But I would actually ask of you that I might take a bone tonight."

Seto paused.

"I too, am weary this evening."

He gestured toward the door. "Allow me to lead you, then."

Waving off his guards, Seto took the pair deep into the palace storerooms, coming eventually to a brightly lit corridor with large, steel doors. Four of his Honour Guard and two Mascare stood by. One Shield nudged another as Seto approached, and the men straightened.

"Open up, gentleman," Seto said.

One of the Mascare and the Captain on duty each produced a key and turned them in the lock to swing the large doors open. Seto accepted a torch from one of his men.

Its light didn't reach the ceiling, but it did illuminate the stacks of bones lining the walls. Several massive ribs loomed, resting on giant logs. Stacks of smaller bones, the smallest rivalling his forearm, were arranged in open boxes. Oddly shaped pieces of spine and other joints lay in massive barrels.

He stopped before one and rested a fingertip on a joint of some kind.

A familiar tingle.

Chelona.

Where was she now? After so long having his father hide the mask away, so long seeing it wasted on Otonos and then lost – and now her echoes filled the bones of the Sea Beast. Or was it more that she had always echoed the Ancient One?

Metti, supported by Guingera on one arm and a smoking bone in the other, let a gasp slip. "What percentage of the Old One does this represent?"

"Between half and a third."

"By all the Gods." She squinted into the shadow. "Is that the head?"

"Yes." He raised the torch and moved toward it. Near as tall as the shadowy ceiling, the snubbed skull, its great mouth full of chipped teeth and large gaps, sat ajar. The black eye-sockets were big enough to stand within.

"Something of it lives still."

Seto turned. "How so?"

"An echo, a memory. It has more purchase on this world than some people I have met."

"It is a precious resource."

"But no-one knows how to use it, do they?"

"To craft a new Greatmask? No. But I mean to ask Danillo Falco when he returns, as Solicci does not know how."

"A shame that such lore could be lost."

"The generations fade everything, knowledge among it. At least four hundred years since we landed – and too much knowledge lost, not in the least to the fire of my great, great, great, great uncle."

"That many greats?"

"Yes. But I have confidence in Danillo, should he live."

"One can hope."

He gestured to the barrel. "Is a joint better than a longer piece?"

"I will start with a joint."

Guingera helped her forward and she gave a shiver as she lifted a piece. Her eyes brightened and steam – not smoke – rose from her fingers. "My." She straightened, standing without assistance now. "This is beyond anything I have ever laid hands upon."

"I am glad to hear it, madam."

Now she did smile, slight though it was. And fleeting. "What news on the Renovar fleet?"

"None. But we prepare."

"You will meet their challenge, Seto. I have confidence in you."

"That is a comfort, Metti."

"You've a reputation for being quite slippery. Cunning."

He laughed. "That I am."

CHAPTER 27

Ain tapped his bowl on the stone floor, a slow pattern of despair.

Until she came back, he wouldn't stop. No matter that Schan had stopped speaking to him, nor that the guards had not returned with proper light in how many days? Or that he snarled at them when they delivered food and water. No matter that the rest of the cells screamed what he assumed were murderous threats.

"Not until she comes back," he whispered. "By the Sands, not until then."

On he tapped.

The rhythm slowed his heart beat. Instead of breathing hard and grinding his teeth, as he had at first, he tapped. He tapped through the hours, only stopping to drink and eat. He tapped as he stared. What were they doing to her? Tap. Was she safe? Tap tap. Cold? Tap tap. Did she call to him, how could he get out, see her? Save her? Tap tap tap.

He tapped on until the cell door swung open, torches blazing around dark figures.

Someone bent and tore the bowl from his hand.

The King stared down at him.

"Where is she?" Ain leapt up, swinging his hand. He

was shoved back and the rasp of steel rang in the cell. Something sharp drew blood at his throat.

"Don't move, Ain," Schan shouted.

He blinked. King Oseto leant over, eye to eye with him. Giovan held the blade and a second Shield stood before Schan. "So, Pathfinder. My offer stands."

"Damn you, where is she?"

"Safe in my rooms. Do you wish to see her again?"

"Yes!"

"More than anything in the world?"

Ain breathed through his nose. "I said 'yes'."

"More than your wife and unborn child?"

"I..." Ain trailed off. More than Silaj? He exhaled heavily and slumped back as a bleak fog lifted. By the Sands. How could he have forgotten her? And Jali. His whole family waited for him. Jedda, Majid, even the Elders. They deserved an explanation, deserved his return. All of them. Even if he would disappoint everyone, both with his failure and the truth – the quest for the Sea Shrine was a lie, and maybe it always had been.

There was nothing for the Medah in Anaskar.

"So, your mind is your own. For the most part," the King said.

"What does that mean?"

"That the bird hasn't completely overwhelmed you. You can still reason at present."

"Well enough not to trust you."

The King raised an eyebrow, then turned to Schan. "What of you, Warrior – do you wish to go home?"

Schan growled. "I wish to die with steel in my hand."

King Oseto shrugged. "Very well." He motioned for the guards to follow him, pausing once the cell was closed. "Arrange for their execution tomorrow," he told

Giovan.

The Shield nodded. "Yes, Your Majesty. Want them to jump the queue?"

"I do. Let's have it finished swiftly."

Ain gripped the bars. "Wait."

The King glanced at him but did not answer. Instead, he turned to leave, orange robes swirling around his legs. He left only the usual single torch and distant guard behind.

Sands, what was happening? How had everything gone so wrong so quickly? "What do we do now?" Ain asked.

Schan frowned at him. "You finally ready to talk?"

"Schan?"

The older man shook his head. "Don't be surprised. Sands, I warned you about that bird. More than once."

"Well she's not our biggest problem now – didn't you hear what he said?"

He snorted. "The King won't kill you. He wants you for something."

"But what about you?"

"He doesn't need me, but that doesn't matter."

"Still want to die here?"

Schan's cheek twitched. "Why return home a failure?"

"And so you want to try and kill the King when they come tomorrow? What if he's telling the truth about setting us free?"

"I hope he is, for your sake. You should go back to the Cloud."

"But you shouldn't?"

"Just look after yourself. And let the bird go; he won't give her up. And you've got a family to think about, remember?"

"I do." The yellow and orange of the bird's feathers. Silaj's dark hair. The clean expanse of the sands. Why couldn't he have both – simply take the bird home? It had enchanted him so deeply. He wanted her, she had hardly left his mind completely, but there was room for other concerns now. "Then you think I should do what he asks?"

"Believe it or not, I don't think this King will cheat you."

"I want you to come with me."

"You might not have a choice."

"Schan, you'll never get close enough. And if you do manage to kill the King, what do you think they'll do to me?"

Schan hesitated. "Afterward then. Once you've given him what he wants and he's set you free. Then I'll strike."

"We don't have to stay in the Cloud or in the Snake Dunes, you know."

"Want to live with the oath-breakers in the West?"

"What about the Mazu Clan?"

Schan paused. "A fair idea, lad." He gave a small smile. "But not for me. My destiny lies here in the chill of endless winter."

Ain had no answer for that. Sands knew he couldn't force Schan from his path, but he wasn't about to let his friend die. "Then I'll have to stop the execution, won't I?"

"You will."

Ain called for the guard but no-one answered, no-one came and in his limited Anaskari, he probably didn't make much sense. Once again, shouts answered from the other cells. He gave up; slumping against a wall.

"When will they come then?"

"Dawn, no doubt."

Ain sighed. There was nothing to do but wait. He closed his eyes.

The clanking of steel woke him. Ain shifted, rubbing sleep from his eyes. He fumbled for his bowl of water – who'd filled it? The water was chill. He splashed some on his face. "Schan."

"I hear it." The warrior rose from the shadows of the cell.

A short man in a black robe and silver collar, wearing a flat mask, led a dozen Shield along the cells. The rasp of steel chains on stone drowned out the stamp of their feet.

When the man in black stopped before the cell, he only pointed.

The guards piled inside, binding Ain and Schan efficiently, ignoring his words. Did any of them even understand Medah? Was Giovan among them? Ain clenched his teeth. If only he knew more Anaskari. "Stop, we want to speak to the King. King Oseto."

No-one responded.

The chains pulled his wrists down. His feet dragged as he was hauled out and marched along the cells, Schan trailing.

"Schan, they're not listening."

"We better come up with something."

Ain shouted for the King again. Someone smacked his head and he fell silent. There had to be a way. The executioner led them through darkened halls, up a flight of stairs and into a long corridor. Light escaped from beneath the edge of a steel door at its end. The path pulsed beneath his every step, a path that did not extend far beyond the door.

When the short man in black opened it, Ain squinted

against the light.

An empty courtyard, enclosed by high stone walls, half in shadow. Not a public execution then. No jeering crowd, no spectacle. And no King Oseto. No-one but the executioner and the group of guard.

An efficient, quiet death.

So long as his neck broke right away.

He shivered, pressing back into one of the guard. A stillness poured from the shadowed rope of the gallows. The stillness of a thousand paths came to a frantic halt here. Buried within the death of those paths were ripples, centred beneath the rope and where feet had kicked, the path had been spraying into the air.

Schan was pushed forward. Ain reached out, but someone smacked his arm down. The warrior did not fight, only sneering at those leading him up the steps.

"Schan, fight them."

"Be strong when I'm done, lad."

The executioner stepped before Schan and made a sharp cutting motion with his hand. Be silent. Ain took a step forward when Schan reached the rope. His expression had not changed.

The man in black fitted the noose over Schan's neck and paused to speak a few words. Then he glanced at Ain before stepping back. His hand went to a lever and Ain thrashed against his captors. The executioner pulled the lever. A trapdoor snapped open beneath Schan's feet. His chains rattled as he fell with a grunt, kicking air.

"No!" Ain shook off restraining arms and dived forward. He barely took two steps before his chains caught on something and he smashed into stone.

Schan struggled, his face turning red.

"Damn you, devil-King, you win," Ain screamed.

He rose to his knees. The King had to be watching, somewhere. "I will do what you ask."

No answer.

"I swear it by the Sands. By my family."

A cry split the air and the executioner spun, drawing a knife and slicing the rope in one motion.

Schan fell to the stones below and Ain slumped in his chains.

CHAPTER 28

Smoke.

Notch sprang from his bedroll, fumbling for his blade in the dim light. Screams and shouts tore through the walls of the hut and the glow of fire burned beneath his curtain.

He burst out into chaos. Flames *swam* in the tree tops and ran across the ground – only they were mute. "What?" Smoke curled about as if stuck in the air, stinging his eyes. Leaves, half-eaten by embers, fluttered like butterflies and beyond the strange, slow-moving fire, the Oynbae struggled with intruders dressed in deep greens, whose veins glowed amber.

Sap-Born.

Dozens swarmed in and around the houses, some carrying torches and others blades, most in pairs. A blast of flame drove him back as he started forward. Beyond his reach, one of the Oynbae leapt to meet a pair of the attackers, jabbing a long knife. The Sap-Man spun, slipping inside the defender's guard and knocking the blade free. He caught the Oynbae by the throat, and after a moment of struggle between the two, a warm light pulsed.

In a flash, an amber statue stood in the Oynbae's place.

The second Sap-Born stepped in, swinging a large hammer. The mid-section of the frozen Oynbae shattered. Luminous amber shards littered the ground as the first Sap-Born fell back, panting. His hammer-man stood over him, weapon raised as he scanned the forest.

A butterfly-eater ran into sight, and seeing the amber torso, tossed off her gloves and leapt for the hammer man. He swung, but she'd already rolled aside, coming to her feet and skipping close enough to cup her hands before him.

She blew and white powder covered his head.

Too slow to recover from his swing, the attacker stumbled back, blinking. His arms went slack and he fell across his still-wearied partner.

The Butterfly-Eater swept in with a blade, cutting the throat of the hammer-man then doing the same for the enfeebled Sap-Born. Notch blinked when she flicked blood from the blade; most of it was yellow. She ran for the nearest skirmish.

Sofia burst from her own dwelling, hair dishevelled. Her eyes widened. "Notch!"

"I'm here."

"What's happening?"

"Sap-Born. Can you use Argeon?"

She drew the mask from her robe and placed it on. "I'll try."

"Find the Oyn-Dir."

He ran forward, sword in one hand and knife in the other. He was no blade master when it came to dual weapons; the knife was more for parrying, but after seeing the Sap-Born in action, he'd take any advantage.

Sofia ran beside him, Argeon's black face seeming to suck in light from the fires. A tree top was engulfed in a slow wave of orange flame, and they fell back. Mute yet, heat pressed against them in the strange firestorm.

He detoured the blaze and paused.

"Which way?" Sofia asked.

He pointed with his blade. "There, the clearing. Stay close."

Notch changed course, moving deeper between homes, flames and smoke. Skirting a blazing stand of trees, he crashed into a pair of attackers. Hammer-man fell to the ground, but the Sap-Born with his glowing veins recovered quickly, a hand catching Notch's throat. Notch dropped his blades and flung his arms open, breaking the man's grip.

He followed up with a blow to the chest, driving his enemy back.

Lucky.

Sofia cried out as he bent to snatch his sword. The hammer-man charged, swinging an overhand blow. Notch brought his blade up and sparks flew when their weapons met. He grunted as he gave ground, deflecting blows. His opponent was quick.

He angled his retreat away from the heat of flames, while trying to keep Sofia in sight as he fended off blows from the snarling man. She was circling away from the Sap-Born but she was in danger. Notch growled. Momentum had to shift. He kept dodging, giving ground, waiting. When the man tired he would strike. Feint and get inside his guard, take advantage of the wide swings.

But the intruder wasn't letting up.

Notch ground his teeth and planted his feet, ducking a massive swing and lashing out with a cut that nicked the man's thigh. A thin strip of red appeared, but hardly slowed him. The hammer whistled in from the side and

Notch threw himself to the ground, rolling as a follow-up blow slammed into the earth, scattering leaves and ash.

He found his feet in time to kick dirt at his enemy, who raised an arm to protect his eyes. It was enough.

Notch leapt forward with a grunt.

His first swing sheared the man's hammer arm at the elbow. Blood spurted as Notch's second swing tore through his opponent's other arm. Notch lunged, impaling the fellow and kicking the body free of his sword, chest heaving. The man's blue eyes emptied before the body hit the ground.

"Sofia!" Notch took a step and stopped.

Two Sofias stood on the path, one of flesh and the other of translucent orange. The orange Sofia stood over the blackened body of the Sap-Born. Upon hearing her name, the spirit-like Sofia disappeared.

"What happened?"

Steam rose from the shrivelled corpse.

"I don't know." Her shoulders trembled. "He came at me and I panicked. I couldn't show Argeon what I wanted and I just...split, like in the Shrine."

He scanned the trees. "And you burnt him?"

"Somehow. He was going to touch me but..." Her voice dipped. "But I caught him."

"You're alive, Sofia. Don't regret killing to survive." She said nothing and he gave her a gentle shake. "Let's keep moving."

Circling a slow-raging fire that had engulfed a hut, Notch led her at last to the clearing where they'd eaten, ringed with fire and clogged with a haze of smoke. In it, the Oynbae had gathered to stand against the attackers. Crowds of Sap-Born and their hammer partners pressed in on a smaller circle. Hunters, warriors and Butterfly-Eaters alike were being struck down. Occasional bursts of powder rose along the front line, slings whirled and bows twanged from both sides.

Even as Notch skidded to a halt inside the tree line, an arrow sped across the clearing. It hurtled toward the dais where the Oyn-Dir stood firm in his yellow. But the man simply crossed his thumbs, fingers splayed, and the air rippled before him. The arrow slowed, finally coming to a halt in the air. The Oyn-Dir sweated as he stood, flanked by the men in white and a handful of green and autumn-clad Oynbae. Was one of them Gelehn?

Whatever other magic the Oyn-Dir worked, Notch couldn't see, but he hoped it was doing something more than protecting the dais.

Despite the Oyn-Dir's power, his people were outnumbered. Amber pulses filled the clearing, glowing in the haze. Cries followed.

"Can you help them?" Notch asked.

Sofia coughed and shook her head. "I don't know how."

"Anything?"

"What if it brings them down on us?"

"Then we fight."

"You mean we die."

He gripped her shoulders. "Would you rather run? Leave these people to their deaths?"

"No."

"Then we have to act."

Sofia nodded but made no move at first. Notch gave her room, putting his back against a charred trunk, keeping an eye on the clearing and the forest around them. The autumn grove shimmered like a summer heatwave.

Even as the watery flames moved slowly; the air was thin. His neck was slick with sweat and his tunic damp.

"I know what to do," Sofia said, whirling to face him.

"Is it safe?"

"Just protect my body."

"I will."

She drew a shuddering breath and went still. The same spirit-Sofia appeared, translucent and tinted orange. It flowed over the ground, heading for the fighting and Notch straightened. At first, the invaders saw nothing.

But when the first one she touched burst into flames, they saw her.

A ripple of fear spread as she wove through the ranks, touching Sap-Born and hammers at random. Each burst into flame, greasy smoke rising. Shouts of confusion rose. Anyone able to lash out at her was rewarded with naught but the passage of a weapon through air.

She glided through their bodies and blades alike, bringing death wherever she passed, until dozens and dozens of fires burned. Sofia's body trembled before him as her spirit continued its grim work.

The ranks of attackers were buckling, as people pushed and shoved in an effort to escape her, trampling each other. The front line stumbled, leaving them open to strikes from the Oynbae. Upon seeing Sofia, the Oyn-Dir rallied his people, pushing back.

Notch's sword arm twitched. If he went out there he'd be overwhelmed. And Sofia's body was vulnerable. His heart thumped regardless. Battle. No other thrill was the same, even if he was always left feeling empty afterward.

Sofia cried out.

He took her by the shoulders. "What is it?"

She said nothing and in the clearing, her spirit kept

burning. Her body was hot to touch and a shudder ran through her limbs.

"Can you hear me?"

A groan.

In the clearing, more screams. He shook her. Up close, her eyes were blazing behind Argeon. "Sofia?"

Her legs buckled and he caught her, fumbling his blade, but she resisted him, shoving at his hands and tearing at her robes. Argeon's glow grew and something creaked from above. Heat buffeted him and he spun, Sofia in his arms.

Burning trees were straining toward him. A sharp splitting followed and he fell back from the branches as blackened leaves spiralled down. His chest tightened. The slow flames were sucking up the air. He retreated further, just as a massive tree crashed to the forest floor. Flames glittered through the air like droplets, slow moving, everywhere. He ran through a shower of fire, spots burning his head and neck as he shielded Sofia.

One flame quivered on Sofia's robe and he set her down, sheathing his blade to swat it out. She'd stopped resisting him, her body growing heavier. He stumbled on, twisting through flame, smoke and the falling tree branches – none of which fell slowly.

The heat punished him.

Notch slowed, coughing. He ducked down to avoid the smoke but couldn't stop. Branches and tree trunks still leaned for them, as if drawn by some force – by Argeon! Where was Sofia's spirit?

Ahead, a tree boomed to the ground and he jumped back. Another smashed down to his left and he flinched, protecting Sofia from the spray of dirt and flame. Yet another crack and he was knocked down, Sofia spilling from his arms. A branch had pinned his leg. Heat seared his skin and he cried out, reaching for her. The world wavered but his fingers found Argeon.

He tore the mask free and lay back gasping.

The heat receded and smoke cleared enough that he saw the trees straighten. They burned yet, but no longer bent toward them. Pain in his leg eased.

Sofia jerked awake beside him, coughing and spluttering. He croaked her name and she crawled closer.

"We have to get out of here," she gasped.

"I'm pinned."

She scrambled to his leg. "It's too large."

Gods, what could he do? "Take my sword and cut it. Or try levering it."

Her eyes were wide. "Won't it break the blade?"

Idiot. Of course it would. "Cut it. We have to try something."

She drew his blade, face full of doubt. "Ready?"

He nodded, cursing as the slow flame spread up his thigh. Sofia placed the sword against the branch then drew it behind her head, swinging it into the wood. The blade bit deep enough to snag. She put her foot against the smouldering branch and heaved.

Stuck.

Leaves rustled. Notch craned his neck from where he lay. A Sap-Born stood before them. His veins already glowed amber and he sneered, flexing his hands. Sofia tugged at the blade as he stalked forward, giving Notch wide berth. Notch clawed at the earth, cursing the man.

The Sap-Born didn't even glance at him.

Sofia jerked at the blade, face twisted.

"Use Argeon," he cried.

She kept pulling on the sword. Had she even heard

him? Her eyes were locked on the amber-man, who was but steps away. Notch heaved at his own leg.

Something pale flashed over Sofia's shoulder. It struck the invader in the face, a puff of powder rising. A Butterfly-Eater followed the flash, streaking forward to knock the disoriented man down. She knelt, drew a blade and drove it into his chest, all in a fluid motion.

Nia.

CHAPTER 29

Notch fell back, closing his eyes to the pain. Rescue.

"Let's get that off you." Nia bent to the log, cupped her hands and blew. White powder doused the flames on the branch. She took a pair of gloves from her belt and pulled them on, and with Sofia's help, hauled the branch off.

Notch gave a cry as patches of skin and cloth tore from his leg. Nia bent at his head, Sofia on the other side. Up close, the worry in Nia's eyes was clear. "We have to leave the Grove."

"What about your father?"

The two helped him up. He winced as he tried his leg. It wasn't broken, he hoped, but putting weight on it hurt enough. He wasn't running anywhere.

Nia wrenched his sword free and handed it to him. One of the edges would be dull now and his pack and whetstone were in his hut. Likely burnt to the ground. "He has already fled," she said.

"After Sofia attacked?"

"No. When the Sap-Born first infiltrated the Grove."

Notch frowned. Sofia's face was a mirror. "But we saw him on the dais, working magic."

"You saw his Echo. Now come." Nia put an arm around him and took his weight, pulling him back onto the trail. What did she mean? An echo of what? He'd been there, he'd been real. He stopped the arrow. Notch cursed when his leg clipped a stone. Time enough to figure it out later. Smoke clung to the trees and flames burned on but Nia detoured both the raging fire and skirmishes. People still fought, but in fewer numbers. In the distance, hunters were driving back a small group of intruders.

By the time they reached a region free of smoke, Notch called for a halt. "I need water."

"Good idea," Sofia said. She kept casting worried glances at him, so he gave her a smile.

"I'm fine."

"This way." Nia changed course, moving down a slope and following the base of a spur to a tiny stream, one that barely filled a narrow rut between tree trunks. Notch lowered himself with a grimace, and no small help from Nia, to drink. The cool water soothed his throat and he sighed.

He splashed water onto his face, wiping away ash and grime.

"Thank you."

Nia helped him up and he leaned against a tree. His leg throbbed and the air stung the raw skin. The edges of the burn were a mangled mess of skin, hair and cloth. He clenched his jaw.

"Does it hurt much?" Sofia asked.

"Enough."

"Here." Nia pulled off her gloves. She crouched

before his leg, cupping her hands. "May I?"

He grinned. "I don't remember you asking before."

She laughed. "This time you'll stay awake." She blew, gently, and a cloud of powder covered his leg. It tingled but the pain receded. Even a deeper ache eased.

"How do you do that?" he asked. Sofia stepped closer.

"Butterfly-Eater secrets," Nia said. She pointed to the trees beyond the spur. "I'll scout ahead. Keep that sword handy."

She slipped into the forest, feet making little sound on the loam. Notch drew his sword and paced the area around the stream, testing his leg. It wasn't strong, but the pain was gone. "This is wondrous."

Sofia raised a hand to her mouth.

He glanced at her. "What?"

"Nia. You're impressed with her, aren't you?"

"I suppose so." What was Sofia talking about? It didn't matter. Her face was drawn, despite her cheer. How much had using Argeon taken out of her? "How do you feel? I haven't asked."

"Oh." She shrugged. "Better now that I've had water."

"It's hard, isn't it? Afterwards."

"Using Argeon?"

"Killing."

Sofia looked away.

He sighed. "I've forgotten most of their faces, but some remain."

"Who?"

"The men and women I've killed."

"Women?"

"Medah women sometimes fought in the war."

"Oh."

"There was another time, a woman. She was a pirate

from somewhere beyond Renovar." He shook his head. "But I'm glad it's always difficult. That's how it should be."

She looked into the trees. "Whenever I touched someone, I felt the fire charge through me and then into them, shrivelling even their spirits." She shivered. "I can remember exactly how burning flesh smells and I tell myself it was Argeon, but I know it was me. I showed him what to do. I burned them."

"Without Argeon you couldn't have done it."

"But I found a way. I knew I couldn't touch them so I showed Argeon a picture of what I wanted. Fire." She shrugged. "It was all around, why not? I don't know if I even expected it to work."

Smoke continued to rise behind them. "And he took it from the trees? From the strange fire?"

"I think so. But I couldn't make him stop. He kept drawing it in. I couldn't get rid of it quick enough."

It explained the trees, why they were drawn to her mask. "It overcame you."

She nodded.

Nia reappeared and waved them forward. "The way to the edge is clear. We have to hurry."

"What about your people?" Notch asked.

"We will survive. Father had already begun moving the Autumn Grove."

The answer didn't make sense but Notch saved his breath for keeping up. Nia set a swift pace, weaving through the trunks, head swivelling often. She paused at another pair of statues, the same pair he'd seen on the way in to the Grove. One headless.

"Where are we going?" Sofia asked.

"Deep into Wiraced. Where Efran and his killers have befouled the sap groves." She made to spit, but stopped.

"My apologies, Lady Sofia. Now is the best time to rescue your father. With so many Sap-Born out of the groves, their defences will be lighter."

"But what about your own father?" she asked.

"You mentioned an echo?" Notch said.

Nia glanced at their backtrail. "Quickly then. Did you notice that the flames burned slowly?"

"Of course."

"The Autumn Grove is an old, old part of the forest. So old that some say it is the whole forest, that its seeds are everywhere if an Oyn-Dir wishes it so. If only he can remember a time that it were so."

"I don't follow," Sofia said.

"You have powerful magic."

"I suppose."

"Well so does my father. His magic is a magic which remembers. And the better that memory, the easier it is for him to make it real. There have been dozens of Autumn Groves over the centuries. Father has already long been preparing the next one. Most of our people are there already, those of us who stayed back, who stayed here, were as much a rear guard as custodians."

Notch shook his head.

"What?"

"You knew the Sap-Born were close? That's too great a risk for you and your father, isn't it?"

"They have been close for a long time. We couldn't know exactly when they would find us."

"And the moment you did, your father started the fire?" Sofia asked.

"No. That was the Sap-Born. But Father slowed it with his magic and began moving the Grove. Next he escaped, taking many of our people. Only volunteers were left behind, to bolster the Echoes."

Notch frowned. "Wait, then were people really dying back there?"

"Of course," Nia snapped. "I told you, volunteers stayed behind to prevent the Sap-Born following."

"But what are echoes?" Sofia asked.

"And how did your father stop the arrow I saw?" Notch added.

"His remembering stopped the arrow. There must have been a tree in its path, at one time in the past. As it began to return, it stopped the arrow."

Notch raised an eyebrow. Impressive magic indeed. "And the Echoes?"

"Perhaps not unlike what Lady Sofia did with her mask. A piece of my father, and some of our warriors, stayed behind when we fled. He is able to remember himself and others. An echo of places they've been, actions they've performed. Sometimes, echoes of any actions taken in the forest."

"So he can raise the dead?" he asked.

She shook her head. "No. It's not that. He can only remember them, and only within the Grove. And further, memories can only do so much." Her voice trailed off before she straightened. "Come, we have to keep moving."

Notch exchanged a glance with Sofia as he fell into line behind Nia. The Oyn-Dir was powerful indeed. A powerful ally or a powerful enemy. He hoped Seto did send someone, even if it was probably too late now. The gesture would be important.

At the edge of the Autumn Grove, Nia raised a hand. "There's someone out there."

"Sap-Born?" Sofia asked.

"I don't think so; they value speed. This one is trying

to be quiet."

Notch held his breath. The green of the Bloodwood beyond the border was silent, sky darkening. "I can't hear anything."

"I've got better hearing than you."

Sofia shrugged. "So let them go and we'll move on."

"I want to be sure, Lady Sofia." Nia slipped into the trees again and Notch took a step after her before giving up. He wouldn't catch her and she'd only get angry with him for trying.

Sounds of a struggle followed, the snap of twigs and then a grunt as a man in forest greens stumbled into the clearing. A sword was belted at his waist and a thin pack slung over his shoulder. He had a weary expression, but determination burned in his gaze.

And he was Anaskari.

Sofia gave a cry, flinging herself forward. "Emilio!"

His eyes widened and he gave a weak smile as he caught her hands. "Sofia. It is wonderful to see you alive." He turned his smile to Notch. "And you, Captain."

Notch moved forward and gripped Emilio's hand, placing him finally. The young Captain who'd been imprisoned by Oson. "Captain no longer, lad."

Emilio glanced around, eyes taking in the statues and the autumn colours. "Can we speak here? Your friend didn't seem happy to see me."

"You're lucky to be alive," Nia said. "I thought you were someone else."

"I agree. There are strange warriors in these woods and unfriendly eyes everywhere."

Nia chuckled.

Emilio's brow furrowed but he continued. "I'm glad to have found you both. Now we can begin the journey home."

Sofia opened her mouth to answer but Notch shook his head. "We can't do that."

"But King Oseto sent us to —"

"Emilio, we can't. I have to find my father and Nia is going to help us," Sofia said.

"I understand. But I swore an oath, My Lady."

Notch tried to keep his voice gentle. "You can't stop us, Captain, and I doubt you truly want to."

Sofia nodded when Emilio hesitated, conflicting emotions running across his face. "And you're exhausted yourself. You need our help."

"I am feeling the strain. We've been tracking you for weeks," he said, casting around for a place to sit. They found a log.

"You mention 'we' as if there were others," Nia said.

"All dead," Emilio said. "Killed by strange men with amber veins. I stole the clothing of one and have been avoiding them ever since, trying to regain your trail. It seemed to double back to this strange place." He rubbed his temples a moment. "I'm surprised I caught up, even though we left just days after you were discovered missing."

"Time moves differently in the Grove," Nia said.

"How many men did Seto send after us?" Notch asked.

"A dozen. Each a good man."

"I'm sorry," Sofia said.

"It was our duty," Emilio said. He accepted a flask of water from Notch and drank.

"How did Seto take it?" Notch asked.

"He was furious. I have never heard such language from a king."

Good. He wasn't too angry then; he was still able to

speak. And curse. "He'll have to get over it."

"I admit, I don't know how I am to proceed from here," Emilio said.

"I can help." Sofia grinned. "As Lord Protector of Anaskar, I'm ordering you to accompany me as my own protector to help rescue my father. There."

Notch squashed down a stab of jealousy. Wasn't *he* her protector? He scratched at his beard. Stupid. It wasn't a contest. She could have more than one protector. And another sword would be welcome. Emilio was part of the Honour Guard; he would be valuable.

The man offered a nod. "It's hard to argue with that, My Lady, but I believe the King still outranks you."

"Then take me back," Sofia said with a shrug. "Only, do so after we find my father. Seto doesn't have to know how long it took you to find me, does he?"

He laughed, his deep voice echoing around the clearing. "Very well. I concede defeat."

Nia looked to Sofia. "Then he's coming with us?"

"Yes."

"Are you up to the journey, Warrior?"

"Yes."

She smiled. "You don't know where."

"I've no doubts about my capability."

Notch stepped closer. "Where are the Sap Groves, exactly, Nia?"

"South east, deeper into Wiraced. The Summer Groves surround the First Tree. It will take only two more days to reach it, but entering the Groves will be difficult. The Sap-Born monitor its borders closely. Freeing Sofia's father will be more difficult still."

"So how do we enter?"

"I know several ways. As to exactly where your father

is kept, I do not know."

"I'll use Argeon to find him. I can spirit-walk, like in the Shrine," Sofia said. Notch noticed a slight tremble in her voice. The Greatmask was unpredictable, but it was probably their best chance.

It wasn't like he could do much to help.

"That will be of much assistance," Nia said.

Emilio processed the information quickly. "Why was your father taken?"

Nia shrugged. "I can only guess that the Sap-Born want him as hostage."

"Efran claimed he'd discovered a secret to defeat the power of the Greatmasks," Notch said.

"That's the last thing he needs. More power," Nia said. "We should keep moving. The Sap-Born won't have given up searching."

Sofia helped Emilio up and the two started after Nia, who headed down the path toward Avaon. Notch followed with a slight frown.

Rear Guard it was, then.

Chapter 30

Despite his show of confidence for Yaev, Kanis did have questions. Vinezi had sold him on attacking Anaskar with acor – on the condition that the big man could deliver on his promise of a city on its knees. It was possible. Probable, even. Walls could not stand against the magical powder.

Kanis would pick over the rich city and Vinezi would get his own revenge, it didn't matter what that entailed exactly, so long as there was enough gold and silk to go around.

And yet...

A little less than a week from the target and a niggling doubt lurked. Kanis had been sure before they left. Without the acor on board, he wouldn't have even lifted anchor let alone made deals with several pirates, not to mention swindling the new Conclave. But Atilus remained obstinate the entire trip, until falling sick – temporarily. Svek had lived up to his own claims, and so now was time for another chat with Vinezi's friend.

He paused before the door to Atilus' cabin. A voice from within; the man was frustrated. Had he cried out for someone to 'answer him'? The words had been indistinct. After a time, Atilus fell silent.

Kanis entered.

The man sat propped up on pillows, a bowl of broth steaming in his lap. A small bone charm – the same one he'd had when sick, sat beside the bowl. What was its purpose? Had he been talking to it?

"Captain."

"Dilar will be fine," Kanis said. He took a stool across from the bed, spreading his legs on the deck to accommodate the roll of the ship. "You are well. Let's talk about the acor."

"Yes, thank you," he said. "As for the acor, not until we are within sight of the city walls."

"Why?"

He laughed, an animal sound. "Be honest, you only see a use for me up to a point."

"And you and Vinezi feel the same about us, don't you?"

"Of course, but we both get something we want. Why jeopardise that?"

"And what do you want?"

"Nothing that would interest a man of your…tastes, rest assured. Silks and jewels will be fine, will they not?"

Kanis raised an eyebrow – but not at the simple barb. "You don't care for gold?"

"It is enough that we have a common goal."

"I don't know if that is true any longer."

He took a spoonful of broth. "I don't recall your being privy to our goals as part of the deal Vinezi struck, do you? But your greed got you here under these conditions." Another spoonful. "Just do your part, dilar."

"I see." If only he could Bind the man. Physically overpowering him would be no feat, but something told Kanis that Atilus' will would not be easy to break.

Stubborn bastard. "And how would you like a new part? Perhaps you could swim alongside us for a while?"

"Then say goodbye to the last secret of the acor."

Kanis folded his arms. "I'll be happy to see the back of you, Atilus."

"Of course." His look expressed the same sentiment. "Have you cared for the acor while I've been ill?"

"Yes."

"It's dry?"

"Yes."

"And the catapult components are –"

Kanis stood. "I know my business, Anaskari."

"Good. Let's hope it stays that way."

Kanis shook his head as he left, closing the door quite firmly – or at least, meaning to. Instead, the door flew from its hinges, clattering to the cabin floor. He poked his head back in. "Sorry about that. Hope you don't need privacy." He smothered a smile. The whole ship knew the man craved solitude.

"I'll be fine," he said through clenched teeth.

"Good. Let's hope you stay that way."

His eyes narrowed. "You'll fix that?"

"Oh, as soon as we can," Kanis said as he walked away. By the time he was topside again, he was beaming.

Skink appeared by his side at once, rising from a pile of nets. "Dilar."

"Skink, find Yaev and bring him here," he said.

The boy ran off.

Kanis crossed the deck, slipping between men and masts on his way to the prow. The tips of the sea-maid masthead, painted bright blue, caught the last of the sun. Had he been bothered, he could have swung out to face the sea-maid and seen a likeness of Flir. Instead, he leant on the rail.

Of all the stupid things he'd done, thinking she'd want to see him was worst of all.

"Why won't you name her?"

Yaev stood behind him, Skink waiting behind in turn. He sent the boy back to his old cabin and turned to Yaev. "Any ideas?"

He shrugged. "Mishalar."

"Fitting, I suppose. But no..."

"What did Atilus have to say for himself?"

"Nothing useful. He wants to see the city walls before he reveals the last step."

"Weasel."

"A weasel's rear end at that." He glanced at the nearest ship, a pirate running green flags from the temperate waters north of Renovar. "Call the Captains to my cabin."

"We're a week away yet."

"Let's check-in. I miss their beautiful faces and I'm sure they've missed mine."

Yaev groaned, but sent a man to run the flags.

By the time the evening meal was ready, Kanis had a full cabin beneath the lanterns. With Skink serving and Yaev sitting in, there was barely room for the other eleven men to find stools around the table.

Once the sound of crunching and clack of cups eased, Kanis stood. The room hushed. Some of the men watched expectantly, expressions reverent. As dilar, he had advantages when it came to leading men. Almost unfair, really. But not every Captain was a believer, and not every Captain a military man. There were pirates and smugglers and even a merchant he'd met in the Far Islands, years ago now.

But all respected his strength. And his vision.

Or so they claimed.

"I trust you ate well, Captains." He glanced at a heavyset man, Hannak. "I know you did, Han." The table laughed, Hannak included. "Let me get to the point of this gathering. A week out and I want to know how we fare. Your stores of acor, your water, your food, your men, is anything amiss? Anything that could threaten our goal."

General murmurs of assurance.

Eventually one man spoke up. Tiroph, an older smuggler. His bald head shone in the warm light and he set aside a drink. "No complaints on my ship, as before, Kanis. But one question. Perhaps an idle one, but if the Anaskari fleet is taken care of as per the information we have, what's to say there isn't another beast in the harbour? Or that the Anaskari don't have another at beck and call."

Again, the table murmured its ascent.

"A fine question. There is a simple answer. The sea beast that ruined the bulk of Anaskar ships was the last of its kind. No more roam the sea."

"You're sure?" another captain asked.

"Yes. Vinezi told me."

Tiroph spread his hands. "But what's his proof?"

"Nothing he showed me, but I suspect he is like me. Powerful. There was something about him beyond a regular man. That I felt. That at least Mishalar told me."

"Good enough for me, dilar," one of the military Captains said.

Another nodded. "No word about another beast in any of these seas since before my grandfather's time, Tiroph."

Tiroph rubbed his chin. "I'd like more myself...but all

sailing is risk."

"It is," Kanis agreed. "If that is all for now, how about I call for some more wine? After all, in a matter of days we will all be disgustingly rich."

CHAPTER 31

Flir paced the waterfront, jaw set.

A light rain misted her eyelashes and the thump of hammers echoed along the street. Another one of Seto's large barricades was being constructed before crowds of shouting people, who were held back by steely lines of Shield, in turn supported by the Vigil. Fire and smoke rose beyond the barricades, staining the morning, as areas choked with dead were put to flame. Grim carts driven by men with heavy faces and hand wrappings had been rolling into such pockets for days, bringing bodies and packing them into homes, shanties and lean-tos, even lain in gaping holes cut into the ground. Some of the drivers were immune, having recovered from the illness. Those few wore no coverings.

"How do you even know everyone got out in time?" a voice shouted.

No-one answered.

"That's our homes-is, what do we do now, damn you?"

"Bet the palace never thought of that."

A rumble of assent.

"We're still dying, you know. This hasn't changed anything, why can't the King save us instead of burning the city?"

Another voice shouted its agreement. "Bet he's not burning the top, is he?"

So far no-one had turned violent while she'd supervised. There was something of defeat in many of the voices, a grief already spent. How many of their loved ones had the illness already taken? From where she stood beneath the shadowy buildings, the sea beast was hidden. Curse it anyway.

Captain Holindo grunted.

"What's wrong?"

He pointed. "Can we be sure? We've mapped the Tier, estimated the illness' spread, but it might not be enough."

"That's what the Storm Singers are for."

"You think the song will work?"

"It helped Bel, at least, before she disappeared."

"That's something."

Wherever Bel was, Flir hoped the girl was safe at least. There was no evidence that anyone had taken her, it appeared she'd fled the palace herself. Was it shame? People had hidden the red rings that covered their skin in Caldtha. Facing Bel's family had been...difficult. Alfeo's face crumbled and their mother simply drifted from the room. Back home had been the same. Confusion, tears, anger. At least Bel's mother had blamed the Beast.

Unlike Mother.

"Has Luik unveiled his idea yet?" Holindo asked.

Flir shook off the memory. "I'm going to meet him once we're done here. In fact, I'd say the sergeant has things in hand. Why don't we go see?"

He nodded and Flir followed him from the barricade.

They'd already checked a dozen barricades, perhaps less than half the total, and only once had the crowd turned ugly so far. Their dissent was quickly managed. Seto listened to her advice, and supplied them well.

Stopping the spread of the illness meant making difficult decisions. Fish remained banned, yet the Vigil still caught fishermen launching boats every night. She couldn't blame the people; what else could they do? Without fish, their income had been taken away and none could afford to buy other foodstuffs.

Outlying farms were being strained and Seto was eating into the treasury, paying generously for caravans and merchant trains from the West. It was trickling in, but there was a real risk that the invasion – if it proved to be as large as she feared – would eventually cut those lines.

By the breach, men still swarmed over the beast's headless carcass. Wagon loads of the flesh were being carted from the staging area. A covered train already headed out of the city gates and into the wasteland. Other wagons took the bones to the palace. Staggering, the amount of bone the colossal beast continued to yield.

Luik and Pevin waited in Holindo's command tent, a pot-bellied man in a black coat beside them. The man's mouth moved without sound – was he counting? The scent of fish was strong in the tent, though neither man's clothing bore evidence of contact with the Sea Beast.

"Good, you're here," Luik said, rising at once. He seemed a little tense. Was he still worried about the illness? He had to know he was immune by now, working so close to the Beast as he had been. He gestured to the counting man. "Renaso's been helping me with our big problem and I think we've come up with something."

"Welcome, Renaso," Holindo said.

"Captain. Lady." He inclined his head and turned to the table in the centre of the room. On it sat a heavy glass bowl with a dark hunk of what could only be flesh from the Sea Beast. Beside it stood a pair of vials. One had yellow liquid, the other clear. He took the coloured vial. "Luik approached me with a clever idea that I thought, at first, was not viable. But I have changed my mind after some experimentation."

"I see," Holindo rasped. "And what did you experiment with?"

"I am a member of a new order, Captain. The Alchemista." He spread his hands. "How best to explain? We're interested in the properties of different substances when mixed."

Acor came to mind. "It sounds dangerous," Flir said.

Renaso held up his hands, which were covered in burns and cuts. "Indeed."

"You should use gloves," she said.

"Oh, we do." He smiled. "Now, this is vitriol, a corrosive liquid." He poured it onto the flesh. It sizzled but nothing much happened, except for the production of an ugly smell. "It will burn through, though not fast enough. Now for the second vial." He stretched an arm over the hunk and tipped, gently. The clear liquid hit and a hiss rose, the black skin and flesh shrivelling right down to the bone.

"Impressive, isn't it?" Luik said. Flir noted he wasn't standing too close to it. Renaso beamed.

"It is. Does it harm the bone or surrounding materials?" Holindo asked, moving closer. Flir joined him, squinting against the lingering acidic fumes.

"At this strength, yes. But I'm working on a proper

ratio. It simply needs to be diluted."

"What's the clear stuff?" Flir asked.

"I apologise, My Lady. But that is a secret for me and the Alchemista, I'm afraid. I trust you understand and I've not offended you."

"Not at all."

"So, it's going to work, isn't it?" Luik said.

"I hope so," Holindo said. "How fast can you produce it?"

Luik answered but Flir beckoned Renaso over. "Renaso. I trust you know how serious this all is. How important to the city's safety."

"Of course, Lady Flir."

"Could we convince you to keep helping us?"

He tilted his head. "Beyond the dissolution of the beast?"

"Yes. I'd like you to investigate something else. Acor."

Renaso took a deep breath. "I'm not sure how to answer. I don't want to appear as an undutiful member of the city."

"What's wrong?"

"I believe acor is an abomination. That it will spell doom for humanity."

Flir appraised him. Perhaps he was right – but it was also bearing down on the city ready to be flung over the walls by her people. "The whole city's in danger. We might need to use it ourselves."

"It would seem a risk."

Flir opened her mouth but stopped. Ordering him would be simple enough. But was it the best way? "A different angle then? Can you discover how else, other than water, we might neutralise it? Or protect against it? Or detect it when hidden?"

"Well..." He tapped his fingertips together. "They all require the same thing, My Lady – learning how to make acor."

"With different results."

He nodded. "Would you have any I could examine, were I to agree?"

"I can arrange it."

"Once I've finished helping with the beast, I will seek you out."

"Visit the palace, I'll leave word."

He gave a short bow and turned to Holindo's beckons.

Flir led Pevin from the tent and back along the glistening streets to a disused square. Once a staging area for the construction of ships, it had more recently been home to surprise markets, temporary dwellings set against crumbling walls and new 'hound-races', where children rode big dogs in a race around a makeshift course.

Apparently the nobility had been betting on the races and the Shield had been brought in to break it up.

But the recent upheaval put a stop to everything. She saw no traces of any organised racing, but then, how would she? The massive space had been cleared earlier, and was now crammed with murmuring bodies. Quiet faces stretched before her like a blinking horde. Only the usual Anaskari tan was tinted green, blue and pale in many places. The cries from babes, many resting on shoulders, crossed the giant square. One man chewed on a piece of lemon, face twisted. It would probably make no difference.

Poor bastards.

Sick as they were, being packed into an overflowing shipyard couldn't help. Behind the walls, nothing like those of the Tier, crowds blocked the streets. Beyond the people who'd climbed the walls to sit atop them, smoke still poured into the grey sky from the burning corpses.

Most were hushed at being so close to the Storm Singers, though whispers still crossed the square.

Abrensi and Lavinia, impressive in blue robes with shining white star insignia, stood on a hastily erected platform. Protected by a row of Shield and Mascare, both on ground level and on the platform, the singers were talking, heads together.

"When will they begin?" Pevin asked.

"Soon I hope. Everyone trusts the Storm Singers, I'd say that's the only reason we haven't had real trouble from the people yet."

"And will the song truly reach the homes beyond?"

"Abrensi has a powerful voice."

"Of course. I seem to remember it from the storm."

What no-one knew was what effect the song would have on so many. Would it be lessened due to the amount of people? The distance? Lavinia and Abrensi had tested the song but hardly on such a scale.

So far, they'd come up with nothing to magnify the reach of their song – and so multiple visits had been proposed. Again, the people of the Lower Tier had grumbled, but listened to Seto's proclamation. Why wouldn't they? If it worked, there was no reason not to attend and return. It meant survival.

Abrensi raised his hands for quiet.

Murmuring faded.

"Sweet citizens of Anaskar, attend to me. I am Abrensi Decena, First Storm Singer, and together with Lavinia Corlini, we will attempt to drive the wretched sickness out, to free you from such insidious bindings. It ought not to hurt, no. All you need do is be calm and listen to our wonderful song."

He turned to Lavinia and together they started, the song soft at first. As it grew in volume, Flir picked Abrensi's voice at a low register, holding steady, as Lavinia's wove around him, nimble.

The tune was wordless but familiar. Of comfort, as if taken from her childhood, old songs from Renovar. When it swelled sighs rose from the crowd. Flir blinked back a tear. Hers was not the only face to taste salt.

The singing repeated its pattern. A child in the crowd straightened his shoulders and a smile spread across a woman's face – off in the distance came a cry of joy, but mostly it was just a swelling of what Flir could only describe as a sense of safety and warmth.

She looked up as hope stirred in her chest. The sun didn't pierce the clouds, but somehow, it would have been right if it had. The rain eased at least.

Abrensi raised his voice and Lavinia matched him. It should have hurt her ears, but Flir simply stood. How far did their voices reach? When he called the Sea Beast from the walls, half the city must have heard it. He wasn't singing as loud or urgently now, but a power lay within. It probably reached right to the harbour.

Would it heal them?

The song echoed in the shipyard and Lavinia slumped in Abrensi's arms. Flir stepped forward, but no-one else had noticed. There were only smiling faces.

A voice soon rose over the din. "My Lord, how do we know we're cured-is?"

Abrensi's voice carried across the square, though he did not shout. "Do you not feel better?"

"I do, My Lord." He sounded surprised.

"Then return tomorrow when we sing again my good fellow."

"Does that mean I'm not fully cured-is?"

Other voices echoed the question. Abrensi, still supporting Lavinia, raised a hand. "Come back tomorrow at this time. Let us be certain. And spread the word. King Oseto has sent us to heal you."

A cheer rose.

Pevin touched her arm at the elbow, using only the back of his hand – typical Renovar deference. He leant in to be heard over the crowd. "Dilar?"

"Don't call me that."

"Of course. I only wanted to ask whether the song... made you think of home?"

"You too?"

"Yes. I quite liked it." His face didn't seem all that pleased.

"You miss Renovar."

"Today, yes."

Flir gave him a look. "So why leave? Why come here with Vinezi and attack the city?"

"Lupo brought us."

"Not Vinezi?"

"No – Vinezi joined us here. I think they knew each other."

Flir pulled him behind the dais where it was quieter. "Why didn't you say this before?"

He rubbed his arm. "I thought you knew. How does it make a difference? We know who was behind everything now."

Flir shrugged. "It might have changed things. Why was Lupo – or Tantos – collecting Renovar to be his men? Is there someone both he and Vinezi knows back home?"

"Dilar, I think it would have made no difference. The Conclave sent us to sow trouble before the invasion and Lupo was happy to use us for that end, as was Vinezi, even if their goals seem to have differed."

"Perhaps."

"And you did everything you could for these people and their city in any event."

"I can't agree with you there." She shrugged. "But finish what you were saying before. Why leave?"

"Because I wanted a different life. At home, I am a third son. My future is no future. Overlooked, unrequited. Barely educated, simply held in reserve. You know the life. With Lupo, I was someone whose decisions actually mattered. I even thought we were helping mistreated countrymen here in Anaskar."

A noble family then. First son was the young lord, second went into the navy or army or sometimes a trade and third – a Servant of the Ice. Responsible for protecting the family home from the ice and snow. A slave to the whims of the white. "So quickly from discontent to aggression?"

He met her eyes and there was a hint of the Pevin who hadn't known her as 'dilar.' "From desperation."

"And now to devotion."

His smile was faint. "Still you cannot trust me."

"Can you accept that I'm no vessel?"

"No."

"There then." Flir clapped her hands together. "Now let's do something useful. I'm going to look for Bel again."

He followed her from the square with a nod.

CHAPTER 32

Ain stood beside the Anaskari King on the great wooden...marvel. Sands, how impossible it had become to concentrate on his task. The wind, the taste of salt on his tongue, the echo of birds with beaks that could half-swallow a child, the power, the vastness.

A ship.

A true sailing ship for the ocean.

He'd read about them, but no words properly described what he encountered and the creaking wooden beast was a tiny thing compared to the giant ocean. Members of the Shield and one of the Mascare stood close by, the heavy steel somehow stifling and yet comforting also.

Because the sea was vast.

An impossibility. How could something stretch so far? Glitter so, be so ceaseless? Such motion – constant motion. It was more powerful than the King's instructions, louder than the cursing and orders from the first mate, whose rasp was the grinding of rock, it smothered the creak of rope and smooth wood.

And it swallowed the paths.

All of them.

He was sleepwalking, so beautiful was the respite.

"Pathfinder?" King Oseto's expression was expectant.

The sea breeze stirred his silvery hair. "Will it work? Can you feel any path?"

A lie was almost tempting, especially after the stunt the King played. Chuckling as he crossed the courtyard to stand over Ain, slumped on cold stone in his chains before the gallows. But Schan was alive and his survival depended, as did Ain's own, on helping the Anaskari devil.

Instead, he told the truth. "I feel nothing. Only the sea."

"Nothing?" King Oseto's eyes burned.

"I haven't felt a path since I set foot on this ship."

The King turned to the Captain and delivered orders in Anaskari. The ship turned toward the jagged coast. Not too close, but the waves crashing against submerged rocks were not so distant anymore.

A small 'beech' as the King called it, mostly made of gravel and slick slabs of stone, lay beyond. The noon remained cool but there was enough sun to catch on something shiny, driven between the rocks on the 'beech.'

Above, sails were being lowered and the ship slowed. Sailors rushed to organise a smaller boat by the railings on what the King called the 'lower deck.'

"Why are we stopping here? So far from land? And there's nothing there besides."

"We're going for a paddle."

"What?"

"So many questions, Pathfinder Ain. You're no longer satisfied with our arrangement?"

"That's not why I'm asking. How can I help if I do not know what to look for?"

"Trust my methods. I don't want you mistaking anything." He gestured. "I believe our boat is ready.

After you."

A small group, the Mask and two of the Shield, along with a pair of sailors, led him to the boat. He climbed in, gripping the edge, and sat at the back while the rest arranged themselves, King Oseto in the front. Next, the boat was lowered by squeaking ropes and touched down on the water. The sailors set to rowing, pulling them away from the ship.

Ain trailed his hand in the water.

Even if the King was crazy for taking such a strange trip, at least the sea was all around. Close. Wondrous. Cold, but a joy. Such peace.

The sailor asked a question. King Oseto replied, making a wide, circular motion with his hand and the boat continued its progress.

"Are we going to land?" Ain asked.

"Can you feel anything now?"

"Nothing."

The King motioned for the boat to change course. Still they rowed, never reaching land and getting closer to the rocks. The sailors switched with the Shield, after some fumbling with the big paddles they continued in a methodical manner, or so it seemed by their discussions, where the ship appeared to function as a marker, crossing parts of the sea before the small 'beech.' The sun crawled down the sky. Ain sipped at the water flask he'd been given and shifted on his seat. The wood had become stone.

The rowers switched again and Ain groaned.

But the sound died in his throat.

"Wait," he cried. "I feel something."

Something lurked beneath the water. Not a path exactly, but something had moved about before the 'beech.' Could it have been a fish? They had no feet to beat a path. And there was a sense of 'power' to the movement. It echoed. It was heavy with years. And decades. Centuries even, he couldn't tell. Couldn't trace it back. It was infinity. The pulse swirled and his stomach churned.

The King leant between the rowers. "Yes?"

"Beneath us – it's passing. Go that way." His stomach eased and he pointed toward land. The rowers complied. "Now to the left."

The hideous echo of ages returned, as did the trouble in his gut. Ain waved the rowers on until it passed. His hand shot up and they turned again, grunting with the effort. Eventually they pinpointed a spot where the echo stopped. It didn't extend in any direction except for back toward the ship and it pulsed harder than before.

"We're directly above something," he said.

The King slapped the edge of the boat, shouting in Anaskari. His face was a mixture of surprise and elation. He gestured to one of the sailors, who nodded, stood and removed his belt, knife and thin shirt. He then slipped into the water with a grimace and took a deep breath before diving down.

His kicking feet splashed the boat and Ain wiped salty water from his lips.

What was down there? The King tapped long fingers on his knee. Had he been able to, Ain didn't doubt the man would be pacing. Ain glanced into the water. How long could the sailor hold his breath?

Long moments passed before the water stirred and the sailor broke the surface with a gasp.

He shook his head as he spoke to the King.

"He found nothing then?"

King Oseto frowned. "No, he's telling me he cannot see well, but there looks like wreckage down there."

"Of what?"

"My father's ship." He turned to the second sailor and motioned to the water.   "Your Majesty." The man removed his own belongings before joining the first diver. Oseto gave more instructions, spreading his hands to mimic a rectangular shape, and both men nodded before diving down again.

Twice more the men dived and resurfaced and twice more they received instructions from the King.

Finally, when the sailors reappeared a third time, they were smiling. In one man's hands rested a sleek black box, steel hinges thick with rust. The pulse was more powerful now that the box was free of the water.

Once the King held it, he fell still. The boat bobbed and rocked when the sailors rejoined and yet he did not move. He only stared at the box, a tiny smile on his face.

"That is what you seek?" Ain asked. He would be free now, if the King kept his word. Unlikely as it was – and yet, he couldn't go through another hanging – real or otherwise.

"It is." He didn't look up.

"And my part of the bargain is now fulfilled?"

"If what I seek is truly inside, then yes."

Ain smothered a spark of hope. Be sure. No celebration until the city was miles behind. "Does it not open?"

"On the ship," he said.

One of the sailors interrupted with what sounded like a curse. He pointed to the ship. A small red flag was flying up the mast and on the rail, the first mate waved twin flags of blood. The King straightened, snapping orders.

The Shield leapt to the seat and began rowing, leaving the shivering sailors and mask to huddle before Ain.

"What's happening?" he called to King Oseto.

"Pirates. Thieves of the sea."

CHAPTER 33

Seto barked orders to Captain Tirang and went directly below decks. The sway of the ship beneath his tread was familiar, but darkly so. Old memories threatened as he locked the door. He shoved each one of them down – the chill of water closing over his head, the rocks hurtling toward him, the rush of waves, all of them.

The Pathfinder he'd left in the custody of Mascare and Shield, who were to take Ain to his cabin. Or cell, really. Ain babbled about honouring a promise and Seto had thrown an assurance over his shoulder.

Through his porthole, he glared at the pirate; for the moment a small shape on the horizon, before crossing the cabin and laying the still-wet case on a table. He lit a lamp and drew his dagger, hefting the blade. Years. More. Decades had passed but now she was returned.

The knife tip came to rest between a rusted hinge. He thumped the heel of his hand on the pommel. Rusted steel snapped. Prying his fingers beneath the lid, he tore it free, final hinge squeaking.

"Chelona." He breathed her name.

She lay inside, her face tinted green from years beneath the sea. Just like the other Greatmasks, a firm mouth and dark eyes looked up at him. But she was beautiful too and his hand trembled as he reached out. Cold when his fingertips grazed bone.

He lifted her and hesitated.

How many dives had he organised, in secret, for how many years? How many storms had his sailors survived now – and all for naught. For all those years he'd been searching in the wrong part of the tiny bay. The wreckage had drifted north west along the reef.

And more the fool his brother had been too, for attempting – at least during the first few years and afterwards only sporadically – the same dives. Seto laughed. How wonderful to defeat the man, now, after so long.

The dark secret of Casa Swordfish – the secret that was no secret in the First Tier – House without Greatmask. Hiding behind its ties to the Storm Singers, its disproportionate representation in ranks of the Shield. Its ties to Falco House.

A knock on his cabin door. "Your Majesty?" Old Snaps, the first mate. His voice was tight. "There's more trouble."

Seto placed Chelona within the steel box and inside the drawer of the writing desk. "Come in, Snaps."

The man limped inside, his canvas shirt open at the neck. White hair curled across his chest, echoed in the white of his beard. His voice still boomed and he had no trouble remaining upright as he pointed above. "Another one, sire. To starboard."

"Show me."

Seto followed him above decks. Sailors with bare feet

and wind-burnt faces skipped out of his way as he strode to the rail. A second ship, this one also running pirate colours, was on the horizon, near to opposite the first. Seto cursed.

"I feel the same." Snaps glowered at one of the ships. "Captain says they'll try to head us off when the wind changes. It'll be a close thing. The one to portside is closer."

"Can we outrun them both?"

"Hard to say. One will try and drive us into the other. We'd have to be a mite more nimble than we are I'm afraid. But Cap has a few tricks up his sleeve."

"Let's go hear about them, then." Seto headed to the helm, where Captain Tirang waited with a hand on the wheel. The helmsman stood beside him. Both men were from Holvard, far west, beyond even Medah, their stocky profiles, broad shoulders and ring-laden hands something of a tell.

"When will they catch us, Captain?" Seto asked.

Captain Tirang squeezed his hands on the wheel. Small jewels set in silver bands caught the light. "Nightfall." His accent was still strong, lengthening the word. "But that's exactly when we'll disappear."

Old Snaps whistled. "Want to try that again, Captain?"

He nodded at his helmsmen, who grinned. "We'll be safe so long as everyone keeps their mouths shut."

"Any idea of who the pirates are?"

"One is probably Falio," the Captain said. "Can't quite see his flag but I think it so."

"The Shark," Snaps added.

Falio, the bastard son of a whore. Seto had lost an expensive cargo to the sea-thief some years back. A tricksome man indeed. Could the lost Greatmask help?

He said nothing. It wouldn't do well to give the men false hope, he might not be able to use Chelona at all – how long now since he'd eavesdropped on Father and Otonos at lessons? And how long now since he'd failed, unable to make her speak?

"Keep me informed then," he said.

"Aye, Your Majesty."

Seto returned to quarters below decks where he motioned for a guard to join him, opening the prisoner's door. The Pathfinder had not outlived his usefulness by any stretch. Seto found Ain pacing his tiny cabin with its hammock and sea chest.

"What news of the pirates?" he asked.

"Two ships seek to stop us."

"Will we escape?"

"By dawn everything will be decided."

"Meaning?"

"Captain Tirang will have evaded them or we will be dead."

"What a comfort that is."

"I trust him. I would not have hired him otherwise."

Ain folded his arms. "And supposing we survive, you will keep your word. Free me and Schan, return the Bird of the Sun?"

"I must thank you for the valuable service you have provided, but I cannot grant you your last request."

"Sands, you are a deceiver, a nurturer of lies. You gave your word. As King of your people."

"That you and your friend would be free, Pathfinder. I said nothing of the Solave. You will have your life, a chance to return home. Forget the bird, it will only lead to your ruin."

Ain sneered. "But not yours?"

"No."

"Ha!"

"I am not ensared, but you are. Else you wouldn't be so angry now." And soon Chelona would protect him, had he need of it. A Bird of the Sun was no match for a Greatmask.

"I'm not –" He stopped himself and took a breath. "Sands, I'm in charge of my own destiny."

"Then, as a reasonably free man," Seto held back a smile, "would you consider completing a bold task?"

"Such as?"

"Carrying a message of peace home."

The Pathfinder's brows drew together. "Peace?"

"Yes. My kingdom cannot be surrounded by enemies and prosper."

"You drove us from our home."

"And tell me, Ain. How did you find your homecoming? Is it what you imagined? Can your entire people survive so far from the desert? Do they even wish to leave it?"

The young man clenched a fist. "That is not for you to decide. And it doesn't change what your people did."

"Nothing can."

"That's your answer?"

"My answer is a question. Will you consider taking a message of peace to the Cloud?"

The Pathfinder turned back to the chest, which was bolted to the floor. He sat on it and put his head in his hands. His shoulders trembled as he laughed. "This is a jest, surely?"

"No jest. Think upon it as we slip between the pirates' trap." Seto left without waiting for a reply. Apparently the peace of the ocean had deserted Ain. The young man was getting a little demanding, another reminder of his powerlessness wouldn't go astray. But later.

In his cabin he returned to the drawer, slid it open and lifted Chelona. How cold beneath his fingertips she was, he'd forgotten already. He checked on one of the ships through the porthole and locked the door before raising the mask. Would she still be there? Would she know him? Care to speak to him?

Seto took a breath and put the mask on.

Darkness.

When he woke it was to more darkness. A thunderstorm raged within his skull. He squeezed his temples with the heel of his hands, rolling on the floor. The ship rocked enough that he stumbled on hands and knees, mask clattering to the wood.

A circle of moonlight poured through the porthole, stinging his eyes.

She rejected him. Nothing had changed. What had Otonos done to her? That pathetic, jealous worm! Seto rose to his knees and his stomach flipped. Vomit splashed onto his hands.

"Ana be damned." He spat bile. Reaching his feet, he gripped the bed – bolted like everything else in his room, and stumbled for a cloth and water barrel. He returned to the vomit and mopped it up with a rueful smile. The Anaskari King, on his hands and knees wiping up vomit on a ship.

Speeding toward pirates.

Powerless to use one of the most powerful artefacts in the world.

He tossed the cloth into a corner and stumbled to Chelona, sliding the mask into his robe. His fingers tapped wood. Strummed absent strings. Even half a song on a harp might have calmed him.

Seto returned above decks. No lamps burned and orders were given in whispers. A flurry of activity went on above, as sailors climbed rope ladders and swung from the rigging. To one side the lights of a pirate ship were considerably closer. He turned and searched for the other, hands on the rail. There. Some distance away yet.

He found Old Snaps, who stood with the helmsman.

"What's happening?" Men were hauling long rolls of what looked like black canvas, it was hard to tell by moonlight only.

"We're dropping the net," he said.

"Are we going to haul the other ships aboard and eat them?"

Snaps chuckled. "Nope. This net is special. There's something woven in it that will help hide us. It does something to the light. Don't really understand it myself, but it usually works."

Seto craned his neck. "Usually?" From the crow's nest, men were throwing out great sheets of netting. A glittering black mesh fell down, covering sails and rigging, rails and splashing softly into the waterline.

"If we keep our traps shut, it will certainly work." Captain Tirang joined them.

"This is the method you've used before?" Seto asked.

"Several times. With the star-netting we'll be safe. We just have to remain quiet and have a little luck from the Blue Vaults."

"Star-netting?"

"Tis so. Our seamstresses back home claim they weave starlight into the rope to help blind our enemies."

"It sounds magnificent. I wonder, since you're returning home soon —"

"They won't sell their secrets, Your Majesty."

"Of course."

"Nearly time," Snaps said.

Tirang nodded. He relayed an order for silence and all activity came to a halt. Only the small creak of wood or rope could be heard as the ship drifted closer to one of the pirates. Their lights were bright and men in a motley assortment of uniform and garish dress, even in the moonlight, lined the rails, peering into the dark.

Seto touched Tirang's shoulder and mimed two ships colliding. He raised an eyebrow.

Tirang shook his head.

That was something.

He held his breath when the ships began to pass, no more than a dozen yards between them. One of the pirates cocked his head. "You hear something?"

His voice was audible over the snap of sails and muttering from other pirates, a man shouting down from the crow's nest. Seto even heard the rasp of a blade on whetstone. Another pirate snorted. "No."

"I thought —"

The man cuffed the first pirate. "Bones. There's nothing out there, use your bleeding eyes."

The man had a hand on his cutlass. "Don't do that again."

"Or what?"

The pirates began to pull away, their argument fading. Seto exhaled.

CHAPTER 34

Darkness cloaked his city.

Even had he looked, the streets could hardly have existed to Seto as his carriage rumbled along. He wanted only sleep. On something that didn't rock.

He sighed when the palace gates ground open and put a hand over Chelona when an argument started. It did not last – royal decree about the closing of gates only extended to those who weren't royal. He was soon striding to his rooms, having ordered Ain sent back to his room under guard, with promises of tomorrow.

He hesitated by the large cage and its heavy drop cloth. The Bird of the Sun would be sleeping, but it still needed to be fed. No-one was allowed to touch or even go near the cage – and only a handful of people even knew where the bird rested – Seto fed the bird himself. Foraging for scraps of meat from a dish – fresh from the kitchens and mostly rabbit and fowl, he dropped pieces into a small tray at the bottom of the cage, lifting the cloth just enough.

Then he let it fall, the pull of the bird washing over him without even a stirring. Too tired.

Two steps from the door to his bedchamber and a knock came.

"Your Majesty, are you there?"

Solicci. Hiding his voice like a true Mascare – though the timbre was familiar enough.

He could say nothing. Just slip into the bed...but if he did, the man would only come back at dawn. Seto checked on Chelona, whom Solicci would not be meeting, hidden in his robe, and raised his voice.

"Come in, Solicci."

His advisor wore mask and robes, but placed the mask aside when the door was closed. "Your Majesty, it is good to see you safely returned to us."

Seto chuckled. "I rather enjoy not being dead myself."

"The nobles will be pleased also."

"Ah." Seto moved to a sideboard and poured a drink. He motioned to Solicci, who declined. "Why don't we sit and you can tell me about it. In brief."

"Well, sire. They worry over issues both small and large. Nemola wishes to place a levy on the people to compensate for the destruction of the fleet, to help rebuild."

"Does he?"

"And there are various disputes and concerns, most related to trade but above all, I believe they – we – are feeling...neglected by our new King."

"That warms my heart, Solicci. But surely that can all wait until tomorrow?"

He inclined his head. "Then would Your Majesty care to take a report?"

"The harvest?"

"Captain Holindo and Luik report that, with the aid of the Alchemista, it will be but days before the last of the flesh is gone."

"Wonderful news." He leant forward, a touch of

energy returning. "And Flir and the Storm Singers?"

"The song appears to be working. The majority of the population who hear it report improvement if not cure. As yet, we haven't unsealed the Gates, but both Lord Abrensi and Lady Lavinia are confident. They still sing daily and crowds remain large."

"Word from Captain Emilio?"

"Nothing new. We estimate that he and his party are still within the Bloodwood."

"Very well. Word of Vinezi?"

"None."

As expected. "And the invasion?"

Solicci straightened. "A messenger bird arrived. Ships have finally been sighted. They are some days away yet, but it is confirmed. The storms have been mild it seems, if the bird managed to reach each island in the chain."

"How many?"

"Ten, maybe more."

"Hardly the full fleet, wouldn't you agree?"

"They will have acor."

"True." Seto sipped his fire-lemon, savouring the burn. His second crucible as King. How would the city fare? "And it's more than we possess, what with how many ships lost to the Beast and how many chasing the pirate fleet?"

"A dozen. And weeks from returning."

"Very well. Tomorrow, accompany me to the corpse. Planning for the fortification of the breech will be finalised."

"Yes, Your Majesty."

He stood. "Thank you and good night, Solicci."

"Of course." The man replaced his mask, bowed and left. Seto finished his drink and paused at a second knock.

"By the Gods." He took another step toward his room.

The knock came again – only with a certain pattern. He admitted a page, who handed over a small piece of paper with a bow. "He has been waiting for you, Your Majesty. In the kitchens."

"Very well." He followed the lad down to the warmth of the kitchens, fuelled by hulking ovens. He'd waved off his guards, but several floors down and he regretted it now. They could have carried him some of the way. What a sight it would have made too, the King of two dominions carried along the halls of his own palace.

A thin man in black sat on a stool, finishing a piece of cheese. The Perfume Rat.

"King Oseto." He stood and swept a low bow, no doubt for the benefit of cooks and their helpers.

Seto waved the man into the corridors, saying nothing until he was behind a closed door – a quiet storeroom. "You have news?"

"No good news I'm afraid."

"Wonderful. Quickly, tell me as I am weary tonight."

"You are very busy, I understand."

"What is amiss?"

"The other Rats and I have come to a decision regarding our place in the city." His nose twitched. "We feel we can no longer work with you as leader, not with your attention so neatly divided, and with such potential for conflicting agendas. Not that we don't appreciate everything you have done."

There. His juggling had failed. Inevitable but most vexing. "I see."

"You don't seem upset."

"I cannot, nor do I wish to stop you." And it was true. It was too much. And he could achieve more as King, and truly, it was his oldest dream. One he'd denied for decades. And yet, a sting lingered. No use trying to deny it. Establishing that sly kingdom had saved him.

The Rat grinned. "Doubt you could, Seto."

"Really, Enso?" Seto gave his own smile when the man flinched. The rat's true name. "Yes, I know all about your true past. You were quite a capable merchant, how surprised your father must have been when you killed him."

"That was an accident!"

"Truly? Now, I trust you realise my reach extends far beyond that which you assume. And let me grant you your freedom – though under conditions I lay out and which will be met, or I will drown every rat in our sewer, do you understand?"

The Perfume Rat swallowed.

"Good. The first is that the Queen's Harper is off-limits unless I invite you. Expect overt moves against the palace and its interests to be answered swiftly and from many sides. Further, nothing has changed in regards to our working to protect the city from the invasion and the apprehension of Vinezi." Seto paused. The rest could wait. "Further stipulations will be issued. See yourself out."

Enso scurried from the room and Seto growled as he pushed himself toward the nearest Mascare passage. Whatever stood between him and four posts, pillows and soft blankets would be crushed.

By the time he reached his rooms he'd stubbed his toe and torn a sleeve on a loose piece of stone, but finally he was mere steps from sleep. The door swung open and Seto froze.

Something was in his bed.

Or someone.

He drew a knife from beneath his robe. All traces of weariness vanquished. "Show yourself."

Nothing.

Seto scanned the room. Empty. For a trap, it was a clumsy one. He took the edge of his blanket and hurled it aside.

A stench drove him back.

Hunks of black, rotting flesh covered his bed – tints of blue catching lamplight from the sitting room. Seto replaced the blanket and roared for his guard.

CHAPTER 35

Seto shouted his commands, motioning for a senior guard to attend. He stood in the hall outside his rooms, a makeshift command centre. While Solicci urged him to keep out of sight, his Honour Guard did exactly as they were told, staying put to watch over him while someone worked at cleaning up pieces of Sea Beast in his bed.

Inside, he'd posted a guard on the bird, just to be sure.

"How many others?" he asked.

"Only one so far, My Liege," the soldier said. "In a corner of a storeroom. Packed into stores of dried fish."

"And they are being burnt?"

"As we speak."

"Good. I want one of the Storm Singers on hand for the search."

He saluted and ran off.

Solicci paced beside him. Seto gave him a look. "Have you solved the problem yet?"

"My King?"

"All that pacing."

The Mascare stopped. "How did they get in?"

"I have an idea of how to discover that."

"The Medah Pathfinder? Do you trust him?"

"No, but I trust the hold the Bird has on him. He will

do as I ask. He won't be able to resist."

"Shall I send for him?"

"Yes. And his warrior."

Solicci strode off. Seto kicked out kinks in his legs. Sleep was gone. A rage replaced it. How had the slimy bastards snuck into the very palace – and his own chambers? Despite being surrounded by steel, with Chelona safely tucked away, it seemed a thousand eyes rested upon him. Exposed – in the depths of his own palace.

If they could get in and out so easily, what else had they done? And where would they strike again? And why hadn't they left an assassin in his room, rather than dead flesh? It didn't make sense. There had to be a chink in the armour somewhere. His best guess was the ways. He'd already sent men to investigate the Three Doors – a passage from First to Second Tier that only the Protector, heads of the houses, Kings and Captain of the Honour Guard ought to know of.

And the keys weren't easy to come by.

But if it wasn't that – how else could they enter? Guile?

A bleary-eyed Ain and a stony-faced Schan were marched up the corridor and Seto ordered them through the press.

"Good morning to you both," he said.

Schan made no reply, but Ain frowned. "Why are we here?"

"Someone has infiltrated the palace, attempting to poison us with the corpse of the Sea Beast."

Ain glanced around, then back to Seto. "And how does that relate to us?"

"I have a new offer to go hand in hand with the first."

Schan shook his head but Ain waited. "Oh?"

"As before, you may leave together at daybreak."

"Or?"

"Or, in exchange for your freedom and the Bird of the Sun – you help me find the path the infiltrators took, and further, you assist me in hunting down a man named Vinezi, who is lurking in the city and is responsible for the turmoil."

At mention of the Bird, Ain's eyes lit up.

Schan gripped his arm. "No. Let's just be rid of this place."

Ain clenched his hands into fists. "But she belongs with me."

"Think of your family."

"I can have both," he gasped out. Ain turned back to Seto, steadying himself with a deep breath. "You have to understand, if I agree, it is not that simple. Not all paths are equal. The assassin's path might be lost."

"I'm willing to take that risk. And I believe they are using an old path. Perhaps an ancient path."

"That will be easier at least."

"Then we have an extension on our original bargain?"

Ain hesitated and Schan folded his arms. But the Pathfinder had already lost. Seto saw as much in the young man's eyes back in the prison. "We have a deal," he said.

"Good." Seto pointed to the Shield. "Now, your escort will accompany you on your search. Begin by mapping the oldest paths inside the palace and report back after dawn."

Ain opened his mouth to reply, but Seto swept by, motioning to a pair of his guard. The men fell into step as he headed down a dark corridor. "Light."

One of his Guard ran back to take a torch from the wall and caught up as they made a turn.

"Your Majesty, should you have more than the two of us with you?" one of the men asked.

"All is well." It wasn't, but he didn't need any more people underfoot.

A layer of dust covered the statues and the frames of the few paintings that remained on the walls. His family, some of them ancestors who'd have set foot on the Old Land. Each with the deep-set eyes and hungry gaze.

Strange that he'd turned into this corridor, of all places in the palace.

The Queen's private rooms.

Of late, belonging to his brother's second wife, Mila. But before that, Otonos' first wife Alessi and before her in turn, Mother had called these halls home. But since Mila had fallen ill and taken back to her mountain family home, no-one used the quarters anymore.

And when Mila took up residence after Alessi's death, before people decided the rooms were cursed, Seto didn't visit anymore either. Not that Mila was a terrible woman but her presence only reinforced the absence of Alessi.

Now he paused by a door he'd paused at many times before, first as a child waiting to see Mother and then as a young fool who thought he was in love, waiting for Alessi. How wrong he was. But she knew him so well – a brighter woman he'd not met. A true loss to the Kingdom. Not that Otonos did anything to save her.

He raised a hand to turn the handle. Unlocked.

"Bring the light."

The guard hesitated.

He sighed. "The rooms are not cursed, simply because Casa Sword-Fish has had an unfortunate history of its

Queens dying."

The men swallowed. "Forgive us, majesty," one said.

"No matter."

Seto led them through a sitting room whose furniture loomed in white shapes, stirring the sheets as he trailed a hand over them. By the chairs at the window he'd argued with Alessi over who was the greater bard, Delissa Gold Tongue or Panaso Cesa. He smiled and moved into the bedchamber where he threw a white sheet onto the floor, revealing a made bed of heavy blankets. Always winter in these rooms.

Here he'd sat on the edge of the bed and listened to Mother tell stories of the Old Land and its enormous cities.

He sat. "Your orders, gentlemen. Send for more men to guard me, but let no-one disturb me until the first hour after dawn. No-one. Not Lord Solicci, not Flir or Luik. No-one. Your heads if you fail."

"We understand, Sire."

"Good. Light something in the next room. And thank you, both."

The men did as ordered and Seto paused. There, that wall. Behind yet another tapestry was a door to the ways. He slid a heavy cabinet across it and leant against it a moment, breathing hard. Next he lifted Chelona from her box, placed her under his pillow and shook out the blankets before stretching atop the bed, closing his eyes. A few hours of unbroken sleep would change everything.

*

Seto's head was a lump when he woke to a knocking on the door.

"Your Majesty, the hour has come."

He called something that could have been an acknowledgement. Stumbling to the cabinet he'd shifted, he fumbled around for Fire-Lemon, cursing when he found none. He rubbed his eyes and gave a rueful shake of his head.

Alessi's chambers.

At least he'd not been murdered while he slept. A small mercy.

Seto moved to the door and stuck his head out. Four different soldiers. "Bring me something to drink. And eat if you could. To my rooms."

"At once, Sire." One of the men hurried off and Seto slipped Chelona into his robes before returning to his own rooms via the conventional passages. The hustle of last night had eased, though pairs of the Shield still searched rooms – their own cloth masks and gloves in place.

Light stained the windows outside and a steady rain had started to fall by the time he finished with breakfast. Sending yet more people scrambling about the palace, he'd have everyone he needed assembled at the breech by the time he arrived.

Solicci met him and the smallest contingent of his Honour Guard he could convince his minders to bring along – a full two dozen men in gleaming armour, Swordfish emblazoned across their chests – at the central doors.

"Your Majesty, I must speak my mind." Solicci's expression was one of worry and disapproval.

"Must you?"

"Yes. You shouldn't have slipped away. How can we protect you?"

"I had guards," Seto said, waving a hand. "Now, has any more been found?"

Solicci sighed. "Two more deposits. One was in the Lord Protector's chambers. We found it only recently, having not thought to check there."

"And the other?"

"Nemola's room, sire."

Seto frowned. "Is that so? And has Nemola or anyone fallen ill?"

"Not yet."

Interesting. Perhaps that explained why the assassination attempt had been almost circumspect? But was the tedious fool truly that resentful? Or resourceful? "Good. And the Pathfinder?"

"He gave us some possibilities, though he is sleeping now. We are investigating." Solicci lowered his voice. "Do you wish to speak with Nemola?"

"It might just be too convenient that he was both targeted and unharmed."

Solicci nodded, setting off. Seto joined him, motioning for a group of the guard to follow. They commandeered the corridors, servants pressing themselves against stone walls, until coming to a halt at Nemola's doors.

Seto cast them open and strode through darkened rooms, following the sound of quiet voices and cutlery.

Open curtains led to a balcony, similar to his own, only smaller of course. A flicker of surprise crossed Nemola's face and Seto allowed a grin in response. It was not the surprise of an unannounced visit from the King.

It was a disappointed surprise.

And that was all Seto needed. Nemola was the one.

There was discomfort in the councillor's bearing too. The man was making an effort not to look at the Honour

Guard. An interrupted breakfast sat between the old man and a servant, who made a bow and left, after a look from his master.

"Your Majesty, you honour me," Nemola said.

"And you do not." No point stretching it out. He gestured to his men, who advanced. One was Giovan. Good.

Nemola blinked, but did not resist when he was taken by the arms. "Sire?"

"My Captain will be questioning you about the rotting flesh found in my rooms. And your own."

He affected confusion. "If I am to help, why am I being detained?"

"The lies grow tiresome. Simply admit you were behind such a clumsy and cowardly attempt on my life and I will spare you."

"I did nothing of the sort," he cried. "I am a target just as much as you, my King."

"I applaud your indignation, but it is hardly necessary." Seto turned to Solicci. "Find the servant who left just before. Question him first, perhaps he'll be more forthright once he's lost a few fingers."

Nemola paled. "No!"

Seto suppressed a smile. Almost too easy. He stopped Solicci, who'd taken a few steps, and motioned for Giovan to help Nemola into his seat. The man grunted when the Captain shoved him back down.

"Who else?" Seto said.

"There are several of us. I will give you their names if you do not hurt my family. Or Pilos. He is innocent."

"You'll have to let me decide who is innocent. How did you bring the flesh into the Palace?"

"We took it from the harbour and snuck it inside via

the ways."

"Who in the Mascare supports you?"

"My family? Pilos and his family?"

"If they are innocent, they will be spared, certainly."

Nemola's eyes narrowed. "Your priorities are wrong, can't you see it? We had no choice, there is so much at stake. You aren't even searching for the acor properly."

Seto shook his head. How odd that he felt little more than a passing regret at the betrayal. "I think you're right, Nem."

"What?"

"I do have better things to do, other than listen to you chastise me for thinking of the whole city, rather than just one part of it. Captain, would you continue the interrogation somewhere quieter? If he isn't utterly forthcoming, be persuasive. I want everyone rounded up, understood?"

"It will be done, sire."

Seto left the room, Solicci and part of the Honour Guard in tow. Outside, the Mascare stepped double time to keep up. "Aren't you concerned about the other dissidents?"

A fair question. And mention of the Mascare could hardly be described as pleasant news. But for now, he had to delegate. Had to think of the whole city. And more, how could he be sure Solicci himself wasn't involved? It remained unlikely, and yet..."Giovan is capable and I believe we should visit the harbour. That is more pressing."

"I'll arrange the carriage."

*

Rain drummed its heavy fingers across the roof as he and Solicci rolled through the city in the royal carriage. Around them, the Honour Guard rode, faces set as water streamed down over them.

"Tell me, Solicci, what news on Lady Cera?"

The man shifted slightly. Betrayal was obviously heavy on both their minds. Especially with mention of Mascare being involved in Nemola's nasty little scheme. "Little. She has fled, but not into the mountains as we first believed. Perhaps the plains before the Bloodwood? We have so few men available now, for her search."

"I still want her found."

"Of course, Your Majesty."

"And your thoughts on the Mascare assisting Nemola?"

"No-one comes to mind, but I will begin investigation."

Seto studied his advisor a moment. No trace of guile in the man's voice at least, but then, such was his training. "Good. The moment you learn something, Solicci."

"Of course, sire."

"And arrange for Ain to bring me his findings in the throne room before I brief the nobles."

He nodded as the carriage came to a halt. Seto opened the door and hopped down to splash across the stones to Captain Holindo's command post. From the shelter of the tent he brushed at his damp shoulders.

The Sea Beast's body, and its stench, was much reduced. Men were working on the main carcass, and its ribs were nearly all gone, but figures also toiled beyond the wall, working on carrying the long tail into the city.

Inside, Seto found Holindo, Luik and Flir seated around a table. As ever, Pevin shadowed her. They had also been joined by Admiral Baliso, whose orange and silver uniform was impeccable. All stood when he entered, Solicci trailing. He waved them down as he took a seat himself. "I didn't sleep well or long, last night, so let's dive right in, shall we? Solicci has brought me up to speed. Well done, all of you. I trust you are aware ships have been sighted and our time is down to days, so swiftly to the next step."

"The breech," Holindo rasped.

"Indeed, Captain. Materials have been in place for some time now, but how long will it take to assemble something solid?"

"We'd need weeks to restore the wall to its former strength, of course. A serviceable wall, perhaps half as thick, could be restored in several days. Less if men worked in shifts all day and all night."

Seto rubbed at his neck. "They will have to."

"Need more than a half-strength wall to deter attackers," Luik said. "We need a surprise."

Flir slapped the table, which rocked. "Exactly. How about your friend, Renaso? Can he mix up some acid? Pour it on them?"

"Will that contaminate the water?" Solicci asked.

Luik shrugged. "I'll find out. No idea if or how much he can produce in that much time. Flir wants him to work on a way to counteract the acor too."

Seto leant forward. "And his progress?"

"I'll find that out too."

"Wait," Flir said. "Shouldn't we start with our ships?"

"We should," Holindo replied. He stood and moved to a table, selecting a rolled chart. Returning, he spread it across the table, accepting daggers to weigh down the corners. Baliso joined him, pointing. "Here is the Renovar fleet, Your Majesty. Numbering perhaps a dozen according to Pevin, at least ten via our own sources.

Possibly carrying up to two thousand men." He arranged carved figurines of bone, pointed at the harbour. The ships led a beautifully painted storm in the Eastern Seas. "Next, the approximate positions of our remaining ships."

Two warships were placed in the harbour, one of which was the *Lancer*, the last remaining royal ship. Another ship Baliso rested along the coast. "Returning from Holvard. Touch and go as to whether it will reach the city in time." Another half-dozen he arranged beyond the Far Islands. "We haven't heard from them yet and nor will we I fear. They are still harrying pirates. Our messages will be too late."

Seto pressed his lips together. What he wouldn't give for another ten warships. Seto gestured to the Renovar on the chart. "Can we afford to be aggressive? Meet them before they reach the city?"

"We'd be outnumbered heavily, and I still might risk it, with our ships. But the acor changes things. I don't know. If they can launch it via catapult, we'd be in trouble. We're generally better armed, but we're slower," the navy captain said.

"Then we need faster ships. Can we outfit merchants?"

"In so little time?" Flir asked.

"Possibly one or two. It might help."

"Begin the process. The Kingdom's coffers are open – be generous but not lavish," he said. To Holindo, "Our ground forces? Can we cover the entire lower wall?"

"It'll be thin. We have perhaps ten thousand men available only, maybe not enough to face catapults of acor and a ground force. We'll have to bolster the numbers with tier militia and they're not trained for a siege. In the past – " He hesitated. "What I am about to say comes from a tactical standpoint, not because I believe it the right course of action."

Seto raised a hand. "I know. Kings have traditionally pulled back to the Second Tier. Less wall to man and it's easier to defend. Though sometimes it has been done at the expense of those in the Lower Tier. I do not wish to do that either, at first."

Flir shook her head. "You both know, we might have to."

Seto paused. Hope was a dangerous substance. One which he had no right to offer. And yet, if it allowed them each to work with more confidence – why hold back? Even if it wasn't the whole truth. It might never come to the Greatmask.

Unlikely.

He looked to Solicci. "I would like to hear from this Alchemisti, Renaso. He is on site. Pevin, you will accompany him."

Solicci bowed and slipped from the tent, taking Pevin with him.

To the Admiral, Seto said, "Admiral Baliso, I need you to organise all captains of suitable vessels. Outline our plans."

"Of course, Your Majesty."

He might well end up telling Solicci later, in private. If the man proved trustworthy. Despite past actions, perhaps the man could be trusted. His loyalty had appeared genuine thus far. Once the three had left, Seto withdrew Chelona from his robe, sliding a black covering from the mask's face.

Gasps filled the tent.

"The Lost Greatmask," he said. "Chelona, of Casa Pesce Spada. Long rumoured amongst those on the First Tier to be stolen. But I have recovered her." He brushed a hand across her cheek. "Not truly lost, she lay instead at the bottom of the ocean for decades, trapped beneath its cold surface since the shipwreck that nearly put an end to me."

"How did you find it?" Flir breathed.

"Later. I must be quick, for I did not wish for Pevin or the Admiral to see it."

"If you say so. And Solicci?"

He met Holindo's eyes, who said nothing. "I have yet to decide."

"I wouldn't trust him that far."

"We shall see." He replaced the cloth and hid the mask once more. "And I should barely need to remind each of you that, for now, this knowledge is to be kept to yourselves. Should we face truly dire circumstances, I would use the Greatmask, though exactly how I have yet to discover." There. Any more and they would not take heart from its discovery.

"This could turn the tide," Holindo said.

Seto spread his hands. "I hope so, though I have never heard of a Greatmask putting out fires."

"It's something," Luik said. "Especially with Notch and Sofia gone."

Seto frowned. "Yes."

Flir nudged Luik, who winced.

"No, it is not Luik's fault, Flir." Seto glanced at the green mass in the bottom corner of the chart. "They chose to desert us."

"I don't think that's what he intended," Flir said.

"We needed the Greatmasks. Sofia and Notch selfishly took them both, whether they intended to deprive us of the masks or not, it is irrelevant as far as the outcome is concerned, don't you think?" He softened his voice.

"But no matter, I found Chelona."

No-one answered and the rain on the tent roof grew loud.

Solicci and Pevin entered with a man in a black coat in tow. He was fairly regular looking – save for his pot belly. It stretched the fabric of his coat, which was shiny. Had it been waxed?

"My King." He went to one knee.

"None of that. You must be Renaso?"

"I am. Lord Solicci asked me to explain a little about the vitriol? You wish to use it in a warlike fashion?"

He nodded. "Please sit."

Renaso did so then tented his hands, tapping his fingers together as he spoke. "It is possible, though it would cause hideous pain. A terrible way to die."

Seto's expression did not change. "We understand."

"Ah. Well, to produce enough to rain down upon the attackers, I do not know if it is possible in the time available."

"How is it produced? Can we speed it along somehow?"

Sweat formed at his temples. "Ah, Your Majesty. The Alchemisti are jealous."

Seto raised his eyebrows. "You're refusing your King?"

He shifted in his seat. "Not refusing, truly. Only, I cannot divulge our secrets. I can, however, make certain requests that would not reveal the whole of the process. If so, we might be able to have a quantity available in time."

"Provide me your list, Renaso of the Alchemisti."

One of his Honour Guard poked his head into the tent. "Sire, a messenger from the palace."

Giovan appeared. "Your Majesty, the Pathfinder's found something he wants you to see."

"Vinezi's path?"

"He seemed confident."

Seto rose. "Holindo, oversee the construction of the wall. It begins the moment the Sea Beast is finished. Luik, Flir, continue your work and report to me this evening."

"Tell us if you find something," Flir said.

"Assuredly."

He slipped from the tent, Solicci following. The rain had eased. He stepped over a iron-grey puddle as he climbed into the nearby carriage. Finally.

"No more hiding, Vinezi."

CHAPTER 36

Vinezi stood before the remnants of his force. Half a dozen men. Half a dozen. Torches crackled on the walls, casting deep shadows across their faces. Bedrolls lined one wall, barrels of water another and the remains of a card game lay on a makeshift table, created he assumed, from remnants found in the lower halls of the mountain fortress. Or perhaps 'hidden temple' was a better description. After all – what else, other than the power of the Gods, did the Pool represent?

According to Julas, he had visited the men often, in order to keep morale high during the regeneration and most importantly, to continue to dangle the promise of power.

But his brother felt it now time for a reminder of that power.

"I am reborn," Vinezi cried in Anaskari.

A shout echoed from the walls and a renewed hope shone from their faces.

His brothers flanked him, making it impossible to pace as he'd have wished, but they were on hand to support him should he falter, unlikely though it was. His joints still ached, true, but enough days had passed that he would have no trouble making the long trip down to the city now. Whether he would be of any use in a physical contest, that was still to be seen. And after the failure of Alvetti it was time to even the odds.

"I know some of you witnessed my death during the escape and that some of you are new to our cause." He met the eyes of each man. Mostly Renovar and Anaskari, but there were two men from the southern forests too. "You will all witness the next phase of my rise to power – I am going to forge a Greatsuit. A simple, incomplete suit at first, but with it I will still have the power to take the bones of the Sea God and begin creating more Suits."

"Like the Greatmasks?" one of the men asked.

"Yes. Only more powerful. And you will each have one but first we must take what little bone is left unguarded at the Harbour. To that end, prepare for a return to the city. We leave in an hour."

Vinezi motioned for Julas to supervise and for Tarvilus to follow.

He ascended the dimly-lit stairs, pausing at the top to catch his breath. He raised a hand to forestall any question from his brother. "I am fine."

In the Regeneration Chamber he strode directly to the pool and the bone fragments lain along its rim. Some pieces were as long as his forearm, some fist-sized and all irregular in shape. Within, remnants of fur and teeth bobbed in the liquid. Other...pieces...leftover from his recovery remained just below the surface, hints of their shape coated in grey and pink.

"I believe I know what the pool is composed of," Tarvilus said. "Blood of a Sea God. Look at the blue colour at the very edge of the pool."

Vinezi leant a little closer, squinting. Tarvilus was right. There was a thin line of blue – as if the pink and grey floated atop. Not unlike oil on water. Another line was revealed under his scrutiny – a watermark on the inside of the stone.

The pool was shrinking.

"Each regeneration comes at a cost," his brother continued. "This pool won't last forever. With no regeneration pools back home and now with the last Sea God dead..."

Vinezi nodded. "You are probably right. And it may be that the missing pages of the Genus discuss it further but there is enough for our purposes at least."

"Do you want me to bring the Crucible closer now?" he asked.

"Yes, but first you need to find an axe."

Tarvilus hesitated. "An axe?"

Vinezi placed a hand on the stone bench. His fingers were tucked into a fist – all save for his smallest finger, which lay across the cold rock. Enough of his memories had returned that they would have been imprinted on the new bone, just as the Genus described. It had certainly been longer than last time. "Insurance."

His eyes widened and then his expression fell. "Then you want me to stay here?"

"I would worry about you otherwise."

"You don't worry about Julas."

"He is better with a sword."

"And I'm better here," Tarvilus replied, a hint of defiance creeping into his voice.

"Exactly, brother. Exactly." He smiled. "Now find your axe. I want to be sure."

Tarvilus nodded and left.

When he returned his expression was still flat but he seemed to have accepted his near-imprisonment in the temple. It was simply the way it had to be. Tarvilus understood better than their younger brother. Regeneration at least – Tarvilus wasn't able to forge a Greatsuit.

That knowledge was for Vinezi alone.

"Ready?" He lifted the axe – more a hatchet – and paused.

"Quickly."

Tarvilus' arm flashed down. Pain exploded and Vinezi screamed as blood spayed. He staunched the flow with a piece of his robe, clenching his other fist over the wound. His brother had already fished the finger out from where it rolled into the pool. He placed it within the Crucible and rested the heavy bone construct on the edge of the pool.

"Where is the *lenasi*?"

"We have none. Julas took the last to repair his leg."

He swore. "Then it wasn't enough."

"He can run now, if he has to."

"No matter. There is still the bone." He glanced at Tarvilus. "I will call for you."

His brother left and Vinezi withdrew his chisel. Its butt bore a steel cap with the waves of Casa Mare and the wooden handle was scuffed and discoloured, years of his sweat worn into the grain.

Without adequate quantities of bone, he had to improvise. Which meant a thinner, less cohesive suit. All he'd truly have would be gauntlets and a partial breastplate. Everything else he'd have to augment from whatever could be found in the harbour. Somewhere in the city below, there was a Witch who had discovered a truth about the fish – after so long living and breeding in the harbour of the Sea God, their bones bore traces of the God's power.

And what better time to harvest bone, while no-one fished.

He gritted his teeth. Block the pain.

The pain was as nothing – the throbbing in the stub – it did not exist.

There was only the old white of bone.

He first carved and chiselled even pieces, using the head of the hatchet to land blows. Blood flecked onto his face and even the smooth white bone, but he did not take the time to wipe it away. Any of it. Concentrate. On the sound of steel on bone, the faint trail of dust that rose after each line cut.

Sweat beaded as he worked and he blinked it away when it trickled down. Just as important as the bone itself, was the ancient pattern he carved. The pattern formed symbols that could have been words but were not legible. In a large piece he could simply carve the pattern as one – here he had to carve the top, the middle and the bottom on three separate pieces of bone. The gauntlet pattern was next – he did not need to refer to the charts, those he'd memorised as a child. The pages of the Genus that dealt with forging, however, those he memorised. And burnt.

When Vinezi finished he sat back to rest a moment. A full suit would have taken longer but he'd done all he could. The pattern did not line up perfectly, but it was close. Whether it was close enough he had yet to discover.

Next, the Crucible.

Each piece he placed within, lining them up before

setting the Crucible aside. A faint glow rose as ancient bone reacted to ancient bone. He peered within. The pieces were moulding together but the glow was fading. Were the patterns too inexact? The bone was quivering, slipping back apart. Try something, fool!

Vinezi lifted the Crucible and placed it in the pool, arms straining.

A blue glow joined the white and the bone solidified and a breastplate formed.

"Ha! See what mere Carver skills can do, Father?"

He withdrew the Crucible and repeated the process with two gauntlets, pulling the final piece of bone armour free before letting the Crucible float into the centre of the pool. He slumped against the wall of the regeneration pool before placing the first bone upon his wounded hand. A warmth spread from the gauntlet and he gasped when it made subtle adjustments, elongating to align with his fingers. The pain disappeared.

Nothing but its own magic seemed to hold it upon his skin – something he had not expected. Most suits were mounted onto clothing manually. For the breastplate he rested it against his robe and the same warmth spread as the bone attached itself. Was the Sea God's blood changing the process?

He stood and let out a roar.

It worked.

Even an imperfect, makeshift suit – a mere three pieces, had worked. He paced. All fatigue was gone from his body. It was as if he had just woken from a deep sleep. He raised a hand then pointed at the hatchet, flicking his wrist.

The blade flew across the room. It struck the wall with a dull clunk and a spark.

He roared again, this time with laughter.

"Vin?"

"Come, Tarvilus – see what I have created." Godhood awaited. And if Marinus did dare follow, he would regret such a foolish move.

*

The endless staircase leading down to the city did not trouble him and nor did the men complain about the long trek down the wide staircase after a demonstration of his power. Power he was willing to promise they would soon share in – even if that were never to happen.

They were not fit. The Anaskari were at least once of noble heritage – but the others, Renovar and Braonn, they were barely human. No history, no honour in their bones. Mere tools, truly.

Halfway down from the temple, they reached the silver and the black doors, the black of which he had not yet been able to fathom. Ecsoli markings were present on both, but they were vague – aside from the note about the temple on the silver. Here Julas stopped and the men spread out a moment.

"Should we check on the *Gigansi*?"

Vinezi shook his head. "On the way back."

"What if he has tired of guarding the Lesser God and fled with it?"

"Unlikely. Besides which, the Lesser God is no loss to us if he has. And we need to move swiftly. Every day is a day closer to Marinus catching up."

Julas chuckled. "Then you do think big brother is following us."

"I would follow, were our roles reversed." He paused

to lower his voice so the others would not hear. "What I don't believe is that he can bring a whole fleet through that maelstrom."

"Hard to believe we passed through ourselves."

"The gamble paid off. We cannot waste this time," Vinezi said.

"And what of Atilus and Kanis?"

"I have spoken to Atilus via bone – they are closing but we will be in control of Anaskar by then. We simply take the acor from the ships at that point and should Marinus appear, he will receive only a bloody surprise."

"And if not? If King Rat and his group hold on?"

"If not, Atilus may still need to sack the city. Whatever it takes, I will have those bones, Julas."

Down they followed the stairs until exiting in the abandoned Mountain God's Temple, its leaves and bird's nests belying a holy place – along with the holes in the roof where morning light poured through. It stung his eyes.

On he took the group, through the cobbled streets and past common Anaskari and Shield alike, before pausing at the harbour to kneel in the direction of the Sea God's body, a dark outline still-visible above the buildings.

Before discovering that Those Who Fled had survived and receiving confirmation about other suspicions, among them the existence of a Harvesting Pool and the survival of a Sea God, he had only ever seen such a creature once, as a child, the day of its Final Harvest. And mother hadn't allowed him to watch the entire process in any event. Instead, she took him back to the Carver's Quarter to continue work on the patterns. His younger brothers had never seen a God before their arrival in Anaskar.

"Where is the grate?" Julas said. His voice was hushed with awe.

"Next street over, My Lord," one of the men said.

"Are you sure? There are dozens of them."

"I'm certain."

They hurried away and Vinezi let his brother open the grate in the ground where it rested near the wall. Just beyond were the wharves and below them, access to the water. And the dead fish and hunks of flesh. Within would lie enough bones to add to the suit. "Remember, we spend day and the night if we must; I will have as much bone as possible. It will be considerably diluted in potency."

"Right," Julas said as he stepped down to the first rung.

Vinezi assigned one man to stand watch before following into the darkness.

Soon. Soon. Soon.

CHAPTER 37

Sofia crouched beside Emilio in the undergrowth, Notch close by. Nia had raised her hand yet again, to signal for silence. She knelt behind a pale tree, hands open before her as a small troop of Sap-Born passed on the trail.

As with each time prior, none of the Sap-Born noticed the intruders.

Their luck, or rather, Nia's skill, held.

Sofia brushed a blood-tipped leaf aside and found her feet when Nia rose and signalled for them to continue.

They slipped further into the Bloodwood. This deep, the light struggled to reach the forest floor. The trees were so much taller, so much older than before. Broad trunks dripped bark and the skittering of small feet on branches drifted down from the canopy. In the dim light, the faces of her companions were pale. Or was it simply a sign of weariness?

Only two days from the edge of the Autumn Grove, having given Avaon wide berth, they were closing in on the Summer Groves, which Nia assured them they would reach by nightfall.

No-one spoke until the Butterfly-Eater led them into a deep hollow. A fallen tree, whose trunk stood taller than Emilio, blocked one side of the depression. The floor was sandy, with tufts of grass and smooth stones, as if a pool had once rested there.

"What now?" Notch asked. His face was set in the growing dark, lined with weariness, but his movements were still sharp enough. Was he hiding an injury? He'd been quiet since Emilio arrived.

Nia flung her pack down and removed blankets and travel rations as she spoke. "Now we set watch and sleep. I want to be well-rested by dawn. Especially if I have to sneak you all inside. You need to learn how to move quietly."

Sofia shared a glance with Emilio, who shrugged. "How do we enter? Is the Grove guarded?"

"Patrolled is a better term perhaps." Nia unwrapped hard bread and took a bite. "The Summer Groves have become their own danger. Animals – and people – who get caught in it die. Another reason to wait for dawn, as even touching it can be dangerous, understood?"

Solemn nods.

"The patrols have no set routine and I expect them to be less frequent with so many Sap-Born out for the attack."

"How much time do we have?" Emilio asked.

"We need to enter, find Sofia's father and leave within hours."

"If he's in there, any ideas on where he might be kept?" Notch asked Nia.

"Efran wouldn't hold him anywhere else. The First Tree lies within the grove, the traditional seat of power for the Braonn. The Grove has now become a place where experiments and strange magics occur. He will be there, deep."

"I'll find out. With Argeon," Sofia said, arranging her own blanket. "I can Spirit-Walk before we go in. Narrow the search."

"Thank you, Lady Sofia," Nia said.

Emilio drank from his flask. "And when we have Lord Danillo? Back to the Autumn Grove?"

"Yes. It will not be where it lay before however. I will have to find it."

Notch paused at his pack. "How?"

"Trust me." Nia smiled. "Now get some sleep, all of you. Sofia, you take first watch, then Emilio, Notch and finally me."

"I can go last if you wish," Notch offered.

"Thank you, but I need to prepare."

Notch nodded, his expression curious. He said nothing, only laying on his blanket and closing his eyes.

Sofia sat with her back to the others once she'd finished her cold meal. The rustling and muttering of everyone settling down soon passed. She shifted as the sand hardened beneath her. How was she going to sleep on sand?

Here the Bloodwood was quieter. A breath of wind passed through leaves in the darkness. Time passed with only an ache in her limbs to keep her company. She shifted often. Damn sand.

She rubbed her eyes when Emilio stirred, turning to face him. Was it his turn already?

"Get some rest, lady," he whispered.

"I will." She hesitated. "Emilio?"

"Yes?"

"Thank you for coming after me. Us I mean. I hope Seto didn't force you?"

"No. I volunteered." Was he smiling?

"I'm glad you did."

She tried to stand but could barely move, so stiff were her limbs. She growled, keeping her voice low. No need to wake the others.

"Here." He helped her up. His hand was warm and a shiver ran across her body.

"Thank you."

"Of course." Did he pause a moment before releasing her? No, she'd imagined his grip lingering. Sofia found her blanket before laying down to close her eyes. It took a long time to grow comfortable on the sand, but she lay flat and still and the tension flowed from her limbs when she did.

"Sofia."

A hand rocked her, gently. Notch stood over her in the pre-dawn grey. The hollow was deeply shadowed. Tall trees loomed in black.

"Time already?" Her head had only just hit her cloak, surely?

"It is. Come, you should eat. Emilio and Nia are scouting."

She tried to turn onto her side and swore. Gods damn all sand! Her limbs were frozen. The stiffness was incredible for just one night. Moving her arm sent a series of loud cracks popping along her whole side. More pops and cracks when she stretched her legs, grimacing.

At least the fevers had ceased.

"Are you hurt?" Notch asked.

"Just stiff from the cold, I guess. And the sand." She packed her blanket away, gritting her teeth as she moved, still blinking out of sleep. The longer she worked, the easier it became to move. By the time she stopped to drink from her flask and chew through more trail rations, her limbs were responding properly. The food was tasteless, but fitting. Who wanted rich food right before sneaking into an enemy's lair?

Whatever happened today she would be ready. She shook her head, a rueful smile directed at the shadows. Fear lurked, but not for her life. At least, not the way she'd expected. What she truly feared was seeing Father again. Learning the truth. Gods, what if Tantos hadn't been lying?

Notch readied himself, running a whetstone over his blade. His expression was dark.

"Is something wrong, Notch?"

He shook his head. "Nothing that shouldn't be wrong."

"What do you mean?"

"I'm just thinking about today. Getting rid of some black thoughts."

She nodded. "The odds are against us."

"They are." He stood and now he grinned as he stretched his arms. "But they always are. The trick is to act anyway."

Leaves rustled. Sofia spun, hand on her belt knife, but it was only Emilio. "Our back trail is clear," he announced.

"Good," Notch said, lowering his own blade.

Nia slipped into the hollow on soundless feet. If Sofia hadn't been facing the direction of the Sap Groves she'd not have noticed the woman. Her eyes were bright; hard to believe she'd taken the last watch. "Quickly. A patrol has just passed."

Sofia raised Argeon to her face. The cold bone widened her eyes. She didn't call his attention, instead keeping the dim forest in focus, falling into step behind Nia.

They wove through the sleeping trees in single file,

crossing several paths and pausing often to listen. When Nia led them up a rise, where the trees thinned somewhat, Sofia found herself breathing hard. Was another patrol of Sap-Born close by? Nia motioned for them to lie at the crest, peering over it to look down through the maze of trunks.

In the growing light, she caught glimpses of what appeared to be a crop. Orderly rows of trees and plants – smaller only compared to the giants that surrounded her – revealed the Summer Grove.

"Wait for the light," Nia whispered. "Any moment now."

Sofia held her breath as the sun peered through the trunks. Gold bloomed as light struck the Summer Grove. Small at first, the glow spread like a blanket. The groves covered much more forest than she first thought, stretching to the limits of her vantage point.

The higher the sun rose the more colour it spread – oranges and ambers swallowing the green in the grove and splashing the trunks where they lay.

"How much does it cover?" Sofia finally broke the hush.

"As deep as it is wide," Nia said. "It seems to be expanding more and more, each time I see it."

"When was that?" Notch asked.

"Near to a year."

"Did you go inside?"

She shook her head. "No. Only to watch." Her face, as Notch and Emilio's, was tinted gold – but for Nia it revealed a strange translucence when the light struck her at a certain angle. The Oynbae turned back to the grove and the moment passed. "If I had entered, maybe we'd have been better prepared for the Sap-Born."

"Or maybe you'd have died," Emilio said. "Instead, you help your people now."

"I hope that is true."

The sun had climbed high enough that the grove of sap trees dulled their light to a soft glow. Individual trees were discernible once more.

"I'm ready," Sofia said.

"We will keep watch," Nia replied. "Be swift."

"I will." Sofia drew Argeon to her and showed him a picture of her spirit-walking the groves.

She blinked.

The amber of the Summer Groves surrounded her.

And so did her friends.

She blocked out the twigs beneath her stomach, the smell of earth and decaying leaves, Notch and Emilio talking softly, until it receded to the edge of her awareness.

Only the grove.

At its edge, each sap tree stood in a neat row, surrounded by sturdy square boxes of wood, trunks bulging against some of them. A thick sap ran down each trunk, down each branch. The wooden boxes collected the amber, so that, when she leant over one, she could see it full to the brim.

Other boxes overflowed, trails of heavy sap running down the sides to cross the path. She wove deeper into the grove. Yet other trees were burdened by great bulging discs of amber, or odd shapes, as if generations of sap had grown upon one another. One plant lay buried so deep that only the tips of its tallest branches grew free.

The whole tree, imprisoned by its own sap.

And yet, it's bark appeared robust and the leaves peering through were smooth and green. At the foot of another tree a mouse lay entombed in the sap, its body twisted.

She shuddered. No time for that. Sofia slipped down the row and turned at the first intersection. More golden rows of sap-trees, boxes overflowing. She made two more turns, making a slow path toward what she judged was the centre – before pausing. There had to be a better way.

Why not spirit-walk as she had with the giant bell in the Shrine? Sofia reached for the nearest tree – pushing her hand – which was unresisting. She stepped forward, foot sliding through a box of sap. Another step and she was inside the tree itself, a golden haze surrounding her, before a third step brought her through to the next row.

Faster.

She ran across the row and leapt through the next tree and the next before coming to a halt. Barely two dozen paces away, a single Sap-man stood on tiptoes. He held a red-hot blade in heavy gloves and beside him stood a glowing brazier on wheels. The man sliced through sap that had crossed boxes, preventing the two trees from becoming a joined mess.

Sofia slipped through the next tree. Find Father. Forget this strange place.

Several rows later and she'd mastered the art of the slow exit, so as not to stumble across any more grove-tenders. She kept angling her path toward the centre.

A child and another Sap-Man waited in the next row.

He bent by the tearful boy, speaking softly. "How did you get here, little one?"

The boy sobbed something about being lost.

"It's too dangerous for you in here. I'll take you back."

Follow them.

Sofia kept pace with the two, gliding close to the sap.

Perfect. If they took her directly to the stronghold, she'd find Father in no time. She'd need markers. The mouse was one. But how many rows had she jumped through since the mouse?

And where exactly had Argeon dropped her off?

She faltered and the couple began to pull away. It was a problem for later, for now she just had to find him. She'd remember. She had to. Sofia caught up to the Sapman and his charge, hopping over a flow of amber that crossed the entire path – something the man had lifted the child over.

Shouting.

Someone leapt to their feet beside her, calling her name. Sofia spun, but the row was empty. The man and child were turning a corner. More shouting and the clash of steel.

Wait.

Her body!

Something crashed into her legs and the Sap Grove disappeared.

CHAPTER 38

Sofia sprang to her feet amidst chaos.

Notch and Emilio fought back to back, surrounded by half a dozen Braonn. Nia stood nearby, blowing clouds of powder at a line of Sap-Born, who climbed the hill.

"Get her out of here," Notch shouted, parrying a blow, but Sofia had no idea who he meant.

By the time Nia's powder reached the Sap-Born, it had obviously lessened in potency, as several came on, veins glowing. Hammer-men kept close behind.

Sofia drew in a breath as she spun. "Back." Her voice boomed and the men surrounding Notch and Emilio stumbled. Notch pressed the advantage, cutting an enemy down and kicking another aside. Emilio was just as quick, blade catching the morning light where it whistled through the air.

Nia grabbed her arm. "Lady Sofia. Can you stop them?"

"I don't know."

"You must try."

Sofia clenched her hands into fists. What could she do? Last time, she'd only used – the trees! Maybe she could incorporate what was around her, as before? She showed Argeon an image of a tree thundering down, scattering the approaching line of Sap-Born.

Nothing happened.

"Quickly."

"It's not working," she cried.

Nia leapt into battle as the men crested the rise. She dived and rolled, powdering one man and leaping away from a giant hammer blow. The veins of Sap-Born pulsed. One reached for her, but she swatted his hand away and ducked inside his reach, driving a knife into his stomach.

Yellow blood flowed as he crumpled.

Sofia drew her knife as Nia sprang away, herding her back. Notch swore from behind them but she didn't take her eyes off the Sap-Born. Why wouldn't Argeon help?

"Stay low," Nia whispered. "If I survive, wrap me in a blanket. All of me – do you understand?" Sofia nodded, but her pulse had doubled. What did Nia mean? The men had surrounded them now, cutting them from the other struggle. Was Emilio safe? She squeezed the handle of her blade.

Nia threw off her jacket and kicked her boots free. The Sap-Born paused, confusion plain on their faces.

"What are you doing?" Sofia hissed.

Nia gave a cry of fury and pain.

Her body changed.

It began to elongate. She spread her arms and they formed pink wings, pant legs tearing as her calves became the bottom halves of her wings – a soft purple. Her under garments ripped as her torso grew larger then slender, her face slipping into an insect-like dot.

"By the Gods," Sofia breathed.

She was a butterfly.

Nia brought her wings together and a wind stirred the leaves. She flapped again and this time, a cloud of powder flew forth. Sofia fell back, shielding her face as the cloud, tinted pink and purple, enveloped the Sap-Born. They cried out, only for choking sounds to follow.

Bodies thumped to the ground.

Nia's wings beat once more and then she collapsed. Sofia coughed, waving at lingering traces of powder as she crawled forward. Nia's wings were near-translucent and her chest barely moved. Her body began to shrink, colours changing until a pale, half-naked woman lay in the rags of her clothing.

Sofia spun. "Notch? Emilio?"

Emilio groaned from where he lay on the ground, bleeding from a gash in his forehead, surrounded by bodies in green. Only four. Where were the others? Notch was no-where to be seen. Sofia dashed across the spur.

"Emilio." She shook his shoulder and his eyes fluttered but he did not wake.

Stupid. Nia first. What had she said? A blanket. Sofia tore through her bag and found a blanket. She wrapped Nia's lower half – even the woman's legs looked see-through – and found a second and third blanket, covering torso and head. She kept the head looser than the others. Hopefully it was the right thing to do.

How long before Nia recovered? Would she recover? Sofia checked each body on the rise. None lived. One man's neck had been cut so deep that the black hole of his throat lay exposed. She turned away. It wouldn't be long before others came to investigate – and where was Notch? The Sap-Born and their Hammer-slaves were all deathly pale, skin coated in powder. Sofia didn't touch it.

She returned to Emilio with water and cleaned his cut. It was not deep. Some tightness in her chest eased.

He had to wake, but shaking him or hissing his name did nothing. Sofia sat back on her heels and stopped – fool! She removed a pale blue vial from her linfa-belt, uncorked it and held it beneath Emilio's nose.

His eyes rolled and he flinched. She replaced the vial as he rose to his arms, coughing. "Sofia?"

"I'm here."

He surveyed the clearing with a frown, fingertips massaging his temples. "Then they took him." He accepted her help to stand. "Where's Nia?"

"There. I think she'll survive. What do you mean? What happened to Notch?"

"When the Braonn saw Nia transform, they changed tactic." He turned to search the ground, hand closing over a yellow pod and raising it. "One of them dropped me with a sling as the other two grabbed Notch."

"Then they wanted a prisoner?"

"It seems so."

"We have to find him, Emilio."

"I know. He'll be in the same place as your father, no doubt."

"I hope so." They needed somewhere to hide and recover. More than that, they needed Nia. "Let's take her to the hollow."

Emilio winced as he bent down, but scooped the blanketed Nia up. Sofia grabbed Nia's pack and added it to her own, before leading him back to the hollow, where she crept to the log, putting her eye against a gap where the wood had began to rot. No-one had followed.

"We'll have to move soon," Emilio said.

Sofia didn't turn from their back trail. "I'll find a place."

Becoming two Sofia's again, her spirit-form ranged out from the hollow while her body stayed put. The forest was still quiet as she passed through trunks and over trails, speeding away from the hollow. A stream trickled through stones and she paused. A narrow opening, a cave? She glided in as far as the light penetrated. Empty and dry. And far enough from the hollow to be safe. If only temporarily.

She closed her eyes and when she opened them, her mask rested against the bark.

"Anything?" Emilio carried Nia.

"A cave. It's some distance away but I doubt we can stay there forever."

"Hopefully until Nia wakes."

Heading through the forest a second time, her feet were calamitous compared to her spirit-walk. Emilio, burdened as he was, fared little better, but no-one appeared to stop them. At the stream, she paused to check their backtrail. A crushed plant, heavy footprints in the leaves. How obvious was it that they'd been this way?

She brushed out their tracks as best she could while Emilio attended to Nia.

He looked up when Sofia returned. "Should we unwrap her?"

Sofia knelt beside him. "I don't know. She didn't say how long for."

"Then we'd better leave her."

She nodded slowly. "How about we eat something?"

Emilio began unpacking the trail rations. He handed her a flask and she accepted it with a skip of her heart.

Alone.

With Emilio. In the cave, the quiet grew. Outside, a single bird chirped as a soft rain dripped from the leaves. She focused on her food. He was so close, their knees near to touching. The only men she'd spent time alone with were family or Lords. Or Notch. And Notch wasn't like Emilio – he was more like Father.

What a time to worry about such things.

"Ah, Emilio." Why couldn't she meet his eyes? She'd seen him glancing at her often, and once, when she caught him, he looked away. If she stayed so near any longer, she'd end up saying or doing something foolish and he'd surely think less of her. "I'm going to do some scouting, can you watch over my body while I do? And tell me if Nia wakes?"

"Of course, it would be my pleasure to watch your body," Emilio said, then flushed. He leapt up, spilling his food. "I apologise, My Lady. I meant only that I would keep you safe."

Sofia gaped a moment, then burst into laughter.

Eventually Emilio laughed too, his deep voice filling the cave. "I'm sorry, My Lady."

She smiled. "Don't be. I'll be back soon."

She called Argeon. Her spirit climbed to its feet and she slipped from the cave mouth, feet making no splash in the stream. She roamed the area around the cave, flitting from tree to tree. No patrols crossed her path, nor did she see anyone in the distance, even gliding back toward the hollow. The bodies had not moved and down in the Grove there was activity, but none of it headed her way. Yet.

But down there somewhere was Father. And now Notch too.

Alive. Both of them. They had to be.

If she could just find them.

CHAPTER 39

The last of the winter sun warmed Notch's face but crisp air stung a cut in his thigh and his head throbbed. Both wrists and ankles burned, ropes straining against them from where he hung – tied to a tree.

Or, what used to be a tree. It was more a massive trunk, far, far greater than anything he'd ever seen. When he twisted his neck, the blackened edge of the tree filled his vision and there was no hint of foliage or branches above. The scent of burnt bark grew strong whenever he shifted, rubbing the charcoal.

The trunk rested in the centre of a fire-blasted square. Blackened stone ringed him, beyond which were yards of stunted, charcoaled trees and heaps of smouldering branches, red embers deep inside. Even the earth was churned and ash-choked in the evening light. A muted glow came from beyond the dead forest; the amber of the Summer Groves.

Two figures approached, one significantly taller than the other.

Efran and Mor.

Both wore forest greens, though Efran's sleeves were rolled up, freeing the glow of his veins. Mor's face was closed as the two came to a halt. Both men were armed, though Efran but lightly, compared to Mor's bow, knives and hand axe hanging from his belt.

Notch stared at them.

Efran snorted. "So, Anaskari. You are captured."

Notch said nothing. Proof that he was useless to Sofia. Some Protector, Notch. At least she had Emilio and Nia – assuming they'd survived the attack.

"And your friends slink around my forest. Tell me why you risk your lives – your Greatmasks, on a single man?"

Tension eased; they were alive. Thank the Gods. "Then Danillo is alive?"

"For now."

Good. The search and journey weren't for nothing. "You won't have them. Sofia will kill you first."

"Possibly." He drew his knife and slapped the pommel into his palm. "Unless I threaten to kill you first? Or better, if I offer to kill Danillo? That will stay her hand."

"Then all three of us will be dead. Mor there too, probably." Notch grimaced. His bodyweight pulled against the bindings, rubbing raw skin.

Mor folded his arms but Efran only smiled. "You are confident."

"If you'd seen what she did to your people in the Autumn Grove, you'd know why."

The smile fell. "What does that mean?"

Notch gestured to his surroundings with his chin. "When we left, they looked a lot like this place, actually."

Efran narrowed his eyes then conferred with Mor a moment. The blond man jogged away, leaving Efran. His boots crunched char as he drew closer, head level with Notch's chest.

He looked up. "How useful do you think you are, soldier?"

Again, Notch gave no reply.

"For if I believe you are useful, you live. If not, you die – after watching Sofia and the others die first. At this moment, you are bait. But I have two portions of bait – I will not need both forever." His arm snapped forward.

A flash of pain and Notch shouted.

The blade protruded from his thigh, blood streaming down his leg. Efran stepped back. "When I return, let's talk about something useful – like your city and your King."

The man strode off without retrieving the weapon.

Notch growled at Efran's back and thumped his own head into the wood. His leg throbbed, the pain hot. "Gods be damned."

It was dark before they returned, torches in hand. As before, only Efran and Mor stood before him. Efran carried a flask of water. Notch traced its movement. He'd dozed, a fitful sleep of exhaustion and pain. The more he dozed, the duller it became.

But now, throat dry and lips cracked, all he could see was that flask in the mongrel's hand. The blade in his leg was a bearable pain, but it was still pain.

"To business then, Captain," Efran said.

"Captain?" Notch rasped.

"Yes. I know it all, Notch. Captain Medoro, hero of the Glass War. Spurned by the palace after saving his King. I can imagine how the nobles delighted in turning on a young man from a mere mountain family, all those years ago."

"I'm hardly old."

Efran laughed. "Your grasp of the important things impresses me. Now, time to demonstrate your usefulness. First question. Where can Anaskar be accessed, aside from the Main and Mountain Gates, the breech and the tunnel beneath the King's Hideaway?"

Notch said nothing.

"Let me warn you. Silence is not an option. I will either assume you don't know – which will be unpleasant for you, or I will assume you are unwilling to answer. Also unpleasant for you."

"I've never had to sneak in to Anaskar." He paused. Talking, even swallowing hurt. "Like a coward."

Efran ripped the knife free.

Notch screamed.

"Better." He tossed the blade to the ground. "Second question. Where can a Captain move about unchallenged?"

More blood trailed down his trembling leg, dripping to the stones. "Water," he croaked.

Efran tossed the flask to Mor, who stretched up, allowing Notch to drink just enough to speak. "Well?"

"These questions," Notch said. "You don't need me for them."

"Answer."

"All Tiers. Within the Palace – not the King's quarters."

He gestured. "Give him another drink, Mor."

Again, the tall man stretched to allow him more water.

"Third question. When can a Captain of the Shield contradict an order from the Mascare?"

What was the man after? Sending an imposter into the palace – as an assassin? Why else all the questions on rankings and movements?

Efran drew a new, thinner blade. "You now have a time limit. Answer swiftly now, or I choose another portion of your body to open."

Notch ground his teeth. "In battle perhaps."

"And a Captain of the King's Honour Guard?"

"Possibly. But no-one in the palace will buy an imposter."

Efran grinned. "Question four. You know the new King well. You've worked with him for years. You know his habits, routines and vulnerabilities. How often does he visit the Queen's Harper?"

"I have no idea, now that he's King." Seto would still be making regular visits, he wouldn't be able to help himself. But Efran could go to the depths of the ocean before Notch gave that information away.

"Notch." Efran shook his head. "Better on the timeliness of your response. But I suspect you're lying."

Notch would have shrugged. How did the bastard know?

"Does he enter the inn via the underground?"

"I've never needed to ask."

Efran's veins pulsed. "And there is the lie."

Notch set his jaw. The other questions must have been to gauge his answers, to provide a base for his truthfulness. Somehow Efran had read him. Yet Notch hadn't changed expression or tone.

No more answers then.

Mor started to walk off at a nod from Efran. "You have more to tell. Good. Since I plan to remain clean, I have sent Mor to collect someone you didn't have the pleasure of meeting the last time you were my prisoner."

"Send my apologies."

Efran chuckled. "Your Lord Protector was spirited too, as I recall."

"Where is he, Efran?"

The man strolled off. "We'll talk again soon."

Notch shifted his weight but it was useless. A slightly different patch of skin began to burn. His stomach was burning too – hunger, for now. Cramps would follow soon enough. And who knew what Efran's torturer was capable of.

The muscles in his thigh throbbed.

He'd faced blades and embers before – scars on the soles of his feet were testament to the beginning of what would have been his last night, had Luik not found him. Stumbling out of the blood-soaked battlefields and collapsing in the waste, after saving Otonos, he'd been easy prey for the Medah.

Notch dozed and shivered.

Again, a fitful time of darkness, aches and burning passed. The scent of charred wood was heavy. At one point, he flinched from light, convinced dawn had already come. But it was only a torch, held close to his face. Black shapes conversed beyond but their words were distant. Muffled. The light passed and he slept again, despite the pain of slumping against the rope.

He jerked awake as something cold splashed over him.

Day had come.

A storm built overhead, its black clouds lurking and a wind stirring ashes in the blasted square.

Efran, Mor and a third man watched him splutter and blink. He licked his lips, savouring the water that dripped from his face. The newest of his interrogators stood closest. The thin man held a glowing knife in a gloved hand. A red-hot brazier rested at his side and beside that in turn, waited a bucket of amber liquid. Sap.

The torturer had a dispassionate expression and wore a collar of amber around his neck. He sliced Notch's pant leg at the shin. Notch flinched as the hot metal burnt his flesh, and this time none of Nia's powder to help.

"Biragn is a patient man, Notch," Efran said. "Don't

feel like you have to give up everything at once."

Notch spat at him, but with so little moisture in his mouth, it wasn't much.

"And save your spit."

Distant thunder boomed. Biragn put his knife into the bucket and drew out a thick glob of sap. It steamed in the cool air and when he applied it to Notch's leg it seared through flesh. Notch screamed again, breathing hard as he strained to break free. His leg had been transformed into a molten stump, or so it felt. The burning wormed into his flesh and he strained to kick.

The torturer stepped back, allowing Efran to move closer. Mor stood by, a satisfied expression on his face.

"Again, Notch. Swiftly and the truth."

"Good idea. You don't have much time left." He was already sweating. And bluffing. If Sofia had been able to rescue him, it would have happened by now. Something must have gone wrong.

"First question. Are there any passages leading from the basement of the Queen's Harper?"

"Gods take you."

Efran flicked a finger to Biragn and spoke softly in Braonn. Notch picked up the word 'more.'

The man spread another scalding line of amber onto the knife, but Efran shook his head. The torturer doubled the amount, said something to Efran, who once again shook his head.

This time Notch bit through his lip with a scream, metallic blood spraying from his mouth as the thick strip of fire ate through his flesh and grazed bone.

Biragn dipped his blade again, hovering it near the knife-wound Efran had already inflicted, but the leader called a halt as lightning flickered on the horizon. "Not just yet. Let's try again. The basement, Notch."

Notch's vision swam and his chest worked hard as he clung to consciousness. He held on, struggling with his bindings. If he could just break free and get his hands around the man's neck. Or get a hold of Biragn's knife.

A Sap-Born ran into view, coming to a halt before Efran. The man's face was pale with shock and he rushed his words, pointing back at the groves. Notch only caught one word.

Dying.

Who was dying?

Efran demanded more information as Mor started forward. The scout replied, voice still hushed, and Efran finally swore. The man spat orders in Braonn and Mor sprinted into the grove with the scout.

Biragn raised an eyebrow but didn't lower his bucket. He simply waited.

Efran nodded to the torturer before following.

Notch faced Biragn. Still the man's expression had not changed. He raised another line of sap, bringing it to hover over the open wound on his leg.

Notch strained all his limbs.

Rope snapped.

His leg shot forward, driving the blade into Biragn's face.

The man screeched as he fell back, clutching his face. Burning skin hissed and the knife clattered to stone. His fumbling feet knocked the bucket down and he fell, white-hot embers tumbling over his legs. The man quickly grew still, the hiss of burning flesh continuing.

Notch smothered his own cry. Jerking his leg forward had shot pain along his whole body. But how had it come free? He craned his neck into a shoulder. There. The sap.

Biragn had put extra on the blade. The excess must have slid down his leg and seared through some of the ropes. He strained against his other bonds but they were too tight. Even when a black rain began to fall, soaking him, he couldn't free any more limbs.

Trapped.

How long before Efran returned?

CHAPTER 40

Flir let a sigh escape. Two days had passed already – all of it fruitless searching, even with Ain's skill at finding old paths. Still not a single step closer to finding Vinezi's trail. She watched Bel's mother, who stood at the kitchen stove, stirring a broth, one hand on the ladle, the other on Alfeo's head where he sat beside her on a stool.

At least here, in the Lower Tier, she could achieve something useful.

"I said it doesn't matter no more, Lady."

Flir frowned. "You don't want me to find her?"

Alfeo shook his head. "It's all right-is, Lady Flir. We've seen her."

"You did?"

His mother nodded. She raised the ladle to taste the stew. "We have. She sent someone to find us and we went to the harbour-is and there she was."

"The harbour? I don't understand. Is she well?"

The older woman gave an odd smile – touched with resignation. And maybe relief too. "Well enough. I'm just happy that she's alive-is."

Alfeo leapt up. "We can go see her, if you like? She stays at the harbour."

"I'd like that," Flir said.

Alfeo led her through the Lower Tier in the morning sun, detouring smoking ruins and barricades lined with stony-faced Shield and Vigil, and down to the Harbour Gate, one side of which remained closed. The Shield once again lined a barricade. A long line of merchants, carts and caravans muttered as they waited beneath the overcast sky, their goods carefully inspected. Flir made to approach the Captain, but Alfeo waved her to a side street.

"Not that way."

He took her to one of the many deep grates, where floodwater would fall down the shaft to eventually escape back to the sea. Alfeo lifted, thin arms straining. He pointed to the ladder rungs. "You don't have to wait as long if we go this way."

"Your mother went down there?"

"She usually waits at the gate-is," he said, a foot on the first rung. "Come on."

Flir followed him down, rungs clammy beneath her palms. "Where does it lead? Is Bel living underground?"

"Not really. It's easier if you just see her. I think someone cut a hole in the stones down here. The tunnel goes to a hole in the big wall-is. A bit like the one the Storm Singer comes out of." He paused. "Here we go."

Flir waited as he swung into a black opening. Was this an entry point for Vinezi perhaps? Impossible to know, but it bore watching. Once Alfeo was clear, she followed. Just what had happened to Bel? The tunnel was dark but a point of light remained visible in the distance. Her boots kicked something soft as she walked. A little way along, Alfeo's steps paused. In the dim light, she saw him turn, stepping through the wall into a second passage. "Watch the step," he said.

A new passage. And much larger by the echo of her voice. "How long have you known about this tunnel, Alfeo?"

"Only a little while-is. We used to use it for fishing at night."

The light grew and Flir squinted. Alfeo stopped at a grated opening, bending down to collect something. Over his back, she saw the grey water of the harbour stretching. She crept forward, peering through the rusted steel.

To her left and above, rose the sheer face of the city walls, coated with grime, and further along, the edge of the wharves, ships at dock, gulls circling. The water was half a dozen feet below, splashing against the stone. Maybe it was an old escape tunnel? She wondered where the second passage originally started. Probably the First Tier. An old passage for the first Kings, back when the Medah attacked frequently?

Alfeo dropped something into the water with a plop. "What was that?"

"A rock. I keep them here now. She'll hear it and come."

"She? What do you mean?"

He pointed to the water. "Oh good. She must have been close by."

A shape moved beneath the surface, moving swiftly up toward them.

Bel's face broke the surface and she smiled as she waved up at them. "Alfeo. And Lady Flir."

Flir's mouth hung open.

Alfeo bent down, lying on the edge of the tunnel. His

head and shoulders squeezed through the gaps in the grate; something Flir wouldn't have been able to manage, not being a child. "How are you feeling, Bel?"

"Wonderful – and there are more of us now."

"That's great!"

"Isn't it? Is Mother well?"

Flir still hadn't closed her mouth. Bel leant back and a slender blue tail with glistening scales flicked water up at them. "Lady, are you all right?"

"I guess I am. What happened?"

Bel shrugged. "That nice song made me feel better-is but it didn't stop what was happening. Maybe it even made things go quicker. I could feel my body trying to change...so I ran away, I didn't want anyone to see. I'm sorry, I hope you weren't all upset."

"We were worried."

"Well, I'm fine now. I love it beneath the sea."

"That's good to know, Bel." Flir glanced at Alfeo's smiling face then back to Bel. "How did you get down here?"

"I'm not sure-is. I just seemed to know where to go, how to get to water."

Alfeo nodded. "And she can swim everywhere now, even underwater. For days and days-is."

Bel laughed. "Maybe not that long."

Another shape grew beside her, then a man broke the surface. He narrowed his eyes as he treaded water. His long hair was plastered to his head and bare shoulders like a dark river. "Bel, this is dangerous." He glared up at them. "Who are you?"

Bel put a hand on his shoulder. "Sanac, it's safe. This is my brother Alfeo and Lady Flir. She saved my life."

The man's expression eased somewhat. "Greetings to

you both."

"Sanac is our leader," Bel said.

"Leader?"

"Of the Sea-People," the man said. He sighed. "I doubt you'd realise this, but ever since the Beast infected the city, people have been changing. Many hid in shame or fear at their changed appearance, and just as many died. Those that made it to the water stay here. And recently, there are those like Bel and I," a fiery red tail broke the surface, "whose transition was made easy and even beautiful, we suspect, by the Storm Singer's song."

"Are there many of you?" Flir asked.

Alfeo leant closer. "Yeah, like, a whole army-is?"

Sanac chuckled. "No. Perhaps a hundred of us. Much less can swim as swiftly as Bel and I, however." A commotion erupted on the wharf. Sanac lowered himself in the water, until only his head was showing. "We should leave."

"All right." Bel smiled up at them one more time. "Come and see me again soon, Alfeo. And you too, My Lady."

Then the two slipped beneath the water.

Alfeo beamed as he stood. "See, she's fine."

"So she is," Flir said, following him into the dark of the tunnel. Just how powerful were the remnants of the Sea Beast?

*

A messenger waited for her at Holindo's staging area, where the colossal shadow of the Sea Beast had finally dwindled down to something that looked manageable. Like a regular whale or two, perhaps.

Seto wanted her and Luik at the palace. At once.

"Lord Luik has already left, My Lady." The messenger gestured to a carriage. "Please, allow me to convey you there."

Something was wrong. Or maybe, for a change, something had gone well. Who knew? At least Bel really did seem happy. Flir hopped into the carriage.

Pevin occupied a seat across from her, face serene. "Dilar."

"Not now, Pevin."

"You seem agitated."

She shrugged. "No more than usual."

"Can I help?"

"Not really." She put a foot up on the seat across from her, resting it beside Pevin. "Tell me, what are you going to do during the invasion, if things don't go well for us?"

He blinked. "Stay with you of course."

"And if I die?"

Now he smiled. "Impossible."

"Do you think so?"

"Mishalar will protect you."

"And you? Will she protect you from the acor?"

"I don't know." He paused. "And as for your hypothetical question, I would seek to avenge your passing."

"You'd kill your countrymen?" She knew the answer but getting a rise out of him would pass some time at least.

"As would you."

"Truly, Pevin?"

"I don't think you understand the extent of my devotion, still."

She glanced out the window, the dark, cold stone

of homes passing. Only she did understand. A young woman back home showed Flir just how deadly such devotion could be – deadly for the poor fool who bought the lie. "I know it too well, Pevin." She met his eyes. "And I hate it."

"It is wondrous, My Lady, for now I –"

"Enough," she snapped.

He fell silent. The rest of the ride passed in silence too, as the carriage bumped its way back to the palace.

She left Pevin outside, as had become customary, and banished frustration with a shake of her head. Or tried to.

Seto waited in his sitting room, pacing. Wayrn stood at the door, his face weary. She greeted him and he smiled. How long had he been under the city now? Hopefully he'd found something. Luik sat in a chair, toying with the handle of his mace. The two Medah were also present. Ain, the young one, still couldn't keep a frown from his face whenever he looked at her. She grinned back. Good, someone who didn't worship her.

"Excellent," Seto said. "You are about to take a little trip."

"Are we?"

"Most of you at least."

"But not you?"

Seto glowered. "I will stay here and see to the defence of the city, among other things. My minders would certainly fall to pieces if I were to actually do something dangerous."

Flir chuckled.

"I'm glad you're amused, Flir." He gestured to the Pathfinder. "Now. Ain has found something. Prepare for what might be a long trip."

"Vinezi?"

Ain replied in his own tongue and Wayrn translated. "There is an ancient path...unused up until recently. It's actually within the Tier wall." Wayrn said. He listened a moment, then summarised. "Ain says he can feel it moving into the mountain but there seems to be no way to access it from the palace grounds."

"Which is where you come in, my dear. If there's no door, I want you to break into the passage. Just don't knock the whole wall down."

Flir laughed. "I'll try."

"Go on then, get to work." He waved his arms as he stood and the group started to file out. Flir shared a look with Luik, who nodded as he left. She paused at the door.

"Seto?"

He turned from the fireplace. "Questions, Flir?"

"Yes. Why aren't you coming with us truly?"

"A question I've asked myself. Tell me, Flir. What would happen if I, as King, were to die?"

"A new King would take your place."

"Not so. The remaining houses would bicker and fight. In their childishness, instead of preparing to repel an invasion, they would doom the city." He paused. "And this is my city now, Flir. I won't have that."

She spread her hands. "Of course. But that's always true. What if you fall down a staircase tonight and break your neck? Same result."

He laughed. "Well said."

"I mean it, Seto. What are you worried about? Why are you letting the nobles push you around?"

Seto sighed. "Flir, you need to go and help Luik and Wayrn."

She folded her arms. "Answer me first."

"Very well." His eyebrows drew together. "No-one has ever pushed me where I do not wish to go. But I am one man only. And not even a young man, we would agree. Yet how many roles do I fill? How many threads need my hand to weave them? How many lives depend upon me? Thousands and thousands and thousands. And how many hours in a single day? How far can I walk each day, how much can I carry? How many decisions need I make – like this one here and now."

She waited.

"I need to stay here and prepare for the attack. To protect my people."

"You have generals for that."

He produced Chelona from his robe. "But only one person for this."

"You're staying back to play with a mask?"

"Gods, Flir!" he shouted. His chest heaved. "There is no 'play' here. This mask, if I can finally learn its use, could save every single life in the city. It is that powerful." He shoved a chair aside, waving his hands. "Have you suddenly become so dense as to forget that?"

He was right. She studied her feet a moment. Mishalar, damn it, he was right as usual. "I'm sorry."

Seto exhaled slowly. "Just do as I say for once, without argument. Find that bastard for me and do it quickly. I want you to return in time for the attack."

"I swear it."

"Oh, and leave Pevin with me. I have a task for him."

"Gladly. What task?"

"Helping your countrymen."

She gave him a look. "That doesn't make sense."

"Those already living in or visiting the city. They're being protected and I want him to help Ambassador

Lallor manage them."

"You mean spy on them and the ambassador."

"The thought crossed my mind, though I suspect Lallor is honest. But who knows what other unsavoury types might have slipped through the net?"

"Other than Vinezi."

He gave her a look that suggested his humour was running dry. "Indeed."

"You trust Pevin for that?"

"As long as you tell him to help me, yes. I can read Pevin if he tries to lie." He waved a hand. "Which I doubt he will."

"He's all yours then."

CHAPTER 41

"Is everything well?" Wayrn asked when she arrived.

The small group stood before a section of the First Tier's wall, close to where it met the face of the mountain. The open lawn had been dug several feet down to reveal a familiar pattern on a stone slab – that of the Mask. A variety of heavy tools had been stacked against the wall.

"Seto had some more instructions," she said.

"Well, here's the opening." He untangled an arm from his cloak, caught by a gust of wind.

"Who dug the symbol free?"

"We did."

"So the earth was undisturbed when Ain found the path?"

"Yes." Wayrn held up a hand. "I know what you're going to say next. That if there was a door here and they used it, how did it open? Wouldn't it have disturbed the earth in some way?"

"Right."

"We've thought of that. It's simple. Ain?"

Ain answered, pointing and spreading his hands in a variety of directions. Once his hands fell still he continued.

"What's he saying?" Luik asked.

Wayrn waited for the Medah to finish. "He says that the path leads to each Tier and extends along more than one wall. Sometimes – no, twice only – it dips into the aqueducts below. Vinezi could have exited at any other point than here. If the man actually came this way."

"Well, let's open it up anyway."

Ain spoke again, miming the turning of a key. Was there frustration in his voice? She waited for Wayrn.

"He said there was a keyhole in the wall when he went up to the Shrine."

Luik knelt and examined the wall, Wayrn helping him. She waited. Nothing. Flir rolled her shoulders. It was going to be up to her; it usually was. She strode to the wall and hefted a hammer and a huge bolt with a wedge end. "Don't worry about that, boys."

They backed away.

Flir twirled the bolt, spinning it around her wrist. Wayrn whistled. She moved down the wall several feet and set the bolt between stones. She tapped it with the hammer. Stone cracked but the bolt stayed in place. She stepped back to get a good swing.

"Am I in line with the door?"

Ain answered.

"He doesn't know," Wayrn said.

"Oh well." She swung. Stone cracked and she swung again, driving the bolt deeper. Next, she drew the hammer back behind her head and rained down a blow that bent the bolt and shattered stone.

"There's a hole," Luik said.

"Good." She swung again, this time aiming for the stone beside the round opening left by the bolt. More shattered fragments littered the ground and she stepped in to rip out a few more blocks. The wall was several layers deep. The more she tore, the bigger the dark opening became.

Flir kicked one more stone in and stood back. "There."

"Impressive as ever," Wayrn said.

"Can't say I'm impressed – I'm getting sick of tunnels and passages."

"When you put it like that, me too," he said.

Luik hefted a pack onto his shoulder and peeked inside. "Door would have opened inward."

"Good to know," Flir said.

He grunted. "Which way first then? Down into the city?"

Flir shook her head. "Into the mountain I think."

"I agree," Wayrn said. "They haven't been seen in the city since the attack. They're hiding, surely?"

"Torches?" Luik handed unlit brands to each member of the party. Within the passage and out of the wind, they lit the torches and started toward the wall. Flir led, torch high. The passage allowed room for several abreast; at least it wasn't cramped. The stonework on the floor and the walls were a match for anything within the palace when it came to craftsmanship.

A set of stairs met them at the point where she judged the wall came up against the Celnos Mountains that flanked the city.

The steps rose up into the black.

Flir sighed as she climbed.

Two landings later and she called a halt. "I need a drink." She uncorked her flask and drank while the others took out their own flasks. Wayrn chomped on a hard biscuit. Ain simply stood and stared after drinking his water and Luik counted torches.

"How many left?" she asked him.

"Enough."

He scratched his neck. "Surprised no-one seems to know about this passage."

"Vinezi must have," Flir replied. She pointed to footprints – many, moving through the dust before them. "Someone's been here recently."

They continued on. Hours passed in the heavy quiet beneath the mountain and new torches were lit. Her calves ached and someone behind her breathed hard. Ain? How much longer would the stair last? Did they have to travel to the top of the mountain?

Finally the stairs opened onto a wide landing. Flir dumped her pack and crossed the dusty floor. Three openings stood at the opposite end of the room. Two were stairs. One set led down, one up and the middle opening continued on a level surface. Mishala, let the path run straight.

"Look here," Wayrn called.

Flir joined the others. Wayrn crouched by a smooth indentation in the stone wall. Tall enough for a man to stand in, it appeared people entered by placing their back to the wall and resting both arms at their sides, with palms open.

Set deep in the points for hand and head were tube-like openings ringed by silver.

Wayrn ran his hand across them. "Flush against the stone. What are they for?"

"Here's another," Luik said.

This one was smaller – set for a woman perhaps. Flir shrugged. "They're strange but I don't think they'll help us."

Wayrn nodded, regret on his face as he joined her in the centre of the room.

"Where to now, Ain?" she asked.

The Medah still glared at her but replied once Wayrn translated. He listened for the answer. "Ain says up. The path down is weakest but the path leading up has been used most recently."

"Of course." Flir thanked the man, who shrugged, and led them higher. By the next landing, one of regular size, she stopped to eat. "It must be noon by now."

"Ah, how far are we going to follow this path?" Wayrn asked.

"Seto only said to be back in time for the invasion," Flir said. "Though he calls it an 'attack' now too."

"That matter? You were suspicious of it yourself at first."

She shrugged. "Maybe I'm just expecting the worst. Ten ships might just be front runners."

"Well, I've packed for a long trip," he said.

Wayrn translated for Ain, who gave a short nod then moved off to sit against a wall, eating his rations.

Flir gestured with her thumb. "Is he angry with all of us or just me?"

"I don't know. He seems lonely."

"Makes sense." Flir took another drink. A familiar feeling. Even now, years after befriending Notch, Luik and Seto, after fighting alongside dozens and dozens of mercenaries, there were still moments when the great white and blue expanse of Renovar called. The crunch of snow or the impossibly clear ice-melt streams.

"Anyone hear that?" Luik lowered his own flask.

The crackle of torches and chewing from Ain filled the room. Flir motioned for him to be quiet, which he did. Nothing.

Luik stood. "A faint echo from above."

Flir walked to the steps and waited. "I don't hear anything, Luik."

"Must have imagined it," he said, but he was frowning.

"Let's keep going anyway. We'll run out of torches eventually and we still have to get back down," she said. "Keep an ear out too."

By the next landing Flir would have been happy to never see another step again. Similar to the last stopping point, strange indentations sat in the walls but only two passages led on. And both of them blocked by serious-looking doors, both tall, one of silver and one black. Onyx perhaps. Each had familiar Masks carved in the centre – actual bone set in the door. Either mask, had it rested on the ground, would have stood taller than Flir.

The Mask on the black door was carved in a frown. Just like Tantos' imposters. Coincidence?

Ain and Wayrn conferred and Flir moved closer. Runes were marked beneath both masks and neither possessed a handle. "Wayrn, can you read these?"

He examined the runes. "No...they seem to have some basic similarities with modern Anaskari writing, but I can't be sure." He handed his torch over and rummaged through his pack until he found a stub of charcoal and a sheet of parchment. "The mask's expression seems pretty clear," he said, copying the runes.

"It does." Flir lifted one of her torches closer for him. "Do you carry that around everywhere you go, Wayrn?"

"Only if I think I'll need it."

"And what does Ain say about the trail?"

Luik finished with the body and joined them.

"That the older path is beyond the silver door."

"And the black one?"

"The newer path goes down there, but it is strange.

I don't quite understand him, but he's not comfortable. He keeps mentioning something about the path 'faltering' but as to exactly what that means, he's not sure. He's certain that down is the most recent." Wayrn finished up and took his torch back. "Will it open?"

Flir stepped over and gave the black door a push. It swung open on silent hinges. Steps led down to darkness. She turned to Wayrn. "Ask Ain if both paths lead to the same place."

Wayrn asked and Ain shook his head. His eyes were a little wide and he seemed to be repeating something beneath his breath.

"We've come this far," Flir said.

Luik shrugged. "Still have plenty of light for now."

Wayrn spoke to Ain, who gave a short response that sounded vaguely affirmative to Flir.

Flir drew her sword. "Weapons ready, all right?"

The rasp of steel answered and she took the first step.

CHAPTER 42

Flir led them down the winding stairwell. Ain and Wayrn brought up the rear, the Pathfinder muttering quietly, but she let him go. It hurt no-one and besides, she was ready for whatever might wait below.

A broad stair, with room for three abreast, the stone beneath her boots was rife with footprints.

She gestured. "That's a lot of traffic."

Luik nodded. "There's something down here he wants."

"This must be why you couldn't find him beneath the city," she called softly to Wayrn.

"Not from lack of trying. I even chased down a Scrapper, you know. Tira and Areth he was filthy."

Flir was glad he couldn't see her smile.

The stair wound on. Once Ain slipped, but caught himself. He stopped muttering then, and it wasn't until they reached another landing and a similar door to the first, that anyone spoke.

"No mask this time," Luik said.

The onyx door was unlocked and beyond, a long

passage lined with stone columns was revealed in the torchlight. Carved into the columns were masks, each with a different emotion. Some barely looked human. Of the closest, one possessed a sharp nose, another wide-set eyes – too wide to be human. Flir didn't step inside, instead pointing.

"Look."

From the opposite end of the corridor came a faint yellow glow.

"Then we're about to meet Vinezi again," Luik said.

"Let's hope so." Flir moved quietly, but set a steady pace. If Vinezi was down here, he was about to get a nasty surprise.

"Wait," Wayrn hissed. He waved his arm. Luik stood across the corridor, peering between the columns. She joined Wayrn. "Another door," he said.

"Over here," Luik said.

Ain spoke softly and Wayrn translated. "The path goes toward the light."

"Which is where we'll go after we check this door. Open it," Flir said.

Wayrn pushed, then stepped inside, torch first. Flir was on his heels. Beyond lay a wide room lined with floor-to-ceiling shelves. A small chair and table sat in the middle. Each shelf contained a small barrel. They must have numbered in the hundreds.

"What's inside?"

Wayrn took a barrel down and pried open the lid with his blade. Inside rested a fine powder. "It's dust," he said. He ran it between thumb and forefinger. "Hmmm. It's very fine. Not acor at least."

Flir waved her blade. "Well, put it back. That's not what we're here for."

He did so, pausing. "Some are missing. It looks like they've been moved recently."

"We'll solve that little mystery another time."

Outside, she shook her head at Luik and he fell into step beside her.

A warm glow slipped from around another door at the end of the corridor – this one of stone but still lined in silver, and slightly ajar. Flir paused. A voice drifted through the door.

A man was singing. His voice was rough and the words were unfamiliar. She raised a hand for silence. He sounded happy.

"I don't recognise the language," Flir said. Which was odd. "And I've come across a few over the years."

Wayrn leant closer to the opening, a frown on his face. "It sounds like..." he trailed off. "Sometimes I think I have it but then...I don't know."

Luik hefted his mace. "Let's just go down and see who's there. Just one voice, right?"

"Sounds like it."

"Good."

Flir inched the door open but as before, the hinges were silent. A short passage, lit by lamplight, came to an open room beyond. Dominated by a huge skull, not unlike the Sea Beast's, the floor was littered with chipped stone and debris, but what caught her eye was something else entirely.

The singer was a giant.

Easily three times the size of Luik, he sat on a row of stone benches, a wooden doll in his giant hand. The bare skin of his chest was dusky, almost molten, like the flame lizards of the Far Islands, patterns fading around his hands and face and along the top of his bald head.

Dark eyes regarded them with shock and his singing broke off.

He stood, head brushing the roof as he drew a huge sickle from his belt. The giant pointed at them with a warning shout.

Flir stood her ground, Luik flanking her. "That almost sounded familiar."

Wayrn jumped forward, holding up his hands and answering in kind.

The giant man paused.

Wayrn spoke again and the strange man lowered his sickle.

Flir picked up a name, Vinezi, and then the conversation quickened. At one point, Wayrn fell back as the giant roared, but the man only slumped onto the stone bench. They spoke further and finally, Wayrn switched back to Anaskari.

"I can hardly believe it." His eyes were a little wide. "This man is Vinezi's prisoner. His name is Alosus and he's been down here for months. He's supposed to guard the path. Or something beyond it I think." He summarised for Ain, whose expression calmed somewhat.

"Like Vinezi's nest?" Luik asked.

"No, something else. But he's hard to understand – he's speaking old Anaskari or something like it."

"Maybe he's been down here longer than he says," Luik said.

Flir glanced at the man, who still held the doll but now only stared at the huge skull mounted on the wall. Alosus' biceps were bigger than Luik's torso. Scrapes covered his shoulders. It must have been a tight squeeze for him at times. "Wayrn, how is Vinezi controlling him?"

"Vinezi has his son as collateral 'back home' but I

don't really understand where that is."

"He doesn't look like home is anywhere close by."

"No."

"Ask him if he knows where Vinezi is."

Wayrn did as instructed. Alosus growled as he replied, Wayrn nodding. "In the little city below," he said.

Luik raised an eyebrow. "Little city?"

Flir joined Wayrn, speaking directly to the giant, introducing herself first. "Alosus, we will help you find your son, if you help us stop Vinezi."

She waited for Wayrn to translate. The big man straightened and a light in his eyes grew. But it faded quickly and he shook his head.

"We can stop him," Flir said.

She waited for Wayrn. This time Alosus snorted, gesturing to her as he spoke. He held up a finger and thumb, barely spaced.

Wayrn opened his mouth but Flir interrupted. "He thinks I'm too small, right?"

"Yes."

She smiled. "Tell him I'll prove it. Tell him I'm stronger than he is."

Alosus laughed.

Flir strode around the centre bench and knelt across from him, placing her elbow on the stone and opening her hand. She looked at him. "Try." She mimed a struggle.

Alosus glanced to her, then to Luik and said something. Wayrn explained. "He said not even the 'small guy' could be strong enough."

Luik only grinned.

Wayrn spoke again to the giant, who finally shrugged. He lumbered over and knelt across from Flir, raising his hand. She clasped his thumb and his fingers engulfed her hand and wrist.

"Ready?" She took the strain.

He gaped. Then she applied pressure and his arm began to descend. He clenched his muscles, slowing her progress but barely. A futile effort; in the end she didn't even get to break into a sweat. When his wrist touched the stone, she let go, leaving him with wide eyes.

She stood, offering him a hand up. He stared at her a moment before giving a slow nod. He took her hand, rose and bowed. When he spoke, his voice was touched with awe.

"He's happy to help us," Wayrn said.

Flir thanked Alosus then turned to the others. "Seto will be pleased for once; we've got Vinezi now."

"We do?" Wayrn asked.

"We do. He's in the city, remember? We just have to go down and set a little trap – he's going to come back this way sooner or later."

CHAPTER 43

Giovan took Seto to the dark, cold cells beneath the palace. Smaller than the city prison, there remained enough room for Seto's purposes. Extra torches had been lit, light catching on the bars of cells.

Five people stood in a single cell, one of which was a Mascare. The front of his robes were stained with blood and his nose was swollen. Trien of House Tartaruga. The young man glared through the bars. The other men were lesser palace functionaries, though one was a council member he recognised – by face if not by name.

"All the names he gave us, Sire," Giovan said.

"And Nemola?" he asked.

"In his own cell."

"And these...traitors. Have they offered you more names?"

"This is all of us," the mask replied.

Seto strode forward. "Truly? This many of you conducted a covert plot which delivered multiple deposits of the Sea Beast unseen into the palace?"

One of the men fell back and others looked away, but

the mask stood firm. "Yes. We alone are responsible for trying to bring about change for the better."

Seto turned to Giovan, a question going unformed. Solicci? His Captain shook his head. Good, no links to Solicci had been found. And as yet, no torture had been administered, as per his wishes. He wanted to see who they were first.

But now there was the possibility of more lies and the necessity of consequences.

"Giovan?"

"Your Majesty?"

"Break their legs."

Cries from the cell.

Giovan gave a short bow, face hard.

"Perhaps they will be more forthcoming if they understand the first price of treason."

"It will be done, Sire."

"Good." Seto left without a backward look. By the time he reached his rooms he was breathing hard through his nose. Gods of the Sea, how had so many come to such folly? Fools. Damn fools.

His hand brushed Chelona where she nestled in his robes.

"And how have you helped me?" he said to the mask. Gods, a day, maybe more, maybe less, before Renovar ships were due to strike and Chelona remained unobtainable. How she taunted him – the violent rejection whenever he placed the mask on.

He lowered himself to the bed.

Earlier he'd woken, for the tenth time that day, on the thick carpet, fire low, after attempting to wear her. She hated him and his family – hated the Swordfish. But why? What had Otonos – or Father perhaps – what had they done?

Stubbornness had achieved precisely nothing. It was time, despite his misgivings, to seek help. Now when both Sofia and her father were unavailable, he needed them most.

Solicci was the only other man with any Greatmask experience in reach.

He was yet to prove himself fully perhaps. And Solicci had been watched. For weeks now, and not one slip up in sight. It was hardly possible to survey the Head of Cavallo House every single moment of every day and night, but Seto's men came close. The fellow either expected to be watched, or was exceptional at hiding his true motives. At least Giovan had found no connection to the betrayers.

Instead, Seto had called for Metti and Abrensi, and when a knock came on his door, he welcomed them not to his sitting room, but the banquet room. A long table inlaid with carven bone sat on polished hardwood floors from the Bloodwood – a hideous expense but typical of Father. The day it was completed, the carpenters left with bags of gold.

Carved Swordfish and crashing waves lined the table and atop rested a modest feast – steaming slabs of beef with a rich sauce and a blood-red wine that waited in an ornate server of treated bone, from which he poured for each guest.

Abrensi thanked him with a sitting bow. "Served a meal by my King – this is an honour."

"Wait until you hear what I have to ask of you," Seto said. He handed a plate to Metti. "For you, my dear." He looked to the impassive form of Guingera, lurking in the shadows beyond the candle light. "Guingera?"

The man shook his head.

Seto nodded. "You'll polish off a small child later, then?"

Guingera grunted but Metti's mouth might have twitched in a smile and Abrensi grinned around a forkful of beef.

Once the meal was close to complete, and he'd heard from Abrensi on the progress made healing the city, Seto lowered his glass. "Now we come to your visit. I have something to share – and something I have debated revealing for some time." He shrugged. "But soon, the city will know. If I could have your assurance, each of you," he looked to Guingera again, "that no word will leave this room before the Renovar attack?"

"Of course." Abrensi gave a small clap. "I admit, you have me quite curious."

"And I," Metti said, as she too gave her agreement.

"I have recovered something precious, something long thought lost." He raised Chelona from where he'd hidden her on his lap. "The Lost Mask of Casa Swordfish."

A stunned silence.

Metti recovered first. "Then *that* is what I have felt of late."

"You can sense her?"

"Yes. She is like a beacon to me – especially now that I know. And to anticipate your next question, I believe few others would sense this. Chelona is different to both Argeon and Osani, who I always felt."

"That brings me to my request. She will not speak to me. I cannot use her to save our people."

Abrensi put down his fork and knife. "Surely Solicci is worth approaching?"

"Perhaps. But I'd like to start with you both."

He shrugged. "I have few, few memories of your father using it and certainly none of your brother. You'd have more surely?"

"It was always easy for him and he used it little, obsessed as he was with warfare." He sighed. "There is no lore, no song?"

"I will search, but I believe not."

"Madam?"

Metti shifted forward. "I could not use it, nor advise you, Your Majesty. When I touch a bone to work my magic, it is left charred and ruined."

"Then can you sense something of her disposition?"

"I will try. Bring her near, but not to touch."

He placed the mask before her. Metti closed her eyes, folding her hands together. Her face, usually still, grew even more motionless if possible. Did her chest even move? Seto realised he was holding his breath.

She murmured something.

The candles danced and Abrensi nibbled on some vegetables.

Her eyes opened and she sighed. "I sense resentment, yes. That, above all else – but she is closed to me for the most part."

"That is all?"

"There is also the image, an echo, perhaps, of a man with your features, only younger. And he wears a beard. Your father?"

"I would say so, yes. He and my brother were last to use her before I stole her."

Abrensi spat his drink. "You stole the Greatmask?" He fumbled for a napkin, daubing the table and the front of his robe. He didn't seem to be achieving much.

Seto chuckled. "Ah. It seems I haven't mentioned that

before?"

"No, my King, most certainly not."

"I stole her when Father passed me over for successor. Because even then, I could not use Chelona. And so I foolishly thought I would take her somewhere and learn how to use her, to prove that I was able. A worthy King. The sea had other plans, of course."

"Then that is the source of the mask's resentment toward you," Metti said.

"I once thought so, but – she wanted me to take her. I know that. When I removed the mask from the setting, in these very rooms – she came to my hand eagerly. I felt the urgency in her; I was her rescuer."

"And she sees a dark shadow of your father perhaps, when you touch her," Abrensi added.

"My revelations aside, my problem is that I do not know if I can reach her."

"Your father may be the key," Metti said. "Though I still suspect that Solicci might aid you more than I or the Storm Singer."

Seto frowned.

Guingera stepped forward at a wave from Metti, helping her stand. "I apologise, Your Majesty, but I must retire already."

He stood, moving around the table to hand her a small package. "Thank you, Metti. You have assisted me well tonight."

"And thank you. Good bye, Lord Abrensi."

Seto walked them to the door to his chambers and returned to see Abrensi pacing by the curtains. The man's face was set and he flexed his hands where they rested behind his back.

"Abrensi?"

He stopped. "Your honesty, accidental as it was, has inspired me, Your Majesty."

"It has?"

"Assuredly. I have...hinted, in the past, at some involvement in the purging of magic-users from Anaskar."

Seto nodded. "Certainly."

"Your father was a tremendous hoarder of secrets, wasn't he? I would be surprised if even two dozen living people knew my fate when I disappeared, and few know now why I had to return." He moved to stand behind a chair again, drumming his fingers along its back. "Do you perhaps remember your father's second Queen?"

"Fiora."

"A fair woman. Too fair, too glittering, too star-like for the likes of me. And yet, we were in love."

"Ah. And that was why they argued so, her and Father."

"Yes. And when she died during childbirth, taking our son with her, I foolishly allowed my grief to show. A single crack in my facade. Just one. Utterly minute. But your father knew. He had me imprisoned and scoured the city as part of his fury. A childish backlash."

"I'm sorry, Abrensi."

"Do not be. The past is gone," he gestured over his shoulder, "back there somewhere. No need for me to go looking for it now." His smile was strained.

"But Father kept you alive. You were too valuable, your blood line," Seto surmised.

"Indeed. And I had no drive to break free and stand against him in his action, so black was my own despair. So heavy my guilt." His voice softened. "To my deep regret, that has been my great mistake."

"And you believe there is a link to my father and the mask here?" Seto said when Abrensi fell silent.

"I do, yes, yes. There is a rumour that he tried to bring Fiora back to life, using the Greatmask."

"He what?"

"I cannot know if it is true. My memory is a spotty thing. And my first weeks in the deepest pit in the city are one big black slab of cold and pain. And despair. By the time I was aware of my surroundings, I had been relocated to the prison."

"If he tried such a thing and Chelona rejected him for trying, then where does that leave me and the city, Storm Singer?"

"In trouble."

"Wonderful advice."

He laughed but it was a resigned one. "Well, I do have one piece. Convince Chelona you are not your father."

"You think she believes that?"

A shrug.

"If I could make her remember that I tried to free her...well done, Lord Abrensi."

"My pleasure, King Oseto."

CHAPTER 44

Sofia returned at Emilio's call. She'd been scouting in spirit form, this time skirting a new cave.

"She's waking," he said, face concerned in the half-light of the cave. Sofia knelt beside the woman, who lay bundled in blankets. Nia's arms and legs stirred, fighting the cloth. Sofia loosened them while Emilio worked on the wrappings around her head.

"I think it's helping," she said. Outside, distant thunder rumbled.

Emilio finished removing the wrapping, securing it beneath her head.

Sofia gave a small gasp. Nia's eyes, nose and mouth were covered by a fine webbing. Little had changed through the night but the woman's arms now rose from the blanket, revealing her breasts. Nia brushed at the webbing, which covered her body too, freeing her face before falling back to blink at the dim light. Sofia raised the blanket to cover Nia's breasts, flushing as she did. Emilio glanced away.

"Don't worry about that," Nia said, her voice weak. "I

need water and food, quickly."

Emilio found fruit and hard bread, holding it while Sofia helped Nia drink. The woman was ravenous, eating two days of her supplies in moments. When she was done, she sat up and flexed her muscles. "Did you manage to save my boots and gloves?"

"We have them," Sofia said. "But you'll need one of my shirts at least." She gave a spare to Nia, who shrugged into it. The grey colour and Anaskari cut looked odd on the woman, but she only smiled. "Thank you, My Lady."

"We've been worried about you," Emilio said.

"I was worried too," Nia grinned. "How long have I been hibernating?"

"Since yesterday."

"Not bad."

Sofia caught herself staring.

"What is it, Lady?"

"I think I made myself forget, but...you became a moth."

"A butterfly, dear lady."

"Ah, yes."

Nia kicked off her blankets, made a sound of displeasure at her torn pant legs, and set about rummaging through her pack, where she soon produced a sewing kit. "My family has its share of secrets."

"It's just hard to accept, now that I think about it."

"Harder than a magical mask of bone? Or men and women whose veins run with sap?"

"Well –"

"Don't worry, Lady Sofia." She threaded a needle then put it between her teeth while she pulled a pant leg together. "We've got work to do anyway."

"Can all of the Oynbae do what you...whatever it was

you did?" Emilio asked.

"I simply sacrificed most of my scales. And just my family can do it." She pulled a thread through. "Are they searching for us?"

"Yes," Sofia said. Scales? Wasn't it powder? She took a breath. Put it aside, Sofia. Notch and Father need help. "We've moved twice, but they haven't found our trail yet. And I've been spirit-walking often. We always have enough warning."

"You do look tired."

Sofia nodded. She supposed she was. But there was no choice. Be tired or dead.

Nia was already onto the next leg. "Well, there's some good news as I see it. Notch should be alive. I suspect they wouldn't have killed him just yet, he's good bait."

"I hope so," Sofia said. If he wasn't alive..."So what can we do? I haven't been able to walk far enough to find him or Father. I have to watch for patrols."

"How far did you get, before the attack?"

"I'm not sure. People were tending to the sap trees and there was a child. One of the gardeners took him away from the trees."

"Hmmm." Nia paused her sewing. "We need a distraction. Something big. Something that draws most of them away from Notch and your father. And you have to find them, Sofia, before we can plan it."

"That could take hours, because I don't know exactly where to look. I have to spirit-walk the whole grove."

"True."

Emilio chuckled. "Not if you were a falcon, you could see everything."

Sofia smiled. "That would make things easier." She paused. "Wait, why can't I?"

"Be a falcon?"

"No. See everything." She stood, pacing the opening. "Argeon is surely powerful enough; I just have to show him what I want. And what I have in mind is a bit like spirit-walking, it should work."

"We'll watch over you."

"All right." Sofia closed her eyes. If it worked, she'd kick herself. Spirit-walking had simply come to mind first, because it was something she could do. And there was so much she couldn't do. She called Argeon and gave him a picture. The Sap Grove from high above, lined in yellow rows with hints of green, the gardeners nothing more than small, dark figures between the lines.

Her vision swam and when it cleared, revealing the grove far below, exactly as she'd imagined, she gave a cry, arms flailing. "I'm flying," she shouted.

"Quietly," Nia hissed. "And you're right here with us."

She was right. It *was* a little like spirit-walking. Sofia still stood in the cave mouth, only part of her didn't, as if only her eyes floated high above the Groves.

Closer.

The landscape blurred and she could make out the top of someone's head. Across. She slid across the sky, focusing on a square to the north east of where she'd entered before.

There.

Another blur and she hung over a blasted courtyard littered with black heaps of branches. A dead tree, a giant, lay in its centre, and someone was tied to the trunk.

Circle.

She spun in the air, coming around to face the figure.

Notch's head was slumped. His wrists and ankles were raw and his face bore dark bruises. A cut in his thigh bled and his muscles twitched, his sleep fitful. But he was alive. Her heart soared.

"And now Father," she whispered.

Up. Her view switched and now she looked for something new, anything other than rows of sap-covered trees. On the horizon storm clouds grew darker.

Across. Closer.

She focused on a larger tree, its surface more green. Fenced in a compound, paved with old stone, the tree was broad enough to house several rooms – the smoke creeping from what had to be a chimney, the leaves around it stained black, the perfect clue.

Lower, to the ground.

Another blur.

Cut into the tree was a large door, bolted and guarded by a pair of Sap-Born, their veins pulsing.

Around. Her view shifted, as if she stood on a sliding platform. The rear of the tree lay unguarded. No one in sight.

"Let me walk now, Argeon." Her spirit-form touched the ground and she dashed to the bark, inching through the blur of brown, gold and white. A room beyond began to resolve. With every step it became clearer, but she stopped before entering – at the point where the room appeared as if through a gauze curtain.

Men sat around a table, their veins quiet. Each held discs of amber, moving them across the painted surface of the table in pre-arranged patterns. Stacks of silver rested off to the side.

In the centre of the floor sat a large round trapdoor of steel. Its handle was wrapped with cloth and its surface painted with unfamiliar runes.

Idle men gambling on guard duty.

Father had to be in the hole. It was just like where she and Notch had been put by Nia. She crouched. There was no way to cross the floor without giving herself away. None of them could touch her, but putting them on guard would be a mistake.

"Argeon, help me sink."

Slowly, she descended through the wood – but had only sunk a few feet when she stopped. She pushed harder but only bounced back up. Sofia slid around, still moving slowly, and tried to sink from a different point in the room.

Nothing.

Her heart skipped a beat. Something strong thwarted her. Father was down there, why else protect the room so? Did they know she could spirit-walk? Unlikely. Perhaps the cell was protected from anyone and everyone? No matter, she'd find out when they went in.

She stepped out of the tree and up into the sky, Argeon fuelling her as she slid back toward Notch. Wind whipped leaves along a path leading to the square, three figures moving toward its burned edge.

Lower.

Efran and the tall man...Mor, joined by a third Braonn. This man carried an array of knives, but also a glowing brazier and a bucket. Burning embers and sap.

She blinked back to the cave.

"I've found them both," Sofia said. "Give me a moment." She spirit-walked a circuit of their cave, and finding no patrols, returned to her body. "We have to hurry. I think they're going to kill Notch now."

"Right. Where is he?" Nia pulled her gloves on. "And what about your father?"

"Notch is tied to an enormous tree trunk to the north

east of the grove." Sofia paused to accept a flask from Emilio.

"A large tree?"

"Yes. It's been burnt and destroyed."

Nia paled. "He goes too far."

"What?"

"Efran has broken the First Tree." Her voice trailed off.

"What does it mean?"

"He has turned his back on everything. Our past. Our future." Her eyes flashed. "He has no reverence."

"We'll stop him," Emilio said.

Sofia nodded. "We will."

"What of your father?" the Captain asked.

"A little way further. Father is inside a large, hollow tree. Down a hole. It's protected by at least six guards and some sort of runes I think, but we can handle them. We can free Notch and head on to find Father."

"You saw your father?" Nia asked.

"No, but he's in there."

"Can you be sure?"

"I couldn't enter the room, even with Argeon. Where else would they hide such an important prisoner?"

"It sounds likely," Emilio said. He buckled on his sword and daggers, handing Nia a bow. "We took this from one of the patrols, you're probably a better shot than I."

Nia shook her head even as she accepted the weapon. "It's risky. What if the hole is empty?"

"Do we have a choice? I don't know how long Notch has and I didn't see anything else that looked likely for Father's cell."

"All right."

"Any luck with the distraction?" Sofia checked her knives, though Argeon would be doing most of the work thankfully. Stabbing and slashing, even to save Notch and Father, wasn't easy.

"Your mask. That's all I can think of," Nia said.

Thunder pealed again and Sofia stopped fiddling with her linfa-belt. "Maybe there is a way."

"How?"

"Follow me, and be ready to run," Sofia moved from the cave. "We need to get closer."

Sofia led them through the forest, crossing paths and leaping streams. The amber of the grove grew ahead. "Faster," she urged. They wove between the trees, approaching a thick screen.

Sofia pushed through the undergrowth, bursting onto an animal trail and skidding to a halt. A pair of Sap-Born stood on the trail. One reached for his weapon but an arrow thudded into his chest.

The other man turned to flee and a second arrow cut him down.

Emilio ran forward with his blade and Sofia looked away. She still heard the sound of each man being run through.

"Better for them not to linger," Nia said.

"Are we close enough?" Emilio asked when he returned.

"No, I have to be touching them I think," she said, and set off again before either could ask another question. Lightning flashed on the horizon above the trees and a wind had picked up. Sofia ran harder, finally slowing at the edge of the first row of Sap Trees.

"Don't touch the sap," she panted.

Nia nodded. "Deep pools will catch you."

They wove through the trees, stopping deep enough to be hidden from view of the forest. Nia stepped over a trail of sap and crouched by the ground, turning her head. "I see no-one for now."

"Keep watch," Sofia said. "I don't know how long this will take. If it works at all." And it had better be quick, for Notch's sake.

"What are you going to do?"

"Distract them, I hope."

She slowed her breathing, though her pulse still raced as she reached toward the nearest sap tree.

Nia caught her hand. "Sofia, stop."

"Trust me, I think this will work. I won't touch the sap."

Nia stepped back and Sofia placed a palm against the cool, hard surface of bark. "Please, Argeon."

She closed her eyes and showed Argeon what she wanted – the illusion of darkness flowing through the trees, pouring out into the sap, all the amber turning to rotten black sludge and flowing across the dirt, and all of it spreading from the centre of the grove like the bloody veins of the leaves.

Sofia shuddered when the mask responded and her stomach churned. Had the sludge passed through her body?

Nia gasped. Sofia opened her eyes as Emilio pulled her back, darkness flowing from the tree before her, spreading rapidly through the row. It worked!

"What have you done?" Nia cried. "Efran may be using them for foul means, but the groves are still precious."

"It's not real," Sofia said. "It's an illusion."

"Truly?" Emilio said, eyes wide. The black had spread to another row, speeding down the lines. From afar, shouts rose. Thunder boomed overhead and the wind rose again, tugging at Sofia's hair as she bent down.

"I'll prove it." She put the edge of her hand against firm sap. The moment it caught, she pulled away, struggling a moment. When she came free, the edge of her hand was a stinging red – little pieces of skin had torn. "See, just an illusion."

"Well, it seems to be working at least," Nia shouted over the wind. "I heard an alarm raised."

"Hopefully it's enough to draw Efran away." She pointed. "If we circle southeast we'll find Notch, right?"

"Let's go," Emilio said.

They ran along the blackening row, turning south and then heading east again. In the distance, the rumble of footsteps and shouting echoed. The courtyard had to be close. Two more rows and a gardener appeared. He paused when he saw them – already wide eyes bulging – then leapt for the next row, slipping between trees. Nia's arrow buzzed down the row and sank into a patch of sap, narrowly missing the man.

His blubbering cries echoed as he fled.

"Leave him," Sofia said. "We have to find Notch."

Finally, she burst into the square, Nia and Emilio on her heels. Wind tossed leaves and ash across the stones and at the huge, blackened trunk, a still-bound Notch lay unmoving.

Sofia called his name.

CHAPTER 45

Someone cried his name. Notch raised his head and blinked sweat from his eyes when the square blurred.

"Notch!" Sofia ran up, ripping her knife free to saw at his bindings.

"Sofia."

Nia stood with a nocked arrow, eyes scanning the square, while Emilio ran forward to help Sofia. The younger man reached up to free Notch's hands, catching him when he fell free with a grunt, pain lancing along his thigh. Emilio lowered him to the ground, gesturing to Sofia, who took his head into her lap as the Captain ran light fingers over his injuries. Notch winced when they touched his wrists.

"We need something for bandages," Emilio said.

Sofia tore strips from her robes and Emilio wrapped his thigh. "Think you can walk?"

Notch grinned. "I have to, don't I?"

"Yes."

He looked to Sofia. "Have you found your father?"

"We're going there now."

"Then we better hurry. Efran will be back, he's gone into the..." Notch frowned at the trees. They were blackened, inky sap spreading from the trunks. Was the entire grove dying? "Did you do that?" he asked.

"It's an illusion," Sofia said.

"Then let's use it. Can someone give me a weapon?"

Nia tossed him a dagger.

"Are you injured?" he asked when he got a better look at her. Tears welled in her eyes but she only shook her head.

"This way," Sofia said. Notch limped after her. His thigh throbbed and he fell behind, swearing at the pain. Emilio dropped back and put an arm under his shoulder. Together they half-ran, half-hopped through rows of fading amber, slowing to navigate dark sap flows.

"How far?" Nia called over the wind.

"We're close," Sofia returned. Notch grunted. He hoped it was right beyond the next row. Nia's powder helped, but dozens of cuts, bruises and wounds plagued him, not in the least his thigh, draining his strength. How long since he'd eaten now? His last sip of water was... yesterday? Without Emilio, he might have fallen several times. Gods, how was he meant to help Sofia now? He muttered another oath.

He shook his head when they paused a moment. "This is dangerous. You can't carry me there and back and I can't help you when we get there. You should hide me somewhere and come back for me."

"That's worse," Nia said. "What if someone finds you first? Or we can't get to you? Bad idea."

Sofia waved them on, only slowing to creep up to the edge of a row. Nia flanked her, bow held ready.

"The compound is beyond the next row," Sofia said. "Before the storm, two men guarded its doors and there were four within."

"If the room is as important as you say, then they'll still

be there," Notch said. "Is there a gate on the compound?"

"Yes, but I'll get them to open it for us."

"How?" Emilio asked. Worry lined his face as he looked at her.

"I'll spirit-walk right through the gates and get their attention," she said. "Then they'll open it to follow me – just be ready. I'll catch up."

"I'll be with you here," Emilio said.

Notch nodded. He tapped Nia's quiver. "Only five left?"

"Unfortunately."

"Save some for the way home."

"I will."

"You can do this, can't you, Notch?" Nia asked.

"I can."

"Here I go." Sofia closed her eyes and a pale blue shadow of her body flitted from the row. Nia followed and Notch kept pace with a clenched jaw. They paused at the end of the row, peering around a bulge of sap.

Sofia's spirit crossed the open ground, heading for a spreading tree concealed within a stone wall. Large wooden gates stood with heavy bolts. She passed through and Nia sprinted across the small clearing. Notch stumbled after her, reaching the wall and leaning against it, chest heaving as thunder rocked the sky.

Nia held her blade ready and Notch had his own dagger in hand.

Sofia's form reappeared and she waited, glancing to them. Her face was set in concentration. The rattle of bolts followed and the gates swung open and a pair of Sap-Born charged Sofia.

Before they reached her, she disappeared. Nia was upon them almost before Sofia's form was gone. Notch lurched forward but Nia was already done with the first man, and had blown a puff of cloud onto the second man's face. She swept his legs out from under him and followed with a knife to the chest.

Sofia and Emilio charged across the clearing. "Help me," Nia said to Emilio, and the two dragged both bodies out of sight as Notch helped Sofia close the gates, his thigh straining.

A neat garden, arranged in circles, stood before the not-too-distant tree. It dominated the compound with its canopy, sweeping down, leaves fluttering in the wind. Sofia led them along the short path to the door, where she stopped.

"Locked. What now?"

Nia handed the bow to Sofia. "Four men inside?"

She nodded.

"Let me try." Emilio stepped back. "It looks quite sturdy." He gave it a good kick. The wood shuddered but didn't budge.

Notch raised his blade, but no sounds came from inside the tree. "Empty?"

"Try again," Sofia urged.

Nia stopped Emilio as he lined up a second time. "Wait." She removed a glove and patted a circle on the wood, her hands swift. Notch watched closely. Did they change colour? She stepped back, replacing her glove. "Now try."

"What did you do?"

"Weakened the wood."

Emilio kicked again. Half the door splintered and he fell back as Nia burst inside. Last into the room, Notch came to an unsteady halt. Empty.

Several chairs and a heavy table; its surface covered

in amber discs. Smooth walls set with dark lamps and a circular trap door in the centre of the floor. Its surface was wrapped with cloth and spidery runes were painted in a circular pattern.

Sofia had already bent by the trapdoor, straining to lift it. She stood back. "It almost moved."

Emilio took her place, spreading his feet across the trapdoor and giving it a heave. The lid slid free with a scrape. The young captain had barely set it down when Sofia leant over the hole.

"Father?" She waved a hand. "I need light."

Notch took a lamp from the wall. "There's nothing to light it with."

Nia bent by a chest resting under the table and Sofia called to her father again, but no reply came from the cell. "He could be unconscious."

"Here." Nia gave him flint and tinder. Once he had the lamp lit, he passed it to Sofia, who held it over the opening. She didn't move at first, and when her head dropped, Notch limped over.

The cell was empty.

CHAPTER 46

For how many hours had he sat in her old room, running the memory through his head? Flir and the others were yet to return – what had they found? Killing Vinezi himself was...a sore point, no matter how hard Seto squashed the thought.

But suddenly, revenge was a luxury and one he could ill afford. A pitiful turn of events. What would Tulio have thought?

No time for that now.

Seto held Chelona in his lap but did not raise her to his face.

Instead he ran the memory over, one more time. A young man dressing in black, waiting in his rooms until the Dead Hour, slipping into the ways to bypass the guards and sneaking into Chelona's room, with a key stolen from Father's desk. Stretching up to touch her cheek, glancing over his shoulder before pulling her down to stare into the hollowed eyes.

Her need to escape had washed over him.

"I'll take you away," he'd told her and slipped back into the hidden passages, then out of the palace and down through the glistening streets with his hood raised and onto the ship with its mutinous crew, men he'd long since counted as his own.

What a young and foolish man he was then.

Seto raised her to his face but paused. Was this attempt twenty? More probably. What an old and foolish man he was now. On the bright side, the blackouts were growing shorter. He placed the mask on.

Darkness.

When he woke, this time sprawled on his bed, Seto groaned. The usual result. But no. There'd been something. A hesitation on her part. Had there been a flicker of doubt before she rejected him?

"Then let us remove that doubt, my dear." Pausing to first drink from a half-empty cup, only water, then moving into the other room to feed the Solave, he strode from his chambers and made for the royal crypt.

Chelona he kept hidden in the deep interior pockets of his robes – the royal orange not to his taste, truly, but comfortable enough. And, unfortunately, splendid for drawing attention.

Solicci bore down on him from an adjacent corridor with General Tadeo in tow. Both had worried expressions. Seto waved them after him as he turned down a corridor. "What is it gentlemen?"

"The wall is near to complete, Your Majesty," Tadeo said. "Our own catapults are in place. They may not be in the best condition but I believe they will hold."

"Then you should both look pleased." He pushed open the door to a stairwell. "Has something gone awry?" His voice echoed.

"Holindo sent us, sire," Solicci said. "He is seeking your permission to...ah, improvise."

He came to a halt. "Out with it, Solicci."

Both men bunched above him, not ready for his

abrupt stop. General Tadeo gave a little laugh. "Well, we don't have enough cut stone to finish the wall. The quarries weren't prepared to repair anything that large. We also have little to hurl at the invaders."

Seto shook his head as he resumed his descent. "And Holindo's solution?"

"To tear down some of the buildings near the Tier wall – factories and work houses mostly. He feels it will be quicker," Solicci explained.

"Grant him my authority."

"And the people?"

"Tell them they will be compensated of course." He chuckled. "Should we survive." He opened another door and crossed a passage to a second stairwell. Neither man made to leave and Tadeo seemed unable to time his question. "General?"

"Yes. Your Majesty, I have my own request."

"Surprise me, Tadeo."

"Ah, we've marshalled every soldier in the city, called in forces from outlying holdings and villages and even the mountains and I'm still not satisfied with the numbers. And frankly, the experience of some of our Vigil – who make up a significant portion of the Lower Tier forces, is not adequate for a siege."

"That is why we're dispersing Shield amongst them." Seto pushed through another door, striding along the passage leading to the Crypts. "Is something else wrong?"

"No. But in light of my concerns, I would like to hire mercenary companies, Your Majesty. They will expect good gold, but they're experienced."

"Thinking with the treasury, I see." Seto stopped at an archway framed by the Swordfish. Too important for the ocean, were the bones of the royal families. "But it is a good idea," Seto added, when the General opened his mouth. "Solicci will arrange the funds."

The General bowed.

"My King." Solicci lowered his voice. "I have discovered something of Nemola's plot."

"Go on," Seto said. A timely test of the man's loyalty. Especially as Solicci did not know of what Giovan had discovered, with the Tartaruga boy.

"A young Mascare has gone missing. From House Tartaruga. His fellows recall him being absent much of late. He was also known to have visited Nemola on occasion."

A good sign. "Enough to investigate further."

"I thought so."

"You have done well."

"Thank you." He paused. "Are you planning on visiting the crypts?"

"I am. In fact –" Seto frowned. Perhaps it was finally time to trust Solicci. "No. Once you've finished with the General, meet me here."

A hint of curiosity lay on his face but he said only, "Yes, Sire."

Seto took a torch from a half-concealed barrel inside the entryway, lit it from a lamp and started down. The Renovar ships were too close, it was time for Solicci to prove his loyalty beyond doubt – and truly, who else could help? Deep recesses, mere shadows beyond his torchlight, held stone coffins. Each coffin contained the long decaying remains of royals five centuries back. Not always the line of the Swordfish either, there were Falco and Cavallo bones too.

At the end of the crypt he stopped to raise his torch.

Three recesses against the back wall, each with a brittle

bone carved above it, the namesake of the decedent. In all cases, a Swordfish. Only, two coffins were empty – their lids smooth and uncarved.

One for Otonos and another for Oson.

But Oson had earned no such resting place and Otonos clung to life yet, such as it was.

The leftmost coffin was thick with dust, his father's relief indistinct. "No-one visits you, Father. Not even Otonos would."

Seto brushed dust from the carven shield, then the stone pommel of the man's sword and finally his face. Dark, sunken eyes and a beard the two features most prominent – the only two features anyone remembered. That and his madness.

"A broader nose than mine, Father."

He removed Chelona. What a fool he must look, alone in the crypt, reintroducing a mask of power to the remnants of a corpse. "Do you remember my father?" he asked her.

She offered no response.

"This is his face." He showed the mask the coffin. "And he is not I. My name is Oseto, and you first met me when I was a young Prince, being groomed for the throne. I held you and you didn't even notice my shaking hands. How busy you seemed. How wondrous – you saw everything, didn't you?"

Seto waited. Nothing.

"If it is true that Father wanted to coerce or force you into an act you did not approve of, let me assure you; I am not he. I want only to protect my city – as you are said to do in times of crisis."

Chelona's eyes were fathomless as he set her on the coffin.

"Will you speak to me?"

Footsteps approached. Seto turned to new light. Solicci arrived, a slight crease to his brow. The man wasn't adept at controlling his face as skilfully as his voice. He probably assumed his expression was composed. Too used to the mask.

"I am here, my King."

"Indeed."

"May I ask why?"

Seto stepped aside, gesturing. "To help me speak with her."

Solicci gaped as he strode forward. "Chelona."

"Yes. And I cannot make her speak. You must help me, Solicci." He took the man by the shoulders. "The city needs her."

CHAPTER 47

Flir sucked in a deep breath. Finally, proper air. Near to a whole day underground and now the late afternoon grey sky, rife with rain clouds, became beautiful.

Alosus paced the grass before the Tier wall while Luik handed out bowls of steaming food – not fish but some manner of bird by its look. She'd already sent Wayrn and Ain to the palace to inform Seto. Now it was time to set a trap. A big one.

"No guarantee he'll come back this way," Luik said around a mouthful. "We didn't explore every tunnel. Might be other entries or exits."

"I know that, but this is the best chance we'll get," she said.

"We'll catch something at least."

"And no mistakes this time. He won't have anywhere to run."

"What have you got in mind?"

She closed her fist. "Surround him. Put him in a wringer."

"Here?"

"No. Further along I think. Let's see where the passage leads, first. Then we can decide where to lay the snare."

"Who's going to watch this great hole then?"

"We can patch it up or post a guard."

"Risky."

"Which?"

He scratched his cheek. A beard was coming in; it made him look even more the mercenary he used to be. "Both. They'll see the patchwork by torchlight, and grow suspicious. Or worse, they'll steer clear of the hole and we'll lose our advantage – or they'll simply trample whoever we leave behind. Then they'll be in the palace grounds, maybe with more acor."

"Fine, but if they could always get in here – why didn't they just break a hole in the wall – or actually use the door?"

"We'd see a hole and then we'd find them." Luik frowned. "And maybe there's no symbol inside the tunnel? If there wasn't, how would they know where to look for a door from the inside?"

"A one-way door?"

"Why not? Seems like a good security step."

Flir put her head inside the hole. Too dark. She re-lit a torch and examined the inside of the wall, further along. Luik was right. No symbol.

"Well?"

She stepped back outside. "Nothing. So the symbols are more important than we thought?"

"Guess so."

"We still need someone to guard this opening."

Luik slapped his thigh. "The Storm Singer."

"That's better. Flank him with some archers and maybe a few of the Mascare and he'll be able to handle anything that comes through the hole."

He glanced at Alosus. "You all right with him while I go and find Abrensi?"

"No problem. Will he still be singing?"

"Probably, but someone will bring him if Seto asks."

"True." Flir made her own hasty meal, offering some to Alosus. In the light of day, his markings were somehow less pronounced, though his odd skin tone remained as vivid. He accepted with words that echoed Anaskari for 'thank you'. He still wore his giant sickle, but the doll was no-where to be seen. Perhaps it was in the bag he wore at his belt, opposite the weapon.

Why had he been singing to it when they found him? And what exactly did Vinezi have the giant guarding down there? No way to know for now, but it had to have something to do with the Sea Beast. She pointed to her eyes, then the opening. He nodded and she went back to guard duty.

The sun was setting, a thin blaze of gold lining the wall before her, when Seto arrived with Luik, Wayrn and Ain in tow. He strode with purpose. "Impressive work, Flir. All of you," he added. When he noticed Alosus, he smiled and spoke a few words, obviously a greeting.

Alosus smiled back and they conversed, Wayrn occasionally joining in. When he finished, the King pointed to the hole. "So this is what Abrensi has to guard? You made quite the mess, Flir."

"You're welcome," she said. "What about Alosus?"

"He is remarkable."

"Where did Vinezi find him?"

"I had a suspicion, the moment Wayrn mentioned him, but it should be obvious – and might explain a lot."

"Tell me."

"He's speaking something close to old Anaskari, so I can understand most of what he says. He's afraid Vinezi will hurt his son, but he's pleased that you have the King 'working for you' as he puts it."

She grinned.

"And what does that tell us, my smiling fool? Who might speak old Anaskari?"

"Old Anaskari people."

"Yes. And?"

Wayrn slapped his forehead as Seto spoke. Flir glanced at Luik, who had an eye on the opening in the wall, and appeared only half-listening. Old Anaskari? The kind of language spoken centuries ago. Which meant...

"I am stupid. They're from across the sea – aren't they?" She rubbed her eyes. That explained everything, right down to Vinezi's uneven accent. "All of them, Vinezi, Alosus here. From the land of your ancestors. Quite a journey, as I understand it."

"Indeed. No ship has reached Ecsoli – or returned to tell so if they did. But it would explain much. Vinezi's knowledge of the city and palace, of Mascare secrets."

"And he's here for bones."

"And we have more than enough of them." Seto exhaled. "Can you catch him, Flir? Alive? There is much more afoot than we first imagined."

"This is our best chance, without flooding the entire mountain with men we can't spare – we can do that later. Alosus said Vinezi was in the city."

"Do you believe him?"

"Yes."

"Then do what you do."

"But, you aren't staying back this time, surely? Everything else is in hand?"

"Not everything. I have an unfinished task," he said, giving her a look, which meant the mask, before continuing, "and your countrymen are close now. I wish to accompany you, Flir. Most keenly. And maybe if I have more success than I expect, I will." He shrugged. "But for now, make your plans and catch him finally."

"I will."

He nodded. "Whatever you need, Flir."

*

With Abrensi and his force camped before the opening in the wall, Flir marched down the sloping tunnel, torch held high. Shadows jumped before her, bouncing from the old stonework. Alosus, Luik and Wayrn trailed her, but no Pevin or Ain this time. Both had other tasks to complete. She'd wanted to scout alone, but Seto wasn't having it.

The sweet old scoundrel.

But any more people in the tunnel and it would be clogged. As it was, Alosus walked with a stoop.

"Let's collapse part of the tunnel. Bury him," Luik said.

"We have to be sure, Luik."

He grunted. "Where are we now?"

"Somewhere under the Second Tier – maybe halfway between the Palace walls and Second wall."

"And that last opening into the aqueduct? I still think we need to watch it."

"If they use it, Abrensi will see them."

"I meant if they start following us."

Flir stopped. "Then switch with Alosus and listen hard."

Another grunt and shuffling as Wayrn explained to

Alosus. They walked on, moving through bends and turns. The only steps were in small groups and there was always another set leading up, somewhere along the way. The path remained roughly even.

And it had been used. Footprints had worn a serious trail in the thick dust on the floor. How long had they been using it? Long enough for Vinezi and his men to learn modern Anaskari? To learn the city. Was months enough? Probably.

But what of the months prior, to prepare and leave the old Anaskari lands? Which no-one had seen or heard from in hundreds of years. Beyond the northern seas. Through the storms and on and on for who knew how long – no ships that searched for it returned.

They climbed another flight of stairs until at the very limit of her torchlight, a door appeared on a landing. She signalled for quiet and crept forward. Reaching the door, she placed her ear against the cold steel.

Nothing.

She whispered. "We're rushing in, all right?"

Flir stepped in and kicked the door from its hinges. She leapt into an empty room. Birds scattered, shrieking through a hole in the roof. Sunset fell into a decrepit space, splashing over streaks of droppings on the stone walls. Nests filled the corners.

A few feathers drifted to the leaf-strewn floor. Papers, torn and water-logged joined them.

She padded to a dust-choked window. The Second Tier stretched beneath her upper storey position, its black rooves and dark windows dusted with orange. Below, people moved about, wrapped in heavy cloaks as the wind swirled around them.

Beyond, sails of the remaining ships were creeping

from the harbour.

"Where are we?" Luik asked.

"Let's find out." She headed for a stairwell. At the bottom waited another rundown room, this one stuffed with shelves and half-ruined books. Stern statues of stone lined the walls, the bearded figures holding giant hammers in both hands.

"Celno."

"The Mountain God," Wayrn said. He snapped his fingers. "We're in the Mountain God's Temple."

"He's not very popular in the city, is he?" Flir said.

"Not for a long time. Gods of the Ocean have been more popular for centuries now. It's seen as 'provincial' to worship Celno, now that the mountain families are out of favour."

"So why use this place? Is there a link? Or just because it's quiet?"

Wayrn shrugged. "Probably nothing beyond its convenience. It has access to the passage within the wall and as you say, few come by here anymore."

Luik pointed to the door. "What about the priests?"

"Let's ask," Flir said.

The corridor beyond was empty, doors leading to simple rooms with little more than old cots inside. One looked to have been slept in, an old bottle of fire lemon on the window sill.

"The priests here don't seem very concerned with their establishment," Wayrn said.

The corridor opened into a wide, circular hall with a high, domed roof. Triangular columns with huge bases lined the room, evenly spaced. From the walls hung carved stone reliefs of Celno and his worshippers working at a forge or hacking rock from a mountain.

Large double doors stood closed, blocking the wind.

A marble floor looked to have been swept recently, revealing a complex mural of coloured pieces that depicted a sun rising over the Peak of Celnos.

"What are you lot doing here?"

A man in rumpled clothes, broom in hand, shuffled out from one of the columns. He affected a stern look, but a hiccup ruined the effect. His eyes widened. "Celno's gut, you're huge," he told Alosus.

Wayrn translated and the giant smiled.

"Who are you?" Flir asked.

He leant on his broom. Up close, he was younger than he appeared, the lines on his face misleading. "You first, girl, you're the uninvited guests." He pointed. "And you won't find anything back there, if you're thieves. And if you want to kill me then let me have another drink first, damn it."

"We're not here to kill you." Flir made introductions and he frowned.

"So I'm not about to die?"

"We'll see," Luik muttered.

Flir shook her head. "No. We just want to ask some questions."

"Oh. All right." He scratched his head then walked back into the columns. Flir waited.

"Is he coming back?" Wayrn said.

Flir followed the man. A steel ladder had been worked into the wall beyond the column, leading up to what might have been a loft. The man's broom lay on the floor. Light bloomed above. She growled. "Are you up there?"

"Who's there?" came the reply.

"This is ridiculous," Flir muttered before lifting her voice. "Come back down."

"Go away. Temple's closed."

"What sort of priest –" She broke off with a sigh. "Luik, would you go and get him for me? I'm afraid I'll wring his neck."

He climbed the ladder. A commotion followed, then Luik appeared, holding the man by his shirt. He dangled the fellow over to the ladder, ignoring the man's protests, and called down. "Ready?"

"What does that mean?" the man said.

Flir spread her hands. "Ready."

Luik dropped him.

The priest screamed and kept screaming even after Flir caught him. She set him on his feet and gave him a shake. "Hey. Listen. We need some answers."

"I'm alive?"

"Yes. Now, what's your name."

"Pins."

Flir opened her mouth to ask if it were true but thought the better of it. "Good. Pins, have you noticed anyone visiting the temple often?"

He snorted. "Not since the Mountain Priests left."

"You're not the temple priest?"

"No. I just look after the place while they're gone back up the mountain. One of them visits every few months to pay me." His expression grew mournful. "It's bare-enough to cover my drink."

"Have you had any other visitors lately?"

"A group of Mascare seem to come in a lot. I'm not sure when it started. My memory's quite hazy." His face brightened. "Maybe we should check on donations?"

"I'm sure they're overflowing. Pins, how many were there?"

"Ten the first time. Then two. I think. Maybe more."

Flir exchanged a glance with Luik before looking back to Pins. "Do they ever have any one else with them? Do they speak to you?"

"They just keep to themselves. One time, I was up because my bladder was full and I..." He trailed off when she raised an eyebrow. "And well, I saw them talking and one of them looked be a southerner, but I can't be sure. Don't they have their own gods?"

"When were they here last?" Wayrn asked.

Pins blinked as he focused on the new speaker. "Ah, last night. Or this morning. No, wait. It was dawn. Or noon." An earnest nod. "Noon."

"Do they often visit twice in one day?"

"Never." Another hiccup. "Sometimes."

Flir turned to the others. "This is the place, we just have to hurry."

Luik glanced around. "Here?"

"Definitely. We'll have to make sure there's only the main entry and the passage but there's space to hide men in the columns and we can cover the exits from outside too. Vinezi won't expect it either."

He cracked his knuckles. "Not if he's been using this place for months."

"What about Pins?"

"He's going back to the palace or somewhere out of the way," Flir said.

"Oh my, the palace? It sounds a treat. I've nothing to wear, you understand," Pins said. A funny look passed over his face, and he bent to empty his stomach onto the floor.

CHAPTER 48

"Gods be damned!" Sofia spun from the empty cell and ran for the half-broken door, skidding to a halt. A line of figures, dozens of Sap-Born and Braonn warriors, poured into the compound. Efran and Mor led them, striding for the tree.

Sofia kicked a chair. Fool. She'd let her desperation to find Father rush them into a trap and now she'd doomed her friends. How pig-headed could she be? She should have made sure he was in the cell.

Time was running out.

"Quick, help me." She grabbed the table. Nia joined her and together they heaved it onto its side and shoved it up against the broken door. A small gap remained, enough to see through.

"What's wrong?" Notch asked.

"Efran," Sofia said.

Nia put her face to the gap. "We're being surrounded. At least thirty men. And most of them Sap-Born."

"What do we do?" Emilio asked. "We can't fight our way out, not with those numbers."

"Can you break the back wall?" Notch asked Nia.

"I doubt it. It's much thicker and it would take too long. Living wood is more difficult."

Notch limped forward. "What about Argeon?"

She shook her head. "I don't know. I can only really spirit-walk. And I don't feel connected to the weather, in here."

"The storm is easing anyway," Nia said.

"Another illusion?" Emilio asked.

Sofia paused. Was the grove still blackened? What could she change here? Nothing really. "They already know we're inside."

"We have to do something," Notch said.

"Stall them," she said. "I need time to think of something."

Notch moved to the door, glanced throughout and turned back, face grim. Sofia clenched fists. What could she try? Argeon was one of the most powerful artefacts in the world – why couldn't he just destroy them?

But even if she knew how, she might never find her father if she killed every last one.

"Give up," Efran shouted. "Save us the trouble of breaking bones if we have to drag you out."

Notch leant against the door. "First man through the door dies, Efran."

"And what of the ten, twenty or hundred after that?" He sounded amused.

"Think a Greatmask can't handle that many?"

"Not in the hands of an amateur."

Notch swore. "Sofia, any ideas?"

"I'm thinking."

Efran shouted again. "Last chance. You have nowhere to run, and no-one can help you." He paused.

"And Sofia, think about your father. And your friends. You're the only one I need alive, you know."

Sofia ran to the door. "I'd be a fool to trust you."

"Then you all die and I have the masks."

"You can't use them."

"Your father will instruct me."

"He'd die first," Sofia shouted back.

"Either way you are still dead and I have the masks."

Sofia froze. More darkness. What if she brought darkness down, the way Tantos had? Could she? She showed Argeon the tree, the compound and the Sap Grove disappearing beneath a cloak of night.

Nothing happened.

A loud sigh came from outside. Efran snapped an order and feet marched toward the tree.

Nia spun. "Lady Sofia."

"I'm trying to bring darkness. We might escape then. Start on the back wall." To Notch and Emilio. "Hold them."

The Butterfly-Eater dashed to the back wall, tearing off her gloves as Notch and Emilio braced themselves against the door. A pounding started, rocking the table. Notch gritted his teeth and Emilio's face was pale.

"Argeon, I need your help." She hissed the words, but no darkness came.

More thumping on the doors.

An axe head appeared in the wood, inches from Notch's own head. He flinched as he fell away, drawing his dagger. Another axe hacked into the door.

"How long, Nia?" Sofia called.

"Too long."

The rest of the door burst open and men piled into the room, barrelling into Notch and joining blades with

Emilio, who attacked with such ferocity that he drove them back momentarily. A pulse of amber flashed and then she covered her face, eyes burning.

When she could see again, Emilio was lying dazed on the ground and Notch knelt at the mercy of a sword point. Even Nia was blinking furiously, surrounded by Sap-Born.

Efran appeared before her.

"Choose, Sofia. Agree to serve me and I will not immediately execute your friends."

She glared at him.

Efran turned to Mor. "Do the Shield first."

"No!" She caught his arm, then flinched away from the glow. "Spare them. I will serve you, Gods be damned."

Her words hung in the room.

Finally he nodded. "Much better."

CHAPTER 49

Ain rubbed his eyes from where he stood at the door to their rooms. How deep into night was it? "You're truly letting us free?"

King Oseto raised an eyebrow from where he waited outside. "Of course. I am a man of my word."

"And the Solave?" Could the Anaskari actually demonstrate honour? Truth? It hardly seemed possible from where he'd sat, locked in admittedly pleasant rooms with Schan, ever since returning from the underground.

The King was flanked by Wayrn, whose expression was dark, and half a dozen Shield, who watched on in silence. The men wore orange in addition to their silver; the Honour Guard.

"She is being escorted to the Mountain Gate as we speak, where my men here will soon convey you both. Please carry this to your Elders." He handed over a letter, sealed with the Anaskari Swordfish. "In addition, I will be sending Wayrn here as my special envoy, further to the gesture of peace."

Peace. Still he played that card, but why? The King

had what he wanted. "The Elders will not be able to read it. And we do not require an envoy." He glanced at Wayrn, whose expression had not brightened.

"It is of course in your writing and Wayrn is happy to be part of such a momentous event." Oseto smiled. "Thank you, Ain for lending me your skills. I have included provisions for your journey. I hope you convey my message with the sincerity in which it has been offered, and that Wayrn is treated with respect as befitting the peace we attempt to achieve."

"I will show them your letter. And Wayrn will not come to harm," he said. Odd that of all the people in Anaskar, Wayrn was most pleasant. Perhaps because he, like the King, could speak Medah properly and so few Anaskari could.

"Thank you, Pathfinder Ain. Giovan and his men will accompany you beyond the Mountain Gate for your protection if you wish. It is best you leave with the cover of darkness, lest the populace grow too curious about you. And do take care of the Solave, she is precious."

Ain bowed, in the Anaskari fashion, a slight frown on his face. Could the man be sincere? Baffling, but all signs pointed to 'yes.' Yet, how long before whatever goodwill the King felt trickled down to the people of the city? If ever?

Schan allowed himself a nod but little else.

The King left and then all that remained was to follow the soldiers from the palace. Giovan took them through the hallways and passages and across the neatly kept, if dark, palace lawns. As ever, the paths thumped beneath his feet. At the main gates, Giovan had them opened by order of the King, and motioned for his men to follow Schan through. He kept Ain back.

Giovan spoke in a soft voice, his Medah accent fair. "Treat his majesty's offer with care, Pathfinder."

Ain stiffened. "Don't insult me."

"It's only an insult if I'm wrong. And I mean both Wayrn and the letter, you understand."

"I will do so."

"Then you and your friend now want peace?"

"I want to go home." With the bird, to see Silaj and his child. And never set foot in Anaskar again.

Giovan stared at him a moment before gesturing to the street. "Then let's get you there."

Ain preceded him into the street. No rain fell from the inky sky but a chill wind cut through his cloak. Schan made no mention of it, but when the Shield formed up around them and headed from the palace walls, Ain found himself glad of it. Even the multitude of paths dimmed somewhat.

Home.

Where was that exactly? Something Wilatt said echoed. *You don't like your current home?*

Only he did. In comparison, Sekkati was a frozen land of stone and ill weather. The only wonderful thing about it was the sea, where all was quiet. Where no paths hissed.

And that was not enough.

He walked on, meeting a carriage, which took them to the Mountain Gate. The driver wore an expression of worry. His face was lined with sleep-wrinkles, Ain noted when he climbed up.

Two Mascare met them at the gate, torches blazing. One held a cage covered in a heavy cloth. Ain leapt from the carriage. Schan's sigh faded as Ain ran to the two red-robed men. The cage was handed over without complaint, and then the masks left the gate. Giovan and Wayrn spoke with the guards and as the large doors ground open, Ain peered under the cloth.

There she was.

Her eyes were closed, but her flame-hued feathers shone in the torchlight. He lowered the cloth with his own long sigh. A knot unravelled in his stomach. She was safe again. Even being near her warmed him through.

"We're taking horses, lad," Schan said. "Hope you can remember how to ride. At least we'll be going slow in the dark."

"Sorry?" Ain saw the horses and nodded. "I'll be fine."

Schan didn't appear convinced, but turned to thank Giovan for the supplies, his voice containing the barest trace of gratitude. Ain loaded the cage, securing it to the packs and climbing into the saddle. It took a moment, but once he had his balance, memories of Jedda teaching him to ride returned and he was able to stay on his horse, which snorted at him as it clopped through the gate.

Ain looked over his shoulder.

The gates were closing, light fading with their grinding, Giovan staring after them.

Freedom. At last, they had escaped the city. Ain made a fist. "We're truly free. The King was not lying."

"Seems not." Schan smiled. He eased his horse down the dark path, face losing some of the tension it had worn for weeks now. Behind him and off to the side, Wayrn rode in silence. Schan's smile didn't last. "Let's hope there's no tricks left for the King to play." He pointed to the cage. "And what are you going to do with that bird? Hard to believe he'd let it go."

"Care for it."

Schan shook his head. "You think she needs that?"

"What do you mean?"

"She's a wild bird, she doesn't need caring for. She needs to be free."

"No. I only just –"

"Be calm, lad. I mean, she needs to be free to hunt and to fly, to choose where she lives. That cage isn't enough. You might not be enough for her."

He'd never thought of that. She did deserve to be free, but not before she was truly safe, away from the city. And she'd want to stay anyway. There was a connection, one that no-one else had. The warmth proved it. "You're right. As soon as we've put some distance between us and the city."

"That's the way."

The mountain path wound down toward distant, invisible foothills according to Wayrn. Ain leant back in the saddle. Finally. The paths faded. So few now, or at least, so few tangents. They simply led down the mountain.

They passed no-one on the road and by dawn, a heavy rain began to fall. Nothing like the rarity of rainfall in the desert. The lightening landscape had begun to blur when they stopped to pitch tents as best they could. Schan kept an eye on Wayrn, expression thoughtful, but the bird took up most of Ain's flagging attention, adding the only scraps of meat provided in their provisions for her tray. Their own meal was cold, despite the cooking implements and supplies they'd been given, but thanks to the rain, there was no way to prepare anything. Nor did anyone seem to have the inclination.

By the time they were underway later that morning, Ain was beyond saddle-sore. "This is awful," he said. "I'd forgotten."

"It'll take time."

"For me to die?"

Schan chuckled. "To grow used to the saddle. We'll walk in a bit and I'll find something to put over the saddle."

Near noon they broke to eat and walk the horses as the rain cleared, leaving a cold wind behind. Ain had checked on the bird regularly, but she always appeared well. He strode across to Wayrn with a flask of water. The man was feeding his mare. He'd spoken little as they travelled and his mood had hardly lifted since leaving the city.

"Wayrn?"

The envoy tried to school his features. "Yes?"

"Take some water."

He accepted it. "Thank you."

Ain hesitated. "You are angry with your King, aren't you?"

"You would be too," he said, corking the flask and returning it.

"Because he is forcing you to be envoy to Medah?"

"Because I can't stay and defend my friends." He shrugged. "And because I resent becoming little more than a hostage, which is what will happen once we reach Cloud Oasis."

Ain paused. It was strange that the King sent only one man as part of his envoy. Why not a party? Something more official. "That is what you believe?"

"Do you not think your Elders will see me as such an opportunity?"

"Possibly."

Schan joined them, his expression unreadable. Was it sympathy perhaps? Or mistrust? "The Elders may believe it an honest gesture, you coming along. A sign of the King's commitment." He paused. "Or they might think you've been sent to spy on us. We remember the last Anaskari 'envoys' and not fondly."

Ain frowned. He didn't remember that. Surely before the Glass War? "Then you think King Oseto's offer of peace is suspect?"

"Just what I need." Wayrn shook his head. "He's sincere, he simply cannot spare the men. The invasion is much on his mind, as you can surely recognise."

"We can," Schan said, glancing at Ain. "Others are just as distracted, I'll admit. But we aren't going to trust you outright, Wayrn."

"I don't expect you to." He returned to tending his mount.

Ain moved away. The glance from Schan was timed well. Perhaps the bird had taken too much of his attention. And why shouldn't she? She was beautiful. Wonderful. And yet, he hadn't considered Wayrn's true purpose. Worse, he'd barely given much thought to Silaj, and he ought to have been thrilled to be heading home. Sands, the bird did have a hold on him.

Was it dangerous? What would he overlook next? An attack?

"Think we're far enough to let her go today?" Schan asked, once he joined him.

He hesitated. "I think the foothills will be best."

"She's a mountain bird, isn't she?"

Ain shrugged. "We found her underground."

"Which I'm guessing is where that camouflage-creature took her."

"I suppose."

"Best to decide soon."

When dusk fell they'd reached the damp of the green

foothills. Ain stood a little way from Schan and Wayrn, who were setting up camp, holding the cage in both hands. The covering was gone and he stared at her.

Each feather a work of art.

The smooth claw, the power in her eyes.

She preened herself, adjusting her grip on the bar. A small tuft of orange slipped from one of the wings. If he kept her now, would she truly become miserable? Of course she would. She deserved to fly.

And if he kept her, would his obsession destroy him?

But if he let her free, would she stay?

Her warmth swirled around him, a deep tingling that extended just to his fingertips as he held her close. How could he give her up? He'd even gotten the better of King Oseto, something he'd not have thought possible.

Ain gripped the cage door. No. He was being childish. Foolish. He had to make a choice. He had to chose his family. He'd been given his life back, how could he lose it to a wild bird, no matter how enchanting?

Jali deserved more.

"And you do, too – don't you?" he said to the bird. "You're safe now, aren't you?"

He glanced around, but the earth was not distorted by strange shadows, by the stalking creature with its colour-changing skin. It must have been trapped back in the city, thankfully. Ain's hand trembled. He took a breath and unhooked the latch, squeezing his eyes shut.

Still he kept the cage door closed.

She deserves better. Jali deserves better.

He swung the bars open.

The Bird of the Sun met his eyes, dark liquid pools. Was there a hint of gratitude there? It hopped to the edge of the cage then leapt into the air with a shrill cry. Ain fell to his knees, a shiver wracking his body. He reached after her but she was circling higher and higher, great wings flapping through a creeping mist. She was leaving.

But wait, she turned...

His heart swelled.

And she circled above but did not stay long, turning. How swiftly she flew. Frozen to his spot on the cold stone, Ain watched her slip away, returning to the mountains.

Just as Schan said.

And maybe King Oseto would have the last laugh after all.

CHAPTER 50

Seto explained his theory to Solicci, this time in the comfort of his chambers, morning sun lancing into the room and splashing across the deep armchairs. "And so she must remember me as Oseto, not as she remembers Casa Swordfish."

Solicci gave a slow nod. "A fair assessment, my King. All Greatmasks must be convinced of the user's worth."

"And do Greatmasks routinely strike down their users?"

"It has happened to me before. I was urging Osani to do something; he wouldn't listen. I pushed – demanded actually, and woke on the floor of my quarters."

"That is somehow reassuring."

Solicci smiled.

"And my path, now?"

"Would be to continue as you have. Call to her, speak to her. Spend time with her – as you cannot do so wearing her, make yourself known to her despite that." Solicci scratched his hook nose. "I have no doubt that the Greatmasks are aware of everything that goes on around them. It is sometimes a matter of being persistent."

"If only there were no other imminent concerns."

"Truly." He paused. "What language have you used, to speak with her?"

"Anaskari as it stands today. You think I should use the old tongue? I don't recall my father or brother doing such a thing."

"Osani preferred it, perhaps Chelona will now?" His face grew pained though his voice remained perfectly calm. Again, Seto was sure Solicci thought he was hiding his facial expressions better than he was.

"Do you miss him?"

"Certainly. The Greatmask is more alive than I can fully fathom. He has a will, and at times I think that will is at odds with itself, at times such purpose would radiate from him."

"I have meant to ask you about him, but so much has diverted that intent. How did Tantos steal and use Osani?"

He spread his hands. "That I fear we may never discover. I would have thought it impossible, but he knew things that no House seems to know. Perhaps more than his father. Just where was Tantos before his return?"

"Sofia did not say."

"Danillo will have some ideas, I believe."

Seto stood and poured two small glasses of fire-lemon. "Allow me to be direct, Solicci."

"I would not dare try and stop you, my King." He sipped.

"Do you regret it?"

Solicci did not need reminding. "Yes."

Seto took his own drink. "Go on."

"To be honest, I hadn't planned to, Sire."

"Indulge me – and take that request as an order," he

grinned.

He sighed. "You know why I tried to seize power?"

"As I understand it, you did not agree with my brother and Danillo, both of whom saw a threat in the East."

"And more the fool I was it seems."

"But Oson?"

"Can you believe that bitterness will drive a man to poor unions?"

"I can." Seto paused. Perhaps it was time to lay a card or two on the table. "Solicci, I want to trust you. Your advice has been valuable and your loyalty appears above reproach, in all things you have acted in my and the city's best interest. Your work with Nemola for instance, or with the council. But my brother may have once felt the same."

Regret flicked across his face. "Then revealing Chelona and seeking me for advice is an act of desperation as much as faith?"

"Should it be?"

He straightened. "No, my King."

"And where have you placed your bitterness, now?"

"Away."

"I hope so, Solicci. Should Danillo return, and Sofia, both will remain Protector and Successor. If that is not a condition you could work with, I would wish to know it now."

"My bitterness was for your brother, in chief."

"And we find more common ground."

"For one, this conversation would have been beyond your brother. His strength of will was his weakness. Inside, he held too many of your father's views. And if I am honest with myself, I believe Queen Alessi deserved better."

Ah. Who in the palace hadn't fallen for her, truly? But that explained it. Always the personal motivations beneath the political ones. But did it make Solicci as trustworthy as he needed to be? As Anaskar needed? "Perhaps we all did." He toyed with his cup. "I appreciate your advice and service, Solicci. Be assured I will call upon you again."

"I will be ready," he said as he stood, made a bow and slipped from the rooms.

Seto glanced at the old box on the mantle. Did it matter which tongue he used? "Chelona, we're running out of time, my dear. If you mean to answer, do it soon."

He rose, locked his quarters and gave express orders not to be disturbed.

Then he slid a heavy desk across the secret entrance to the old ways and opened the box, removing Chelona. Her dark sockets were unfathomable.

This time he would break through.

He raised the mask and stared into her eyes.

"Chelona, hear me," he said, using the old tongue. "I am not here to force your hand. I am not here in a misguided attempt to bend you to my will. I am not here as Casa Swordfish. I am here as Oseto, the young man who tried to save you. And I need help, our city needs me. You are one of her protectors – help me now, I entreat you."

Did she grow warmer in his hands?

Seto raised the mask to his face.

And screamed.

CHAPTER 51

Sofia woke in a cold stone building. Its walls were lined with small windows of stained glass – or was it sap? Light pressed within. Where...? She groaned. Captured. The same room Efran had dumped her in before ignoring her completely. After failing to break her way out, she'd slumped onto the bed and...fallen asleep.

And now, to rub salt into the wound of her failure, her limbs were like steel rods; her arms dull as lead. When she moved her neck it creaked. It was getting worse. Was it the *lenasi*? It had to be something else.

No way to know and no-one to ask. She was alone. Were Notch and the others alive?

An unlit fireplace stood opposite her bed, which was naught but rustling straw. She slid her body around, breathing hard. Pain lanced her limbs. By the time she reached a half sitting position sweat had formed at her temples.

"Gods," she groaned. The unresponsiveness in her limbs went beyond anything the *lenasi* had caused.

She needed Argeon. Or Osani. Immediately.

A door opened and Efran entered, a smile on his face. "I'm glad to see you awake at last."

"Where...are my...friends?" she asked, the words difficult to form. Even her jaw was tight! "And my... masks."

"Both are safe for now." He knelt before her, blue eyes intent. "I see you are in pain. Why? Did your little stunt with the grove cost you?"

If she answered he'd only use it against her.

He stood. "Then I will leave now and finish off your friends. Starting with the ever-defiant Notch, I think."

"I need a mask," she ground out. "They protect me... from my addiction."

"Do they? What are you addicted to?"

The more words she forced out the easier speaking became. Quickly, finish the lie with a half-truth. The whole truth was something else, something worse perhaps – if her frozen limbs were anything to go by. "*Lenasi*...I wear them and it alleviates the pain."

"This is a poor ploy, Sofia – and my stores are hardly open to you."

"I suffer whether you believe me or not."

He narrowed his eyes. "Prove it."

"Osani. The plain mask. I cannot use it, it's not tied to my House." She trembled as another wave of pain shot along her limbs. "If you want...a useful servant, you'll have to believe me." She raised her hand with some difficulty and grabbed his arm. "Or you can watch me die."

Efran hadn't stopped her from grabbing him. No doubt he was confident that his strange power protected him, but he removed her hand gently now. "Very well, Sofia. I will return with Osani and test the truth of your words. I know enough to find what you have said about the houses familiar. Something your father mentioned perhaps?" He paused. "But should you lie, and attempt or even succeed in attacking me, your friends will die. You understand, don't you?"

"Yes."

He stood. "Good."

Sofia made it to her hands and knees once he left, struggling with each movement. Next she lifted a single leg, bringing her knee up and placing her foot flat on the floor. Finally she lifted her head and pushed up. Her back creaked and she gave another cry, biting the inside of her cheek.

Swearing, she reached her feet and stretched out her chest with a grimace. Pulling her shoulders back and flexing her muscles was slowly increasing her flexibility but her body was slick with sweat beneath her robe. A trail ran down her neck and her hair was damp.

Footsteps beyond the door announced Efran before he entered. This time his veins glowed amber and he carried Osani.

He lifted an eyebrow when he saw her but said nothing, only handing the mask over. Sofia ground her teeth as she reached out and placed it on her face.

Pain vanished.

She slumped, a groan of relief escaping.

Efran had watched her carefully, but when she made no move to attack, and simply stood still and slowed her breathing, the glow in his veins eased. "I see."

"I told you. I need to wear a mask."

"Yes, you did."

"Now I will see my friends. And my father."

"In time, yes."

"Now. I can hardly take you at your word, can I?"

He laughed. "A fair point but there is no time. You have work to complete first."

"Work?"

"You can eat now, however. You must be hungry."

What was going on? His eyes had not changed; he wanted her as a slave. He wanted the masks, he held to his purpose. His offer was simply part of ensuring her compliance, but his game was a long one. And it wasn't anything Tantos hadn't already tried when posing as Lupo.

"Show me this work."

"Come along then."

He led her through a narrow hall, lined with doors and clear windows. A heavy mist cloaked the outside and a set of stairs waited at its end. The murmur of voices rose from below but he did not take her down. Instead, he opened the last door and showed her inside.

A young Anaskari woman sat at a table, poring over a large book. Her brow was creased in concentration as her quill wove across the page. She looked up, pushing long black hair from her face. "Father."

Sofia blinked. Not Anaskari.

He went to her and touched her cheek. "Catrin. How are your studies progressing?"

"Well enough." Her gaze drifted to Sofia. "Is this her?"

"Yes." He gestured. "Meet Lady Sofia, my dear. Successor and keeper of the Greatmask Argeon."

"Hello, Sofia." Her Anaskari was faultless.

Sofia frowned at Efran. "What is this charade?"

Catrin answered. "Father is preparing me for the most important journey of my life. Of our people's lives."

Efran put a hand on her shoulder. "And you will help

her, Sofia."

Sofia tensed. Something Derrani said, before he died. He'd accused Tantos of being blind about Gianna. He'd called her Gyana. A Braonn imposter. "You're going to send her into the city, because she looks Anaskari. As what, an assassin? Your own daughter – how old is she? How could you do that?"

He shrugged. "She is only a little younger than you. Certainly old enough to undertake such a great task."

"I want to go." Catrin added. "And I'm so glad you're going to help me."

"No, I'm not."

Efran shook his head. "Remember our arrangement, Sofia? You will help my daughter. You will tell her everything she needs to know. You will finish her education, the customs, the phrases, the history, the life of a noble. You will give her all the little details only a native can provide, thereby finishing her transformation." He met her eyes. "You know what will happen should you refuse."

Sofia glared at the smiling pair.

CHAPTER 52

Flir signalled to Luik, mostly a pale smudge against the darkness, who nodded then melted into the shadows across the hall. Moonlight slipped through the gap in the closed doors, a line slicing the sunburst mosaic.

Luik was joined by dozens of Shield and a row of Mascare, all concealed within the shadowy columns. On her side of the room waited her own line of soldiers and archers, spreading to encircle the empty hall.

Archers also lurked in the loft. Pins, she'd safely stowed away in the palace, having already sent him back with Wayrn – who'd not been happy about being left out. No point getting Pins killed and if Wayrn was hurt Seto would be furious. And if she was honest, a night ambush wasn't Wayrn's speciality.

Last was Alosus, at the mouth of the stair. He waited for Flir's signal. The giant had been prepared to act as bait. Or was it just a way to taunt Vinezi? He was eager to 'send Vinezi to the White Embers.' Flir didn't ask what they were, but the resolve in his eyes was clear.

And now the slippery bastard was within reach.

Their luck had held; she'd been able to get into position before Vinezi tried to use the passage again, something she'd not been sure would be possible. But lookouts posted on the floor above reported seeing a small group approaching the temple and now all she had to do was spring the trap.

Muffled voices echoed outside. Flir drew her blade and held her breath. Alosus stepped onto the mosaic and waited, arms folded.

The doors swung open and a small party, half a dozen, entered the temple. Several stopped to flick rainwater from their cloaks while others lit torches. One was speaking in an agitated tone, his Renovar accent clear.

"But who is responsible?"

A new voice, Vinezi, answered. "Whether we are responsible or not, something's been woken. It won't matter once we have more bones."

Flir strained her ears. What had been woken?

Once light filled the room, Vinezi froze, demanding a torch. He strode forward, shouting in Old Anaskari.

Alosus answered, voice firm.

Vinezi continued his tirade. Flir watched, choosing her moment. The others needed to move further into the hall. Vinezi's face appeared odd – had he aged? Or was it just the torchlight? Part of his cheek appeared grey. What did it mean? Did a different man stand in the hall?

Or was the dead man in the cell an incredible decoy?

Or a brother, as Luik favoured?

No. There was a conceit to the way he walked, the way he demanded answers from Alosus. Only Vinezi, the man who'd blown up the Pig and stayed around to gloat, who'd taunted them so often, would speak that way. The man in the cell, the man Seto had captured, was a decoy.

Finally the other men moved further into the room – and by their torches she could see, few were Renovar. The others had Anaskari colouring. Which meant they were doubtless from the old land or new recruits.

Time.

Flir stepped out of shadow. "Come to pray, Vinezi?"

He spun, and his men threw back their cloaks to reach for weapons. The temple door slammed shut as her men outside sealed Vinezi in. A line of Shield stepped into the light. Archers drew their beads and swordsmen held blades ready, as men fell into position, blocking escape. Luik grinned at the prisoners and Alosus drew his sickle.

"What a warm welcome," Vinezi said, expression dark.

"I'll give you a simple choice. You and your friends die right now or surrender right now," Flir said. She took another step forward.

"Is there no third option?"

"None."

"Very well." He threw his cloak to the floor. A network of bones had been woven into his clothing. Many appeared to be fish bones, though some were larger. A single large bone had formed something of a breastplate and thinner pieces ran across his hands and up his forearms, in such a way as not to restrict movement.

A necklace of odd pieces ringed his neck and when he raised his free hand, bones clattered on bracelets.

"Ready for that third option?"

Bones like those from the Sea Beast?

"Fire!" Flir gave the order too late. Bows snapped but Vinezi was already moving. He swept his arm in a line and Flir and her row of men were flung to the ground. Arrows went astray, several striking Vinezi's men.

She found her feet and charged. Luik's line bore down

on the man, but Vinezi swept another arm, torch blazing, and they too were cast to the ground. Even Alosus was driven back, though he kept his feet.

Shouting echoed throughout the temple and the ring of blades followed, as Vinezi's men were engaged. Flir stood before Vinezi, who raised an eyebrow at her. "Aren't you plucky?"

She drove forward and he brought his hands up sharply.

Stone erupted and she rolled aside.

Alosus threw his sickle but Vinezi deflected it with more bone magic. The giant charged after his throw, grasping Vinezi by the throat then flinging the big man across the room.

Again, Vinezi's magic protected him, even as he bounced from a column. He leapt to his feet and swung his arms again. This time stone flashed from shadow, smashing into the Shield and his own men alike. Hoarse screams followed. Flir ducked as another piece sped by her head.

She leapt after him, sword whistling. Vinezi raised an arm and her blade stopped, inches from his arm. "You cannot stop me, girl."

"Let me decide that." She put more pressure on and his eyes widened as she drove his arm down. She lashed out with her free hand, cracking bone with a blow to the lower rib. He collapsed with a roar, his torch hitting the floor in a burst of sparks, even as more stone flew across the room.

Flir leapt back.

A second piece swept her legs out and she grunted as she hit the floor. That was going to bruise.

Another scream as yet more stone flashed, this time

slamming down from the roof to crush a man's head. A shaft of moonlight poured into the hole and an arrow sped across the gap. It bounced off Vinezi as he found his feet. Flir scrambled after him but the man was stopped by Alosus, whose giant hand engulfed his arm.

Luik appeared, swinging his mace.

It bounced off Vinezi's back without causing the man to even stumble.

"The stomach." Flir shouted.

Vinezi struggled with Alosus, whose face was twisted in a snarl as he tried to drive his fist into Vinezi, unable to beat the magic.

Cracking sounds came from above.

Huge slabs of stone crashed down from the roof, burying struggling men. Flir dived away, her cry lost in the roar. She tumbled into the columns, chest heaving. Stone continued to rain down on the mosaic, light, wind and rain pouring in after. Some few Shield had fallen back to the safety of the columns and the archers in the loft were safe, but the temple floor was littered with bodies.

Hints of armour and red robes were visible among the rubble. An arm twitched in one pile and she stepped around trails of blood as she made her way to the centre of the heap, where Vinezi and Alosus had stood.

Stone shifted as she neared. She crouched, but no more debris flew across the room, instead, part of the pile creaked, beginning to sink. A hole in the floor? Flir dashed forward.

There! Mottled skin. Alosus, still covered in stone, was sliding toward the centre of the hole. She caught his arm and pulled him back from the edge, swearing when she noticed a hint of fabric and bone slipping away beyond him. She carried Alosus to the columns, laying him flat.

His chest rose and fell but his body was heavily bruised. Had he survived simply because he was strong, or close to Vinezi when the man pulled the roof in?

She motioned to one of the surviving Shield, who'd rushed forward.

"Help him. And search for survivors."

Flir scanned the rubble until she found Luik. He'd escaped most of the wreckage but he was unconscious. She brushed aside some large pieces of stone – they'd leave serious bruises – then moved him to the clear space near Alosus. His eyes fluttered.

"Luik?"

He groaned. "I'm alive. Go get him."

She stood. "Someone bring a healer, right away."

"Where are you going, lady?" one of her men asked.

"After Vinezi."

"You think he's alive?"

"Not for long."

CHAPTER 53

Near to a week out of the city they passed Anaskari wagons, stirring grey dust of the Wasteland. Ain stood back, a frown on his face as each one, half a dozen in all, rumbled by.

The frown wasn't only because he missed the Bird of the Sun.

Morning sun beat down on rotten flesh that dripped from the rear of the wagon beds, empty now. They'd doubtless been to dump the remains of the Sea Beast in the Waste. Did that mean the place would soon be diseased? Just what everyone needed.

Only a token force of Shield rode with the drivers and when Wayrn spoke with them, they carried on without bothering Ain or Schan.

"They've been dumping the flesh in the Wards, which we'll reach by nightfall," Wayrn reported.

"What will that do to them?"

"I don't know. Surely nothing?"

"We'll find out soon enough," Schan said. "I'd be more concerned about what the Wards might do to us."

"I've never seen them," Wayrn said. "How dangerous are they? I understand they no longer actively attack travellers?"

"No, but some folk simply never return after going inside."

He nodded, looking into the distance. "And then?"

"Two weeks to the Cloud once we pass the Wards, hopefully no big sandstorms to slow us either."

"Something to look forward to then."

They resumed their journey. By noon the path to Tanija and the caves of the Mazu Clan appeared, dark ridges rising in the distance. Ain paused to water his horse, taking a few sips from his own flask. Their stores were generous. Despite the strength of the path beneath his feet, he wouldn't need to find a well before the Wards and a detour to see Tanija probably wasn't necessary.

Though he would have liked to see the man and his family.

Wayrn left the road, taking only a few steps into the rock-strewn Waste, a hand raised to shield his eyes. "Something shimmers in the distance. Another illusion from the sun?"

Ain joined him, Schan not far behind. Wayrn pointed to a rock formation, tall as a man, that stood in a half-circle. Heat waves blurred the distant stone.

"It's nothing," Schan said.

"I suppose." Ain turned away, but spun back when a flash of red caught his eye. Wait... Nothing. Only the heat waves and the drab grey of the wasteland. He squinted. Still nothing.

"Coming, lad?" Schan asked.

"Sorry." Ain returned to his horse and on they rode, Schan leading and Wayrn between them. The Braonn kept glancing over his shoulder. Ain soon joined him. Was there a new disturbance, closer, wavering in the air?

Sands!

It could have been the creature that stalked him on his first journey. Or, more accurately, stalked the Bird of the Sun. But that one had been more camouflaged. This figure was different – and yes – there it was again. A hint of red in the heat waves.

"Schan." His pulse quickened. Something about the waves...they were...unnatural. His horse stamped a foot in the sand. Wayrn's own mount snorted. "It's changing."

A wisp of shadows, black and red entwined, formed in the waves.

"Ride," Schan called, and wheeled his mount. Gravel and dust flew as Wayrn followed, and Ain snapped his own reins, his horse happy to comply. He glanced over his shoulder. The wisps had solidified, wavering as they kept pace.

"Faster," Ain shouted.

They tore into the Waste, the path magnified beneath them. Each hoof beat was like a thunderclap and his chest heaved. Still the thing kept pace and worse, began to gain on them.

Schan angled toward the still distant ridges and Ain cried out but his friend didn't turn, instead taking them toward more treacherous patches of the waste, the rockier, uneven paths heading toward the hills.

When Ain next turned, he saw a second swirling mess – this charging in from the west. Dust storm. The grey wall was closing, creeping yet, but still dangerous. Another curse. Had the Sands abandoned them?

The wavering wisps grew closer still. He steered his mount around a sharp dip, breathing hard. Schan had sought higher ground and Wayrn was close behind, but Ain's detour was taking him away from them. The blur of grey stone and gravel slowed beneath his horse's hooves as he angled back toward the others, picking through rough terrain. The howl of wind rose and the red and black menace poured forth its panic – how had it come so close so quickly?

Even the dust storm was too near.

The horse stumbled into a hole. Ain clutched at the reins but it was too late, he was already flying through the air. He crashed to the ground with a cry, groaning even as he rolled to his feet, a dull throb spreading along his hip.

The storm swallowed his horse and he fell back when it screamed. He spun. Where were the stalking wisps? Gone. Yet from inside the screen of dust that rose around him, darkening the sun, was the sound of ripping fabric, of puncturing sounds and of flesh being torn from bone.

Darklings!

The true Mazu clan. Those who stole blood to fuel their sinister magic, those whom had supposedly died out centuries ago.

He fell back, slapping hands over his ears as the horse screamed on.

Dust everywhere.

Ain fled, stumbling over rocks and ridges, heading toward where he'd last seen Schan. The paths were drowned beneath him, only a thudding echo – and yet, if he slowed...yes, there. A way forward. Only, a strange path, nothing he'd ever felt. An opposite force, a path that didn't exist in the thump of feet passing, but in peace, one pulling him along, away from the strange creature.

Half-blinded by the swirling dust, he drew his cloak

over his mouth and surrendered to the strange path.

And no longer did he stumble. No rocks caught his feet, no dips or welts in the earth to catch him, just every step firm and true. Even the wind and dust, even in the dim light, even with the ache in his hip, he travelled swiftly. A dark mass appeared ahead – safety. The path drew him closer.

The new path led away from the menace but the creature pursued him still. Was it truly a darkling? There was no way to know without getting too close.

Ain ran. Still he did not trip, even when the earth sloped down, his every step was sure until he came to a large cave mouth and ducked inside, coughing as he collapsed on cold sand, scrambling back into the dark.

The mysterious creature followed. The unease it created ranged before it like invisible vines, crawling up the path. Ain squeezed his eyes shut. "Sands protect me." If he could ride out the storm in safety, there'd be a chance. He thrust his hands into the sand and imagined the path closing, disappearing in the grey of the waste.

And it changed!

No more hiss of animal feet across the sand, no more vines crawling over the path, not even the hint of peace, just a sense of closing. As if the path itself had disintegrated into sand and was scattered by the wind.

The coloured wisps of death faltered, slowing. Its frustration ran along the path, a violent ripple, but he held firm. Keep the path closed, Ain. Keep it closed. Pressure built. It was trying to break down his defence.

He began to tremble. It pushed harder and his image of the empty, pathless waste wavered.

Ain dug deeper into the sand, clenching his teeth. "No."

And then it was gone.

He fell back, chest heaving. It was gone and he was safe.

CHAPTER 54

When had he screamed last? As a boy? Or a young man, hurtling toward white waves and black rock?

Seto gasped for breath, hands gripping the tiny desk that floated in a black void. The deep thunder of silence surrounded him, pressed against his skin. The pain had gone, but he hadn't woken. A regular click echoed in the hush. Very precise but faint. Bone on bone?

A woman appeared before him and he flinched. She wore a simple hooded gown of green that brushed her toes, but her face was blank. Only skin covered the front of her head, with grooves for eyes and mouth – and a slight protuberance in place of a nose.

Little Oseto.

He blinked at the force of her voice, though it was beautiful too. Who did it remind him of? "Chelona?"

I remember your uncertain clasp. The flutter of your heart.

"Lady, you truly remember me? I have been trying to reach you."

The blank face leant closer. *A barely adequate search, Oseto. How long did you leave me at the bottom of the restless ocean? After promising so much.*

Seto gasped. Her displeasure poured forth in waves that twisted his very insides. He shuddered, knuckles white where he gripped the desk. "I was injured, most severely." He managed. "It took time to grow in strength and power, before I was able to hire ships in secret."

All this I know. But you should never have stopped, Oseto. Not until I was found.

"I apologise for failing you. Forgive me."

That I haven't decided. She drifted closer, seating herself opposite him and placing smooth hands on the table. Right down to the curved nails, they were perfect. *You were to free me from your grasping family.*

"Yes."

And yet your actions are so similar.

"Lady?"

Like all of your kind, you wish to use me for small ends.

The turmoil in his stomach eased. He wiped his brow. "Forgive me again, but is there no agreement between you and my line – like the other Houses? I thought any assistance you offered was willing."

Willing, yes, but all agreements are individual. Do you not even know the details of your own House's servitude?

Servitude? "It has been over five hundred years, My Lady and my family has been lax with its records it seems. Or perhaps my father simply wanted me ignorant." He frowned. "Of what servitude do we speak?"

Five hundred years is not a long span, Oseto. Disapproval. *Your line serves me as I served you.*

"Then can we not help each other?"

Once, I believed we could. Now I am not sure. When you took me, Little Oseto, I wondered. Was your line finally living up to its promise?

"What promise, My Lady?"

The Sacrifice.

A chill. "Which would involve?"

Do not fear. You are fulfilling your end of the bargain.

"I am?"

By joining me here while the transformation occurs. Has so little of our agreement truly been documented? Passed down?

"Again, I fear it has been hidden from me, by design."

Her voice softened. *That is unfortunate — I had assumed you knew, which is why you took me.*

"I took you because..." He hesitated. Did she care? Would she want to hear something else? He almost snorted. As if he could hide anything from her. "I wanted to prove myself to my father. A pointless endeavour in more ways than one, My Lady. What is the Sacrifice I must commit so that we may work together again? I did not know my line had failed you so."

It is not a failure, so much as a delay, now that you are here. She reached out to take his hands and he screamed as his vision darkened. *It will pass, little one.*

When he could see again the pain receded, though it remained, and Chelona had not released him. "Have I angered you, My Lady?"

No. The pain will not last, but it is necessary. Your kind are fragile, I will admit. But I will ease you during the Sacrifice.

"Thank you," he managed. Things were getting out of hand. "But I still do not understand the Sacrifice."

A sigh of patience wavering. *Very well. I will show you.*

Her face and body dissolved and in its place appeared a huge carcass, on a windswept beach. Seto gasped from where he observed the scene. A sea beast lay on its side, half-submerged in foamy water. Its scales shimmered gold and the giant eye was open, sightless.

Two figures approached, their dress antiquated and the swords at their belts had the look of bronze. The elder man's head was shaven and his face deeply lined around the mouth and beneath the eyes.

"The Old Land?" he guessed.

Only to you, Little Oseto. You witness a discovery by Lucisan and his son that will lead to the first arrangement between humans and my own predecessors.

Bones clicked before he could ask another question, changing the scene. A younger man, with similar creased features, sat in a cave furnished with benches, tools and braziers. Behind his workbench, a large rib bone lay mounted to the wall.

Twice the man cocked his head while he worked on something Seto couldn't see, then resumed his labours. Finally, after a third pause, a slight furrow to his brow, he stood and faced the rib bone. Slowly his expression changed from confusion to rapture, and he nodded at the bone.

Then he lifted it to his bench and raised a chisel, again, titling his head again, now as if listening, and then began to carve.

Bones clicked.

The same man stood beneath a bright moon overlooking a still lake. In his hands he held a mask of bone, which he stared at for a long moment before placing upon his face. A Greatmask – but like no other. Heavy brows and deep sockets, long fangs and a row of horns along the forehead, it had a dark aspect.

Seto whispered. "Is that the first Greatmask?"

After a fashion.

"But it looks nothing like ours, nothing like Vitahu."

Vitahu was not the first. And of more relevance, know that

Cianal entered into a different understanding than ours.

Bones clicked.

Sunset over a battle and Cianal charged a line, twin swords severing limbs and heads, blows flinging men across a chaotic but silent battlefield. Silent for Seto at least. The carver fought on, untouchable – Greatmask free of blood or mud.

Bones clicked.

Cianal stood on a hill overlooking a port city, a horde of soldiers at his back. He raised his hand and the sea churned, rising to swallow the city.

Bones clicked.

Cianals' screaming face, hands outstretched. Flames shot forth and Seto's vantage point widened to encompass a line of men in a great hall, each wearing gold crowns, and each burned to cinders.

Bones clicked.

Cianal lying on a bed in a white robe, his face a map of wrinkles, hair thin and grey, attended by a single man – his son, by the distinctive creases around his mouth. Cianal placed the Greatmask on and beckoned his son closer.

When the boy pulled back, Cianal's chest no longer rose and fell.

Bones clicked.

Cianal's son stood in a large cave, torch held high. Bones lined the walls.

And so down through his line and the lines of his children was the first Greatmask passed, along with the others he had made.

A scene of other beaches, other beasts and other men carving, flashed before Seto's eyes. Time passed and the men aged, some passing the masks down on deathbeds, some losing them, some dying, clawing over them with bloody hands until –

Bones clicked.

Another young man, now in heavy plate armour, sat beside yet another dying father in a quiet room, cold sunlight pouring in from a high window. He and the older man shared a sad smile, both knew his time was upon them.

And then, in the time it took Seto to blink, the man passed and the son closed his father's eyes, drew up a white sheet and knelt in prayer or grief. When done, he took up a Greatmask from his father's side and placed it on his face, shoulders heavy.

The mask was the first horned Greatmask.

And then he threw his head back and screamed – in what seemed to be joy. He thrust his fists into the air and laughed and laughed.

"What is this?" Seto asked.

That is Cianal taking possession of one of his descendants, as per the arrangement he struck with his great-grandson. The first Sacrifice.

The image faded and Chelona reappeared, surrounded by the darkness once more.

"But how?"

Cianal discovered that the bones of the 'Gods' as you might term them, could be quite porous – even that a small piece of them, such as a mask, might come to absorb and house the memory, the spirit, of a human.

Seto narrowed his eyes. "Then on his deathbed..."

Yes. He passed into the Mask. And from that point on, directed and helped his children, if in a much less formal fashion than ours. Yet the desire for life was too strong. He was soon unhappy.

"So he made a deal with his great-grandson – he would only continue to act as a tool of power if he could one day take a body for his own."

Chelona nodded. *And now ten generations of Casa Swordfish have passed and it is your turn. I have served your line faithfully. In accordance with the true order of the world, I have not meddled in the affairs of death, I have observed other great laws that are not important now. All other tasks I have performed.*

The true order? When Father tried to resurrect Fiora? Seto flinched as bolt of pain shot up his arms. She was continuing the Sacrifice!

"Is there no other way?"

No. It is time for the Sacrifice to begin. Your body will be mine to shape and to use, and your mind absorbed into the Mask, where you will serve with each of the others, contributing to the lineage of power and knowledge, preserving and sustaining. Be at ease, be proud. You will live forever.

Seto's chest constricted.

CHAPTER 55

Sofia stood on her toes and prodded the sap-window with her shoe. It was safer to touch, more set than sap in the grove. She pushed harder and golden light passed through as the sap stretched, coating her boot. And then it stopped. She pulled back, fighting the amber until her shoe burst free.

There was no way out.

Her room was guarded day and night and Efran refused to let her see either her friends or her father. She had to find a way. Either that or kill him. Only all she had was Osani. And he wasn't answering, nor would he.

She rested her head in a basin of water, the coolness of the water easing her headache. Pushing her dripping hair back, Sofia returned to her table. Now that teaching Catrin was underway, Efran afforded her furniture. A proper cot and table and chair, even a change of clothes. Aside from her red robes, she now possessed a simple tunic and pants in forest green.

The door opened and a Sap-Born placed a tray on her table and left without a word. She ate the fruit and nuts, drinking down the milk that came with it and sighed. Someone would be along to escort her to Catrin's rooms shortly.

While waiting, Sofia probed Osani. He was a mountain side, sealed off. No hand holds to scale, there was only the sense of his distance and age. No calls were answered, not even a flicker. How could she even begin to find a way in?

The door opened again. It was Catrin herself. Sofia smothered a groan. Damn the girl, she was too cheerful. Her father had obviously raised his daughter to be a mindless parrot of his views. Was the girl's mother any better?

"Are you ready, Lady Sofia?"

"I am." She followed Catrin to the room by the stairs and took her chair, silent. Portraits of the Bloodwood lined the walls and a small pot of sap sat on a bench beneath a window. It seemed to comfort the girl, who checked on it regularly.

Catrin readied her notes. "I think we've covered the palace quite well. Tell me more about the city itself. The tiers. How would I move about as a noblewoman?"

Sofia met Catrin's eyes. "What does your mother think of this?"

The girl's expression grew dismissive. "The woman who birthed me hardly matters. She's no more important than the others."

"Others?"

She laughed. "Isn't it obvious by looking at me? We have Anaskari women here, Lady. They assist Father."

Sofia's stomach churned. 'Assist.' Poor women, what kind of hell were their lives? She would help them – once she found Father. And Notch. Sofia sneered at the girl's placid expression. "So you truly want me to help you die?"

"What do you mean?"

"You will die. When you reach Anaskar, you will fail."

"Everyone dies." She smiled, raising an arm, whose veins pulsed once. "And besides. I'm confident I can achieve the goal of freedom for my people."

"You are young. Do you really think assassinating King Oseto is going to magically achieve that?"

"Hardly. It's a first step."

"It's a false step. Anyone you murder will be replaced. And if Anaskar learns who sent the assassin, your forest will be razed."

"But that won't be easy." She waved a hand. "Anaskar has no Greatmasks —they're here with you. Or, more accurately, with Father. And the Sap has made us strong."

"Someone will see through your act."

"Would you, if you didn't know who I really was?" Catrin didn't wait for an answer. "It doesn't matter anyway. Back to the tiers."

Sofia folded her arms. "No."

"No?"

"Tell Efran that I've waited long enough. I will see my father and my friends before I sit through one more of these lessons."

Catrin regarded her a long moment before leaving the room. Sofia snorted. Who did the girl think she was?

Efran appeared quickly. "What is this?"

She stood. "My compliance relies on my acceptance of the fact that both my friends and father live. Demonstrate your side of the bargain."

Efran narrowed his eyes. "You are quite demanding today."

"Father, let her see them." Catrin took his hand.

He glanced at her, then back to Sofia. "Fine. Catrin will take you to see them – but you will make up the lost time this evening."

"Very well." Sofia said.

"It wasn't a request." He grunted as he left, face lined with a new weariness. Good, there was something she could exploit there. Or at least, there would be if she could figure it out. Patience.

"Come on." Catrin took a cloak from the back of her chair. "I'll take you now. Get it done with."

She followed her captor out and down the stairs. "Your father seems agitated."

"He's working and doesn't like interruptions."

"On what?"

"Safer ways to use the sap."

Sofia paused at the bottom of the stair. Sap-Born and Braonn crowded a wide room. Most sat and talked, mugs in hand, but a good deal gathered around small tables with pools of amber in the centre. Holding their hands over the pools, they took turns swirling or raising the sap with their palms – each without actually touching it. Their veins pulsed as they worked, brows furrowed.

But Catrin did not linger, instead exiting the building into air cold enough to pink Sofia's cheeks. Trees grew close around the building and Sofia finally caught her bearings. The grove was not too distant, and it appeared her prison was tucked in at the edge of a small clearing, its roof covered in generations of decaying leaves.

"Where are we going?" she asked.

Catrin strode along a dirt trail leading between the trunks. "It's not far."

She was right.

The trail turned and another building appeared. It too, was snug against trees and low-lying branches. A pair of sappers stood guarding a heavy wooden door. There were no windows. Catrin motioned to them and they stood aside, one opening the door.

Inside, a bare room a single lamp glowed, casting light on four poles that had been driven into the dirt floor. Her friends stood tied to three of the poles and a cold brazier sat before them.

Notch was bruised, dried blood long since caked down the side of his face. Emilio had a similar half-healed cut across his forehead and his tunic was spotted with blood. Nia looked paler than usual and did not stir, but at their entrance, Notch's head sprung up. "Sofia."

She ran forward, wrapping her arms around him. He ducked his head down to her own. "Are you well?" he asked.

"Fine. You?"

"He hasn't done anything serious yet. You've struck some sort of deal?"

"I train his little assassin and he doesn't kill any of you."

"Of course. And your father?"

"I'm seeing him next."

"You have Osani?"

She shook her head. "I still cannot use him."

Catrin cleared her throat. Sofia turned to face her. "Is there a time limit on my visit?"

The younger girl raised an eyebrow, exactly like her father, but stepped outside.

Notch grinned. "You getting your way already, then?"

"Of course." She tried to return his grin but seeing them all prisoner...what cheer was there truly? "How are the others?"

"Emilio is angry and Nia is grim, but she's working on something. She's exhausted but you should be able to wake Emilio."

"All right." She lowered her voice. "They have me in a large building beyond the trail. Top floor." Next she moved to Emilio and shook his shoulder, calling his name. He flinched when he woke, but his eyes lit up when he saw her. "You're safe, My Lady."

"As are you. I've bought us some time."

"Ah, that is why we live yet. We will find a way to escape, lady."

Catrin entered and cleared her throat again. Sofia gave Emilio a smile meant to hearten him before checking on Nia, whose chest rose and fell. Up close, the skin on her face was once again darkly translucent.

Sofia took one last look at them before she left.

Catrin turned back toward the larger building. "I've changed my mind. That's enough for today. We're wasting time."

Sofia stopped. "Where is my father?"

"You're not letting this go, are you?"

"Would you?"

Catrin pursed her lips. "Fine. But you won't like it."

CHAPTER 56

The glow of Anaskar had been growing on the black horizon for hours.

"Not long now," Yaev said. He wore chest armour and furs now, helmet's nose guard blocking his face. It gave him a grim aspect. Kanis wore only his vest and leathers but had belted on a heavy hammer.

The catapults were being readied and acor transported above decks. Each man carrying the dangerous powder had strict instructions to keep it closed up.

"Indeed." Excitement stirred. Everything would be decided soon. The wealthiest city in the known world soon to be open to him – a third and final dream had confirmed as much. He could take hold of a worthy future. Yet despite the anticipation, there was Flir beneath it all. Would she be there, on the walls? Or striding the streets? Soon he'd know.

He turned to Skink, who stood by silently. A perfect slave really. "Skink, I want you to listen."

"Yes, dilar."

"If we do not return, find a way home to Renovar.

Steal passage if you must. See your family, wait for me with them. Those are my wishes."

"Are you, sure, dilar? How will I serve you?"

"By doing as I have said. Now go and open the drawer in my desk and bring me the bottle within."

"At once, dilar."

No sooner had the boy ran off than a pair of sailors escorted Atilus to the prow. "So, we're closer than I thought," he said, eyes on the horizon.

"A matter of hours."

"Then I will take my leave and pack, as I'll be disembarking soon. Ready a longboat with several days' water and supplies."

Kanis frowned. "What are you talking about?"

"My instructions are to leave the ship before you reach the bay itself. But don't worry," he said. His expression was tight – what was he hiding? "I'll give you the final instruction before I go."

Kanis nodded to his men, who hurried off to ready the boat.

"Still trust him?" Yaev asked.

"No, but I'll kill him in his damn boat if he tries something." Did the sudden departure have anything to do with that bone charm?

By the time everything was ready the glow on the horizon had bloomed into a yellow beacon. Individual lights were visible beyond city walls, rising like a mountain itself, proud against the black of the sky.

Atilus sat in the longboat, now dressed in his own red robes, waiting for it to hit the black water. Kanis leant over the rail. "Well?"

"The final step is to load the acor and fire it into the city. Follow up with a fireball."

Kanis clenched a fist. "You told us that already."

The longboat touched down. The man smirked up at him in the lantern light. "And that's all you need to know to finish the attack." He took his oars and dipped them into the water. "I hope we do not meet again, Kanis."

"That's the information you demanded to be healed for?" he shouted.

He called back. "I never trusted you, dilar – why did you trust me?"

Yaev was swearing for archers, but Kanis put a hand on his arm. "No, let me." He flipped his hammer into his hand and took aim, drawing his arm back then hurling down. The weapon flashed across the water and shattered the long boat's stern, tearing through to the water.

A cry of dismay followed.

"Hope you're a good swimmer," Kanis shouted, then left the railing and the sinking boat behind. Atilus still hadn't shared everything – not about the acor, but about whatever else it was that had been troubling him.

But the city of Anaskar and its riches waited. And if Mishalar truly did smile upon him, he would see Flir again. There was no doubt she would survive whatever battle ensued. He doubted even acor could stop her. Slow her down maybe, but not stop.

As to what he'd say, he had no idea.

CHAPTER 57

Flir splashed along the dark tunnel, torchlight wild on the walls.

Somehow, the weasel had made his own hole in the temple floor. And she'd made a mistake. A lot of men died. Flir thumped the tunnel wall and a brick splashed down.

She hurried on.

Twice, the passage left the aqueducts and crossed the streets in the Second Tier, but each time she followed muddy footprints, a few spots of blood and even a fragment of bone. She was lucky it hadn't rained today – and yet, it made no difference in the end.

He escaped.

The passage opened into a large chamber. Its walls were lined with green slime and a pitiful channel ran through its centre, trickling into a drain. Light fell through grates high above, pouring in cool blue bars. Insects were black shapes where they crossed.

A spot of blood rested on the stone at her feet.

She drew her blade. There were no exits on floor level,

only thin grates. A ladder led up to one of the grates in the ceiling but it was broken halfway. Did a shadow move in one of the corners?

"Come out, Vinezi."

Silence.

Then a figure limped into the torchlight. He scowled as he splashed to the centre of the room. His bone-lined clothing was ripped in places and many pieces were missing. His necklace remained intact but a makeshift bandage covered his thigh, red seeping through the fabric.

"So. We reach a stand-off," he said.

"It's not a standoff because I have all the advantages."

"Do you?"

She pointed with her sword. "Yes. You would have tried your stone trick by now, if you could. Where did you steal the bone from?"

He snorted. "Stealing? Worse, I have been forced to harvest from the harbour to make this," he sneered at his own costume, "paltry suit. And you are correct. It is spent – something both surprising and disappointing."

"Then meet your fate, Vinezi." She took another step forward. "It's finished; you should have stayed in the Old Land."

"Congratulations. You've figured out that much, from Alosus I imagine? Perhaps you are not all as stupid here as I suspected."

"Want to bargain?"

"My life for that of Alosus' son?"

"Something like that."

He shook his head, but he was smiling. "It's not much of a bargain, I must admit. I'd only be cheating you." He raised a hand, showing his missing finger.

"What does that mean?"

"I wonder if you found a body in your prison, dear White Lady?"

"Your decoy."

He laughed, then sprang forward – a knife appearing in his hand. Flir deflected his blow, then hiked her knee to kick him in the chest. He flew across the chamber, slamming onto the earth and sliding into the wall. He hit with a groan.

She followed him across the floor. "What are you talking about?"

He reached one knee, slashing with his blade, keeping her back. He said nothing, only drawing a knife and pressing an attack as he rose. What he lacked in strength, he made up for in speed, even wounded.

It was the desperation that burned in his eyes.

Flir gave ground, parrying as she did. "You won't win this fight."

Still no answer.

Flir pushed back, knocking one of his blades from his grip. He faltered momentarily, before launching what had to be a final attack. He hurled his bulk forward, arms raised to deliver a massive overhand blow, swinging down. Flir brought up her own sword in a reflexive action, impaling him to the hilt.

"Damn you!" She hadn't expected such a foolish move. There was no way she'd be willing to let him land such a blow and he knew it. She needed him alive. The light in his eyes faded as he slid off her blade, slumping to the water. It pooled around him as his bulk blocked the flow, now coloured red.

"Mishalar, what was that?" He'd done everything but throw himself upon her sword and all without reluctance or fear. The decoy, what did it mean? And why was his missing finger important? She was overlooking something. Everyone was.

There was no elation. Only questions. Somehow, he'd managed to have the final say. "You filthy worm."

Time to haul him out in any event. Flir grabbed one of Vinezi's arms and gave a tug. A wet rip followed and she stumbled, his arm in her hand. Gods, she hadn't pulled that hard, had she? Flir held the limb up to the torch, bone bracelet rattling.

The skin of his forearm – everywhere but his hand – was furry rather than hairy. "What's this?" She leant closer to his body. The discolouration of skin was confined to one cheek and jaw and on the opposite side of his face his stubble was heavier than the discoloured patch. An odd swirl of darkness rested beneath the skin under one of his vacant eyes. Yet more mysteries! Damn the weasel. Even in death he taunted them. Dumping the torch and grabbing him by the shoulders, Flir hauled Vinezi from the chamber and started back up the dark tunnel.

"You better be worth the trouble," she told the corpse.

*

In the Harper, Flir rolled Vinezi's body down the basement stairs, tossing the arm after. Next she gave orders to one of Seto's men and ran outside to pay the wagon-driver who'd helped her.

"You sure you don't want me to send a grim-cart around?" He scratched his head.

"Thank you, but he's where he should be. It's what his family would have wanted."

Flir then sent a runner to the palace. Seto needed to see the body. Next she could check on Luik and the others but she'd stop for a quick drink first. After all, she'd earned it.

She'd barely taken two mouthfuls when a message-bearer arrived. His eyes were wide and he gasped for air as he looked around.

"Lady Flir?"

"I'm here."

"At last." He rushed over, handing her a scroll. "Urgent. From Captain Holindo."

Unsealed. She unrolled it and read the hasty script. Four words only. She whispered them. "The invasion has begun."

"Get to the palace," she told him, and tore from the room. Her feet pounded on the cobblestones as she wove through shouting people and horses who flicked their tails and snorted, leaping clear over a cart that had toppled, spilling lemons into the street.

What was everyone doing? The gates were closed. "Stay in your homes," she shouted.

Flir was breathing hard by the time she found herself running through the staging area. Packed with soldiers, the glint of torchlight on breastplates flashed and the hum of a crowd bounced off the walls. General Tadeo shouted orders, giving his runners a shove as he sent them along the wall. The last of the Sea Beast, a large section of spine, was being hauled away and the demolition of nearby buildings and construction of the wall stood complete. New stone and mortar did not appear as sturdy. The pieces were generally much smaller than the old wall, but it was better than nothing. The scaffold supporting the makeshift archer's platforms were stronger-looking than anything that had been erected around the beast at least.

Captain Holindo waved to her from one of the platforms. She took the stairs two at a time and gripped the parapet beside an older Shield. White sails lay on the horizon, bright on a dark ocean. More rain was due, its scent heavy in the air. She squinted. "How many?"

"Dozen or so." The Shield spat. "Be here in a few hours, I'd say, Lady."

"And we'll send them back."

Holindo arrived, joined by Renaso. "It's time," the Captain said.

"And are we ready?"

He shook his head. "No, but we have to be nonetheless."

"Renaso? What about the vitriol and the acor powder?"

"We have some acid but it is not enough to defend even a fifth of the wall for any significant time. As for the acor, we have failed. Its secrets elude us as yet. Neutralising it will have to be done with water."

"Then that is what we'll do," Flir said.

"Forgive me."

"Don't apologise." She slapped his shoulder, causing him to stumble. "It's not your fault the city's being attacked."

Holindo stared across the water. "I've called a final meeting with General Tadeo, Admiral Baliso and the King. Would you join us?"

She nodded. "I sent your runner on to Seto."

"Good. That will be the second."

She frowned. "The first hasn't returned?"

"Not yet, and I sent him some time ago." Holindo turned back to the staging area. "No, wait. There's someone."

A boy in palace livery slipped through the press of silver, blue and the King's orange as soldiers rushed about, stacking bushels of arrows and vats of oil. He hopped over a stack of blades and climbed the stair. At the top, he spun, eyes wild. As soon as he saw them, he sprinted the final steps.

"Captain, Lady." He paused to catch his breath. "Lord Solicci requires you at the palace."

"What's happened?" she asked.

"It's King Oseto – no-one can wake him," he blurted.

CHAPTER 58

Ain woke, flinching from the light.

The interior of the cave was hushed and outside the wind had died. No sense of the strange, stalking shade – or darkling – remained. Only the ever-present thump of the paths. He was safe.

Outside, orange light bled across the waste.

He swallowed, throat dry. When he moved, his hip ached. The flesh was tender, no doubt a colourful bruise was spreading. He'd have to hurry; he needed water, he needed to find Schan and Wayrn. Ain worked out a few kinks from sleeping on sand, then exited the cave, limping at first. Paths spread around him. To the west, to home, the path headed into the fiery sun, a powerful thunder of hooves and countless boots.

North were lesser paths, but that was the direction he would take. He was much closer, by estimation, to the Caves of the Mazu, than home. Schan would have deduced the same and headed there too.

If he and Wayrn survived.

He climbed the slope, standing on the ridge that

protected the depression and its cave, where he paused. His poor horse. If the creature that tore it apart lurked nearby, could he fool it again? Closing a path was not something he'd ever been able to do – nor had reason to attempt. It was unheard of, as was the idea that a path could draw him from danger.

He scanned the dust and sand, distant dunes shadowed.

No sign of the darkling.

Ain hurried toward the caves, legs straining as he swallowed again. The path was strong enough but the clear pool he and Schan had found would not be on the Anaskari side of the Wasteland.

Sands, let there be a well.

Because surely there were no supplies left by the corpse of his horse? The ripping fabric and puncturing sounds echoed. No, it was a risk. If he even found it. He needed to reach the caves.

Ain followed the path as the sun set, not stopping when darkness fell around him, purple fading to a black that was scattered with stars. Bright dust above, dull dust below, he noted as his boots stirred the earth. He'd slowed in the dark, but didn't trip as often as he expected.

Instead, his throat grew sore and mouth dry. Even in the relative cool of the winter night sweat formed at his temples and beneath his eyes as he walked. He wiped at it periodically. Thankfully, it was better than being blasted in the day or having a dust storm choke him.

Or being stalked by darklings.

Another hour at least passed before he witnessed a change in the landscape. Even in darkness the ridges of rock that surrounded Tanija's caves were visible, rising to block out the stars on the horizon. He was close.

Yet his steps faltered.

The path split beneath his feet. One was the regular thrum of footfalls, and the other the newer, gentle urging, the same as he'd felt last night. A draw toward safety – but it turned away from the caves.

He stopped, running a tongue over parched lips.

If he ignored the path to safety, there was every chance he'd be abandoning Schan and Wayrn. If they'd reached the caves and were in danger, they needed him. It was surely less likely that the path pulling at him led to safety and Schan. No, the Sands were not that merciful.

He turned away from the path that seemed to promise safety, that had done just that only last night, and set his thirsty steps for the Caves of the Mazu.

*

Before dawn broke he collapsed beside a well, tearing at the coverings and heaving the bucket up where he dunked his face within. Coolness spread across his skin, tickling his ears as it trickled down the back of his neck. He swallowed a mouthful then slumped into the stone with a sigh, pushing back slick hair.

Finally.

He drank again as grey light grew around the depression. The path faded beneath his relief and he stood to turn a slow circle. Tanija's caves could not be far now. A few of the ridges thrusting up from the stony ground were familiar in design if not specifics. Uneven ground was cracked and broken. Behind him, distant now, were echoes of the peaceful path, it's urging all but gone.

"Sands preserve me." He took one more long drink, replaced the bucket and covered the well before resuming his journey.

By mid-morning he was thirsty again, but he was smiling too. The slope before him wound down into the great crater protecting Tanija's caves. Light fell halfway down the walls, shining into shadowed openings and leaving the very bottom dark. Veins of quartz caught the sun from where it wove through the walls, something he hadn't marked during his last visit.

Ain traced them with his eyes as he descended. Beautiful. His steps rang loud when he increased his pace; the almost-echo of the generations of feet beneath him of comfort. Were Schan and Wayrn already here? There were recent footfalls in the path. Tanija would have welcomed them, even Wayrn, probably.

A bird screeched overhead, voice echoing. Not the Solave.

He stopped. There were no other sounds.

Ain drew his belt knife. Nothing about the path below appeared disturbed, yet why were there no sounds and not even a hint of movement? The first cave opening was some distance away yet. He stepped closer to the rock face and continued at a slower pace, drawing to a complete halt when he neared the opening.

A faint buzzing came from within.

Ain gripped his blade, inching closer. What if it was a darkling, lying in wait? No fear poured from the opening; it was all his own trepidation. Sands, he was a fool. Darklings didn't buzz. Desert wasps, flies and even mosquitoes buzzed in the dark of night, but not the creature that devoured his horse.

Look inside or flee, Ain.

He leapt into the cave mouth. Shadow covered half the interior, a blank wall of rock and an open door. From inside the buzzing had been joined by an unpleasant odour. Slow, flickering light grew as he crept forward. Using the tip of his blade, he pushed the wooden door open and stepped inside – and wretched.

Bodies.

Covered in blood, torn, their faces were distorted in the dying lamplight. Filthy insects circled and crawled, tiny feet frantic as they swarmed around open wounds. He fell back, squeezing his eyes shut.

Had their bones been protruding, as if erupting from the very flesh?

He stumbled back onto the ramp, a shudder running the length of his body. The poor souls, had darklings come after all? Tanija had thought it safe, certain the Mazu were no more. It certainly appeared to be the sort of damage the creature would inflict. They had to be one and the same. Darkling and wisps of death.

Ain wound deeper down the walkway, checking houses as he did. Most he did not enter, the sound of flies enough. One was empty save for a boy, his head shaven like the rest of his people, half his rib cage visible through his tunic. Ain forced himself through the doorway to draw the curtain, then continued on until he came to Tanija's home.

The door hung off a single hinge but no stench and no flies.

Nor, he found as he walked through the empty rooms, any sign of life. He exhaled as he searched. They were alive, surely? A chair lay overturned and Tanija's children had not drawn up the blankets on their beds, but nothing else was amiss. From the faint glow of embers in the stove he lit a wick for a lamp and headed down the passage opposite the entry.

Everything was neat in the rooms where he and Schan had stayed. Ain slipped back into the passage and found its end. Another door – only this one of stone. According to Tanija, there were caves deeper beneath the earth, which led to Mazu symbols, carven columns, places the man's grandparents explored but abandoned.

Had something awoken in its depths? Did a chill seep from beneath the door? He pushed against it but it did not budge, even with his whole weight.

Ain returned to the walkway and continued his search. The quiet was complete, again, only the scrape of his feet on stone. Yet new paths pulsed beneath him, their urgency becoming clear the lower he went. Not every home concealed bodies, just as many were empty. Some of Tanija's people had survived. Or fled at the very least.

But still he found no-one.

Ain completed a circuit of the ground level, checking caves, only pausing to take water from a jug in one home and to eat a handful of nuts and a strip of salted meat in another. He hoped they'd forgive him. Here fewer caves contained bodies, yet many had stone doors hidden behind the living quarters.

All were sealed but one.

He pushed and stone ground on stone, revealing a black square of nothing. New paths surged into its darkness.

Ain raised his lamp.

CHAPTER 59

Chelona's face was taking on features.

A fine nose and the shadow of eyes. The suggestion of a mouth even. The longer she held him, the better defined it became. At first, only the whisper of a line across the bottom of her face. A slight upturning for the nose.

You are doing well, Little Oseto.

"I never agreed to this, My Lady."

Your line did. Her voice grew hard. *And when your immediate forebears begged that I pass them over for someone stronger, I agreed, knowing that you were indeed stronger of mind and of will, and knowing that you would soon come.*

"My father did what?"

Offered you in his stead, and in that of your sibling. When you came of age, you were to begin this process.

The old bastard – and coward!

Or had the old fool been just as shocked to learn of a pact made decades, centuries before his birth? Seto should have known. "So, the blackouts were not rejections of me. You were trying to fulfil the contract."

When you lost me to the ocean I had thought to turn from your line. I admit, my first attempts to bring you here were clumsy, but I have developed a more gentle touch now.

"My Lady, there must be a way to extend our arrangement."

There is not.

Seto clenched his teeth. He'd started to sweat. "I am old."

You are young.

"But my body is not, please, look closer. Remember, a human lifespan is not like a Greatmask's. You would not have a long or fruitful life in my body."

Nothing.

Her face continued to change. Were there hints for the whites of an eye now? "Chelona? My Lady?" His skin tingled, as if a hand caressed him.

This is unacceptable! Her voice thundered in his mind.

"I cannot change that, but there is a way. I could find someone else – someone young?" His stomach heaved. Proof that he was no better than his father.

But he did not take his offer back.

Such a bargain has been made before, Little Oseto.

"If I lie you can take me – there must be some way you can monitor me perhaps? To follow me in my attempts."

Of course. Was she amused? *If I agree, you understand only the line of Casa Swordfish is able to make the Sacrifice.*

"Blood of our line lives yet."

Then you will find them. And quickly, for your own life hangs in balance now. And if you do attempt a betrayal such as the one made by your father, my displeasure will fall upon you. I am watching.

He shivered. "Yes, My Lady."

CHAPTER 60

All around, amber oozed. Some of the flows glistened, and Sofia had to hop over trails without running into low-hanging branches. It was almost like a golden roof in places – and she even had to crawl at one point. Catrin herself grumbled when she first bent down. This deep in the grove the gardeners had not visited in some time, it seemed. Or maybe it was only days, who knew how fast the sap grew?

"Most of this is fresh, be careful," Catrin said.

Sofia slid between the buried boxes. "How far now?"

"Close."

"Is there another building hidden on this side of the grove?"

"There is," Catrin said. "Father has a room there."

They wove on between globs and trails of yellow, a faint rustle of leaves overhead, as the occasional free branch shifted.

"Here," Catrin said, moving aside and gesturing.

Sofia nearly stumbled back into the sap. A large tree stood buried in amber, so thick that someone could have rested within it easily.

And someone did.

Her father stood encased in sap.

He wore no under-mask and his face was set in a snarl, hands bunched into fists. His robe was half open, empty linfa-belt visible. Frozen.

"No!"

"He's alive."

Sofia made a choking sound. How could it be true? It had appeared as though..."What?"

"The Sap preserves him. If you move closer, you can hear his heart."

Sofia strode to the surface and strained her ear. At first, only the whisper of wind and Catrin's shifting and then, finally, a faint thump. A long pause. Thump. His heart was still beating. Slowly, but he was alive.

"See? He's fine, let's go now."

Sofia whirled. "What have you done?"

"What we must. Father put him there as leverage weeks ago. He tried to escape too many times and we already had most of the information we needed." She strode closer, a frown on her face. "But he's alive and safe. What else do you want?"

The blasted girl was bored. Catrin tapped her foot and there was even a little sigh. Sofia trembled. How dare she?

She shoved Catrin. Hard.

Caught off guard, the younger girl stumbled back into the sap with a cry. Sofia pounced. She swung her fist, knuckles cracking into the girl's cheek. A shockwave flew up her wrist but she didn't stop, pushing Catrin into the sap.

Her captor struggled but her torso was already half-submerged.

"Get me out," she hissed, clawing at Sofia's arms.

Sofia stepped back. "No." She caught one of Catrin's flailing arms and shoved it into the sap. The edges caught Sofia's skin and welts appeared when she tore herself free.

Catrin's face was red from strain, but her efforts were useless. The Sap had enveloped her up to the neck. Sofia leant close. "You're getting off easy, compared to what I'm going to do to your father for this."

"Bitch! When I get out of here –" Amber closed over her face and she was still.

Sofia heaved a deep breath. "I'll be long gone."

She moved back to her father and raised her hand, fingers hovering before the surface. "Just a little longer, Father. I'll return."

She dashed through the trees, head swivelling down each row. Light grew in the forest, scraping the distant edges of the grove but as yet, no gardeners were about.

Somehow, she had to find Argeon. Nothing else would work. She couldn't face down all the Sap-Born and Braonn, Mor and Efran, while rescuing Notch, Emilio and Nia. Where was the Greatmask? She needed help.

When the prison came into view, its grey blocks shadowed beneath trunks of the more ordered sap-trees, she circled to the rear. She took barely half a breath on her way. The back of the building was dark and thick with loam; damp leaves barely rustled beneath her feet.

Two guards and a locked door. No windows.

And she had no weapons. Only the Mask – which she couldn't use.

"Damn you, Osani." If only he would respond.

Shouting came from the trees. She tensed. It was

Efran. Asking after her and his daughter. The guards explained and the man swore. "Go, search for them."

Footsteps receded.

That took care of the guards. But how to enter the room? She waited a moment longer before slinking along the wall and peering round the stonework, the blocks chill against her shoulder. The backs of the guard and Efran were slipping into the grove, each moving in a different direction.

She dashed to the door and tried it. Locked of course.

Smash it down? There were only a few old branches nearby, each rotten and grey. A large stone poked from the loam. She brushed the leaves and dirt aside, heaving it from the earth.

Sharp edges. Good. But it would make too much noise, surely? Maybe it didn't matter, if she was fast. Sofia raised the stone over her head, elbows wobbling, then hurled it at the wood.

A crack split the air. The stone bounced back to thud into the earth and a deep split was revealed in the door. Sofia leapt forward and kicked at it until a panel came free. She tore at the wood, jamming an arm inside to fling a bar free. The door swung open and she leapt into the room, shutting it as best she could before spinning to the shocked faces of her friends.

"We have to hurry."

"How did you escape?" Notch asked. She ran to his side and tore at the ropes. Too tight. She swore. "Efran's daughter took me into the grove to show me Father. He's alive but he's trapped in the Sap." She faltered. "I don't know how we're going to get him out."

"Argeon," Emilio said.

"If I can find him." She thumped a fist against her

thigh. "I need something sharp."

"There." Notch gestured with his chin. Against the wall stood a stand of knives, some with serrated edges, some with hooks. None appeared pleasant. She snatched one up and sliced through the ropes, freeing them one at a time.

As they rubbed feeling into their limbs, she checked on the door. So far, no-one approached. But how long did they have?

"I don't know –"

Shouts. Too late. She spun. "Nia, can we escape out the back?"

"I can't use my powder on stone."

Notch armed himself, tossing a blade to Emilio then Nia. "We have to get out, one way or another." He strode forward.

"There's too many," Sofia stopped him.

"Then we'll lead them away – Emilio, go with Sofia. Find the mask and free her father. Circle around to the hollow. If we're not there, we'll be heading east." He glanced at Nia.

"East," she affirmed.

"It's too dangerous," Sofia said. "We should stay together."

"We don't have time. And we can't fight the whole Grove. The best chance is to lead them away. Nia?"

"I know a place," she said, joining him at the door. Notch glanced over his shoulder, meeting Emilio's eyes.

"I'll look after her," the Captain said.

He nodded and burst from the room. Emilio was on Nia's heels and Sofia leapt into the rising sun. Notch and Nia struggled with Sap-Born, ducking and slashing. One man went down and another pulsed, but Nia stopped him with a burst of powder.

"Go," Notch roared, fending off another blow. At any minute, dozens of men would pour from the larger building. "Sofia, go. Your father needs you."

She blinked back tears as Emilio dragged her away, behind the prison and into the trees. They slid down a slope, feet tearing the loam. At the bottom, he pulled her along a game trail, circling back toward the large building. She glanced over her shoulder as they climbed, but Notch and Nia were lost in the trees. Emilio bunkered in the undergrowth, waving her down with him.

"We can't waste this chance."

"I know."

That Notch and Nia might buy it with their lives was a thought she kept unspoken, though it remained between them. Why did Notch have to be so stubborn? But Father needed her too. She ground her teeth and peered through the leaves.

Dozens of Sap-Born now poured from the building. Once they stopped, she waited a moment before touching Emilio's shoulder. "Ready?" He crossed the small clearing to press himself up against the wall then waved her over, using the heavy, curved blade he'd taken from the torturer's rack.

He ducked beneath the windows and she followed, keeping low. At the door Emilio paused.

"I'm going to move quickly. Let me deal with any remaining men, My Lady."

"I will."

"Good." He glanced around and she followed his gaze. No-one. "Where am I going?" he asked.

"Upstairs. Efran has a room there."

"And Argeon is inside?"

"I hope so."

He frowned but said only, "And I. Ready?"

"Yes."

He shoved the door open and sprang into the room. Two men looked up from where they stood, stringing bows. Before they could draw weapons, Emilio had leapt across the room. His superior reach was all the advantage he needed. His knife whipped out and tore through one man's throat. Catching the second man's wrist, he pulled the fellow close enough to drive his head into the man's nose. A crunch put a stop to the glow in the Sap-Born's veins, as he fell back with a curse, yellow blood pouring down his face.

Emilio's knife cut his voice short.

He dashed for the stairs and Sofia climbed after him, her own blade held ready.

"That door," she pointed, once they'd reached the landing.

He tried the handle but shook his head before stepping back to give it a kick. Splinters flew. Inside lay austere furniture and a large mirror, its edges lined with paintings of trees and interlocking circles. At the foot of the bed lay a small chest and a cupboard crossed a corner. Emilio tore open the doors, but she saw only clothes over his shoulder.

Sofia bent to the chest. A steel lock caught the clasp. Argeon was within. How she knew, it didn't matter. She beat at the lock with the hilt of her blade. "It's not working."

"Find a key." He checked the bed, tossing a pillow aside. Sofia shifted the chest itself, then slid the mirror aside. A small panel of wood lay ajar. She pressed it and the panel popped open. Inside lay a small box, which she opened. A few scraps of paper and a row of jewels so blue that her eyes widened.

But no key.

"Emilio."

He paused a moment then snapped his fingers. "I'll return." He slipped from the room and the sound of doors opening and closing followed. Sofia stood, knife ready. His footsteps soon returned and he entered, a large axe in hand.

"Careful," she said.

"I will be," he said as he moved to the chest. He drew the axe back and swung, shattering the lock with a grunt.

Sofia knelt and threw back the broken lid.

Argeon lay encased in amber.

CHAPTER 61

Flir shook Seto gently. His head still wobbled where he lay on the expansive bed. Ridiculous. Now that she'd finally caught Vinezi for him...what else could go wrong?

"We've tried that, My Lady." Solicci said, his worry not fully clouding the frustration in his manner.

"I hope that's not the only thing you tried."

"Of course not. The healers can do nothing. Not even Mayla. She's off concocting a new draught and I'm searching for the Storm Singers now."

"It's the mask, isn't it?"

"I believe so." Both stood alone in the King's bedchamber. Wind howled outside and rain rattled the windows. A gust flew down the fireplace.

"Can you do something?"

"No. I have tried to remove it. Something untoward is happening...but he breathes at least."

"And where are Abrensi and Lavinia?"

"Finishing with another song. The last one before the invasion it seems."

Flir rubbed her neck. "There's nothing I can do, is there?"

"Not truly."

"Then I'm going back to the wall. Holindo's in charge

of the men, you're in charge here and I'm in charge of everyone, right?"

"Until his majesty wakes."

She gave him a grin. "I don't want the job, Solicci."

"I understand."

"Send word if he wakes."

"Of course."

"And get someone over to the Harper to move a body up here, I don't want it going missing."

"A body, Lady?"

"Yes. And it's heavy, so be sure to send men with stout backs."

"Vinezi?" he breathed.

"I imagine he has another surprise in store for us, but for now, I think I put a stop to him."

He straightened. "I'll send men at once."

She strode to the door but he stopped her. "Be safe."

"Sentiment, Solicci?"

He smiled. "Some."

"You too." She charged down the corridors. The ships would be within firing range in hours. Less. And still too much to be set in motion.

By the time she found a mount, fought the crowds and handed the reins off to a soldier in the camp, she was breathing hard. Too much running, even with a horse to do half the work. She signalled to Holindo, who joined her with a worried look on his face. "How is he?"

"It's the mask. Solicci has sent for the Storm Singers."

"That's something."

She nodded. "I nearly forgot to mention, but I killed Vinezi."

His eyes widened. "Just like that?"

"Well, it wasn't simple exactly, but it might have been

too easy. I'm having the body sent to the palace, to be safe. He mentioned 'waking something' too, which worries me. But we'll talk about it if we survive the invasion. Right now, let's gather everyone in your tent. We have to act as if Seto won't recover in time." Which he better. She'd kill him if he didn't.

Holindo sent runners and she watched a group of Shield haul a huge vat toward the wall. Thin trails of steam escaped from the edges of its lid. It moved on a wheeled platform, crunching to a halt beneath a system of ropes and pulleys. Men rushed to affix hooks to the vat and stood back, faces ruddy in the torchlight, signalling to those above, where space had been cleared for the vitriol to rest.

Further along, catapults loomed. To her eye, they didn't appear as sturdy as they ought, the timber and steel having an aged quality. In fact, they were smaller than modern catapults. How long since they'd been used? How many decades since an attack had even been attempted via the harbour? Piles of rubble were heaped nearby, the great arms creaking under the weight of their loads.

Maybe they ought to be flinging some of the acor from beneath the palace at the ships. Not a lot of margin for error – once it hit the water...

"Did you catch him?" a voice said, speaking quietly.

She blinked. Luik stood behind her, arms folded. A bruise crept across his forearms and though it was hard to be sure, it looked as though dried blood matted his short hair.

"Yes. Have you seen a healer?"

"I'm well enough," he grunted. "Where's the bastard now?"

"His body's in the basement of the Queen's Harper."

"Good."

"Maybe."

"Something wrong?"

"It's strange. At the end, when he knew he was caught, he threw himself on my blade."

"Think he's mad? Or he knew he was finished?"

"He has to be a little mad, but I think it was confidence too. He still has something in store for us, Luik. I know it."

"Wouldn't surprise me."

"Where have you been? Any survivors in the temple?"

"Just our men. I've been wandering the city."

"Useful."

"Not like that. We're preparing, in part, for regular siege, focusing on the walls, right?"

"Because of the breach."

"Right. But what about when they send acor over the wall?"

"That's what Holindo's fire-crews are for, that's why we've been searching for hidden acor for weeks."

"I know, but we should have given the fire-crews more time to prepare. We need better lines from the wells. We should have been planning how to use seawater somehow. We have to support them better."

"I agree, but how ready can they be? You remember the Pig. How could we prepare them for that?"

He shrugged. "We should have done more."

"You might be right. Where's Alosus?"

"Guarding the Tier wall in the palace."

"Good idea."

"What about Seto? Rumours are starting that he's died."

"Idiots." She lowered her voice. "The mask has done something to him but Abrensi's going to try and wake him." She caught sight of General Tadeo and Admiral Baliso heading for the tan command tent and started after them.

He kept pace, despite a slight limp. "So what's the plan?"

"Same as before, only now I'm in charge."

He chuckled. "How's that different from usual?"

She swiped at him but he ducked away, still grinning. Big fool. "Very clever. Let's just focus on how we get through the siege."

"Right."

Holindo's command tent was crowded with grim faces. The Captain was listening to the Admiral. "Our ships are ready but the Renovar fleet is larger than we hoped. We're not going to be as effective as I wished, even with the refit. But if we can attack their catapults, we'll sink them."

"It will have to be enough. Our catapults?"

"Ready. They are old but I'm praying they are good for several volleys – at least, for all the material we have to throw at them."

Tadeo leant forward. "I hesitate to ask, but can the Storm Singers help?"

"Possibly," Flir said. "I'd never want them to take part in any fighting. If we have to pull back to the First Tier we might engage them. If there is anything they can do."

Luik straightened. "Can they call a storm to disrupt the ships?"

Holindo called for a runner. "Let's find out."

"Let's hope," the Admiral said. "How long now?"

"An hour or so."

An older soldier dressed in the blue of the city Vigil cleared his throat. "If I might speak, My Lords?"

Holindo nodded. "No ceremony here, Meloc."

"Some of the people are heading underground. They think they will be safe from the explosions."

"Do we want to discourage that?" General Tadeo asked.

Flir frowned. "Did every explosion in the city breach the ground itself?"

"Some did. But we can't tell how potent each strike of acor will be," Luik added.

"They're in danger no matter where they seek shelter," Holindo said. "Don't stop them, just keep them off the streets as planned."

"We will."

"And when the breaches occur?" The General asked.

Holindo sighed. "I know, Tadeo. Falling back to the Second Tier is still an option."

"But its walls will be just as susceptible."

"But easier to defend."

Meloc stiffened. "That means sacrificing the population of the Lower Tier."

Silence.

"Unfortunately, yes," Holindo said. He paused to chew on some more herbs. "Either that, or everyone dies during a press of bodies at the Antico Gates. As it is, we're having to clear makeshift ladders at the Lower Tier walls too often. People are constantly trying to flee the city. And if we do fall back, the attackers will be within the walls anyway. And once supply lines are cut, we won't be able to support the population within the Second Tier."

"What about the Mountain Gate?"

"It still won't solve the problem of how to bring thousands of people through the Antico Gate while under attack."

"Then we should have moved them in days ago."

"The men on the walls need something to defend other than empty buildings," Tadeo said.

"And they won't be any safer in either Tier," Flir said. "Not with the ships flinging acor at us."

Meloc shook his head but fell silent.

Holindo clapped his hands together. "Let's all get to work then."

"Everyone is to support Admiral Baliso during the siege," Flir said. "And Luik will be leading the fire-crews. Report to me or Captain Holindo. In the event of both our deaths, General Tadeo. Understood?"

"Yes, My Lady," the room said.

CHAPTER 62

Sofia swore at the lump of sap. Her knife barely made a scratch, so hard was the amber.

Emilio ran to the door to listen. "What now?"

The gardeners. She spun. "They melt the sap with embers and hot knives."

He checked the hall. "Let's go." Sofia hauled the square of sap after him. At the bottom of the stairs, she held back a moment while Emilio checked the door. "No-one."

They slipped around the building, sneaking into the trees sheltering it. Hints of other structures were visible through the leaves, thatch rooving and heavy boards. A breath of smoke hung in the trees. The saw-marks looked fresh, even from their position. A child's voice echoed.

She pointed. "Look."

"Are the gardeners within?"

"I don't know. Last I saw them was within the grove itself."

"We go there first."

They crossed the small clearing and entered the

grove, stepping over a typical trail of sap. Emilio knelt a moment, head swivelling to peer beneath the rows. "Left." He took off again and Sofia followed, bumping into him when he stopped again.

"Be ready."

Emilio sprang into the next row. Sofia skidded after him, unable to keep up. He was already sprinting over the dirt and sap. The gardener fell back at the sight, overturning his brazier.

Embers hissed in dirt as Emilio swung his axe. The Braonn raised his own glowing knife but too late. Emilio's weapon hacked through the raised arm and the man screamed as blood flashed. The Shield twisted and followed-up with a second blow, this one digging into the man's neck.

The gardener collapsed, axe still lodged in his body. Sofia averted her eyes.

"Quickly."

She ran to his side as he jerked a glove free from the man's hand then passed it over. Sofia shuddered when she pulled it on, but took the blade from the dirt and began carving sap from Argeon, turning her back to the bleeding corpse. The glowing steel parted the amber with ease. She cut the corners away, then sliced the longer edge of the square on each side.

"Should we do this somewhere else?" she asked, wincing when her hand slipped too close to the glowing blade.

"Better to finish quickly." He held the axe again, its head bloody. "I'm watching."

More sap fell away. She breathed slower the closer she came to the bone itself. Careful. Don't push too hard. She ran the tip of the blade around his face. Next came the inside of the eyes. Shifting the knife, she shaved at the cheeks and mouth, flipping him to cut into the block of sap stuck inside.

"How goes it?" Emilio asked.

"Like being a Carver again – I should be able to wear it soon."

She kept slicing and shaving, but the curve of the mask obstructed her movements. And she needed most of it gone, else she'd have the mask stuck to her face.

Shouts.

A group of men in forest greens charged up the row. Emilio shifted his feet, taking on a wide stance, weapon ready. "Hurry, My Lady."

She cut away a few more pieces and stood. Four men. Armed with swords and bows. One man had pulled an arrow from his quiver. Emilio bent and snatched up a stone, hurling it at the bowman just as he drew. It struck his throat and the arrow flew wide as he pitched forward.

But another Braonn was already nocking his own arrow.

Sofia tucked Osani away and raised Argeon to her face. Still-warm traces and globs of sap stung her skin and she fought tears, even as she shouted.

"No!"

The bow string snapped and Emilio stumbled, a shaft caught in his shoulder.

He stood his ground. "Run, Sofia."

There was another way. Spirit-walking would not stop arrows. But maybe now, Argeon would hear her. She showed him darkness, the grove snapping into black.

As before, nothing.

"No, please," she cried.

And then Tantos was there in the dark, smiling at her.

Like this. His voice was the same, a touch of amusement as he showed her. For Argeon, there was no night and day. He saw everything.

You want him to blink, for lack of a better word. Tantos told her. *His blinks are slow.*

She showed Argeon and night fell.

CHAPTER 63

Flir glared at the ships in the darkness, their lights illuminating white sails. The decks were a flurry of activity as men rushed to set the acor on the catapults, or turn the ships to meet Admiral Baliso, who bore down on them in his cutter. Another ship joined him, this one a refitted merchant and significantly slower, its rails also lined with archers. Each man held burning arrows.

The plan was simple if risky.

Explode the ships where they floated, by intercepting their launch. There was no way for their few ships to stop the attack, but if they could at least do some damage it had to make a difference.

One of the Shield shifted beside her, armour scraping. His face was hard in the torchlight. Both hands were crossed on the pommel of a blade, its point resting in a crack in the makeshift platform. "Damn those pale bastards," he muttered. Then he flushed. "Begging your pardon, My Lady."

"Don't be sorry," Flir said. "I don't want them here either."

He mumbled another apology and moved off.

Luik chuckled. "You scared him away."

"Too bad it won't work for that lot out there."

"Any word from the Storm Singers?"

"None."

He grunted. "We do it the hard way then."

"There's no other way in battle, Luik."

"True." He pointed. "Look."

But she was already watching. A shout rose along the wall, demanding readiness. One of the enemy catapults drew back, its contents a glowing blaze. Baliso bore down on the Renovar fleet and his other ship split off to intercept one of the enemy vessels attempting to outflank them. "They're heading for the wrong catapult."

Luik slapped the parapet. "He sees it."

The Admiral changed course, slipping around to strafe the line, cutting away from the second ship. Heavy fire followed *The Seahawk* but his archers unleashed a volley of their own flaming arrows. They peppered the decks and sails, but the full force concentrated on a catapult – loaded with acor.

"Did it work?"

Flir shook her head. "It doesn't seem –"

A roar echoed across the water as orange light exploded into the dark. Pieces of burning wreckage flew through the air, leaving behind a smouldering skeleton of ruin. Men, some aflame, leapt into the water as the ship sank. Nearby vessels were a hive of activity, as lines of sailors and soldiers rushed to put a stop to small fires, protecting the volatile acor.

Cheers burst from the wall and Flir joined them until the snap of catapults crossed the harbour. One of the Renovar ships finally sent its cargo into the air, where it flew high above the wall to hurtle down and crash into the Second Tier streets. The rumble reached them on the Lower Tier and another ship was right behind, this one sending a blazing comet screaming overhead.

It landed with a thud and barely a breath passed before the explosion rocked the very city. A giant column of flame rose, smoke pouring into the night. Screams followed and Flir took half a step before Luik stopped her. His face was grim.

"We have men up there," he shouted.

She swore. "Luik, you're right. We're not prepared for this."

The old catapults on their own walls returned fire, hurling forth the rubble with a creaking boom. The makeshift shot arched into the air but fell short, splashing into the harbour. Curses rang out and another volley came from one of their catapults, this one wiping the rigging clear on a Renovar ship.

The wall erupted into cheers again, but on the water Baliso was in trouble. His merchant ship was on fire, men leaping from the sides. One of the Renovar ships was in trouble too, but the *The Seahawk* now had two cutters on its tail. Baliso twisted around the bay, archers returning fire, but it would be a losing battle. And the cutters didn't need to sink *The Seahawk*. All they had to do was protect the larger ships.

The Renovar fleet had been reduced to eight ships but they'd not been idle.

Two more enemy catapults cracked and another cargo of acor and flames shot into the night to smash down into the city, this time deeper into the Lower Tier. The explosion buffeted the walls and Flir squinted against the light. "Mishalar," she breathed. Entire buildings had disappeared. It was unnatural. Before she could turn back to the water, another volley struck the city – punching through a section of the Second Tier wall.

"They're not going to stop," she shouted to Luik.

On the comets came. Men on the walls shouted in despair and the lines below burst into action, hurling bucket after bucket at the flames. Already the blaze had started to spread. How many men would be able to fight when there were so many fires to deal with?

Their own catapults snapped back. Most hit true this time, but none of the targets sank; the cargo spread in the air, the amounts too small to sink the warships, even if they did scatter the decks and slow the attack. Worse, the Anaskari forces were already running out of rubble to hurl back.

"Tell Holindo I'm going out there," she said, running for the stair.

Luik gave chase, wincing as he caught her. "What?"

Flir pointed at the water. "Out there. See to the fires, Luik."

On ground level she pushed through the crowds of men in armour. "What's happening out there?" A young man asked. His eyes were wide and sweat dampened his hair.

"Hold your positions," she said. "They haven't sent longboats yet."

Luik caught her shoulder again. "Damn it, Flir. What do you think you can do?"

"Sink those ships myself if I have to."

"That's not funny."

"I'm not joking. I can do it."

"How?"

"I don't know yet. But I'll know once I get there." She reached up to take his shoulders. "Look after everyone here."

He hung his head. "I'll try."

"Good." Flir took a few steps but a whistling overhead stopped her. Acor smashed into a row of homes, barely a street over from the wall. Powder hung in the air like a screen. "Down," she screamed, ducking behind a stack of supplies. Fire rained and a moment later, the explosion boomed. It tore through the buildings, showering the staging area with burning debris.

Shaking her head to stop the ringing, which didn't work, she leapt from behind the stack.

Scattered pockets of flame burned. Smoke poured from the ground in orange columns and jumbles of wood and stone were littered with black tiles. The street across from them had borne the brunt of the damage – most buildings left with only foundations. Cries for help grew.

Men were regaining their feet to assist others. A few bodies did not rise, but causalities were light. She sneered at herself. What a thing to think. Luik rose from where he'd crouched nearby, and met her eyes. "Stay alive, do you hear me?" she said.

He nodded, then limped off to help.

Flir snatched a hand-saw from a nearby bench, charged from the staging area and skidded along the streets. Where was that grate? Near the wall, beyond the harbour gates.

A figure appeared ahead and she slowed. Pevin, running toward her. "Dilar, are you safe?"

"It's an invasion, Pevin, so no, I'm not. What are you doing here?"

"I'm here to help."

"How exactly?"

He faltered. "Well, to be near you. To protect you."

She opened her mouth to send him back, but shook

her head. He wouldn't listen anyway. Better to keep him in sight. "Just don't get yourself killed."

"I won't."

"Follow me then. And tell me what you learnt."

"Ambassador Lallor is sincere in his efforts to help people. I didn't recognise any of my former colleagues."

"That's something, I suppose."

She led him along dark streets at a sprint, boots echoing on the cobblestones. Whenever she saw people, Flir shouted for them to stay indoors. They obeyed. On a corner she found a man stumbling along, his steps unsteady. The fool was drunk.

"Keep off the street, it's not safe."

"What?" He blinked at her, then Pevin.

She took an arm and led him to an old building. Its door was locked. She thumped on it, wood creaking. It soon opened a crack, a frowning face revealed. "Who is it?"

"Let him in. It's too dangerous out here."

The frown deepened. "He's drunk, lady."

Flir pushed lightly, driving the door open and shoving the drunk inside. "Don't leave the building."

She didn't wait for an answer, pulling Pevin across the street and running closer to the wall. The grate had to be near now. When Alfeo led her to it last time –

Heat flung her to the ground.

Flir rolled, covering her head as flame roared, the ground shaking beneath her. Something crashed into her leg and she cursed. The heat eased and she reached her knees, Pevin pulling her the rest of the way up. His face was shocked in the red light. Another strike had hit, this one close enough to collapse the building she'd just left. She charged forward, coughing as a gust of smoke funnelled down the street. Heat, a red glow from a fire, no more than a few houses away, sucked the air from her lungs and she faltered. The moment the wind changed she ran forward again, Pevin close behind.

"We have to help," she shouted.

Half the building had collapsed, piles of stone heaped against the portions still standing. She climbed the pile and heaved a hunk of stone aside, then another and another until a hole appeared. She called inside but no-one answered.

"It's no use," Pevin said.

One more cry and she climbed down, foot slipping on something soft. She righted herself and groaned. An ankle protruded from the rubble, clothing torn and blood staining the stone around it. Flir leapt to the ground. There was nothing else to do.

She ran on until she saw the grate.

"Finally."

"This?" Pevin didn't appear thrilled.

"Down we go." Tearing it open, she began her descent. How were little Alfeo and his mother coping? And Bel? Light above faded to a faint orange blush when she stopped at the opening and swung inside, waiting for Pevin then jogging forward with her hands trailing the wall as guides. She slowed when light flickered ahead.

Two people huddled over a candle.

One of the figures stood, a blade catching the flickering light. "Who goes there?"

Alfeo and his mother.

"Flir."

"Lady?" He stepped closer, turning back. "Mother, it's Lady Flir-is."

"I hear you, son."

Alfeo's face was tight with worry and his mother's eyes listless. "We came here when the ships appeared."

"Good thinking, Alfeo." She motioned to Pevin, who stayed quiet. "This man is a friend."

He smiled. "See, Mother? I told you."

"Yes, dear."

"Have you seen Bel?" Flir asked, moving closer to the grate. It was a tight squeeze, but Alfeo and his mother made room. Across the water, another pair of blazing comets flew at the walls. Was there any more acor? The tremors had stopped. Maybe it didn't matter – who knew how much of the city was afire now? There was no return fire from their walls and longboats had already left the enemy ships, the red glow of fire reflecting from armour packed into each boat.

"Bel hasn't come yet. We don't think she can hear us," Alfeo said.

"We have to keep trying, right away."

"Why?"

"Because I need to speak with her and Sanac. I want them to take me out there."

Alfeo's mother snorted. "Lady, you must be daft-is. What are you going to do all by yourself?"

"Sink every one of those ships."

CHAPTER 64

Sofia crouched, cutting off a gasp. The darkness was complete but the scrape of boots and frightened mutters from the Sap-Born were almost too loud.

"Tantos?" she whispered.

Nothing.

Had he truly been there, or had she imagined it? Delusion and desperation perhaps. The sense of him had been so sudden, nothing like before. But it didn't matter. She stiffened when blue outlines appeared from the dark, then pale white outlines of the trees and yellow shimmering. The sap. Emilio's glow was frozen in place before her, she reached out and took his hand. He flinched but she pulled him down, squeezing his hand.

His muscles relaxed. She whispered in his ear. "I can see. Come with me."

Taking slow steps, they crept from the row. She glanced over her shoulder but the outlines of the Sap-Born had not moved far. Their hissing and arguing covered any incidental sounds she and Emilio made.

The longer she walked, the further the world resolved

itself into more shades. More detail. A greater depth of colour, more between the outlines. Still, there was no sky, only black.

"Is it still dark?" She knew the answer from his steps. But hearing his voice was something she wanted suddenly.

"Yes."

"Are you in much pain?"

"Enough."

"I can wrap it now if you like?"

"It'd take too much time to cut the arrow. I cannot simply pull it, the head is barbed."

"We'll hurry then."

She led him through the grove, bypassing another gardener – his knife and orange-glowing brazier sending off waves of heat as he crept about – and ever-closer to her father. Every outline was similar enough that it would have been hard to find him again, but his outline cut through all the others – a fiery blue that came into view as she narrowed her eyes.

Almost as if she was focusing deeper into the dark landscape.

A smaller blue shape glowed off to the side. Catrin. That was someone going no-where. Sofia slowed as the yellow shapes grew denser.

"Are we close?" Emilio asked.

"Yes. The sap is thick here. I have to give up the darkness for a time." Not only was the fresh sap a danger, but she doubted she could use the glowing knife safely without seeing the world as it was.

"Argeon, open your eyes," she whispered.

The world snapped into true shades. The depths of the Sap Grove glowed amber with the wintery sun. She gave a gasp when she saw Emilio properly. Blood soaked his shoulder from where the arrow protruded and his face was deathly white.

"We have to do something."

"First, your father."

Sofia hesitated.

"Hurry, they'll be searching for us again."

She crawled through the sap arch, turning to help him stand. His eyes widened when he saw her father in his tomb of amber, then Catrin, her foot protruding from her own cell of sap. "And they are alive?"

"I could hear Father's heartbeat before."

"How will you free him?"

She paused. "I thought I'd use the gardener's knife. Your axe?"

His mouth tightened. "I doubt either would be enough. The Greatmask?"

"Argeon, help me," she said. His attention swung to her. How quickly they worked together now. She showed him a picture of her father, standing beside her, not a single piece of sap left.

But nothing happened.

Could she melt it? But there was no heat to draw upon, not with the winter sky above.

"Tantos, are you there?"

Emilio gave her a look, but she ignored him.

"Please, where have you gone?"

Sister. The sense of him was immediate. Concern touched with a kind of detached amusement.

"How can I free Father? Please."

Assuming I want to help you?

She squashed down the fear, as tears formed. How could he still hurt her so? "For me, if you care for me at all, Tantos."

Silence.

"Please, Brother."

A sigh. *Very well. But know that I will not stay when he is conscious. And that I won't be able to help you forever.*

"What do you mean?"

I am still becoming part of Argeon, my sense of self, my memories, everything about me is being absorbed. Didn't Father tell you?

"No." She shivered. "I don't know anything about this."

Still Father hides things from you – you need to understand the true history of the Greatmasks.

"Like what? That you're becoming Argeon?"

In a way. The Greatmasks require a Sacrifice. It's part of what sustains them, and lends them such knowledge. Generations may pass before it's needed, but at my and Father's estimation, were I – or you – to bear children, one of them would have had to pay the price.

Sofia shivered. "Our children?"

No matter now. I took it upon myself to pay, though it's taken longer than I imagined. I drift in and out of awareness, Sofia. Sometimes I am myself, sometimes I seem to be many more people at the same time.

"I didn't know." When was Father going to tell her such things?

Worry not. I have done what must be done. Now, did you know our great, great grandfather was a skilled healer?

"Will Father need healing?"

Possibly, but your friend first. Tell Emilio to come closer.

Emilio had been working as she spoke; he'd already cut off the shaft and torn strips of clothing for a bandage. He had half an eye on the trees around them. As yet, there was no sound of pursuit. "Emilio, I think Argeon can help you," she said, moving to his side.

Watch, Sofia.

Her hands worked without her will, tearing at his tunic, brushing his hands away and taking hold of the remaining shaft.

"Sofia?"

"Trust me, Emilio."

I'll cheat now. Tantos said, and the wood beneath her fingers disintegrated. Then her hands hovered over the wound and the arrow head slipped free with a wince from Emilio. But the head had changed shape, losing its barbs.

She barely understood what happened next, as her hands moved in a whirlwind of activity, probing, wiping, dressing the wound and tying a bandage in such a way that supported but restricted movement to his shoulder.

Then her hands were her own again.

Done. Thanks Great, Great Grandfather Dilagi. Now for Father.

"How did you do that?" Emilio asked. "And thank you."

"I don't know."

We're going to melt the sap now. A pause. *What about the girl?*

"She's where she needs to be." No doubt Efran would have a way to remove her anyway. A better idea would be to have Tantos shove her in deeper. Or kill her? Sofia didn't even know if she could. Whatever Catrin was, she was still a girl. And there wasn't time anyway – the sap born, or Efran himself, could appear at any moment.

Very well. Get ready to catch him. And goodbye, sister.

"Wait, Tantos?"

No answer. She stepped forward and raised her arms. The sap began to steam, the hard surface running like water. It pooled below but Argeon diverted the stream before it reached her feet, sending it coursing back into the grove. Still the amber drained away, a small river flowing from the tree's base.

The tip of a finger came free first. Next Father's whole hand and then his arm and leg emerged from the amber. The sap continued to melt and where his robe or skin became visible, it was bone dry.

Finally his face was free and his body slipped forward, oozing from the sap. Sofia caught him, straining under his weight as the last of the sap drained away, then lowered him to the ground. Tears streamed down her face and she pulled her father close. His heartbeat thudded against her ear. She lifted her head.

His limbs had relaxed and his expression eased, but his eyes remained open and he did not speak.

"Father?"

Nothing.

Emilio knelt beside her. "He's alive, isn't he?"

"His heart is strong." Sofia clenched her fists. "Tantos?"

Still nothing. She spun at distant shouts. Men were co-ordinating a search, their voices loud. Should she bring the darkness back? How far from the edge of the grove were they? The Sap tree her father had been encased beside was still melting, shrivelling down to black, shuddering as it steamed.

"Can you wake him?" Emilio asked.

"Let me try."

Argeon was quiet again, lacking any hint of Tantos, though perhaps he was there, distant, but observing. Was that a trace of anger too? The Greatmask, its sense of self much more layered now that she'd recognised Tantos, was a swirling mix of traits and half-images, of faces and hands, unified by the solidarity, the crippling age of the bone itself.

Wake, Father. She showed Argeon an image of her father moving his arms, sitting up and breathing easy, his face alive with a smile.

But nothing changed.

The voices in the grove grew louder.

Emilio put a hand on her shoulder. "We should leave. I can carry him."

"Wait." Sofia raised a hand to touch Argeon. "Let me try one more thing." She pulled the mask free, tearing at her skin, then paused above her father's face. What if Tantos still lurked within, what if he tried to hurt Father? He'd said goodbye but he'd had no trouble lying before.

Osani.

She withdrew the mask and placed it on her father's face. She waited.

Nothing.

"It's not working, is it?" Emilio said.

"I don't think so. And why would it? Casa Cavallo."

She removed Osani and took Argeon. His blackened face was stern as ever. There was nothing left to try. Please, Tantos, leave him be. She rested the bone on her father's face and sat back, holding her breath.

CHAPTER 65

Seto opened his eyes.

His room was dim, only a single lamp burned. He lifted Chelona from his face and sat up. Silk stirred beneath him as his body sank into his bed.

"My King?"

Movement in the shadow and another lamp bloomed. Solicci held a cup. Seto accepted it and drank. Cool water. "Thank you."

"How do you feel?"

"Well enough." It was true. Some stiffness from laying still, but overall he was fine...and yet, there she was. On the edge of his consciousness. Watching as promised. What an awful bargain he had struck. "What day is it?"

"The attack has started and the city burns," Solicci said, voice heavy.

Seto shot to his feet, wobbling a moment. "Show me." He strode after his advisor, stopping as the man threw open curtains and then glass doors to one of the wide balconies.

The city was a swathe of orange and red, smoke pumping into the night sky. "Like ugly orange worms," he breathed.

Both tiers were choked with flame. It spewed from

gaping holes in the city itself, buildings crumbling and debris littering streets. Soldiers and city-folk held lines from wells, but few blazes appeared under control.

Further chaos reigned in the Lower Tier.

Soldiers from Renovar had taken the gates and were snaking into the city. Pockets of fighting occurred, small shapes whose shouts and cries were inaudible, lost in smoke and flame. The walls were still manned, but the defence spread across too many fronts. Now that the enemy was within the city, there was no point holding an entire wall. As yet, none had reached the Second Tier, but just as worrisome was one of the flaming masses raging near the gate.

In the harbour, Renovar ships sat like fat spiders waiting to feast.

Another catapult shot forth its deadly cargo, this time spearing down to explode in a shower of flame, engulfing a Second Tier square. Faint screams rose.

Seto hurled the cup from the balcony. "Enough."

He dashed to the bed and took Chelona.

Her presence loomed near as he placed her on and returned to the balcony. "Chelona, My Lady, please stop these fires."

Little Oseto. Do you wish to alter our arrangement?

"I wish to stop the city from burning, My Lady."

Not until you have arranged a Sacrifice. As agreed. And as we have discovered, you cannot offer yourself – you will die in the transition. Find a replacement.

He opened his mouth but said nothing. Thousands of people were dead or dying below. His city burned. An unreasonable enemy brought murder and fire and he was denied even the chance to stop it with a single – if momentous and noble – gesture.

"I don't know if there is time, My Lady."

Then hurry, youngling. The next time I hear from you, I expect it to be with a new Sacrifice.

He removed the Greatmask. "The city will burn, Solicci."

"There is no way?"

"She has demanded a Sacrifice."

Solicci raised an eyebrow. "So soon?"

"Does Osani require less?"

"No. But Osani is younger than the other masks. Our Sacrifice is not due for several generations yet. Did your father never speak of the Sacrifice to you?"

"No."

"Ah."

Seto placed the mask in his robes and turned back to the burning city. If only there were some distant relative, living close. The few remnants of the extended Swordfish line were scattered beyond Anaskar – the Far Islands and one in Renovar if he remembered correctly. But not even a single bastard at hand in the city.

He straightened. "Wait."

"What?"

"Follow me, Solicci."

Otonos.

CHAPTER 66

Flir waited and Anaskar burned, orange reflected in the water. The Renovar ships still hurled acor and burning loads at the city, though their frequency was less. Probably the men had to load from stores below decks – she couldn't imagine they'd expected the Anaskari fleet to be so decimated.

"They're taking their time now," Pevin said.

"Or being careful." After all, they worked with serious powder.

"I think she's coming-is," Alfeo said.

Flir turned to the water. Only darkness, until a small figure broke the surface. Bel didn't wear her usual smile. Instead her face was worried, even as she greeted everyone. "I'm glad you're all safe."

"For now," Flir said. She glanced at Pevin. She'd warned him but his eyes were still a little wide. "Are you and the Sea-People safe?"

"Yes. We've been staying well away from the people collecting bones-is and the ones fighting."

Bones? Vinezi and his people. But no time for that now. "Bel, that's part of why I wanted to speak with you. I need to get to those ships."

Pevin shifted but said nothing.

"Really?" Bel said.

She nodded. "And I need your help."

"My Lady, we don't have any ships."

"No, but what if you asked Sanac to help me somehow. Is it possible?"

Bel gave a shrug. "I don't know. But I can ask, I'll be back soon." She slipped below the surface and her blue tail gave a little splash.

Alfeo was still smiling. "She looks well, doesn't she, Mother?"

"Yes, dear."

"Lady, how are you going to stop the ships?"

She stared at their hulls, strong on the waterline. "I'm going to break them from beneath the water."

His eyes grew wide in the poor light. "All by yourself?"

"Yes. Unless you want to come?"

He gave a weak laugh. "Well, not truly-is." He looked at her. "What will you use?"

"This." She held up the saw.

Bel surfaced before he could answer, a large man beside her. Not Sanac, but a smiling fellow with broad shoulders. "This is Fedi. He can help you."

"So, you want to go for a swim?"

"I do."

"Right. Better lose the boots," Fedi told her.

"Give me a moment." She removed them, then her sword. That left just the hand saw and knife. Both of which she'd need.

"It's cold," he warned when she put her hands on the grate.

"Colder than the ice flows of Renovar?" A chill seeped into her soles but it was nothing like home.

He chuckled. "Maybe not that cold."

Pevin touched her arm with the back of his hand. "Forgive me, dilar, but it is too dangerous."

"Pevin."

He did not remove his hand.

"I need you to make sure Alfeo and his mother stay safe. That is my wish."

His brow creased. "This isn't fair. I have to protect you."

"You have to obey me." Poor guy. In all his years in Renovar, holding to his faith, he probably never expected to actually meet an object of his worship. And she must have been a shock to him. "Pevin, I'm asking you as Flir. Please."

He bowed his head. "Be safe."

"Worry about them out there."

She wrenched the grate open and squeezed through, perching a moment on the edge before leaping down. She hit the icy water with a gasp, surrounded by darkness and thrashing bubbles tinted orange.

Surfacing, Flir swam to Fedi and Bel. Maybe it was colder than she'd expected. But she kept her teeth from chattering. "So, how do we do this?"

Fedi scratched his head. "Bel?"

"Maybe if she wears something? It could help her beneath the water-is?"

"Like?"

Bel sighed. "Well...Can you wait a little while? This one's not close by," she said, slipping beneath the water.

Flir waited with a frown. They could have worked it out before letting her jump in. Alfeo crept closer. "Ah, Fedi?"

"Yes, lad?"

"What does everyone eat down there?"

He laughed. "Same as you. Little fish, mostly. Sometimes seaweed."

"And it doesn't taste bad? You know, raw?"

"At first, but now I'm used to it. When I was like you, I used to love hot food, but no longer."

"When did you join the Sea-People?" Flir asked, treading water, keeping her hands moving in circles. Where was Bel? How long would it take? People were still dying.

"Not long after I fell sick. Sanac and I were among the first. In fact, we ate a lot of the flesh from the Beast once we started to change."

"You what?" Alfeo said.

Flir gagged.

Fedi shrugged. "It was natural. We simply saw it and ate. I should have been revolted I guess, but...I wasn't. It was as if we were meant to do so. Like the Great Father wanted us to devour his body."

"Truly?"

"Yes."

"But why?"

"I've no idea. Sanac has several theories but I'm not sure, myself." He fell silent, not speaking again until Bel returned. When her small face broke the water she was smiling. "All right. I think this will work." She held a piece of bone. "Can I borrow your knife?"

"Of course."

Bel took several strands of her hair then sliced them free, threading the bone through and tying the hair, making a necklace. "Wear this. You'll be able to swim longer-is."

Flir placed the bone over her head. Bel's hair was strong, like cord, only softer. A tingle spread from where the bone rested against her chest. "How do you know this will work?"

"I have a feeling."

"That's all?"

"Well, there's something else," Bel said. "It's from one of the Sea People. He died a few days ago. Sometimes it happens...I don't think everyone is happy about the change-is."

Fedi nodded but said nothing.

"Only a few days ago?"

"Something...ate his flesh I think." Bel looked toward the ships. "He wouldn't mind though, not if it helps."

"Are you all right?"

"Yes. Want to try it out?"

"I'm ready."

"Then hold on to us," she said.

"And let us know when you need air," Fedi added.

Flir gave a wave to Alfeo and Pevin, whose face was set. She took a deep breath then ducked beneath the water, kicking away from the wall. Bel and Fedi each took a wrist and drove forward, dragging her through the water.

Their tails shimmered before her and she kicked, but doubted it added to their speed.

When her breath ran short, she tugged on their arms. Fedi pulled her up to the surface and she sucked in air. The ships were much closer. Over her shoulder, the walls lay distant and the opening had grown tiny. They'd nearly crossed half the distance already.

"Are you well?" he asked.

"No problems yet." Taking another breath, she dived down and once again, Bel and Fedi drew her through the cold water. They soon paused, and Bel pointed ahead and mimed empty space closing with her hands, then waved as she and Fedi pulled away.

How close? Flir broke the surface quietly and drew in air. The hulls of the ships rose before her, close enough to see the faces of sailors rushing along the decks. Sails flapped in the night breeze and even as she prepared to dive once more, another catapult's arm shot forward. Dark objects, barrels of acor no doubt, flew toward the city walls.

Longboats sat low on the water, crammed with soldiers, the creak of oars lost in the chaos. They'd reach the wharves and swarm into the city soon enough. Holindo would have to stop them. She had ships to sink.

The question was whether it was even possible.

Time to find out.

Flir slipped beneath the water once more and swam to the nearest ship, guided first by light from the flaming city then by the rough tops of barnacles. Sliding lower, she fought the water to drive her knife into the wood. She kept hacking until she'd made an opening for the saw, then got to work.

Once she'd made enough holes to tear away entire planks, she moved to another part of the ship and repeated the process before returning for air, breaking the surface with as little noise as possible.

No-one bothered to look down, so busy were they with the catapults, ears clogged with shouted orders. She glared at the waterline. The ship didn't seem to be sinking fast, if at all. It was big – three masts, how much would she have to tear open? Flir slipped below again and repeated the process, ripping yet more planks from the hull.

Once more she repeated the process, and this time,

while treading water she smiled. The ship was definitely sinking. Slowly, but certainly. Flir swam to another ship, took a deep breath and dived once more to work with knife and saw. By the time she'd pulled a good dozen planks free, she was seeing spots. Pushing off, Flir swam for the surface and sucked in air.

The first ship had ceased its attack and was resting quite low in the harbour.

Maybe she could hit it again, to speed the process up?

"What's this, then?"

Something slipped over her neck and she thrashed against rope. Something else caught one of her arms and she kicked herself up to half-turn in the water. Renovar sailors had hooked her from where they stood at the rail, poles fixed with loops resting in their hands, faces a mixture of shock and anger.

She jerked on one of the poles and a man flew into the water with a cry.

Tensing as she prepared to fling a second man into the sea, she swore when another loop caught her neck, despite her struggles. It cut her air but she wrenched another pole free. Two more took its place.

Something struck her head. She cried out, vision swimming as she slumped against the ropes.

"Imbeciles!" A voice roared. "Alive, do you hear me? Alive."

She fought the poles as they raised her, tugging at the loop around her neck until a strong hand caught her wrist.

She frowned.

A strong hand?

Her captor called for help. His face was blurry; he looked down on her from where sailors dangled him over the side, one man each holding a leg. They pulled him up and she went with him, the man dragging her over the side easily once he had his feet.

She clenched her jaw, wiping at her eyes.

A strong hand.

"Well, Flir. I have to say. You're the last person I expected to see swimming the harbour with a handsaw."

That voice! Her vision cleared enough for her to drop the saw. "Mishalar's Heart."

Kanis stood before her, eyes glittering with surprise.

CHAPTER 67

Notch charged through the trees. Grey trunks flashed. "This way," Nia called.

He changed course, clambering over a fallen log. Shouts still trailed and another arrow hissed by. He ducked onto the new trail, catching up to Nia. Her chest heaved as she climbed an incline.

At its top, they crouched to peer back. "We're in trouble," Notch said. His own breath came hard and his legs trembled. Too long tied as a prisoner. He ground his teeth at the pain radiating from his thigh. To hell with them. He wasn't going to make it easy.

Sap-Born converged on their back trail, pouring out of the grove from a host of directions. They numbered over a score and he couldn't be sure, but it seemed Efran led one of the groups.

"At least we've drawn them away," Nia said.

"Let's give them another clue then." He hurled a dead branch down the slope. The search parties altered their course and he dashed after Nia, angling toward a heavy stand of trees. She slipped through the branches and he followed, cloak snagging, pulling him up. He jerked it free and ran on.

Shouts of pursuit followed.

Nia shouted over her shoulder. "I have an idea."

"Good."

She stopped at a point where the path, now much more defined than a game trail, broke into three. In one direction the way was overgrown, but the other options were somewhat better travelled. She tugged her gloves free and clapped her hands twice, sharply. From this puff of powder two butterflies appeared, one pink and the other purple. They hovered before her and she blew one down each path. As they flew, tiny hints of powder drifted toward the earth.

"Decoys?" Notch said.

"Yes. Each will last long enough to mislead them. See how they begin to disintegrate? But impressions of our 'passing' appear already."

Both gouges in loam and leaves and evidence of trampled grass appeared, where before the trails had been unbroken. Impressive magic indeed. "And the third fork?"

"Leads to a place few Braonn seek to enter. We will draw our share of them nonetheless." She started down the path.

Here the way was overgrown and the shrubbery thicker, more concentrated. Creeping vines covered stumps, stones and tree alike. Somewhere a thin stream trickled, but he did not see it as he ran. Twice they were forced to leap – or in his case climb – fallen branches. These too, were buried in vines. Tiny red eyes blinked from the shadows, shying away as he climbed.

The trail curved around a heavy stand of trees, their trunks scarred by crude carvings – howling faces and unfamiliar, blocky runes. "Warnings?" he asked as they passed.

"Yes. From the Ulag."

The Black Raiders, who'd pillaged the Bloodwood for hundreds of years. Until the Anaskari wiped them out. Or so the legends went. A trickle of water murmured beneath their footfalls. "Are we close to the Sarough River?"

"Somewhat." Nia took him from the trail, pulling back a branch. A canopy was revealed, and a little way along it, a stream cut through the forest floor, barely a few feet wide. A space clear of leaves lay beneath one of the trunks, dirt edged with fur.

Nia bent to drink deeply. Notch followed suit, then she led them back to the trail.

"Have you been here before?"

"Only once. As a child. Father thought it necessary, to learn our history."

Notch nodded. He strained his ears, but their back trail was quiet for the time being. Ahead, a low stone wall appeared, but like nearly everything else in this part of the Bloodwood, vines crawled across its weathered surface. Nia stopped at an empty opening, where a gate must have once stood. Beyond waited rows of tombstones. More vines covered them, but many were broken and stained an ugly brown.

Old blood. It had worked its way deep into the pores of the stones.

Nia wove into the cemetery with soft steps. She passed each grave without turning her head, moving toward a small building. Notch paused by one of the tombstones. Old Braonn writing. Back when they built with stone by choice, before the Anaskari came.

Much of the writing had been smashed away. Stone fragments lay half-buried in the dirt, obscured by dead leaves and green shoots. He brushed some of the vine back. A bolt had been driven into the tombstone, its head marked with a wave-like symbol.

He touched it and fell back as a rush of nausea hit.

"Notch?"

He shook his head. Strange. "I'm here." He stood and joined her at the building. A small temple, open to the trees above, its columns carved to resemble trees. As with all other stone in the graveyard, it was splattered with old blood. Vines spiralled up, tiny white flowers budding. "What is this place?"

Nia turned a slow circle, feet scraping on dusty stone. "Here my ancestors worshipped and buried our dead. We did not show true respect to the forest then but there was harmony for centuries at least. Until the Ulag came. What they could not take, they simply destroyed." She walked deeper, stopping at a circle of stone chairs several rows deep. All faced an empty space where interlocking circles were set in the floor, darker stone used. And this time, not the echo of blood.

"It's said their brutality was unmatched."

"It is true. Did you know, they wormed their foul magic into the very tombstones that we could not even clean them?"

He shook his head but it explained the ill-feeling that came from touching the bolt.

Voices called to one another.

"Here they come," Notch said. He drew the serrated torturer's knife he'd taken.

"Ready?"

"A good night's sleep and a decent meal would have been nice."

"If we survive this, I'll look after both." She gave him

a look.

His pulse gave a skip. Did she mean...? He should have been able to recognise when a woman was interested in him. Idiot.

Nia was amused now. She patted his cheek. "Come, Warrior. It hasn't been that long, surely?"

He had to laugh. "Shouldn't we worry about the Sap-Born first?"

"We should."

"So how do we handle them?"

"For a large group...I'll surprise them. Pick off as many as you can; they'll be stunned. Then, lead them back here, into the temple."

"Here?"

"I feel better here." She shrugged. "And we can use the columns as barriers."

"And a small group?"

"Let them spread out so we can pick them off. Come here if you're in trouble."

Did it really matter where they made a stand? Probably worse to do it out in the open of the cemetery. "All right."

They moved between the graves, crouching down behind one of the taller, vine-covered headstones. Nia waved him across the path, where he concealed himself behind a similar stone. His leg throbbed but he ignored it as he waited.

Voices neared. Someone wanted the group to spread out. He heard at least four distinct voices, the tension clear even at a distance. Nia raised two hands, one with only her thumb showing. Six. She made a motion for him to circle away from the temple and put a finger to her lips.

He signalled back and crept to the next headstone. He peered around the vines. A pair of Sap-Born headed toward him, angling to his left. Birds had stilled and the thump of his heart was like a hammer within his chest. Surely they'd hear it.

The first pair chose the middle path and two more veered right, heading deep into the cemetery. He whispered a curse. Efran led the pair in the middle. Notch ducked to another tombstone, this one with a low stone wall surrounding it. More of a family crypt. With each move he came closer to heading his prey off. No choice but to act fast. If either made a sound, they'd draw the others down.

Both men held swords. Their eyes roved and they took careful steps. Notch grabbed a piece of headstone and held his breath. Just a little closer now.

A leg came into view and he inched around the crypt until he approached their backs. He glided forward but froze when one man paused. He started to turn and Notch leapt. He swung the hunk of stone down, cracking the man's skull and spinning on the second man, jabbing the knife into his side.

Notch jammed a hand over the man's mouth, pulling him down before he could cry out. The fellow struggled, his veins beginning to glow but it faded quickly. Notch removed the blade, smeared with amber-coloured blood, checking on his victim. "Gods," he whispered. A young man. Stupid kid.

But then, how old was he when he joined the Shield?

Notch checked the first man. A huge dent lay in the back of his head, blood weeping to the earth. Without honour, but the job was done.

He circled behind the temple. Neither Efran nor the other pair were visible between the stones. Had Nia already taken care of her two? He crept closer, his foot slipping on a loose stone. He froze. Mere feet away was one of the openings, the green of a vine climbing.

Movement beyond the wall. Someone was within the temple. He inched nearer, crouching as he peered around the edge. Efran paced between the chairs, a second Sap-Born close by – only on the opposite side of the temple. Efran's veins pulsed and he shook his head.

"They're here somewhere."

"Maybe," the other man replied.

"We keep looking." Efran left the temple, passing through the opposite columns. Notch followed. He'd barely taken three steps when the second man gave a shout. Notch sprinted as best he could, crossing the temple and bursting into the cemetery. Efran's man was down, powder faint in the air over his body.

Nia circled Efran, keeping a headstone between them. Her face was set in a glare. Efran grinned, light from his veins spreading until the whole of his body glowed.

Bad news.

Notch bent to take the short sword from the body and approached.

"Captain Notch?" Efran slowed. "What a surprise. But I am glad to see you both. Have you come to sacrifice yourself along with the lovely Nia?"

"You're alone, Efran."

The man laughed. "I'm trouble enough, believe me."

Nia met his eye, then gave a slight nod, before hopping onto the headstone, where she leapt into the air, arms spread with a scream.

Efran fell back, his glow pulsing even as Notch charged. He slowed when her clothing tore and her limbs elongated, so quickly that he could have imagined it. Yet long before she began her descent, a stunning, giant butterfly took her place, and with a huge downbeat of her wings, she buffeted Efran.

The man raised his hands. Another wing beat and powder coated him as he stumbled.

Go, idiot, go!

Notch cursed himself even as he sprang forward again, swinging his blade in a vicious arc. The weapon tore into Efran's torso, lodging deep. Efran wheeled, tearing the sword from Notch's grasp. Sap pulsed and the blade turned pure yellow. Efran battered the weapon and it shattered, half still deep in his body.

But he did not fall.

Instead, he advanced on Notch, who gaped as he gave ground, knife ready. Efran moved slowly and his hands were raised. Was he blinded? Notch ducked away. Behind the leader of the Sap Men, Nia hovered. She couldn't hit him with powder again, not without coating Notch.

He feinted.

Efran reacted, slowly.

And yet, if Notch made a mistake, he'd be a statue of sap. Could the man even be stopped? Maybe the head. Notch came up against tombstone. Efran lunged.

He dived from his good leg, rolling to his feet in time to see the headstone explode in a shower of amber. Efran climbed to his feet. The man's glow had grown so great Notch had to squint. Nia swooped in and coated the leader of the Sap-Born again. He fell to one knee in a daze.

This time her flight dipped as she backed away. Her wings showed patches of translucence. She couldn't keep it up. Notch belted his knife and hauled a slap of stone above his head. Heaving it at Efran, his stomach flipped when the slab shattered in an amber shower.

Could Efran even be touched anymore? "Nia, we have to leave," he shouted.

She hovered but didn't turn from the man, instead hitting him again with her powder. Efran slumped to both knees, hands deep in the ground as he heaved for breath. An amber glow began to spread from the man, infusing dirt, vine and stone alike.

Notch fell back, cut off from Nia. Her wing beats were faltering but she coated Efran a fourth time and dipped even lower. She'd used too much powder. "Nia!" He started forward but the amber blocked him and she was already too close.

A wingtip brushed the glow.

Amber shot along her body. It froze her outstretched wings, froze her whole shape in a terrible flash that left only a softly glowing statue of a butterfly in her place.

CHAPTER 68

Ain strode deeper into the earth.

His lamp wasn't going to last forever and already he'd descended two flights of stairs and bypassed several side passages, two of which were blocked by closed doors and one which led back up, and as the newest footfalls led down, he was not willing to change course.

The Sands had truly cursed him.

It wasn't enough that he was underground again, the weight of all that stone above pressing down, but he was alone without food or water, only one lamp and naught but a knife to defend himself against the darkling – or worse, darklings. Surely more than one creature had to have been involved in killing so many of Tanija's people? Else more would have escaped.

The passage opened before him. A vaulted ceiling watched over tall columns, each marked at the base with the curved outline and twin triangles within, sign of the Mazu clan. The columns glittered in his lamp light – more quartz? He didn't check, instead hurrying through the open area. The path led to an archway and another set of stairs leading down.

It was a short flight.

At its bottom the path split in two, spreading around a set of double doors, again in stone, and again closed, marked with the Mazu symbol. By the shape of the paths, both choices appeared to curve around the central chamber, which was much larger than he first assumed.

Up ahead, something small lay against the wall.

Ain slowed his approach, kneeling when the lamplight caught on a water flask. A long gash had emptied the water, though the stone was dry beneath it. It was a sign at least, the path was not deceiving him. Tanija's people had come this way.

He walked on, counting his paces. Forty before the tunnel curved again, revealing another set of doors, these a mirror of those at the opposite end. Across from the closed doors were another set of stairs, these leading down.

But the most recent footfalls of the path went into the giant chamber he'd circled. Ain pushed on the doors. Nothing. He leant harder, putting the lamp down and straining until it gave a distance so small he might have imagined it. Ain slumped against the stone a moment, wincing when he bumped his hip.

If he couldn't open the door he'd have to go back up. Or down further. Neither option appealed. The path went through the doors, that was his best chance.

Wait, did voices murmur beyond?

Ain held his breath. Yes, voices – speaking with urgency but not panic. He smacked the hilt of his blade against the stone and shouted. "Ho, can anyone hear me?"

The voices stopped.

"My name is Ain and I'm a Pathfinder from the Cloud Oasis." He paused, waiting for a reply. When none came he added, "I'm looking for my friends. Can you help me?"

Footsteps approached and once again, voices conferred, hushed. Then the doors swung open and two men in long white coats and black pants were revealed. Both men were older, their features, down to the grey in their short hair, almost identical. So too were the heavy belts they wore, weighted with hammers and other tools.

"Come with us, quickly," one said, his accent strong and unfamiliar. The men were Medah, and yet none of the Clans spoke in such a manner.

"Wait, have you seen my friends, the people who live in the caves above?" he asked.

"No time, not safe." The other dragged Ain into the giant chamber.

"But I –" He stopped. In the centre of the room, more grand than any of the surrounding columns, was a huge, trunk-like shaft of stone and quartz, running from floor to roof. Parts of it were still dark stone, but the majority was clear quartz tinted with gold – as if a sword were being unsheathed and the blade running into the stone floor.

But what made him stop was the figures rising within the quartz, standing calmly on a platform of some sort. They continued up and into the roof, disappearing in moments.

"It's hollow," he said.

"Come." The same man tugged at his arm and he followed them across a tiled floor, the images interlocking triangles. Light grew as they neared, until the quartz shone as a torch, spilling fractured light across the room.

He blinked, shielding his eyes when they stopped

before the quartz. Eventually the light dulled, though it remained luminous. Ain closed his mouth; he'd been gaping at it.

"Who made this?"

The first man strode to the quartz and pulled open a wide door, the heaviness of its construction clear by the effort it took. No hinges were visible.

"Your friends are above," the man said, pointing.

A surge of relief. "And they are well?"

The men exchanged glances before the first replied. "Most."

His relief dissolved. "What do you mean? Is someone hurt?"

The second man turned his head, as if hearing something Ain could not. He ran several steps toward the doors, then flung an arm at the quartz. "Go," he roared.

Ain was dragged inside, the second man rushing in after, pulling the door closed. Both men had tensed. One clutched a hammer and the other's jaw worked.

"What's happening?"

"Old Ones."

Before Ain could ask more, the other man shouted something to the roof, the words unfamiliar. High above, the shaft rose toward a point of light, winking as if something or someone passed before it. The platform had began its descent.

"There!"

Something had slipped through the doors, racing toward them. A shadowy thing, wisps of red coursed through it. From behind came another and Ain fell back as the first creature flashed across the remaining distance, crashing into the door.

The quartz barely shook, but the thing did not appear hurt. It struck again, joined by its fellow. Yet again, the quartz held.

"Can they break it?" Ain asked.

The first man shook his head, eyes never leaving the darklings.

Up close they were still things of shadow, but hints of white flashed within and whenever the creatures paused, wisps of red began to solidify. The shapes were never the same. Once he thought a long-fingered hand appeared and after another attack, he could have sworn he saw a gaping mouth, large enough to swallow a man whole.

He inched back from the door. Above, the platform continued its steady descent.

The darklings continued to slam themselves against the quartz, but not even a scratch appeared on the surface. Neither man had relaxed truly, but when the platform finally touched down behind them, Ain noticed an easing to their shoulders.

The first man shouted up again and the platform began to rise.

Below, the darklings soon grew smaller but Ain sucked in a breath as a third creature joined the first two. And then another and another, until at least a dozen of them milled about below, the red flaring.

"They cannot follow," the second man said. But he was frowning down at them.

"What?"

"Their numbers grow."

The platform continued to rise and Ain shivered. One of the creatures was enough.

Light grew above, the small square soon resolving into a wide opening, beyond which lay a spacious courtyard of stone, protected by a ridge of dark rock. Men dressed in a similar fashion to his saviours were shifting heavy wooden chests and stone carvings from a staging area beside a great wheel and cog, to an open cart. Stout horses waited for their masters to finish working where the cart stood before another broad opening in stone, this leading gently down.

"Are we safe here?"

The second man shrugged. "Most of the time."

Reassuring. "And where is here?" Ain asked as he stepped from the platform. He nearly missed the reply, as the sense of a path returned. On the trip up the quartz it had receded to become no more than a faint pulse.

"Above Haven, our home," the first man said. "You will find your friends below."

"Thank you, and thank you for saving me," he said.

"Welcome."

He gestured to the cart. "What of your carvings?" Many were more patterns than figures. "You risked your lives for them?"

"They are part of us." He pointed to the slope. "Down to your friends."

His guides set a quick pace, passing the men who worked at the cart, none of which gave Ain a second glance, and moving down the slope and back into the shade. The path was ancient. The search behind the old caves, the quartz and the darklings had distracted him, but now the feet of thousands pummelled his senses. Not unlike the path leading to the Sea Shrine in Sekkati.

Another circle of light appeared below, and when they reached it his eyes widened. An intricate carving arched the exit, Mazu symbols hidden between other patterns. In the centre were a pair of open hands carved from quartz. He couldn't fully suppress a shudder. How many stories about the Mazu Clan featured them stealing the hands of their victims?

But Haven did not appear to be a place of horror.

Beyond the exit a broad trail ran alongside a ridge that led down into a series of brick homes, tiles on the rooves a deep red. Light flashed from windows as the sun beat down, oppressive even in winter. Grey clouds crept up behind it, smothering the blue. All seemed peaceful enough.

A figure limped from one of the houses and waved.

Schan.

He ran into the village and caught Schan by the shoulders, grinning like a fool. "You're safe, thank the Sands."

Schan grinned back. "And you, lad. We looked for you."

"It doesn't matter." He glanced over his shoulder to where his guides drew near. "Can you believe that quartz?"

Schan shook his head. "Not truly."

"And so this is the Mazu Clan then?"

"Yes, though they are not what I expected." He shifted his leg, wincing. "And you've met the twins, Rejam and Predi."

"Yes, they saved me from the darklings. Are you hurt?"

"I'm fine. They've taken good care of me."

"And Wayrn and Tanija and his people, are they here too?"

Schan's face darkened. "Yes, but all is not well. You saw the caves?"

Ain nodded.

"The envoy is alive and so is Tanija, but his children died from their wounds here." He shook his head. "We thought they would survive at first."

"Oh." Ain's heart missed a beat as Bemm and Sae's laughter echoed. Gone now. "Tanija and Ashia must be broken."

"They are being brave for the survivors, but the grief is there. They'll be happy to see you safe." He started toward the village. "But there's something you must see first. Someone has been asking for you. He claims to have a message."

"Here?"

"I can hardly believe it myself, but let me show you."

"Schan, who is it?"

"Best for you to see it with your own eyes."

Schan took him down a winding street, moving through the village, which was a lot larger than he first thought, and past people dressed as the twins, many at work with pieces of quartz. A few raised their heads and smiled as they passed, and children peered from behind their doors, eyes big with curiosity.

Finally, Schan stopped beneath another arch set in the rock face of the same ridge that protected the town, cutting it off from the rest of the Wastelands.

Beyond a narrow opening waited a triangular chamber. It extended out to a smooth wall of quartz, which caught light from somewhere above the shadowy roof. Tiered benches of stone lined the room. The paved stones leading to the wall were swept clean, not even the hint of a weed peeked up.

"Here?"

"The wall," Schan said.

Ain moved closer. The wall was actually four pillars of quartz carefully fitted together, and while each were luminous, the first was cloudy compared to the others.

He peered closer.

"You have to touch it," Schan said quietly.

He extended his hand, placing a palm on the smooth surface and blinking when the milky clouds swirled. A figure resolved and Ain gasped.

"Ibranu."

"Of course it is." The old Engineer's expression was hardly patient. His outline was touched with blue, just as the spirits in the Wards.

He gave Ain a look and then mouthed words but none were clear. After a moment, the spirit shook his head and pointed to Ain, then to his eyes. Watch.

More clouds swirled and the carcass of the sea beast appeared in the Anaskar harbour, followed by the empty, giant bones in the desert. Ain straightened. Of course; another beast! Right on the heels of the desert came a wall of fire, devouring a city, then came water, swallowing islands, people screaming, then ice and snow falling, burying a third city.

And then nothing.

Ain turned back to Schan when Ibranu didn't reappear. "What does it mean?"

"Trouble, lad. For the whole world, it seems."

"And Ibranu wants me to stop it? Sands, how?"

Schan shrugged. "No idea. But I'll do my best to help."

CHAPTER 69

Seto tore open the door to his brother's chamber, flinging tables and canisters aside at the bed. "Light," he called over the smashing of glass. Otonos was a pale smudge against his royal pillows.

Behind him Solicci banked the sleeping fire and fumbled with a lamp.

His brother's sunken face was skull-like in the new light. And still. Awfully still. Seto put a hand to Otonos' neck and waited.

Nothing.

"Damn you!" he shouted. How dare the fool die on him now – when had he slunk into death? Seto slammed a fist into his palm. He needed to know if there was a hidden child, legitimate or not – someone close-by, something, anything better than a distant relative, all but inaccessible in the winter.

"He is gone?"

"Yes. The fool."

"He held on a long time."

"Not long enough," Seto snapped. Solicci said nothing. The King sighed, walking from the room. "If he had lived long enough..." No matter. Nothing had changed; he had still to find a young replacement for the Sacrifice.

And before that, survive the attack, save his city.

Back on his balcony he raised Chelona again, but did not wear her. Could he do it? Become part of the Greatmask? Live forever? Or at least, until he found a way to steal someone's body as Chelona herself, or whoever she once was, planned to do? Was it even possible? The Swordfish line might die with him. He sneered at the Renovar ships, but it was directed at himself. The line would certainly die with him.

Unless he could find someone else.

One to take Chelona's place, one to continue the line. If it mattered. And maybe it didn't? Who was to say Sofia's House, or even Solicci's House, couldn't take over guardianship of the city? And do a better job.

He glowered at the flames.

Should there be any city left to protect.

And he could stop it all, he was sure. Chelona's power was...considerable. With her, he could blast the fire away, sink the ships, turn back the attackers. And all it would cost was a single life. If he was willing to make the choice for someone else. "You old fool," he whispered.

"My Liege?"

"Nothing." He replaced the mask within his robe. "Solicci, find me a good horse."

"It's too dangerous for the King to –"

"I can't very well do nothing, can I?"

Solicci opened his mouth to argue but offered no reply. His brow furrowed and he strode to the balcony rail. "Look there."

Dawn was creeping across the sky, its light streaking forth. Riding before it on a rising wind were a host of blue sails. Easily two dozen ships bore down on the Renovar fleet, one of which was sitting quite low in the water.

"Who are they?"

"No-one I recognise. Not with blue sails – and those prows. They seem old-fashioned. Blockier."

"True."

The newcomers flew at the Renovar ships, splitting apart to encircle the small fleet. Catapults ceased firing and though it was near impossible to see from such a distance, it seemed men scrambled to take up positions to repel boarders. Only most of the soldiers were already in the city. One of the straggling longboats was smashed by a blue-sailed ship. The Captain hadn't slowed at all.

"They're going to save us," Solicci said.

Seto said nothing.

All along the rails of the blue ships, figures stood poised to leap across the water to the Renovar. Only, for the most part, the distances were great. But each small figure made the leap, causing chaos on the boards. Their blue cloaks quickly overwhelmed whatever forces remained.

The process repeated itself all around, all save for the sinking ship. That the newcomers ignored.

"They've finished the invasion."

"They have," Seto said. He leant forward. "But who are they?"

"I would say –"

Fire roared into the dawn sky. Seto blinked and Solicci fell back. The ship furthest from the wharves was lost in a floating ball of flame, the nearest two blue-sailed ships afire too.

"One of them must have set off the acor," Solicci observed.

"We have to get down there."

"I'll arrange the Honour Guard."

"And find Abrensi too," Seto said as he ran for his knives. Who knew who had come? He had a suspicion but it wasn't possible...was it? Whoever it was, there was no way to learn their intent from a balcony.

*

Several times his troop was forced to detour flaming buildings that blocked the way. Swathes of black smoke crossed the streets. At every turn people had to be herded back into their homes. Once, Seto ordered his party stop to help battle a growing fire that threatened a pair of inns.

He watched his men douse the flames with a frown.

Solicci moved his horse alongside. "Still no word of Lord Abrensi. Nor Lavinia."

"It is disturbing that neither can be found."

"I have men searching the palace."

"Then that's all we can do for now," Seto said. "These newcomers in the harbour will have to come first."

Nearest the fires, bodies lay unmoving. Many were covered in char and ash.

At the broken Antico Gate a skirmish raged. Renovar soldiers, their grey furs thick against the wind, hacked at a band of Shield and Vigil with a variety of axes. Seto ordered his men forward and they turned the tide quickly enough.

He dismounted and joined Giovan, who stood before a sergeant from the defenders. "How goes the defence of the city?" Giovan asked.

"Hard to say, Captain." The man's eyes widened when he noticed Seto. "Your Majesty." He tried to bow but one of his knees buckled.

Giovan caught him.

Seto waved a hand. "No need for that, go on."

"Well, we can't be sure but the Lower Tier is probably overrun. With so much of it on fire, we can't coordinate properly."

Seto put a hand on his shoulder. "You are doing all you should. Go, rest your men a moment."

He bent at one of the Renovar bodies. Perhaps a little shorter than a typical Anaskari man, his blond hair and beard were thick, woven with chips of stone marked with bold runes. His pale skin was splattered with blood and his armour ringed with furs. At his belt hung a hand axe, a larger double-headed blade lying beside his open hand – it too smeared with blood.

"Why are they here then, Majesty?" Giovan asked.

"I do not know."

Seto remounted and they wound their way down toward the harbour. Several more skirmishes ensued, but they met no larger groups. Instead, only scattered soldiers, many who'd taken to looting. Those men he had shot on sight – his archer was kept busy.

Not once did he even come close to actual fighting, so dedicated was his guard. It was both heartening and a touch disappointing. Along the way he even collected stray soldiers, and by the time he finally neared the smoking ruins of the staging area, large groups of Vigil and Shield had joined his party. If only he'd thought to bring Alosus as well, then they'd have really been impressive.

Dead littered the stones. Shield and Renovar alike. Some of the bodies nearest the wall, now breached once more, were dark, shrivelled things. Acid burns.

Seto glared across the water, fire reflected in its

darkness.

A new longboat had been sent forth, this one flying a small blue flag from the prow. Beyond, the sinking ship's decks had almost dipped beneath the surface and the Renovar fleet was finished. Men were being cast overboard, their cries faint and the splashes barely audible.

"Form up," Giovan ordered. Soldiers arranged themselves in a wedge, supporting Seto where he stood on the broken ground before the crumbled walls. Smoke still rose from patches of the earth where the acor had landed.

"What are they wearing?" The Captain pointed.

"It's hard to see. Something white hides beneath their cloaks," Solicci said.

Chelona's presence neared, as if she'd swooped in from somewhere to focus on the newcomers. "By the Gods." Seto breathed. Close enough now, he could see one man who stood high on the prow, cloak thrown back, hands upon his hips. The stranger wore a Greatmask.

As did each of his fellows.

Seto's guard shifted, but held their ground, hands on weapons as a ripple of power seemed to flow from the strangers.

The longboat nosed its way between other, empty longboats driven onto the wreckage of wharf and stone, and the men leapt out, striding forward to halt mere paces from Seto and his formation.

The leader pointed, then asked a question. Seto stared, unable to answer at first. The fellow's chest was covered in what looked like an external ribcage, bones moulded into something of a breastplate. Even his hands were covered in bone pieces carved to resemble long gauntlets.

The white bone caught the orange light of flame and destruction.

The man repeated his question and Seto heard the words properly. Old Anaskari. The stranger wanted to know who he addressed.

"King Oseto, Casa Pesce Spada. And who are you?" He answered in kind.

The leader's head tilted. "I am Prince Marinus of Casa Mare. You speak strangely, King Oseto. Do you mark my words well?"

"I do, Prince Marinus. Though not all with me will. To their ears, you speak 'old' Anaskari."

He laughed. "Then it is true, you are descendants of Those Who Fled?"

"We are." Seto looked to the Renovar. "And we appreciate what you have done in the harbour."

"Do you?" He turned, perhaps to admire the work of his fleet. "You may not for long, King Oseto."

"Why is that?"

"Because we are not here as rescuers, but conquerors." The Prince said. "We are here for the bones of the last Sea God and for the fugitive you harbour. Turn him and the bones over and I will spare your lives."

"Fugitive?"

"Vinezi Mare." He sneered. "My brother."

CHAPTER 70

Flir stood her ground. No-one on the ship but Kanis would be even half a problem but enough held bows that she had to be careful. Water dripped to the decks as she waited.

Kanis flashed his most self-confident smile, but she thought she caught a hint of doubt in his eyes. "Well then, you better come below so we can talk...in private." He started toward a ladder.

The sailors snickered.

"No."

Silence. Kanis stopped. He turned. Once again, his dimples appeared, but he was shaking his head. "Flir. Think this through. My ship, my men, my word is law. You like breathing, don't you?"

She didn't answer. The smug bastard. How in the world had he gotten mixed up in war? That wasn't his style. He was a liar and a thief, but not a war-pig. "You've really lost that much respect for yourself?"

"Said the mercenary."

Flir threw up her hands. "Fine. Let's go and talk."

"Thank you." He led her below decks and the smell of garlic drifted up from the galley. The decks rolled gently as she followed him down a dim hall. His muscled arms were smooth in the light, shoulders bare under a grey vest of furs.

A shiver of home, just looking at him.

He opened a door and motioned for her to enter first. She seated herself at a large table. The room was a haze of costumes and the table was covered in maps, but all she really saw was Kanis.

"What the hell are you doing here?"

He sighed when he sat, as if the answer were all too obvious. "Taking a better life, of course. Like you did, only on a grand scale."

"With acor?"

"It's necessary. Unpleasant but necessary." He shook his head. "I still can't believe you're here. Care to change out of those soaking clothes?"

She raised an eyebrow. "Don't try that."

"Don't blame me. I've missed you."

She snorted.

"No, I have."

"Enough, Kanis. What's really going on? Acor, cooperating with scum like Vinezi?"

"Another necessary unpleasant thing, that man. But our ends aligned for a time."

Was he surprised that she knew of Vinezi? He reached beneath the desk and brought a pair of glasses and a dark bottle of brandy. "So, Flir. Tell me what you've been up to these years. I heard only rumours at home."

She slapped the tabletop, hard enough to shake it. "You want to chat like old friends while you're attacking my city?"

"Well, I'm not planning on stealing the city itself. Just enough to change my life for good – you remember feeling like that, don't you?"

"That's not important."

A thumping on the door interrupted. "Kanis. We're under attack," someone shouted.

He stood. "From who?"

"No idea, just get out here. They've got blue sails, that's all we can tell."

Kanis swore, throwing his chair back. He snatched a large axe – it looked like something a giant would use, and charged to the door, where he paused. "You coming?"

"Whoever it is might free me."

He grinned. "Or kill you." Then he was gone.

Flir thumped her thigh. He was right – she needed a weapon. She turned, scanning the walls. Nothing. Kanis barely had anything else in the room. There – a chair leg. Giving it a wrench, she broke it free, thumped part of the base from the leg and ran above.

She gaped.

The fighting was over.

A few sailors lay still on the decks. Surrounding the rest of the ashen-faced Renovar were men in blue cloaks and behind them, hulking figures with mottled skin. Like Alosus.

But even they were half-realised shapes.

Instead, it was the men in blue cloaks she saw. Each wore a Greatmask. And more, each wore a breastplate that looked to be part moulded bone, part ribcage. Many wore bone affixed to the outside of their gloves too. Like Vinezi, only far more sophisticated.

None spoke, as in the centre of the deck, one of the newcomers stood with hands spread. One hand turned in circles and another was open, fingers splayed. Before him, a blubbering sailor turned on his heel, completing pointless circles. He moved to the motion of the stranger.

The open hand appeared to be holding Kanis back, despite the distance between the two. Kanis' face was flushed with fury, jaw clenched.

Flir finally recovered.

She hurled the chair leg at the man controlling the sailor. It flew across the deck and shattered the mask.

The sailor collapsed and lay gasping on the deck.

But the man in the mask crumbled to the ground and the row of blue-cloaked strangers roared with laughter. Hands caught her arms. She flung them off, shoving a giant aside. That stopped the laughter, and suddenly she was frozen in place.

One of the other Greatmasks had turned to her, a hand raised. Frozen, just like Kanis. She met his eyes and there was the old rage. She could have smiled, he hated being denied anything.

The mask lowered his hand and Flir felt pressure to kneel – only it came from inside. As if her very bones were being compelled to move. She fought, starting to sweat almost immediately, until she hit the deck with a crack.

The man she'd struck was climbing to his feet, splinters of bone on his clothing and a cut beneath his eye. Blood ran freely down his tan skin, and he strode toward her with a snarl. One of his companions stopped him. They exchanged heated words. Other Greatmasks turned to watch. The two shouted some more and then it was over.

Broken-mask backed away and the one who'd intervened turned to her.

Only darkness lay in his gaze.

CHAPTER 71

Sofia's hand hovered over the mask on Father's face. Again nothing had happened. All that was left was to –

A groan.

He was waking! Argeon glowed luminous as her father stirred. She took his hand and squeezed.

"Thank Ana," Emilio said.

"Father, can you hear me?"

His head twitched. "Sofia?" His voice was rough from disuse but he returned pressure on her hand. She fell into his arms, sudden tears welcome. He was alive. Somehow, everything had gone right. An ache returned to her body. So swiftly it returned, the stiffness. Inside she groaned, but pulled back and replaced Osani. The pain vanished.

"Sofia, how did you...Osani? Emilio?"

"Yes, My Lord." He was smiling.

Voices from the groves began to converge. Sofia stood and helped her father up. He was unsteady at first, but he kicked out his legs and rolled his shoulders. "We should talk later," Sofia said. She hugged him again. "The Sap-Born aren't going away."

He scanned the trees, a hand on her head. "No. They aren't. Let me deal with them. Then we can free Efran's concubines and leave," her father continued.

"Concubines?"

"Slaves truly." He rubbed at his arms and legs, stretching with a frown. "Efran keeps Anaskari women in a village beyond the groves."

The homes she and Emilio had seen. "To breed assassins?"

"Yes." He trailed off as he turned in a slow circle. He'd obviously been tracking the voices but stopped when he noticed Catrin. "Such as her." He stepped forward but did not reach out to the sap. "How did this happen?"

"I put her there," Sofia said.

"We should hurry," Emilio said, scrambling beneath the sap.

Her father held her gaze a moment longer, and there was pride and sorrow mixed in his eyes where they glittered behind Argeon, then bent to crawl through the opening after Emilio.

Sofia followed. She'd barely found her feet when a group of men ran up the row, weapons raised. Only two had veins that glowed. Her father stood before them and raised a hand. The men slowed. One dropped his weapon and shouted about "something holding his body."

Danillo pushed his hand down and the Braonn stumbled, falling to their knees and cursing as they toppled. Several threw hands out to break their fall, then pushed back, as if trying to force heavy weights from their backs.

Only it was useless.

Her father kept his arm rigid and the men stayed in the dirt and sap. "They are trapped."

"Is Argeon doing that?" Sofia asked.

"Yes." He hesitated. "We don't want them following. Sofia, promise me something."

"Father?"

"Do not repeat this Compelling. Nor what I am about to do."

"What do you mean? I don't understand."

He said nothing, only took a deep breath and brought his hands together in a sharp clap.

Sap-Born screamed over the sound of snapping bones.

The men continued to scream after her father dropped his arm and Sofia's stomach churned. What had he done? Emilio's own face was pale.

"Quickly." Father led them down another row, moving swiftly as his awakening limbs would allow, if his half-stooped run was an indicator. But no doubt Argeon would be helping him.

Cool air stung her eyes – they must have been wide. "By the Gods, Father, what happened back there?"

"What was necessary. This way." He turned down another row and soon enough, they were leaving the grove. She didn't remember even half the turns. How had Argeon – Father – done such a horrible thing?

The tree line beyond the grove thinned around a winding trail.

Ahead, the thatched rooves of houses peeked through the leaves. Smudges hung in the air, the scent of wood smoke strong. The trail opened to a line of small houses – the ones she and Emilio had seen before. They'd been knocked together with rough joints and the wood was freshly cut, at least, until the end of the row, where several older houses stood, one with a stone base.

Braonn women and children stepped from the houses to watch them stride up the street. They wore thick robes but their expressions were flat and uncaring. Even the children's curiosity was dulled. The sight of three Anaskari, two in Greatmasks, one carrying a bloodstained axe, ought to have provoked more fear.

A few people did return indoors at first sight, but most simply stared.

"This is where he holds them," her father said when he paused at the door to the stone building. He gestured over his shoulder. "The rest are near slaves, best I can discern."

"No-one is guarded?" Emilio asked.

"The guards may be searching for us, but then, many of the residents are drugged." He pushed the door open. "As are the women in here."

Within waited a single room, wide, with makeshift divisions; a couple of chairs and a blanket, a stack of crates, sometimes only a pile of clothing. The women and children, most little ones young enough to carry, were Anaskari. One of them was probably Catrin's mother but Sofia couldn't be sure. Many had bruised or dirty faces when they stood. A few lay sleeping and one woman turned her head at the new light, squinting with drowsing eyes.

Another woman, with dark hair tied into a tail, stood, arms folded. "Who are you?"

"Gather those who can walk. Help the others here to me," her father commanded.

The woman glared. "Why?"

"Because we are taking you home."

Sofia added her own voice. "Surely you can trust us?"

Her head turned but her eyes did not meet Sofia's. She looked slightly off to the side. "How do I know that? I can hear your voices. You're Anaskari at least, but that don't mean nothing here."

"I am Lord Danillo, Protector of Anaskar. I can help clear your minds of the drug, but only if you do as I say and prepare to leave. And quickly." Argeon lent his voice power and the woman trembled, but started to move. "Go, help them," he said. Emilio moved off to gather women and children, helping them stand or collect warm clothing.

Sofia stayed behind.

"Father, what happened to those men back in the Grove?"

"Sofia, there will be time to speak on this later."

"Will there?" Still he brushed her off. Would it be the same when she asked her next question? "And what of Tantos, Father?"

He faced her. "Let us get these women to safety first."

She shook her head. "Fine. I'll help them."

Once the prisoners were ready, many carrying no more than a blanket or a child, she followed Father as he led the women from the village and into the forest.

"Where are we headed?" she asked him.

"The eastern edge of the Bloodwood, where I hope to find a boat. It will be quicker than travelling the entire forest and less open to attack," he said, though the few warriors they encountered as they travelled were driven away, either by his voice or the Compelling. But she still watched the forest. The Sap-Born could strike at any time.

Notch and Nia.

How could she forget?

Sofia held back, letting women stumble past, motioning to Emilio, who'd taken position of rear guard. "We have to find Notch and Nia."

"Gods." He turned back, then took a deep breath.

"But these people need us. Maybe more."

"They're not in danger. Not with Father here to protect them."

"And who will protect him?" He kept his voice gentle. "Notch and Nia can take care of each other. I do worry about them, but we have to trust them."

"If you worry, then let's leave now. Who knows what's happened? It's already been hours. The light is failing."

He hesitated.

"You can help me."

"Of course, My Lady. But the Lord Protector...surely he needs us yet? These prisoners are vulnerable. Even your father must sleep. What if he were to be attacked, alone, at night?"

Sofia cursed. He was right. "But we can't just leave Notch."

Emilio snapped his fingers. "Spirit-Walk. Perhaps they're hiding somewhere close."

"Good idea." The notion quickened her pulse. Wearing Argeon again would feel...right. How strange that was now.

She turned but Emilio touched her arm. "My Lady?"

"Emilio?"

"They may not..." He could not meet her eyes at first. "I want to warn you. About Notch and Nia. They may not be well." He drew in a breath. "Or alive."

Sofia reached up to touch his cheek. How sweet he was. "I know, Captain. And thank you."

She jogged along the line.

Time to wear Argeon once more. And time for Father to finally tell the truth.

She joined him as he led the women along the trail. Ahead, the glitter of water through the trees. The rushing of a river eased itself between the trunks.

"Father?"

"There will be a better time to discuss it, Petal."

Sofia frowned, even as her heart warmed. She was hardly 'Petal' anymore and yet, how many times had she imagined him calling her so? Missed it when alone or when searching, imagining his hand on her shoulder, checking on her as she drifted off to sleep.

"You're wrong, Father."

Argeon stared down at her. "You have become like your mother." His voice was fond.

No. It wasn't the time for memories. "We have to talk. About everything, what happened to the Braonn, to Tantos and more – I need to find my friends, Notch and Nia. I need to use Argeon, Father. I can Spirit-Walk and find them. They're in danger from Efran."

He slowed but, "At the Aforna," was all he said.

"Fine, at the river." She replied, though he'd already turned back to the trail. Better than nothing, and yet, he remained guarded, even with her. It wasn't right. Just how much had he hidden from her? Had Tantos lied? Did Father feel him in Argeon?

The green of the Bloodwood didn't have any answers.

Sofia fell back to check on the blind woman, Alcina, who was being led by one of the younger of Efran's prisoners.

"Are you well?" she asked.

"Well enough. It's nice to feel the air on my face." Alcina turned her head toward Sofia. "You are still tense. Because of your father. I hear it in your voice."

"I am."

"He's afraid of disappointing you. I hear that in his voice."

Sofia had no answer. Was that what he feared, truly?

Alcina seemed to accept her confusion, giving a small smile before walking on, as Sofia slowed further. She stepped off the trail a moment, letting the women pass. Their faces were weary but a light shone in their eyes, one that had been absent in their tiny village. Their hair was wild and faces smudged with grime, the hands reaching out to steady or hold little ones just as dirty. Efran had mistreated them beyond the dirt and bruises. How many of the children stumbling along the trail were his?

She shuddered.

Emilio touched her shoulder and she jumped.

"Sorry, My Lady. Did you speak with your father?"

"When we reach the river."

"I will watch over the women then."

She returned to the head of the group as they broke the tree line. The women and children spread upon the banks of Aforna River in a small clearing, the trees growing right up to the waterline, leaves arching over to brush the dark surface. White ripples crossed from bank to bank when the wind picked up.

"Rest a moment," her father told the women. "We will find you food and –"

"We can help, you know," one of the women said.

"Of course. Do not stray far. Emilio?"

Emilio joined a pair of women heading into the trees, meeting Sofia's eyes a moment. She nodded and turned back to her father, but Alcina was already asking him a question.

"And just how are we going to escape?"

"By boat or raft," he said. "I will find something suitable."

"And how is that?" One of the other women said.

"The Braonn could come at any moment and there's no boats here."

"Worry not. The Greatmask will aid me."

The woman accepted his word and moved to the water to drink. Sofia's own mouth was dry, but she stood before him and removed Osani.

"Face to Face, Father. And the truth."

"It may not be safe for me to remove the Greatmask, but I will answer you."

"Very well." The old anger was building. Now that he was safe, now that he was speaking, she had to know who had lied. "Father, he's dead."

He knew who she meant. He took her hands. "I know, Petal."

"No. I mean, truly dead. He died weeks ago, in the city."

His grip slackened. "How?" was all he said.

She tossed his hands aside. "You knew he lived?"

A nod.

"How could you?"

The blind woman stormed forward. "If you are truly here to save us, then stop this."

Her father turned away. "Of course. We are here to help. Tell the women to bring everything they find here. We will not be far."

"I hope so." Alcina left, again aided by another woman.

"Come then, Sofia." He lifted Argeon from his face and motioned that she move away from the clearing. He stopped at a point where the women remained in sight. "What did he tell you?"

She folded her arms. "You first."

"I had to protect you. My only daughter."

"I don't need protecting now."

A deep sigh. "Your brother was blind, Sofia, before he left. He would no longer listen to reason. Could not see his duty. Gyana had fooled him mind and heart."

"And so you had Derrani kill her, then hid him away as a tailor?"

He hesitated.

"Tantos told me everything, Father."

"Everything as he saw it, no doubt. Petal, it is my duty to Protect the King, the people of Anaskar. As it will be yours. Even if that means hurting people I love."

"And were you going to kill Tantos too, before he fled?"

He straightened. "Do not pass judgment when you do not understand."

"You weren't there when he died, mad from his obsession, cursing you as Argeon sucked the life from his body," she cried.

Her father loomed over her. "He was still my son, Sofia."

Some of the women paused their foraging to watch. She lowered her voice. "Then why didn't you forgive him? Why did you drive him away?"

"Because I could no longer trust him."

"And me?"

"No, never think that." He reached out to take her shoulders. "Of course I trust you. You're all I have left, Sofia."

She caught his hands and used them for support, squeezing her eyes shut to fight off tears. "Then why did you lie?"

"I had to protect you from him, from what he was becoming."

"You don't have to do that anymore."

"I will always protect you, you know that."

"Then trust me to understand whatever you must do."

"And would you have accepted what I did to protect my King from assassination, to protect my city from war? Driven your brother away? Made the difficult choices?"

Sofia wiped at her face. Had she not tried and failed to make a difficult choice with Catrin? Hopefully the little monster was still encased in amber. "I don't know. You didn't give me the chance."

He held her close. "I'm sorry."

"No more hiding things, Father. Not between us," she said into his shoulder.

"Of course."

Gods, she hoped he meant it.

*

A quiet fell over them as she stood in his arms. Finally, after so long searching. So long not knowing, so long squashing her fear down, never letting it take control. His familiar scent and the steady beat of his heart.

"Sofia." He pulled back.

"Yes?"

"You asked about what happened with the men in the Grove? I grieve to say it is something you must know, if you are to wear a Greatmask."

A chill from the echo of snapping bones. "What was it?"

"I Compelled them. Compelled their bones with Argeon."

"You mean..."

"Yes. Compelling is the true power of the Greatmasks." He shook his head. "How naïve I was, Sofia, to think I knew the Greatmasks well."

"But you do."

"No. I foolishly thought that the extent of 'Compelling' was what could be done with the status, the awe and even the control we exert with our voices, the power it lends to spoken commands. How wrong I was." He shook his head. "Compelling is much more than that – something I have had the misfortune of perfecting during my imprisonment here. Though 'perfecting' is a stretch. You must not attempt it unless I guide you."

"Father, no. You want me to practise doing that? To people? That's what you did?"

"I had a choice between experimenting for Efran or death."

"Ana." Her stomach turned. "How dangerous is it?"

"Had I less control, the Compelling might have hurt you and Emilio. Or anyone nearby."

"But I don't understand. How did Efran learn of something you as Protector did not know?"

"I could never discover."

She shook her head. "I don't want to do that."

"I hope you will never need to." He pulled back and smiled, holding Argeon out. "Now find your friends and show me, clever girl, how to 'Spirit-Walk'. Argeon has never shared with me such a thing."

She accepted the mask. Despite the growing stiffness in her joints, a little glow formed in her chest. Something Father didn't know? Perhaps Argeon had warmed to her after all.

"I don't know how to explain it, but my spirit roams while my body stays in place."

He checked on the women, who were talking amongst themselves, then turned back to Sofia. "Show me and I will try after you."

Argeon was cool, as ever, and the moment she put him on, the stiffness eased.

Sofia!

Metti's voice burst into her mind.

"Metti?"

Sofia. The city is under attack by men in Greatmasks! Where are you?

"What?" She nearly choked on the word. More Greatmasks?

They have come from across the sea – your ancestors. They each wear Greatmasks and suits of bone. No-one can stand against them and they have control of the city. You must return.

"Are you safe? What about the others?"

For now but I don't know –

Silence.

A chill ran across her skin. "Metti? Can you hear me?"

"Sofia, what's happening?" her father asked. "Is Metti in danger?"

She returned Argeon. "I don't know. She said that our ancestors attacked the city."

"Our ancestors?"

"And that they all wear Greatmasks. I thought there were no more masks?"

"Gather our charges, we have to leave." He replaced Argeon. "And give me Osani too, Petal. He will need to speak with you now, whether he wishes it or not."

GREATMASK PREVIEW

Book 3 of the Bone Mask Trilogy

CHAPTER 1

Notch climbed to his feet, legs wobbling as he caught his breath. All around, the hush of the forest pressed heavy upon his shoulders. Water dripped from green leaves with red tips, as a soft rain worked its way down the branches. An amber butterfly seemed to float in the air – yet the tip of its wing had brushed the molten earth upon Efran's death. The forest floor had cooled to a muted yellow and only the suggestion of the man remained there, now no more than a single bubble frozen in amber.

Was she gone?

He kicked a rock onto the yellow loam but it was

not enveloped and no flash of light followed. Safe. He trudged forward. Nia's wings were frozen in mid-beat; he reached out but didn't touch her.

"Celno, what now?"

He had to take her back to the Grove. Only Nia's father could help, her father or Sofia maybe. And she was safe with Emilio and her own father, if everything had gone well. Another prayer to the Mountain God.

But how?

Notch bent by the contact point. Could he hurt Nia by trying to move her? Would she shatter? He had to be gentle; more gentle than a soldier's brash hands. His wounded leg wouldn't make things any easier either. The ache had returned and without battle's adrenaline, his limp returned with it. If he could find a way back to the Autumn Grove and avoid any patrols... if she wasn't already dead... Notch made a fist, his arm shaking.

He lowered it. Act or die; that was the measure of a soldier's life.

"Let this work." He drew his knife and carefully cut a circular piece of amber around the tip of her wing, one hand raised to support her. He dropped the knife as she came free, holding Nia as best he could, the shape and smoothness of her wings difficult to grip.

A sense of warmth tingled his fingertips. Was it a sign of life? It dimmed and he swore. She had to go home. The Oyn-Dir was a powerful magic user; surely he could save her. He placed Nia down, gentle, but still he winced when a wing scraped against the amber floor. She held and he sighed, scooping up his knife before lifting her again and limping between the headstones.

He stopped to take a sword from one of the bodies, then moved on.

The Sap Groves lay west and the Autumn Grove last lay to the north, back toward where he and Sofia had entered the Bloodwood. But that was before the attack, and Nia said her father was moving the grove. Impossible, but he could doubtless do it, even if it didn't quite make sense. Therefore any direction – any leading away from the Sap Grove – was as good as another.

By the time he reached the crossroad where Nia's magic had led the Sap-Born away, he was breathing hard. He needed water and food. From memory, the Aforna River was less than a day's walk, but he had no boat and heading northeast and eventually into the sea wouldn't help.

He chose a path and walked on. The forest was quiet save for his footfalls and breathing. Nia grew no heavier, but no lighter either. He often had to bend and twist to navigate overhanging branches, and at a fallen log he rested Nia against the loam before climbing up only to reach back and lift her.

By dusk, he'd stopped in a wide hollow ringed by trees. He sat back to rest within it, stretching out his leg. The whole thing burned inside. He'd found one tiny stream and filled his stomach, but still no food. He reached his knees and took the time to cover Nia with leaves and a single fallen branch. It wasn't much, but within the hollow it would be hard to see her from the path – the trail itself having an overgrown look. At the very least, he'd put some distance between himself and the graveyard.

Mor would be searching for them. It might not be soon, but when the man found the remains of Efran, the hunt would begin.

From the darkening trees came a raspy cry. It was echoed by another, this one further away. Again, the first rasp cut through the quiet. Its twin replied, closer now. Notch propped himself against a tree and drew his stolen sword.

More rasping.

He made it to one knee then paused when a silvery creature slipped into the hollow. Its slender body, about the size of a dog's, appeared to collect the remaining light. Were those scales or leathery skin? He gripped his blade. Low to the ground, the creature walked on all fours and weaved an elongated, bird-like head. The eyes were thin slits of white.

It shuddered, opening a mouth to release that heaving rasp.

An echo.

Notch flinched when a second creature joined the first.

It too was slender and luminous. Its feet ended in splayed, hand-like appendages. Even in the dying light the length was visible, twice that of a man's hand-span. One leapt to a tree, clinging to the bark and raising a single foot to flex long toes. The other kept its narrow white eyes trained on him.

He slid his back up the trunk, reaching his feet. The first creature stretched to the next tree, its long head twisted to watch him as it moved. The other shuffled closer, feet soundless on the leaves. [Never]

Nia rested between them. Could he fend them off without shattering her? One misstep and whatever slim hope remained would be gone. And if he died, she was just as likely to remain frozen forever. Such a fate might be hers no matter what he did.

"Think faster," he muttered.

If he attacked one, the other would strike. But if he

was quick...Notch growled. No choice. He leapt from his good leg, slashing at the grounded creature. It slipped back, easily avoiding his strike – but not with speed, more that its body twisted just enough for the blade to miss.

He spun at a rasp.

The second creature bore down on him, feet outstretched. He lifted his blade but the creature hit, knocking it free and sending them tumbling into a trunk. A foot wrapped around his shoulder and he screamed as a chill bit into his clothing. He fought to keep the rasping mouth from his face, it was open wide enough to swallow his whole head. Two other limbs wrapped around him, one burning into his wounded leg and the other planting itself on his chest.

He cried out again; the points of its feet were like ice.

Notch thrashed but it was too strong. A sweet-smelling liquid dripped from its mouth, slicking his skin and splattering onto his chest. Fumes rose and he blinked back tears. If he let go, the mouth would cover him. Could he reach his knife?

The hollow darkened. Notch coughed at the fumes. More slime dripped free, sweet but cloying. The mouth drew closer. He pushed back but his strength was gone and he gasped a curse, sucking in a good dose of the fumes.

Nothing followed.

*

He woke to the rasping in darkness.

Somehow he was alive but he couldn't move. Air tore at his nose and throat, both so raw that swallowing hurt. A sweetness lingered on the air. Something, not ropes, bound him. A thick...substance...its chill clinging to the skin. It coated his limbs and he shivered, barely moving, yet the muted spasm ran along his entire body.

Something shifted and light poured after it, filtered green. He blinked until his vision cleared. Sunlight through leaves bathed him. He lay in a large nest that had been carved from the hollow of a Bloodwood tree. The rasping came from one of the creatures; it was curled along the nest, its leathery body collecting the light to give off a faint glow.

The head nestled into its chest, giant feet wrapping parts of its body. The rasp was softer, regular. It was sleeping. Notch strained against the slime but to no avail. He twisted his head. Where was the other one? Had it been blocking the entrance to the tree?

The sleeping creature twitched.

Notch frowned as the twitching continued, coming from the feet. Why hadn't the creatures killed him? Unless... "Gods, no," he managed.

One of the finger-like toes peeled back. Something small and silver peeked out, tiny white hints of eyes. A baby crawled forward, pausing to open its mouth. Testing the air? It moved closer, pausing again, mouth opening, then repeated the process. Halfway across the floor tiny, razor sharp teeth snapped from its beak-like mouth. It reached Notch's side and he strained against the hard slime.

Useless.

The creature hovered over his hand, then snapped its mouth down. Tiny teeth tore into his skin, blood welling. He cursed and it flinched back, scurrying for the safety of its mother. It disappeared beneath the foot and Notch heaved a sigh of relief, only for it to catch in his throat.

The creature peered out once again, stepping forth with a sibling in tow. And then another. And a fourth. And fifth. Six, seven, eight, he swore as a swarm began to flow from beneath the mother. Few were more than a hand tall, but all bore sharp teeth.

And that was why the parents hadn't killed him.

He was food for their spawn.

A NOTE FROM ASHLEY

Hi! I hope you enjoyed *The Lost Mask* and thanks for reading.

I'd like to ask if you could help me out by leaving an honest review of the book at your place of purchase? Long or short, bad or good, it all helps!

AND if you'd like to sign up to my newsletter you'll receive *The Amber Isle* for free, the first title in my second epic fantasy series.

Further, you'll also be the first to know when *Greatmask* (Book 3 of The Bone Mask Trilogy) is released. You'll also have first access to preview chapters and pre-release editions of the book, in addition to being automatically added into the draw for giveaways.

Ashley

ACKNOWLEDGMENTS

As ever, thank you first to my wife Brooke – no way could I write without you.

And also to my families for years of support and for believing in me, for urging me to succeed.

Thanks also to those awesome folk who were kind enough to beta all or parts of the *The Lost Mask* and send me feedback: Cheryl, Aderyn, Erena, Zeta and legendary readers like Jen, Sean and Maddelena who were willing to read an ARC and who gave me more invaluable feedback.

Once again I need to thank the 'Alchemy Writers' – Rebekah, Cheryl and Tess – for support, advice and for their patience which I am fortunate enough not to have exhausted (yet)!

Thanks again to the team at Snapping Turtle Books, who worked on the first edition of this book. A big thank you also to Vivid Cover for the brilliant work on both *The Lost Mask* and *City of Masks*! and the entire series.

Thanks also to anyone anywhere who might have picked up any of my books!

Ashley

ABOUT ASHLEY

Ashley Capes is an Australian novelist, poet and teacher. *City of Masks* is his first novel and the follow up is *The Lost Mask*. The trilogy will be complete with *Greatmask* in 2016. Ashley is also the author of five poetry collections and various other novels. He loves Studio Ghibli films and strongly believes Nausicaa is one of the greatest heroines out there.

Visit his blogs at *www.cityofmasks.com* & *www.ashleycapes.com* or follow him on twitter @Ash_Capes.

Other titles by Ashley:

The Bone Mask Trilogy
1. *City of Masks*
2. *The Lost Mask*
3. *Greatmask (forthcoming)*

Book of Never
1. *The Amber Isle*
2. *A Forest of Eyes*
3. *River God*
4. *The Peaks of Autumn*
5. *Imperial Towers (forthcoming)*
0. *Never (Prequel to The Amber Isle)*

CPSIA information can be obtained
at www.ICGtesting.com
Printed in the USA
FSHW020053130620
70794FS